TEXMEX

by Clabe Taylor

TEXMEX

A Spymasters Literary Guild Series Book

Legacy Publishers

PO BOX 62442
Virginia Beach, VA 23466
www.legacypublishers.net
www.spymastersguild.com

Library of Congress Control Number: 2012948678

ISBN 978-0-615-68911-1

Cover illustration by Adam Carabet

Printed and bound in the United States of America.

"If I owned Hell and Texas, I would rent out Texas and live in Hell."

Philip Sheridan

CHAPTER 1

Hal Wilson looked up nervously from his clipboard and recognized the gold-colored International Harvester cab and the light blue license plates from Sinaloa. The 80-foot long tractor trailer with "GRUPO ZIMA" emblazoned on both sides in red letters spewed rank diesel exhaust as it inched across the World Trade International Bridge and slowly approached the U.S. Customs inspection station in Laredo, Texas. No matter how many times he had been through the drill over the past three years, Hal's pulse always raced when he caught sight of the rig and his throat constricted, making it hard to swallow.

The phone call had come the night before during an old rerun of "Border Wars" on television. Hal had listened without comment to the familiar accent and the instructions which never seemed to vary. The conspiratorial double-talk made him smile, but he got the message and knew what to look for the following day. It wasn't a difficult thing to do, hardly an inconvenience, really. As shift supervisor, Hal was able to float among all twelve inspection booths in operation each day and keep an eye out for the Grupo Zima truck.

With nearly 3,000 eighteen-wheelers entering the United States daily through the Laredo crossing, the U.S. Customs Service could only inspect a small fraction of the commercial traffic coming across the bridge from Mexico. Hal provided risk insurance against the outside chance an overzealous inspector would try to inspect this particular truck. Tuition bills for two kids at Texas Tech University strained Hal's budget and he welcomed the extra cash.

Hal approached the driver and gave a perfunctory look at the truck's bill of lading. As usual, the shipping documents were in perfect order. Sometimes he idly wondered what was really in the trucks but decided long ago he'd rather not know.

"Tomatoes, uh?   Where are you heading this time?" he asked casually.

"To Dallas, *señor*," answered the Mexican driver obligingly.

"*Bueno*, everything looks good. *Qué tenga buen viaje.*"

"*Muchas gracias*," replied the driver and slowly eased the truck forward through the inspection lane and across the bridge.

Hal knew the drill. Tomorrow he would have breakfast at a little Mexican dive on Rio Grande Street. When he opened the menu the waiter handed him, Hal would find an envelope stuffed with $100 bills. Fifty of them, to be exact. Lord knows he needed the cash. Hal knew he wasn't the only one making a little extra money on the side. Who cared if another truck load of *mota* made it across the border? He sure didn't.

***

The two men sat motionless under a tall mesquite tree in an overgrazed pasture of Buffel grass. They were exhausted after walking for two days without eating. They crossed the Rio Grande the night before and drank the last of the water in their canteens that morning. It was unspeakably hot even in the shade. The smell of cow manure wafted over them in waves on the humid breeze, and the air shimmered in the distance above the hot asphalt of Farm-to-Market Road 359 about ten miles east of Laredo. They lay in the dry grass waiting for dusk when they could move about without fear of being discovered by *La Migra*. Grass burrs pricked through the thin cotton of their threadbare shirts, and fire ants crawled up their trouser legs, stinging without provocation and making sensitive skin itch and burn. The men were miserable in the muggy heat.

"There's a stock tank just over the rise, you know." Rodrigo pointed towards the herd of crossbred tiger-stripe cattle grazing in the distance.

"Can't risk it yet. We can fill our canteens when the sun goes down." Mario was adamant. He was older by two years and the unspoken leader of the two.

"You think the water will make us sick?" asked Rodrigo.

"Maybe, but we can't go much longer without it."

"When can we start looking for work?" Rodrigo was impatient.

"*Tranquilo, mano,*" he warned. "We need to put some distance between us and the border first. Try to rest."

They waited. As the afternoon waned, the heat began to dissipate, and the shadows lengthened mercifully around the dense thicket where they lay. They leaned up against the trunk of the tall mesquite tree and gauged the time by the height of the sun above the distant horizon. The persistent high-pitched drone of the cicadas in the sparse mesquite trees was hypnotic and they dozed fitfully, nodding awake to swat at the greenhead horse flies that landed on their exposed skin and bit painfully. With dusk approaching, Mario and Rodrigo gathered their meager belongings and prepared to make a dash to the stock tank to fill their canteens.

Voices from the highway startled them and they looked towards the road, trying to identify the source of the commotion. A white Crown Victoria with a green logo on the side had stopped on the shoulder of the highway, and two men in uniforms were placing orange cones across the eastbound lane. They were speaking loudly in English.

"*¡Mierda!*" cursed Mario. "Of all the luck! What's *La Migra* doing here? *¡A la verga!*"

"*¿Qué hacemos?*" asked Rodrigo.

They watched two men in uniforms set up a roadblock. Border Patrol, for sure. They would be stopping vehicles to check for illegals.

"We wait till they leave," answered Mario with resignation, and the two crouched low behind the trunk of the mesquite tree to lessen their chances of discovery. They were a scant seventy-five yards from the highway.

Mario and Rodrigo watched in uneasy silence as the agents began stopping vehicles coming from Laredo. For a half hour neither man moved or said a word. They still hadn't taken their eyes off the highway when an eighteen-wheeler slowly approached the roadblock from the west. The sun glinted off the gold-colored International Harvester cab. They could make out the words "GRUPO ZIMA" in huge red letters on the side of the trailer. They heard the *"whoosh"* from the air brakes as the truck obediently ground to a halt in front of the orange cones.

"Probably a load of vegetables from Sinaloa. My cousin works for that company," whispered Mario.

As he and Rodrigo watched, one agent disappeared on the far side of the cab, apparently talking with the driver. They heard the slam of the cab door and saw the agent and the truck driver reappear a few seconds later at the rear of the trailer where the second Border Patrol agent was already waiting. One of the agents motioned with his arm at the rear door of the trailer, and the driver obligingly climbed on the truck and rolled open the door. The rumbling rattle of steel on steel was loud and jarring in the quiet of the approaching dusk.

Mario knew something was wrong when the driver jumped down from the back of the trailer and ran frantically towards the front of the truck. The Border Patrol agents reacted quickly. They both went for their handguns, and the agent closest to the driver sprinted after him. He took one step and appeared to lose his footing. His body spun spasmodically to the left, his arm outstretched as if appealing to an inattentive and callous God, and he fell awkwardly to the ground. A split second later the staccato thunder of automatic weapons fire from the hidden shooters inside the trailer reached the Mexicans under the tree. The other agent had barely cleared his pistol from a government-issue leather holster when he took the first round squarely in the chest and staggered backwards. The impact of dozens of 7.62 caliber rounds fired at point blank range tossed his body about like a rag doll. It was over in five seconds. Mario and Rodrigo watched in stunned silence. The cattle resumed grazing, and the echoes from the brief gun battle scurried across the flat mesquite plain and became fainter and then died in the thick South Texas air.

The two wetbacks hugged the ground in terror, ignoring the fire ants stinging their ankles and wrists. They watched in disbelief as armed gunmen leaped out of the trailer and carried the bodies of the dead Border Patrol agents back to their Crown Victoria and tossed them unceremoniously in the back seat. Others hurriedly stripped the car of two shotguns and the vehicle's radio receiver and transmitter and carried them back to the trailer. Finally, as the truck began to pull away slowly, two gunmen poured gasoline inside the Crown Victoria, tossed in a match, and ran back to the trailer where they were pulled on board by their obliging comrades-in-arms. As the truck increased speed, heading rapidly eastward, the Crown Victoria suddenly exploded in an inferno of flame and black smoke. Scarcely three minutes had passed since the truck shuddered to a reluctant stop in front of the Border Patrol's makeshift checkpoint. The scene had played out in lurid Hollywood fashion, and each actor had performed his role to perfection.

Mario counted fifteen heavily armed gunmen but knew there had to be more inside the trailer. Eyes wide, uncomprehending and near panic, he and Rodrigo wasted no time. They hurriedly shouldered their backpacks and broke into a slow lumbering run away from the highway and the scene of the brutal murders, all thoughts of water and food and work suddenly inconsequential and frivolous.

CHAPTER 2

Creed Tucker didn't take shit from anyone. He didn't have to. He owned most of the land between Cotulla and Catarina way over in Dimmit County; something like 35,000 acres, give or take a few thousand. That still meant something in South Texas.

Land for a cattle rancher in the Brush Country north of the Rio Grande had always been like a securities portfolio for a Dallas investment banker. It was the key to an unspoken membership in the good-old-boys' fraternity of the landed gentry. This was South Texas aristocracy, and it didn't matter whether the land was inherited, stolen, or bought with a lifetime's worth of hard work and perspiration. Land ownership was the vivid reflection of a rancher's manhood, of whether he had a pair of *cojones* or not. Creed had both the acreage and the balls and everyone knew it.

Most mornings after Creed and his sons finished the first round of chores on the ranch, he drove his beat-up white Chevy pickup five miles north into Cotulla for a cup of coffee at Angelina's Café and a Tex-Mex breakfast of his own invention: rice and pinto beans with cornbread covered with green *tomatillo* sauce, the hotter the better. Creed knew that his wife Guadalupe didn't take offense at his preference to have breakfast in town. He used the time to meet with the few remaining Anglo ranchers in La Salle County to discuss strategies and share information. Today Creed went along with his wife's advice to take his two sons along as bodyguards. He could tell she was grateful and his usual condescending smile in her direction didn't seem to rankle as it normally did. It was getting dangerous for Creed to go out alone whether he wanted to recognize that reality or not.

"Matlock!" Creed stood by the open door of his truck and called hoarsely to his elder son who stood inside the screen porch, washing his hands in a white enamel basin that had been in the Tucker household as long as Creed could remember.

"On my way, Dad...relax!"

"Just humor an old man, will you? Where the hell's Scrap? Tell your little brother to get a move on."

"Scrap's hung-over. You saw him feeding cattle this morning. The boy's in pain. Take it easy on him."

Five minutes later the three of them sat in the front seat of the truck while Koot, an ornery three-year old Blue Heeler, rode in back. One 12-gauge shotgun and an SKS assault rifle adorned the gun rack on the back window. They knew it didn't hurt to advertise these days.

At Angelina's Café, Matlock and Scrap got a table near the front door where they sat with their weapons discreetly hidden under the table. Creed sat at a smaller table at the rear of the café with his back to the wall, talking with a rancher he'd known most of his life. There used to be five or six of them that met for breakfast every morning. That was before. Now almost everyone else had fled the county: moved north of the Nueces River, driven off by the Mexican drug trafficking gangs and the anti-Anglo ordinances of the newly elected radical Hispanic municipal governments.

Creed couldn't understand the reluctance of the authorities in Austin to confront the growing security problem but he suspected the worst. Drug money had changed the moral and political landscape along the border forever, and now the poison was creeping north like the tell-tale red lines of a rapidly spreading necrosis.

"Not taking any chances, are you Creed?" James Brazzle nodded over towards the entrance to Angelina's where Matlock and Scrap sat picking at their *huevos rancheros* and watching the street.

"Not any more. Not since that little dust-up we had a couple of weeks ago," answered Creed, glancing over at his boys. "You heard about that, I imagine."

"*Un café más cuando tengas tiempo, por favor,*" called James, waving his empty coffee cup at one of the Mexican waitresses as she walked by bringing several orders of steaming *chilaquiles* to a Hispanic family sitting at the adjacent table.

"Shit, James," said Creed, hiding a grin. "I didn't know you spoke Spanish!"

"I don't," he said. "You know that. Hell, if English was good enough for Jesus Christ, it ought to be good enough for everyone, don't you think?"

Creed tried to wipe a smile off his face. James' drawl always became much more pronounced in the presence of his friend, but Creed knew what few people in the small town of Cotulla were privy to. James Brazzle was a retired CIA officer with a Master's Degree in Latin American studies from Georgetown University. His Spanish would put to shame any of the newly elected Hispanic mayors or city council members in the county, but Creed knew he enjoyed playing the role of redneck rancher. It suited his sense of irony. Creed played along; there was little enough to laugh at these days, and he was more than happy to humor his old friend.

"Yeah, I heard about what happened," replied James, getting back to their conversation. "Heard you winged one of them sons o' bitches."

"Not exactly," said Creed. "We didn't get one, but Koot did."

"Koot?" asked Brazzle.

"Yeah, my Blue Heeler," answered Creed. He pointed outside where Koot sat patiently in the bed of the pickup, waiting for his humans to return.

"What exactly happened?" James asked.

"They wanted to lease some of my land."

"Who did?"

"The damn Mexican drug traffickers, that's who," answered Creed.

"What the hell for?"

"To build an airstrip," explained Creed.

"How do you know they were drug traffickers?" asked James.

"You ever see anyone in Cotulla want to pay for anything in cash? A suitcase full of cash?"

James laughed. "Alright, I see what you mean. Did you report it to the DEA in Laredo or to the sheriff in Cotulla?"

"Yeah, they said they'd investigate. You know what that means."

"Those worthless bastards," James mumbled. "Sometimes I think they're all working for the cartel."

Creed took a bite of cornbread, dripping thick globs of *salsa verde* on his plate and lowered his voice.

"After I turned down their offer, we knew they'd come after us. Figured it'd be at night, and we got ready. We caught four of them crossing the pasture near the interstate at midnight about a week ago, and we lit 'em up like deer with spotlights from three pickup trucks. You never seen a bunch of Mexicans run so fast. We fired in the air above their heads just to scare them, but Koot took it all kind of seriously."

"Hell, I'd give my right arm for a dog like that," interjected James.

Creed looked at James with feigned derision. "Who're you trying to kid? Your wife and her West Highland Terrier wouldn't let you have a real dog. Besides, a Blue Heeler wouldn't take kindly to all that shampooing and grooming. I bet you put perfume on that thing!"

James just shrugged his shoulders and laughed.

"So, what did Koot do?" James asked.

"Well, Koot treed one of the Mexicans."

"Ain't that some shit!" James leaned back in his chair, slapped his knee, and laughed.

"We kept the wetback locked up in the tack room till morning. He wouldn't say a word to us, and we brought him into Cotulla the next day. But that corrupt sonofabitch Sheriff Martinez let him go about an hour after we left. Said there wasn't enough evidence to hold him. Martinez probably already bought himself a new bass boat with the money he got for that chicken-shit decision."

Creed turned to spit on the floor but thought better of it and sent a thin stream of unappetizing brown tobacco juice into his empty Styrofoam coffee cup.

"So now they have two reasons to be pissed at you," said James. "How much money did they offer you, anyway?"

"How about a hundred thousand dollars to put the airstrip on my ranch...and then a monthly stipend?"

"I'll be damned!" said James. "Where'd you hide the money?" He shook his head laughing.

"I wish it were that simple," said Creed.

"What do you mean?" asked James. "The way I see it, you either take the money or you don't."

"You can't deal with the cartel," Creed stated categorically. "Can't even talk with them. You give an inch, and those bastards will take a mile and then some. But if you don't give them what they want, they'll kill you. I'm on their list now. That's why my bodyguards have breakfast with me nowadays." Creed nodded towards his sons. "Guadalupe will hardly let me out of the house without them."

"Well, if you turned them down, they'll just find someone else who needs the money a little more, or who's a little more scared," said James. "They'll find a way to get what they want, you can count on it. Even the DEA can't stop them. Sometimes I think they don't even want to."

Creed nodded his head in agreement. "Why would they? Then they'd be out of a job."

He leaned back in his chair, balancing on two legs and made a dismissive gesture with his right hand, flicking his wrist as if he were swatting at an annoying insect.

"Personally, I think the war on drugs is the cause of a lot of the problems we've got today," Creed continued, "but I sure as hell won't deal with the drug traffickers...don't like the feds much more, but at least they're not as likely to shoot if you piss 'em off," Creed continued.

James froze with a forkful of refried beans poised in mid-air and propped his elbow on the table.

"What are you saying? You'd rather see drugs legalized?" he asked.

Creed paused, surprised at the question. He reached for a toothpick and poked absentmindedly at his front teeth, looking back at James and considering his response.

"Frankly, I don't much care either way. I just want to be able to live and work on my ranch without the traffickers or the feds telling me what to do," he said finally.

"My sentiments exactly," said James.

"At least we agree on something," Creed said and smiled sadly. "You know, my family settled this country five generations ago. What am I supposed to do? Turn my back and walk away from it all? I don't think so. Wouldn't be able to look at myself in the mirror. Shit, it's hard enough as it is."

"I'll agree with you on that...about the mirror, that is," said James.

"So the question is, what can *we* do?" asked Creed, ignoring James' attempt at humor.

"Maybe you ought to talk with your old friend Rudy Gutierrez. Isn't he part of that Hispanic rights movement down in Laredo? What are they calling themselves? The National Front for something or another."

"Yeah, the National Front for the Liberation of Texas," answered Creed. "A bunch of crazy old Brown Beret radicals from the 60s for the most part. I wish ol' Rudy hadn't got involved with them."

"Can't you talk some sense into him? You two served together, didn't you?" asked James.

Creed emptied his coffee cup and stood up and stretched. He nodded to Matlock and Scrap who discreetly collected their weapons from under the table and moved to the exit, eying the street cautiously.

"That was a long time ago, James. Rudy still doesn't much like Anglos after what happened to him in Vietnam even after all these years, but I just can't imagine he'd have hooked up with the traffickers. He's a good man."

"Still, it probably wouldn't hurt to look him up," said James.

"Yeah, maybe so." said Creed." James put on his cowboy hat and wiped his mouth with a napkin and folded it neatly under the side of his plate.

"I'm starting to think like my father and grandfather did when they got old. They were horrified at what the world had become and they longed for a time that was gone and would never be again," said James.

Creed reached into the front pocket of his blue-checkered shirt for a pinch of Red Man as James held the door open and the South Texas air collided with them like a wall of wet heat.

"I'd have to agree with them," said Creed. "You can hardly walk the streets of any town in South Texas nowadays unless you're armed."

"We're fighting a losing battle," said James with a frown. "We're outnumbered, outgunned, and the politicians in Austin are sticking their heads in the sand like ostriches. Afraid to help us out for fear of losing the Hispanic vote."

Creed looked up and down the street and paused.

"We're practically living in a war zone, and they're worried about the Hispanic vote." He shook his head in disgust. "We stole this country from Mexico back in 1845...can't deny that. But they're gonna take it back, sure as shit. You just watch."

CHAPTER 3

Lester Van Slyke hadn't slept well in weeks. He would wake up in the middle of the night with a headache and the vague recollection of an irksome dream he couldn't quite reconstruct. The dreams made him feel guilty and somehow unclean. He felt like a feral animal being tracked, hunted, and finally cornered. Of course, Lester was far from feral. The only wild thing Lester had ever done in his life was to accept money from that Mexican government official last year. In return for turning a blind eye to some bloated election rolls in South Texas, the balance in Lester's new offshore bank account in the British Virgin Islands had increased steadily, and up till last month he had been eying that house on Lake Travis his wife liked so much.

But now the damned greasers wanted more and more from him, and the few Anglos left down in Webb and La Salle counties were raising hell. The Hispanic landslide in the last municipal elections all over South Texas raised too many eyebrows and his critics were asking questions. In fact, a delegation of concerned Anglo citizens was arriving today to discuss allegations of election fraud. They would be meeting with the governor as well to discuss the security situation and the recent murders of two Border Patrol agents. As head of the Texas Election Commission, Lester finally would have to address the fraud issue publicly. It wasn't going to be a good day. In fact, he was in deep shit, and he knew it.

***

The three-pickup truck caravan of Anglo ranchers made its way steadily north towards Austin along Interstate 35 from San Antonio. If you didn't count Koot and a Catahoula Cur in the third truck, there were eight of them. They were meeting with the Texas secretary of state in the morning and the governor in the afternoon. Afterwards, if the politicians' answers did not satisfy the ranchers, there would be a press conference covered by all the local TV news channels. James Brazzle had tried to use his old contacts in Washington to get CNN interested, but Wolf and the crew were more interested in a photograph of a New Jersey congressman's penis an underage campaign volunteer received in her email inbox. "Yeah, CNN has its priorities straight," Brazzle had commented at the time with a sneer.

The press conference was admittedly a risky maneuver. It would piss off both the Hispanic majority in their counties and the Anglo politicians in Austin, but the ranchers figured they had nothing to lose. The execution-style murder of the two Border Patrol agents near Laredo and the attempted raid on Creed Tucker's ranch headquarters had tipped the scales. It was time to act.

"I'm not sure why we're bothering with this charade," said Creed. He sat in the driver's seat of the lead pickup and sipped a bottle of cold Dr. Pepper.

"We're covering our asses, Creed," said James. "It's just one of the things we've got to do before we take things into our own hands."

"What are we, some kind of vigilante posse?" Creed liked to pose rhetorical questions.

"Extreme situations call for extreme measures," replied Brazzle. "You'll get your chance, Creed. Let's take it slow right now."

"James, why don't you do the talking at the meetings today?" proposed Creed. "You're a silver-tongued old SOB.

You'd represent us well."

"Hell no, Creed, that's what you're here for," Brazzle stated emphatically. "Everybody knows and respects you here in South Texas. People don't remember me. I was gone too long. But I need to keep a low profile anyway. If the Hispanics down in the valley get the Mexican government to do a name trace on me, I'll have a gang of *sicario* killers gunning me down in broad daylight at the Super Walmart in Laredo."

"May come to that anyway," James. "We're too old and there's too few of us to put up any meaningful resistance," said Creed.

"When and if the time comes, we'll have help," Brazzle said mysteriously.

Creed exchanged glances with James but kept silent. James never talked much about his work for the government, but Creed knew he wasn't one to waste his breath or make idle promises. He didn't doubt that James had some contingency plans for almost any eventuality.

James had been different from the rest of them even as a kid. He had never wanted to participate in the generic games of "war" they used to play on the banks of that creek that flowed into the Nueces River. He condescended to play only if he could be in charge. He would draw up detailed battle plans with reconnaissance patrols, supply lines, air support, and unconditional surrenders. When his friends were reading *Riders of the Purple Sage* by Zane Grey, James read *The Prince* by Machiavelli. It hadn't surprised anyone when James left Texas after he got out of the army and didn't come back for thirty-five years. But he still was the same old bull rider Creed remembered from their rodeo days, and he knew he could count on James when the chips were down. Creed sensed that events would put them both to the test very soon.

The ranchers parked their pickups in a garage on Congress

St. and walked to the Rusk Building where Lester Van Slyke had scheduled their meeting. The sunlight played games on the modernistic reflective blue glass walls of the office building. Passersby in business suits and ties looked at the group of middle-aged ranchers in cowboy hats and boots with amusement. Austin was still the capital of Texas, but it wasn't the town it used to be.

When Lester Van Slyke finally appeared in the conference room where the ranchers had been waiting for over thirty minutes, nobody stood up to greet him. They didn't take kindly to the secretary of state making them wait or to his haughty demeanor. Creed Tucker had no intention of wasting time with meaningless chit chat. That had never been his forte, and on a day like this, small talk was the farthest thing from his mind.

"Do you know Texas history, Mr. Van Slyke?" began Creed acerbically. He continued without waiting for a response. "Because if you did, I don't think you and your fellow politicians would sit up here in Austin behind your mahogany desks and ignore what's happening in South Texas!"

The secretary looked down his nose through a pair of prescription reading glasses at Creed.

"Mr. Tucker, we're perfectly aware of what's going on in the southern counties, and we are following the situation very carefully," replied Lester. "But as far as Texas history is concerned, I consider myself somewhat of an expert. Are you referring to anything in particular?" he asked smugly.

"I sure as hell am," retorted Creed, already beginning to lose his temper. "The Nueces River," he said as if that should explain everything. He looked around victoriously at his companions sitting at the conference table as if he had driven a point home in a high school debate.

"What about the Nueces River, Mr. Tucker? It's about 315 miles long, rises in the Edwards Plateau, and flows into the

Gulf of Mexico." Van Slyke sat imperiously in his padded leather chair at the head of the long conference table.

Creed stared back at him without flinching and with enmity he didn't try to conceal. Van Slyke dropped his eyes and ostentatiously adjusted his blue swirl enamel cuff links.

"That used to be the northern border of Mexico and the FNLT and their backers in Mexico City aim to make it that way again. Are you blind?" Creed tapped his fingers on the conference table in exasperation, and his elegant Lucchese crocodile boots drummed impatiently on the floor.

"And what is this FNLT?" asked the Secretary of State.

Creed looked at him incredulously and almost hissed in response.

"You're telling me you're in charge of elections in the state of Texas, and you don't know what the FNLT is?"

"I seem to have read something about it," said Slyke nervously.

"The *Frente Nacional para la Liberación de Tejas* is running things in South Texas. Austin doesn't mean shit to a tree down there. You Anglo politicians are irrelevant south of the Nueces River!"

"Mr. Tucker, would you mind translating that? We speak English in this part of the country."

"You won't for long if you keep your heads stuck up your asses," snapped Creed. "The National Front for the Liberation of Texas is made up of drug traffickers, M-13, and Zeta gangbangers, and corrupt Mexican and Texan politicians. They're using intimidation, election fraud, bribes, and outright violence to take over South Texas. Anglo residents and federal and local officials have been threatened and murdered, and neither Austin nor Washington seems to recognize the problem or want to do anything about it. A lot of the Anglos have left already, but some of us have our roots there and would rather die defending our land than leave with our tails between our legs. Why have Texas elected officials done nothing to help us, Mr. Van Slyke? Who's on the take up here?"

Creed was beside himself and stood up and pounded his fist on the wooden table for emphasis. The cattle ranchers were not impressed with the trappings of Van Slyke's position in the Texas state government, and they didn't take kindly to his meaningless platitudes. Van Slyke's hands trembled visibly, and he appeared to be at a loss for words.

"Mr. Creed, I appreciate your updating me on what's going on in South Texas. I can assure you that we will look into your allegations very carefully. I promise you that I will speak personally with the governor about the situation." Van Slyke stood up, letting his visitors know that the audience had come to an end.

"The name is Tucker, by the way," said Creed. "Don't bother to talk with the governor. We'll be seeing him in an hour. You haven't heard the last of this."

Van Slyke turned and walked out of the conference room as quickly as possible.

Creed turned to look at the others and then sat down in the soft leather chair, his fists clenched with anger, partly at himself for losing his temper. James Brazzle sighed and shook his head.

"Never were much at diplomacy, were you Creed?"

CHAPTER 4

Guadalupe wasn't expecting to hear from her husband before he returned from Austin later that evening, and she certainly wasn't worried when he didn't call. Creed refused to use a cell phone, and there was nothing she had been able to do to change his mind. The Broken "T", though, was beginning to resemble a remote outpost in Comanche country since many of their Anglo and Hispanic neighbors had fled. Creed's instinctual aversion to digital devices eventually could have security implications for her, and Guadalupe intended to remind him of that when he returned. Creed's sons, of course, never left her alone intentionally, but the ranch was huge and sometimes they ventured out of radio range.

Creed had divorced his boys' mother when Scrap was just three years old after he caught her in bed with the ranch manager. She had been an alcoholic and always looking for the greener grass on the other side of the hill. The ranch manager had been a key member of the Broken "T" outfit for many years, but that hadn't saved him from the dire retribution of an enraged husband. Creed hadn't lifted a hand against his wife, but the ranch manager had never recovered from the beating and was destined to spend the rest of his life walking with the help of a cane. In South Texas in those days, catching your wife *in flagrante* with another man was justification for practically anything, and Creed hadn't even been charged with assault. Had the foreman died, which he almost did, the judge would have ruled the beating "justifiable homicide".

Creed met Guadalupe a few years later in a Mexican café in Laredo where she worked as a waitress. The two were married within six months, and Guadalupe gave birth to a daughter the following year. Little Alba gave a new purpose to Creed's life and was probably the only thing on earth that could have dismantled the wall he had erected around himself since his divorce. Most of his friends had written the irascible old man off as a lost cause and avoided him whenever possible. They considered the change in Creed miraculous and recognized Guadalupe and Alba as the cure.

Alba grew up bilingual and could have been a poster child for cultural diversity, a term Creed had never heard of but instinctively fostered. Her exotic good looks were the talk of La Salle County, but she had few suitors even as a seventeen-year old senior in high school. The local boys were intimidated by Creed, and few of them could have passed muster as a suitor to his only daughter. If one ever got past Creed, he'd still have to face the gauntlet of Matlock and Scrap. Given that grim reality, Alba joked that she was destined to be an old maid.

Late in the afternoon Guadalupe and Alba were working in the kitchen, throwing together the ingredients for a large batch of tortilla soup. A small portable television with a pair of rabbit ears on top stood on the counter, and out of the corner of her eye Guadalupe watched a rerun of *Rosalinda,* a popular Mexican soap opera starring Thalia.

"Momma, I don't know how you can watch that garbage," ventured Alba in English.

"Mi amor, ¿por qué no me hablas en español?" asked Guadalupe. Since she had entered high school, Alba rarely spoke Spanish to her anymore.

"Because we're living in the United States...and because some of the kids make fun of me for being half-Mexican," she blurted out.

Guadalupe laughed out loud.

"That's just plain ignorance," she declared. "Your father used to call me a 'wetback' when he got mad, but then he married me. The *gringos* don't always say what they really mean."

Guadalupe glanced at the round electric clock that hung over the sink. It was past five o'clock, still the heat of the day in South Texas but beginning to get late. She had been so busy preparing the broth, frying corn tortillas, and grating cheese for the tortilla soup that she hadn't noticed how the afternoon had flown by. Matlock and Scrap also would be driving up before too long after they finished their chores. She looked forward to them all sitting down together for dinner as a family and wasn't concerned about Creed running late or the boys' absence from the compound. Then she heard the first burst of semi-automatic weapons fire.

***

"What's your take on everything, James?" asked Creed as they approached the northern boundary of the Broken "T" Land & Cattle Company ranch.

James had drifted off to sleep, his Resistol straw hat pulled down over his eyes. He sat up with a start at the sound of his name, and Creed waited for him to collect his thoughts. Meanwhile, Creed stopped the truck and rolled out of the driver side of the cab and opened the pipe gate, walking across the iron grating of a cattle guard so full of dirt and debris it no longer served any practical purpose. He got back in, rolled the truck forward, and got out of the truck again and shut and locked the gate behind. When he climbed back in the pickup, James was still rubbing his eyes, trying to wake up.

Prickly pear cactus and scraggly mesquite trees were the predominant features of the barren, cauterized landscape on either side of the road. Despite the lengthy drought South Texas was experiencing, the Brahma-cross cattle somehow were still able to find some dried-up stubble left over from the normally plentiful native grasses. Creed hadn't started feeding hay yet but he would soon. It was unspeakably hot and the country needed rain badly.

The men hadn't spoken much since the disappointing meeting with the governor of Texas. It was one thing to have to listen to thirty minutes of political banalities from a politician. They had expected that, but when the Texas Rangers broke up their press conference at the direct order of the governor, who threatened to charge the ranchers with "inciting the people of South Texas to riot", the men were at a loss for words.

"You want my candid opinion?" replied James, wide awake now and clinching his jaw. Creed recognized the mannerism from years back and knew that James was about to give him his uncensored version of the truth. Brazzle never minced words despite his years in the "diplomatic" service. It's impossible to eradicate a South Texas upbringing even if you live half your life abroad.

"Well, a little candor probably wouldn't hurt, James," responded Creed. "It might be an improvement on your usual line of bullshit."

"Okay, son, here it is. To begin with, I think the FNLT has made some significant inroads in Austin," stated James emphatically. "Just don't know how deep the rot is."

"No shit, James." Creed spit out the window. "That Van Slyke character is as dirty as they come."

"Agreed." James nodded his head. "I suspected it before," he added. "There's no way so many Hispanics registered to vote in the municipals last month or that the vote could have been so overwhelmingly one-sided in favor of radical Hispanic candidates. I'll lay even money that if we could look at the election rolls, we'd find that the Front used the same kind of tactics the PRI used for decades in Mexico. Van Slyke must have known about it, but chose to ignore it. I think we all know why. I'd love to take a look at his bank statements...all of them."

"What the hell's the PRI, and what tactics are you talking about?" asked Creed.

James glanced quickly over at Creed and almost laughed.

"Sorry, I forget sometimes what an ignorant redneck you are, Creed."

Unless you knew him, Brazzle's dry humor often seemed to come down on the acerbic side of friendly. Creed could take it as well as dish it out, though. He was used to James' barbs and just waited for him to answer.

"The PRI is the Institutional Revolutionary Party. They had the monopoly on political power in Mexico for more than seventy years and wrote the instruction manual on electoral fraud. I mean to tell you they used every tactic you can imagine: registering dead people to vote, corrupt financing of election campaigns, threatening and intimidating voters. You name it, they used it. It looks like the FNLT learned from the PRI. Personally, I think they're taking orders from somebody in Mexico City."

"That's what I told Van Slyke, but I thought I was exaggerating. There'd be political implications to that, I'd think," responded Creed. "Something Washington couldn't ignore. Can you prove it, James?"

"Not yet, but I'm working on it," James replied.

"I thought you weren't concerned about all those tattooed gangbangers with their Glocks and Brownings stuffed down the back of their baggy jeans driving around Cotulla like they owned the place."

Creed slowed down to let a skinny wayward calf get out of the way of the truck.

"I wasn't so much when I thought they were just a bunch

of street corner dope dealers. That was before they killed the two Border Patrol agents and made a move on your ranch, Creed. Now I realize the National Front has some organization behind it and that we're facing something more than just a grassroots Hispanic rights movement. Sometimes it's not that easy to connect the dots."

"Well, if you've connected them, enlighten me, will you?" demanded Creed.

"I don't have anything more than theories right now, Creed, but I know this is more than just a little spillover violence from cartel turf battles in Mexico."

"Come on, James. Isn't it obvious? It's a turf battle alright, but it's our turf they're after."

"Yeah, I'll buy that, but who's behind it? That's the answer I'm looking for. The thugs on the street aren't calling the shots. Whoever's running this operation wears a suit and breathes the rarified air of financial and political power. They probably have offices in Mexico City and who knows where else."

The two men sat in silence in the pickup as it rocked from side to side on the uneven gravel road and Creed negotiated the familiar gauntlet of ruts and potholes. Creed refused to use the air conditioning in his pickup and he insisted everyone suffer along with him. The sticky heat made the men's skin itch, and the back of their shirts was dark with moisture and hugged their bodies like plastic cling wrap.

As the white pickup truck followed the rough road around a sharp bend to the right and emerged from behind a thicket of mesquite trees, Creed saw a plume of white smoke rising in the distance above ranch headquarters.

"What the hell?" said James in a concerned voice.

"That better not be what I think it is," said Creed and stomped on the old Chevy's accelerator.

CHAPTER 5

Mario and Rodrigo spent three harrowing days walking and hitchhiking in a northerly direction, putting as much distance as possible between themselves and the scene of the gruesome murders they inadvertently witnessed. The incident had shaken Rodrigo, whose relatively sheltered life until now had centered around training horses on a large *hacienda* in the Mexican state of Guanajuato. He'd heard talk of the violence along the border with Texas but thought the stories were exaggerated. Now he knew they weren't. It was worse than he could have imagined.

They traveled at night and hunkered down during the day, hiding in deserted outbuildings or thorny mesquite thickets, keeping an eye out for rattlesnakes and scorpions and any sign of the Border Patrol. A kind Mexican family gave them a ride in their rattletrap 1989 Ford pickup north along Interstate 35 almost to Artesia Wells and offered them a supply of corn tortillas and beans. That night Mario and Rodrigo split a bottle of Modelo Especial they bought at a gas station convenience store and relaxed for the first time in a week.

On the fourth day towards dawn, Mario and Rodrigo crawled through a barb wire fence into the Broken "T" Land & Cattle Company ranch. They made their way cautiously through the pastures cluttered with scrub vegetation and the occasional wide-eyed Brahma-bred cow and they filled their canteens in a trough fed by an old Chicago Aermotor windmill. They shared the water with several liver-spotted calves and a confused white-tail doe that ran from them at first and then stood eying them suspiciously from a safe distance. They came to a gravel road and followed it to a large hay barn in sight of the main residence. Mario rolled back the heavy metal door and they squeezed through the opening, sliding the door shut behind them. The aluminum barn was clean inside and they saw 800-lb. round bales of hay from irrigated fields of coastal bermuda neatly stacked three high on one side. Other than a few elusive field mice and an ill-tempered old striped tomcat that eyed them suspiciously, Mario and Rodrigo were alone and they climbed up on top of the bales and spread their clothes out over the scratchy hay and lay down to rest.

"This ranch might be what we're looking for," said Mario. "Look at these round bales. This is good hay."

"Are we far enough from the border yet?" asked Rodrigo.

"Not really. Maybe sixty, sixty-five miles at the most, but we're running out of money."

Rodrigo reached across the hay to his jeans and pulled a money clip from the left rear pocket. He pulled out the few remaining crumpled bills and started to count them.

"I've still got twenty dollars or so," he said.

"Yeah, I've got ten left, but money doesn't go far up here."

"How long will this last us?" asked Rodrigo.

"Couple of days, maybe more if we could buy a pot and cook some rice and beans."

"Maybe we should keep going north towards San Antonio," Rodrigo suggested.

"The more time we spend on the road, the more likely *La Migra* will find us," Mario said. "Besides, we might not find a job right away. It's probably time to start looking."

He rolled on his back and stretched, groaning with pleasure.

"*¡Hombre, qué rico!* Best bed we've had since we left Guanajuato."

"So what do you want to do?" asked Rodrigo.

"Sleep," said Mario.

"What about work?"

"What about it?"

"Are we going to ask the *patron* here for a job?"

"We can try," said Mario. "But let's rest a little first."

"They have horses here, you know." said Rodrigo.

"How can you tell? I didn't see any."

"Look at those square bales across the barn."

Mario propped himself up on his elbows and looked at where Rodrigo was pointing. On the other side of the barn he saw stacks of light green square bales tied up with baling wire. Hundreds of them.

"This *patron* has good horses or else he'd just feed them round bales like the cows," said Rodrigo.

"So?"

"Maybe he needs a horse trainer. That's what I did in Guanajuato, you know."

"You any good?" asked Mario.

"I know horses. I trained for all the *charros* from Leon and Irapuato."

"*¿De veras?*"

"*Claro.* My father put me on a horse when I was four years old. I've been riding ever since," said Rodrigo. "I could probably teach these *gringos* a thing or two," said Rodrigo.

"Maybe, maybe not."

"What do you mean?" asked Rodrigo.

"*Gringos* think Mexicans are too rough on horses. Usually a *patron* in Texas won't let one of us ride his good horses, much less train them," explained Mario.

"They'll see. I've got a light hand," said Rodrigo.

"Hey, can you do me a favor?" asked Mario.

"Sure, what do you need?"

"Shut up. I can hardly keep my eyes open."

They were dozing off as Creed and James Brazzle drove away from ranch headquarters towards the highway on their way to Austin. They could hear the diesel engine of Creed's dually pickup as it roared by outside the barn. They slept for several hours and could have slept all day, but the metal structure conducted heat, and by early afternoon when they woke up, it was stifling and their t-shirts were soaked with sweat.

"*¡Hijole!*" exclaimed Rodrigo as he gasped for oxygen in the suffocating atmosphere of the barn. "I've got to get some air," he said and started to climb down from the stack of round bales.

"Wait a minute," cautioned Mario and he put his finger to his lips, warning Rodrigo to be silent.

"What's the matter?" asked Rodrigo.

"I thought I heard something," said Mario.

A vague *thump-thump* that sounded almost like distant thunder or explosions gradually became more distinct and increased in volume, and they recognized and soon could almost feel the pulsating bass of a car stereo blasting at full volume. The sound of music grew louder, and they heard the high-pitched whine of diesel engines approaching in low gear...then shouts and short bursts from semi-automatic weapons. The two Mexicans looked at each other in alarm.

"*¡Puta! ¿Aquí también?*" Rodrigo couldn't believe it. They clambered down from the top of the bales where they had fallen asleep and ran to the door of the barn which stood slightly ajar. They peered out of the door and saw two black SUVs circling the barn at high speed, skidding and churning up clouds of blowing dirt. Rap music in Spanish blared from both vehicles, and several Mexicans with baseball caps on backwards were hanging out of the back windows firing their weapons indiscriminately into the air. Shots ricocheted off the barn door, and Rodrigo and Mario retreated apprehensively to the rear of the barn where they took cover behind the first tier of round bales.

"Who are these *cabrones?"* asked Rodrigo looking at Mario in utter confusion.

"They're probably *narcos,* but what are they doing here? Keep your head down," Mario ordered.

The SUVs raced around the barn for another minute and then the engines slowed and the firing stopped. Mario and Rodrigo heard the metallic rumbling of the barn door as it slid open, and they burrowed deeper into the stack of hay bales at the far end of the aluminum structure.

A voice cried out in Spanish. "Throw it. Let's get out of here!"

The barn door slid shut and they heard car doors slam before a deafening explosion sent shrapnel zinging around the barn's interior and left them disoriented. When they looked up, the barn was filling with acrid smoke, and flames were spreading in the dry hay over by the door. Their ears rung painfully and they each mouthed words the other couldn't hear.

***

At the first sound of gunfire, Guadalupe took the frying corn tortillas off the gas burner of the kitchen stove and ran to the gun rack in the living room and retrieved two Model 770 Remington deer rifles. She grabbed a box of .30-06 cartridges and handed one of the rifles to Alba. They both heard the explosion from the living room and ran to the front porch and saw dense smoke pouring out of the barn. She and Alba stood helplessly and watched the two SUVs disappear in a cloud of dust. Ragged volleys of gunfire reverberated across the flat plain before gradually fading and dissipating in the distance.

Guadalupe had already raised Matlock on the radio and knew that he and Scrap would be arriving in about fifteen minutes from where they had been repairing cross fence in a pasture south of the house. She also knew that wouldn't be in time to save the hay they needed to get the cattle through the winter. They could always sell off enough land to the developers to cover their feed costs, she thought to herself as she and Alba flew down the steps from the front porch carrying the rifles and then raced towards the barn. She just hoped Creed wouldn't do anything stupid. He was tough; no doubt about it, but not a match for the Zetas or whoever these criminals were.

She and Alba ran past the front door of the barn, coughing from the harsh smoke which burned their eyes and made their chests hurt. They headed for the water spigot and hose that ran from the well Creed drilled last year. As they ran around the far corner of the barn where the hose lay, they almost collided with two young Mexican men who were running towards them, frantically uncoiling the hose which was already starting to spew water. There was no time for questions. Guadalupe sprinted to the barn door, and with Alba's help, slid it open. Mario ran inside carrying the hose and directed the high-pressure stream of water on the flames. Rodrigo flailed at the flames on the other side of the bay with a gunny sack he had found outside the barn. In fifteen desperate minutes the two Mexicans managed to douse the fire and emerged from the barn wheezing and with chests heaving from their efforts.

"The fire's out," said Mario in Spanish, gasping to catch his breath. "You should probably get a tractor with a hay fork and move the bales that got wet."

Guadalupe looked at the two boys, their faces blackened with soot from the fire and eyes bloodshot from the smoke.

"*¿Quiénes son ustedes?*" she asked although she already knew the answer.

"We're *vaqueros*. Looking for work."

"*Bueno,* you might have come to the right place...and at the right time," she added.

CHAPTER 6

Francisco "Pancho" Salcido gazed out of the air-conditioned study of his home in the hills east of Culiacán, Sinaloa. He watched the crew of construction workers put the finishing touches on his two-lane Olympic-size swimming pool, an ostentatious touch to an otherwise modest ranch house. The workers labored under the watchful eyes of Salcido's security guards: eight former federal police officers armed with brand new M4 carbines which a National Guard Armory in South Texas had recently "donated" to the cause.

Salcido sat back in his overstuffed leather chair. He inhaled deeply on a Cuban Montecristo cigar. He twirled the ring band around his little finger and admired the brand's logo: a triangle of six swords surrounding a fleur-de-lis. Francisco looked forward to swimming in the new pool for exercise and he knew he needed to lose weight. Now wasn't the time to forget about his health. Things were going too well for him to be slowed down by nagging health problems. His doctor had advised him to exercise more and to watch his diet. For once, he planned to listen to the man's advice.

Salcido had taken huge risks over the past few years and spent enormous sums of money. It all had finally paid off, and in a big way. Candidates he backed had won the gubernatorial elections in most of the northern states of Mexico, and his own people held influential positions in the state governments and the Federal Police throughout the country. He had dozens of key politicians on his payroll, and no important decision in Mexico City was taken without consulting his opinion. To do otherwise could be deleterious to one's health.

Francisco grinned to himself as he recalled the multiple

reorganizations of the Federal Police force that had taken place over the last decade. He remembered the estimates the Mexican government made, alleging that 20% of the police force worked as enforcers for the Sinaloa cartel. Twenty percent? he thought to himself. *"Carajo!"* he cursed mildly. It was more like 75%, and his own cousin ran the organization and reported to him daily.

Salcido's own success in the drug trade was not surprising. His uncle has been Manuel Salcido Uzueta, the infamous, "Cochiloco", drug lord extraordinaire, whose escapades to this day are celebrated in Mexican folklore and *narcocorridos*. Francisco had worked his way up in the Cochiloco organization. He had incorporated his uncle's positive innovations into his own organization but eschewed what he saw as excessive greed and violence. Violence always had to have a purpose or else it was just cruelty. Francisco Salcido did not think of himself as a cruel man. He was pragmatic, but not a bully.

His cell phone rang. Francisco glanced at the number and grunted in acknowledgement. It was the attorney general calling from Mexico City.

"¿Quíhubole, carnal?" Salcido greeted the caller warmly. The attorney general had become one of the wealthiest men in Mexico thanks to him, and Salcido had come to genuinely like and respect him. "Félix Aguilar is a man of honor who keeps his word," Francisco commented frequently to his lieutenants. The fact that Aguilar betrayed daily the men who looked to him for leadership did not occur to Salcido. Francisco generously rewarded those who supported him and ruthlessly eliminated those that didn't. That's all he knew.

"Hola, Pancho. ¿Que pasó?"

"Nada, compa. Just sitting here waiting for your phone call," replied Salcido.

"I thought you would like to know...the legal attaché from the American Embassy...you know, the FBI representative.

Well, he came to see me today to discuss the unfortunate incident last week that took the lives of the two *Migra* agents."

Salcido sat up in his chair. He wondered how long it would take the *gringos* to look for a Mexican connection to the murders.

"And what does Mexico have to do with a crime committed in Texas?" he asked. "I'm afraid I don't understand the reason for the American's visit," Francisco said, feigning innocence.

"The *gringos* are not stupid, my friend. Naïve, of course, but they're like the proverbial mule. If you hit them over the head with a two-by-four, you'll get their attention. Looks like you got their attention, *compa*," said the attorney general.

"*Escuchame, carnal,*" replied Salcido. You forget yourself. I'm a simple businessman. I export tomatoes to the United States. Your inference is out of place and not appreciated."

"Forgive me, Pancho," said the attorney general. "I didn't mean to imply anything."

Salcido smiled to himself. The attorney general did not know how right he was. The FNLT had requested Francisco's assistance several weeks ago. The National Front needed more muscle to enforce some of its more radical policies. Salcido exported many things to the United States including the Sinaloa cartel soldiers who lately had been pouring into South Texas in eighteen wheelers belonging to the Zima Group. Why send them over in ones and twos when a single tractor trailer could take an entire platoon across the border? As long as the *gringos* in Austin turned a blind eye to his ambitions, he would take advantage of their inaction. After all, that inaction was costing him a lot of money in strategically placed bribes and incentive payments.

The history of the *norteamericanos* in Texas and Mexico provided the only lessons Francisco needed. Power and brute force were everything. With the border secured in Texas and the real political power in South Texas wrested from the

Anglos, there would be no limit to Salcido's influence. His uncle would have been proud of him.

"So, what did you tell the *cabrón*?" asked Salcido.

"What you would expect of a loyal friend and Mexican patriot," replied the attorney general, relieved that Salcido's anger had subsided. "I asked him for proof that Mexico was involved in the incident. When he failed to produce any evidence, I told him that crime in Texas was an internal matter for the Americans, and that they should clean up their own house before trying to blame all their problems on Mexico."

"That's why we get along so well, *carnal,*" interjected Salcido. "I couldn't have put it better myself. We're both politicians, only I don't have to run for election."

"I agree, Pancho. We do think alike," said the attorney general. "The FBI officer was not very happy when he left my office."

"The *gringos* are never happy unless we dance like puppets to their music and kiss their asses," said Salcido.

"This one even had the gall to threaten me."

"What did he say?"

"Oh, just the usual: hints of a reduction in foreign aid for our narcotics eradication program if Mexico doesn't do more to stop the export of drugs and violence to the United States."

"I can guess how you answered that," said Salcido.

"Yes, I *did* happen to mention that most of all the weapons we seize from the traffickers come from the United States."

"And of course the obligatory complaint about *gringo* demand for drugs fueling the problem?"

"Naturally," said Aguilar. "I know my role by heart."

"You have a brilliant future ahead of you, my friend. I will make sure of that. How's the campaign going?"

The presidential elections were scarcely six months away, and Félix Aguilar was already the unspoken forerunner. His extraordinary "success" in the fight against the drug traffickers and organized crime had made his candidacy the talk of Mexico City. Salcido thought it was ironic that the Mexican voters attached such significance to the drug seizures he and Aguilar staged for political gain.

"I can't complain. The latest polls have me ahead with almost 69% of the vote. I'm even polling well among the leftist parties. Everyone's tired of the violence. They see me as the savior."

"That means our strategy is working," said Salcido. "It's a wonder what campaign financing can do, isn't it?"

"What is it the *norteamericanos* say? Money talks and bullshit walks?"

"Ha, for once I agree with them," said Salcido.

"When can you come to Mexico City? asked the attorney general. We need to meet."

"What for?" Salcido asked.

"Things are heating up in South Texas. I have some ideas to discuss with you."

"I do have to meet with my banker. Let me call my pilot and see if we can fly over tomorrow."

"That would be perfect."

CHAPTER 7

Creed Tucker had to admit it. Hiring those two wetbacks was one of the best things he had done in recent memory. Of course, he didn't really have much of a say in the matter when you got right down to it. Creed saw that much on Guadalupe's face when his pickup skidded to a stop in front of the smoke-filled barn. She announced in a voice that disallowed further discussion that Rodrigo and Mario would be working on the ranch and living in the bunkhouse. The smoking barn and their black, sooty faces told the whole story.

That was two weeks ago. Since then, even Scrap and Matlock had given their stamp of approval to the two Mexicans, especially to Rodrigo. That boy was the best hand with young horses Scrap or his father had ever seen. Creed had gotten into the habit of watching Rodrigo work the two-year olds at first light before it got too hot to ride. He would walk all stiff and bow-legged down to the corrals and take a seat in the narrow bleachers overlooking the round pen. He'd watch Rodrigo work his magic and sip hot coffee from a ceramic coffee cup decorated with images of bucking horses and barbed wire. Guadalupe had the cup made especially for him to celebrate their tenth anniversary, and Creed had kept it ever since and refused to drink out of anything else.

Rodrigo had a gift. That couldn't be denied. Even Scrap, an accomplished horse trainer in his own right, watched Rodrigo in awe. From the moment the boy walked into the dusty, cedar-post round pen, he established an almost mystical connection with the colts he worked. Even the rankest colts submitted to his calm and assured manner within minutes.

What bothered Creed, though, was that he seemed to have

the same effect on Alba. Creed was far from a racist. Hell, he was married to a Mexican, but he didn't know if he liked the way Rodrigo and Alba looked at each other. He needed to speak to both of them, he reckoned. Alba was being too coquettish and forward, and Rodrigo came up with too many excuses to be close to the barn where he could see Alba more often. The two spoke Spanish together most of the time, but Alba was already teaching him English. The boy picked it up quickly. He was a smart one.

"Rodrigo," called Creed, as the boy dismounted and tightened the cinch on a two-year old Little Peppy-bred gelding. "When will you have that colt ready for the buyer to ride?" he asked in Spanish.

"He's ready now, *patron*. Anybody can ride him now, even Alba," Rodrigo said smiling.

"Alba's been riding since she was four. She can ride almost as well as you," Creed exaggerated. "Let me know when the colt is ready for Mario. Then I'll call the buyer."

Rodrigo nodded his head and Creed couldn't help but notice him look guiltily over at Mario who was saddling the next colt for Rodrigo to ride. Mario had called the shots during their trek northward, but things had subtly changed between the two friends since their arrival at the ranch. Rodrigo was the top hand on the Broken "T", and everyone knew it. Creed could tell Mario had a chip on his shoulder and resented the attention everyone lavished on Rodrigo.

Creed knew Mario might move on and look for a job elsewhere, but a job in Texas was worth more than vanity and hurt feelings nowadays. It wasn't just the paycheck or a place to sleep or a plate of rice and beans. South Texas had become a dangerous place, and his job on the Broken "T" was a refuge from the uncertainty that reigned beyond the boundaries of the ranch. Creed hoped Mario would just swallow his pride and stay on for the time being.

Creed climbed down from the bleachers and headed back toward the house, his cowboy boots shuffling in the dust. It was still early, but the sun in this part of the country was merciless, and most living creatures on the Broken "T" were already seeking shade under sparse mesquite or oak trees: meager relief at best, but better than nothing. He had already broken a sweat, and the back of his blue denim shirt was soaking wet.

A red Dodge Ram extended-cab pickup sped up the graded drive from the barn and stopped abruptly in front of the house sending gravel spewing in all directions. Creed recognized James Brazzle climbing out of the truck and adjusting his straw hat.

Wonder what this is about? he thought to himself with growing unease.

"You heard the news?" called out James, without even greeting his old friend. He pulled his hat down over his eyes and squinted at Creed in the bright sunlight.

"Good morning to you too," said Creed. He couldn't abide bad manners and he was irritated at James' violation of their unwritten social code.

"Sorry, Creed," James ventured with an embarrassed nod. "It's just that I'm not used to being stopped by a bunch of Mexicans in uniforms on this side of the border and having my truck searched for contraband."

"What in God's name are you talking about?" asked Creed. "You been smoking some of that shit your wetbacks buy in Laredo?"

"Hell no, you just don't get off your ranch enough and you never watch the news. You don't even know what's going on fifteen miles up the road," retorted James.

Creed stared at James, who strangely was wearing a holster with his M1911 Browning .45 caliber pistol. That got Creed's attention more than his friend's excited hyperbole. At least, Creed was hoping it was hyperbole. If James was packing, though, the situation must have gone south in a hurry.

"Come on inside," Creed offered. "Let's find out what the hell you've been up to."

The two friends sat around the coffee table in the living room with the ceiling fan clanking above them. The screen windows were open and the humid air from outside was heating up fast. Creed refused to use the air conditioner before noon. He viewed the artificially cooled air as a concession to the twenty-first century and an admission he was softer than his father and grandfather had been.

"Go ahead, James," Creed suggested.

James stood up and hung his cowboy hat on a steer-horn hat rack on the wall. His spurs clicked on the Saltillo tile floor as he slowly paced back and forth.

"Well, I'm not sure what you know and what you don't," began James.

"Just give me the background in a nutshell, and then tell me what happened today."

"However you'd like your medicine, Creed," said James, trying to accommodate the increasingly grouchy rancher.

"Two days ago *El Frente*, the National Front for the Liberation of Texas, issued a statement publically condemning the inability of the local and state police forces to stop the violence. They announced that their own paramilitary forces would be patrolling the streets and highways in South Texas and warned the police not to interfere."

"Jesus Christ," said Creed. "They create the problem to start with and then pretend they're outraged the police can't do anything about it. The bastards are clever. And on what authority did they make this announcement?"

James snorted. "Creed, you need to watch the damned

news. This is dated intelligence, my friend."

"Keep talking," Creed said.

"On the dubious authority of the 'Hispanic Majority Committee' composed of most of the mayors in South Texas," stated Brazzle without emotion. "The mayors apparently asked the Front to reestablish law and order in South Texas."

"The Hispanic Majority Committee? Never heard of it." replied Creed. "It all sounds a bit like Hitler in the 1930s."

James turned and looked at Creed solemnly.

"There's even talk of holding a referendum on autonomy for South Texas, but so far it's only talk. They're still afraid the governor might come to his senses and send in the National Guard to restore order. Frankly, I'm not so sure he will."

"And what the hell is that snake Van Slyke saying up in Austin?" asked Creed. "This kind of thing can't take place without the approval of the Texas Election Commission, I reckon. For that matter, Washington's not going to sit by and let this kind of thing happen either."

"Yeah, you're right, Creed, or you should be. But all our friends up in Austin have said is that they're looking into the constitutionality of the referendum. Haven't heard a peep out of Washington."

"That figures," grumbled Creed.

"The bastards have set up a checkpoint at the I-35 business exit into Cotulla. They're wearing military uniforms with the letters R.A.T.S. on their hats. They're calling themselves border guards of the Autonomous Republic of South Texas!"

Creed gawked at James in disbelief.

"R.A.T.S? Well, at least the abbreviation in translation hits the nail on the head, doesn't it?" laughed Creed. "*La República Autónoma de Tejas del Sur!* Haven't they jumped the gun on this a bit? You said they were only talking about holding a referendum, right?"

"I asked about that. In Spanish, of course. They refused to speak English with me. They just said they were just following orders from *El Frente*," James said.

"Hell, this is nothing less than an invasion of sovereign U.S. territory by the cartels. Can't anyone besides us see that?" Creed raised his voice and looked at James practically in desperation.

Brazzle shook his head.

"You're preaching to the choir, Creed. I wouldn't be surprised if those thugs at the checkpoint were soldiers for the Sinaloa cartel or the Zetas and their uniforms made in Mexico!"

"I think they've gone too far now. The governor won't have any choice but to come in with the National Guard," said Creed.

"Maybe, maybe not," said James.

"Yeah, I'm not so sure either," said Creed. "He's thinking more about reelection than his responsibilities to Texas. I just hope he's not on the take too."

Creed turned and looked at James.

"Well, Brazzle, you old CIA coot. You said if and when the time came, we'd have help. Don't you think the time has arrived?"

CHAPTER 8

James Brazzle felt like a poker player whose hand has been called. Not that he was bluffing. One thing he did have to show for his long years in the CIA were contacts: and plenty of them. But his generation of CIA case officers was mostly retired now. Some lived abroad, addicts to a dissolute, cosmopolitan lifestyle and cheap local booze. A surprising number lived in the suburbs of Washington D.C., as if their proximity to Langley somehow kept them in the loop and fed their adrenalin addiction. Most had aged badly. It was an unhealthy way to live, and the heavy drinking, smoking, late nights, and marital strife had taken their toll on many of his now middle-aged colleagues.

But to a man, everyone he called had the same thing to say: the CIA did not plan to get embroiled in any domestic affair. Despite the circumstantial evidence implicating the Mexican cartels in the anti-Anglo initiatives in South Texas, the Democratic administration in Washington had issued unambiguous instructions for Langley not to get involved. Washington viewed this as a domestic affair and outside the CIA's bailiwick. Why the FBI was sitting on its hands, nobody could say. There was also the issue of states' rights to be considered. The consensus was that it was Austin's prerogative to deal with the crisis itself or to request federal assistance. So far, the state government had done neither.

Domestic affair? Circumstantial evidence? That smacked of political correctness taken to the extreme, Brazzle thought. Even a high school sophomore could use the latest Google Earth satellite photography and see the R.A.T.S. checkpoints along the Nueces River. Surely, that alone would raise some eyebrows in Washington. Talk about a referendum to establish an autonomous region in South Texas should evoke memories of secession and would have to raise suspicions of electoral fraud. Was he expected to believe that Washington didn't have a steady stream of intelligence pouring in from a multitude of sources regarding the extraordinary developments in South Texas over the last six months? James knew there were other considerations at play, but outside of the probability that a few key officials in Washington and Austin were padding their bank accounts with cartel money, he had no answers.

That left Mako Sloane. Not exactly a poster boy for political correctness, Mako and his team of former covert operatives had set up a headquarters on a country estate outside of Chantilly, Virginia. Rumor had it they were freelancing: intelligence gathering or paramilitary services to the highest bidder. Somehow, "mercenary" status didn't quite fit Mako Sloane. James suspected there was more to it than that.

Brazzle and Sloane went back a long way, almost as far back as James did with Creed Tucker. James first met Mako at a rodeo in San Angelo, Texas when they were sixteen. James had been a bull rider, and Mako was riding saddle broncs. They were both wild as shithouse rats in those days and had even made a few drunken, late-night sojourns together to the Chicken Ranch, the infamous "Best Little Whorehouse in Texas" outside of La Grange. They saw each other in the army and a few years later had a good laugh when they literally ran into each other in a men's room at CIA headquarters.

They had gone their separate ways then, but a decade later James found himself working with the Contras in Nicaragua and taking orders from none other than Mako Sloane, who by then was already a legend in the Agency. Brazzle recognized pure, distilled genius when he saw it and watched in disbelieving admiration as Sloane played his role as unofficial envoy to the Sandinista government, hobnobbing with Daniel Ortega and his cronies as if it was something he did every day. The Reagan crowd was uncomfortable with Sloane's personal relationship with Ortega but didn't mind the intelligence bonanza the friendship provided.

Brazzle lost track of Mako Sloane after that, but the rumors persisted. He knew Sloane was making a name for himself in Moscow, but nothing more. Then, inexplicably, there was his transfer to Afghanistan after 9/11 and his mysterious disappearance. The U.S. government reported he was dead. Seven years later, those who had known him were shocked when Mako turned up in perfect health and a free man as he emerged from the bowels of the federal prison system. But there're some things you just don't ask about.

That all sounded like Mako, he thought, even federal prison. Mako's penchant for simplistic, usually violent solutions and his sense of personal invincibility were usually a guarantee for controversy of one kind or another despite his long string of operational successes. Brazzle had heard a Russian penetration of the Agency had been involved in Mako's downfall and that he had been convicted on trumped up charges to silence him. About what, nobody seemed to know. For James Brazzle it was enough to know that Mako Sloane was back. He didn't care whether he had the backing of the Central Intelligence Agency or not. He would have trusted Sloane under any circumstances and he needed the man's help even though he knew he'd have to keep Mako on a tight leash.

Sloane wasn't an easy one to track down, though. Brazzle made at least a dozen phone calls before one of his old colleagues who used to work the Soviet / East European target gave him the private cell number of Drake Herrin. Herrin was a CIA legend in his own right. He had been Sloane's direct supervisor and mentor during the Moscow years, and Brazzle had once known him well. It was a starting point, at least, the only lead James really had. Allegedly, Herrin was working again with Mako.

"James, I wondered when I'd hear from you," said Drake Herrin the following day when Brazzle finally reached him.

"I've been expecting your call. I figured you had retired to your family's ranch down there in South Texas and might be feeling a bit edgy by now."

"You should have played chess, Drake," replied Brazzle, gratified that Drake still remembered him so well. "You always did see a couple of moves ahead. Have you been following what's going on down here? Washington's been awful quiet."

"Quiet doesn't mean idle," Drake declared. "Washington's treading a fine line here. The administration doesn't like threats to the sovereignty of the United States, but they've got to respect Texas' right to run its own affairs. They're sitting on the fence right now waiting for Governor Throckmorton to make his move."

"Drake, something stinks up in Austin. The governor should have made his move long ago. If the administration waits much longer, it'll be dealing with a *fait accompli.* You'll need a visa to drive from San Antonio to Laredo."

"Listen to me, James," suggested Drake. "Can you meet me at the airport in San Antonio tomorrow? I'd like to take a look at this first hand. Mako's down in Managua trying to put out some fires before they get started. Hugo Chavez flew in from Caracas yesterday to see Ortega. Mako's delivering the message for Nicaragua and Venezuela to stay out of this. The Front doesn't need any money. As far as we can tell, they're getting all they need from the Sinaloa cartel, but Chavez and Ortega are rattling swords and threatening to offer military aid to the Front in a show of Latino solidarity. If that happens, things could careen out of control real fast."

"The sooner, the better, Drake. Call me when you have your itinerary."

***

The three men sat in rattan rocking chairs arranged in a tight semi-circle on the first floor veranda of the Mediterranean-style villa with red ceramic roof tiles. The tiles were fashionably discolored by streaks of black mold which created the impression of old money and respectability. The fronds of the two tall palm trees bracketing the house rustled and undulated in the persistent offshore breeze that originated to the east from Lake Nicaragua and blew relentlessly across the narrow isthmus towards the Pacific Ocean. Armed soldiers stood guard at ten-meter intervals around the villa, and the occasional crackle of monosyllabic radio transmissions was jarring and somehow incongruous in the otherwise idyllic tropical setting.

President of Venezuela Hugo Chavez leaned back in the thick cushions of the wicker rocking chair and sipped a tall rum and coke made with 12-year Flor de Caña dark rum. He looked over at Daniel Ortega, the recently reelected president of Nicaragua, and then stared with open animosity at the American who was patiently waiting for a response.

"Venezuela will always support the principle of self-determination," Chavez suddenly declared. "Our suggestion to the *gringo* government would be: let the people decide. Don't interfere with the referendum and respect the results. *¿Qué no, Comandante?*"

Chavez gestured towards Daniel Ortega with upturned palms and Ortega nodded his head in agreement. It didn't matter what Chavez proposed. Ortega's support was a given. The president of Nicaragua had become a Chavez puppet over the past few years. The Sandinistas in Nicaragua looked to Chavez for strategic leadership, oil, and financial aid. In return, they danced to his fiddle. Chavez and Ortega both waited for the American's reply.

Mako Sloane stared at Chavez and inwardly shuddered. The man's resemblance to a pig was disconcerting.

"You know, *Señor Presidente*," began Mako. "There are

several principles I think we can agree on. We too support self-determination. After all, who except the citizens of a country have the right to make decisions about their own lives and the type of government they have? But secondly, I think we also can agree that those decisions need to be made by the local inhabitants themselves without outside interference. When that outside support comes from a drug cartel in a neighboring country in the form of cash, arms, and cartel soldiers, the legitimacy of any claims to self-determination fades. ¿Qué no?" asked Mako rhetorically.

The Venezuelan president's response lasted a full twenty-five minutes. He regaled Mako with a rambling tirade against American imperialism that the veteran CIA officer had heard dozens of times before; maybe not from Chavez, but from leftist tyrants of one ilk or another on three continents. Mako found it harder and harder to keep his eyes open. Hugo's capacity for pompous oratory took Mako back to his days in the USSR and the bombastic speeches the communist party leaders used to give about the West.

But this was a private meeting arranged at one of Daniel Ortega's many Pacific coast retreats near the resort town of San Juan del Sur. No interpreters were present. The two Latin American presidents were speaking Spanish with an unofficial envoy from the United States. They both knew what organization he represented. Because of his unofficial status and longstanding personal relationship with Daniel Ortega, Mako didn't feel obligated to follow strict diplomatic protocol. In fact, he had made his career violating most of the niceties of negotiation and diplomacy and saw no reason to change now at his age. He waved his hand and cut off the Venezuelan president who was obviously taken aback by Sloane's abrupt manner.

"What is the meaning of this, Mr. Sloane?" asked Chavez, sitting up straight in his bamboo chair.

"Let's not bullshit each other, Hugo," said Mako, dropping

all pretenses to civility. "Here's my message. If you provide weapons directly or indirectly to the National Front for the Liberation of Texas, there will be hell to pay...quite literally." Mako looked at an increasingly enraged Hugo Chavez without emotion. "If you have any questions about me or whom I represent, ask Daniel. He's known me for almost thirty years," said Mako as he casually got up from his chair and walked down the stairs to a small parking area where his driver was waiting in his rented Range Rover under a giant *genícero* tree.

CHAPTER 9

If Creed had second thoughts about sending Rodrigo and Mario into Cotulla for supplies, he didn't let on. There really hadn't been any choice when you came right down to it. Matlock and Scrap were already doing double-duty: patrolling the southern border of the ranch and looking for strays at the same time. They had taken Koot with them to drive any stubborn cows they might find out of the dense, thorny brush. That Blue Heeler was worth his weight in gold, both as a cow dog and as a bodyguard to protect Guadalupe and Alba.

Creed couldn't send the girls out by themselves any more. It was too dangerous now. And then to top it all off, he had gone and gotten himself kicked by that goofy Brahma cow and could barely walk. Mario was supposed to be holding the rope with the cow's left rear leg in the air so she wouldn't kick. Creed was trying to milk the cow to get as much colostrum he could for her newborn calf they'd had to pull. The rope had slipped out of Mario's hand, and the cow had taken advantage of the lapse to deliver a jack-hammer hard kick to Creed's thigh. Creed had gone down like a sack of potatoes and he hadn't been up since.

That was a week ago. The colorful blue and yellow hues of the bruise now covered Creed's leg from the knee up. He had cursed Mario up one side of the barn and down the other through clenched teeth. Mario had just kept his eyes on the ground and muttered, *"Disculpe, patron."*

***

Rodrigo was at the wheel of the old pickup as he and Mario drove up the interstate towards Cotulla. Mario had a smile on his face as broad as Texas itself. He was thrilled to be out in the truck without the *patron* or his sons. They passed the checkpoint on the Nueces without incident. It used to be that anybody with a dark complexion could expect to be stopped and harassed by the authorities practically anywhere in Texas. Now it was an advantage to look Latino, at least in South Texas. The guards at the checkpoint in the R.A.T.S. uniforms hadn't even asked to see their identification.

"Still working for that old *gringo*?" one of them had asked. He recognized Rodrigo from previous crossings with either Creed or his sons.

"It's not so bad," answered Rodrigo. "Puts rice and beans on your plate," he smiled good-naturedly.

"How about you?" the guard pointed to Mario. "We're always looking for good men. How about it? Know how to handle one of these?" The guard motioned with his head, indicating the M4 he carried on a sling in front of him.

"Yeah, I know how to shoot," Mario said.

The guard took out a wad of green bills from his uniform pocket and flashed them at Mario. "I bet you could use some of this, couldn't you?"

"*Hijole,*" said Mario. "You can say that again."

"Well, when you get tired of kissing that old *gringo's* ass, come see us."

"I will," said Mario. "It might be sooner rather than later."

"*Mario, no seas pendejo.* We've got a good job and the Tuckers are *buena gente.* They're good to us, *carnal.*" Rodrigo pulled forward in the pickup and waved to the guards.

"Maybe to you. The old man cussed me out good the other day."

"I would've too. That old cow damn near broke his leg."

"*¡Callate, buey!*" laughed Mario. "I told the old fart I was sorry."

In Cotulla they made the rounds, stopping at Super S to pick up groceries from a long list Guadalupe had drawn up and at the La Salle Feed Store for 20% protein cubes for the cattle. The dry grass filled the cows' bellies, but they needed some protein to keep weight on in the summer. Wherever they went in town, they were eyed suspiciously by the Anglo shopkeepers, at least the ones left, and by the older, long-time Hispanic residents of Cotulla. Two young Mexican men in a pickup to their minds could spell only one thing: a R.A.T.S. patrol.

According to the results of a ballot proposition during the last election, the counties in South Texas voted overwhelmingly to declare Spanish the official language between the Rio Grande and Nueces rivers. The new law required stores to conduct business in Spanish and mandated sanctions for violators. Not knowing Spanish did not qualify as an excuse. Roving bands of Latino gangbangers accompanied by one or two uniformed and armed R.A.T.S. "soldiers" patrolled Cotulla's streets after dark exacting retribution for alleged breaches of the new ordinance. The exodus of Anglos from Cotulla continued unabated, but there were still some hard-core holdouts who refused to abandon their property and faded dreams of prosperity.

The two Broken "T" ranch hands got out of the pickup at the feed store and went in to pay for the protein cubes. The old Anglo at the counter nodded silently to them.

"*¿Qué quieren?*" he asked in heavily accented Spanish.

"*Buenas tardes, señor.* We need some protein cubes for the cattle," continued Rodrigo in English. He had been practicing the phrase all week with Alba.

"*¿Cuántos sacos?*" asked the old shopkeeper in Spanish.

"One hundred, please," replied Rodrigo stubbornly in English.

Rodrigo was eager to try out his new English vocabulary, but the Anglo shop owner viewed his smiling face and attempts to speak broken English as a provocation. Rodrigo cringed at the man's belabored attempts to speak and write up a sales receipt in Spanish.

"*Señor*, Rodrigo said calmly, *"Usted puede hablar inglés conmigo. No soy del Frente.* You can speak English with me. I'm not with the Front.*"*

The old man looked at him without responding and continued his tortured attempts at Spanish. Rodrigo just shook his head and paid for the feed. Mario watched the episode with satisfaction.

"*¡Tienen miedo estos gringos de la Raza!"* Rodrigo whispered on their way out to the truck.

"Yeah, they're scared, Mario. They've lost control here in South Texas."

"I hope they all leave," said Mario.

"You can't be serious."

"Sure, I am. Then we wouldn't have to work for just a few bucks a day. We'd be our own bosses."

"Great idea, Mario. I guess you have money to buy a ranch and a herd of cattle and tractors and trucks and feed and fertilizer?"

"I'm just tired of always doing what they say," said Mario.

"If they're paying you, you do what they say...it's that simple."

"Texas used to be part of Mexico, you know. It was part of Coahuila."

"Yeah, but that was a long time ago. Before that Mexico

used to be part of Spain. Are we supposed to give it back too?" Rodrigo was losing his patience. "Anyway, you can't change history."

"The National Front is trying to."

"Yeah, well let's see how far they get. I don't want to fight the Tejanos."

A half hour later after splurging for lunch at Uncle Moe's, they began the trip back to the Tucker ranch. Rodrigo drove the pickup slowly with the extended bed full of groceries and their flatbed trailer loaded down with 50 lb. sacks of cubes for the cattle. A new shift had come on duty at the checkpoint and they didn't recognize the new guards: all sullen and tattooed, wearing sunglasses and backwards baseball caps with the letters R.A.T.S. stenciled on the front. Rodrigo eased the pickup truck up to the barrier and stopped.

Several of the guards walked towards them and one of them circled the truck and trailer.

"What's the Broken 'T'?" he asked in Spanish, pointing to the logo stenciled on the side of the truck.

"That's the ranch where we work," said Rodrigo.

"Is that a *gringo* ranch?"

"The owner's white and his wife is Mexican," answered Rodrigo.

"Got any beer?" one of the guards asked.

"Not today, friend," answered Rodrigo. "Too much work to think about drinking."

"Well, if you don't have any beer, let me see your import permit for the sacks of feed."

"Ha, that's a good one," laughed Rodrigo.

"*No mames, buey,*" answered the guard. "Where's your permit?"

"What permit? We're in Texas," Rodrigo responded.

"You were in Texas, but now you're crossing the border into *La República Autónoma de Tejas del Sur.* You need an import permit." The guard looked at Rodrigo grimly. Mario sat quietly, staring out the window at the guard's semi-automatic weapon and uniform.

"Well, I don't know anything about an import permit. We just came through here last week with a load of feed and didn't need one." The other R.A.T.S. guards heard the raised voices and gathered in a semi-circle behind the one doing all the talking. There were five of them.

"Get out of the truck, *puto!"* ordered the guard and suddenly jerked open the cab door. Two other uniformed guards stepped forward and grabbed Rodrigo by his shirt and dragged him out of the truck, his prized cowboy boots dragging toe down in the dirt. He felt the back of his shirt rip about the same time he felt a tremendous blow to the side of his face. One of the R.A.T.S. uniformed guards had kicked him below his left ear. Another lifted Rodrigo up by his armpits to make him a better target for the punches that rained down upon his head, face, and midsection.

He'd been beaten up worse. At a cockfight one night in Leon the year before, he had gotten drunk and danced with the girlfriend of a local *narco.* He hadn't known the girl was with anybody, and she hadn't let on, but nobody had cared when he tried to explain. That was the first time his nose had been broken. The R.A.T.S. guards broke it for the second time.

Mario stayed in the truck cab, paralyzed with a cold fear that nauseated him. His mouth hung open in dumb bewilderment.

"You work for the *gringos,* you need an import permit. *¿Entendido?"* The guards threw Rodrigo half-conscious and bleeding into the back of the pickup and ordered Mario to take the wheel. His hands were shaking as he drove away from the checkpoint.

CHAPTER 10

"The commissioner's here," whispered the uniformed customs official, sticking his head into Hal Wilson's office and then hurrying back to the inspection lane on the bridge.

Hal stared straight ahead at the closed door in wide-eyed, uncomprehending silence and then slammed his fist down on the desk and cursed out loud, bubbly spittle spraying the top document on the pile of papers in front of him. This was the hard way to learn about bad luck, he thought although Hal knew he was in way too deep for there to be an easy way. But why had the commissioner picked today of all days to show up unannounced and conduct a surprise inspection of the Laredo border crossing? And if it was going to be today, why the hell did it have to be now?

The phone call had come at the usual time the night before. Another Grupo Zima truck would be coming across the border in the afternoon, the caller said. All Hal had to do was make sure it wasn't searched, just like he had done dozens of times before. That wasn't too difficult for a shift supervisor, was it?

Until today, Hal had been on a mind-boggling run of good fortune. The phone calls were coming almost every day, and he looked forward to his Mexican breakfast every morning and especially the bulging envelopes the waiter handed him inside the menu. Maybe it was greed or maybe it was just the relief that he would be able to pay the expensive college tuition for his kids after all. He was proud they were Red Raiders. Hell, if he'd had this extra income a few years ago, they could have been Longhorns.

And now this. Shit! There it was...right on schedule, inching its way across the bridge in a long column of Mexican eighteen wheelers. Not now, for God's sake! He felt like his head would burst and his breathing was shallow and quick. For a fleeting second, Hal's mind conjured up a 30-year old image from the First Baptist Church in Del Rio and the tall, cadaverous preacher's dire admonitions about eternal damnation. The preacher hadn't mentioned that damnation might come in the form of an eighteen wheeler crossing the international bridge from Mexico.

The International Harvester cab hauling the long trailer with the giant red letters and the Grupo Zima logo on each side slowly eased forward in the inspection lane, getting closer and closer to the booth where the commissioner was in animated conversation with a rookie customs inspector. In desperation, Hal walked quickly towards the commissioner, hoping to distract him.

***

Commissioner Frank Garza had worked his way up the ladder. He was first-generation Mexican-American, and he was proud of his U.S. citizenship and would just as soon forget his Mexican heritage. He'd wear his U.S. passport on his chest instead of his blue and gold Department of Homeland Security badge if he could. His parents had picked fruit in the Rio Grande Valley but had worked hard; hard enough to send him to college. Maybe not to one of the more prestigious state universities, but he did get a bachelor's degree in criminal justice from Pan American University in Edinburg, Texas. Much later, the government had paid for his master's degree from the University of Texas. Garza knew he had made the grade then, and even the scornful looks of the rich Anglos at UT, sons and daughters of doctors, lawyers, and crooked Texas politicians, didn't take away his sense of accomplishment. Anyway, Frank knew he wasn't competing with them. The U.S. government wanted a few token Mexicans in positions of authority, and Frank didn't mind being one.

Garza noticed Hal hurrying towards him and wondered what the unimaginative bureaucrat wanted with him now.

***

Hal reached the booth just as the International Harvester applied its air brakes to stop for the young customs inspector and the commissioner who had followed him out to the truck. Hal called out to the commissioner, but his shout was drowned out by the hissing air of the truck's brakes and the squealing and creaking of the aging chassis. The commissioner was putting the young inspector through his paces and wanted to see the rookie in action: to see a graduate of the new training program perform. Hal tried to interrupt the conversation, intending to take the commissioner on a tour of the facility, but Garza waved him off dismissively.

"Not now, Wilson," said the commissioner, the irritation plain in his voice. Hal followed helplessly behind the two, a creeping panic now adding to the gnawing fear that demanded decisive action but dulled his reason. Hal was scared. Scared shitless. Not of what might happen today if the rookie inspector decided to show off for the commissioner and open the trailer, but of what would happen tomorrow, afterwards. Hal feared his Mexican benefactors far more than he feared anything the U.S. government might throw at him, were his mendacious betrayal to be discovered.

Hal stood to the side with his arms helplessly at his side and watched as the young inspector carefully examined the trucker's documents. The driver looked over at Hal with the unspoken question on his lips. He had made this trip many times and knew that the middle-aged *gringo* with the belly overhang was supposed to be checking his documents. Hal looked back at him, his face frozen in a paralyzed grimace.

The commissioner looked over the rookie's shoulder.

"Let's run the license plate of the truck and see what we come up with," Commissioner Garza suggested.

The rookie instructed the driver to wait for him and walked briskly with the commissioner to the booth where he entered the truck's license plate into the data base.

"Okay, look here," commented the Commissioner, studying the truck's profile which had appeared on the monitor's screen. "Interesting...this eighteen wheeler has made about one trip every two weeks or so for the past two years carrying tomatoes to Dallas, Houston, and San Antonio. But, look at this...it's never actually been inspected. Not even once!"

"Shall we open her up?" suggested the young inspector.

"Your call," replied the commissioner. "It's your show."

"Let's do it," decided the rookie and the two returned to the truck.

"Get out of the truck, please, and open the back," he instructed the driver who was now visibly nervous. The driver had no choice, however, and climbed awkwardly down from his high perch in the cab. He walked around to the rear of the truck and activated the roller door with an electric switch on the side of the truck. The high-pitched whine of a small electric motor and the creaking of the door as it opened reverberated in Hal's ears. He watched, spellbound. A perfect storm of bad luck and unlikely coincidences had conspired against him.

The commissioner was the first to react.

"What in the world?" he said under his breath. "Wilson, close down the inspection booths and call for all available agents!" the commissioner ordered. He drew his handgun and shouted, "*¡De rodilla!* On your knees. Hands behind your head!"

The rookie drew his gun as well and looked into the trailer

in disbelief at the mass of huddled bodies crowded together, squirming, pushing, and falling to their knees. They were packed shoulder to shoulder like pickled okra in a jar. A low murmur from within increased in volume until there were apocalyptic shouts and screams of panic.

"*¡Qué no disparen!*" shouted someone, and the cry was repeated over and over. "*¡Qué no disparen!* Don't shoot!"

Getting to their knees like the commissioner ordered was easier said than done. There was simply no room, and the stowaways began tripping and falling over each other like dominos in an uncontrollable chain reaction; like a house of cards collapsing from its own weight.

Reinforcements started to arrive, and the commissioner himself supervised the arrests. Hal leaped into the trailer and began searching the stowaways for weapons and drugs. He counted over one hundred and twenty Mexicans: men and women of all ages, shapes and sizes. They were escorted one by one to three waiting school buses that had been commandeered to transport the prisoners to the detainee center. The customs and border patrol agents ran out of handcuffs after the count reached twenty-two.

***

The incident was bizarre and unprecedented. The commissioner had never heard of an attempt to cross so many illegals into Texas at one time. The driver claimed innocence, of course. During the interrogation he swore he knew nothing about his actual cargo. He thought he was hauling tomatoes, or so he said. Even when Hal reported to the commissioner that each illegal had been carrying the same set of forged U.S. identification papers, it didn't dawn on Garza that this was anything more than a well-organized and massive attempt by an industrious *coyote* to smuggle the maximum number of illegals possible across the border.

When he glanced at the list of documents found on each of the Mexicans, he did a double take. Now this *was* something new. Besides Texas driver's licenses, U.S. passports, and miscellaneous Blockbuster and Costco membership cards, each detainee had a copy of his own Texas voter certificate.

With talk about the referendum in South Texas heating up, Frank Garza knew exactly what he had inadvertently discovered. He picked up the phone and dialed Lester Van Slyke's direct line in Austin. The head of the Texas Election Commission needed to know about this. Hal clenched his buttocks together, trying desperately to keep his bowels under control.

CHAPTER 11

Alba always looked forward to Rodrigo returning from his errands in Cotulla. The Broken "T" always seemed empty somehow without him around. She loved just knowing he was nearby, and it was comforting to see him loping circles on one of the two-year olds down in the cedar-post round pen. She couldn't really explain it, but the young Mexican's lack of guile and his quiet independence resonated with her. It probably didn't hurt that he had the good looks of Omar Sharif either. The high school football players who had pursued her this past year seemed strangely bland in comparison: mass-produced, predictable, and, quite frankly, just too Anglo. Rodrigo made her proud of her own Mexican roots, and she loved speaking Spanish with him and teaching him English.

Alba stood next to Guadalupe in the kitchen kneading dough for flour tortillas and rolling the one-inch diameter balls into the required shape. Guadalupe snapped her fingers when she was ready, took the flat raw tortilla from Alba's extended hand, and cooked each of them about thirty seconds per side in the cast-iron *comal.* Mexican *norteña* music played softly from an old-fashioned transistor radio on the window sill. An oscillating fan purred quietly on the counter. It was another hot day, and the gas stove along with the cooking tortillas made the kitchen uncomfortably hot. Beads of sweat formed on Alba's forehead as she hummed along with the music. She glanced out of the kitchen window past the barn to a cloud of dust approaching the house from the distant highway.

"Here come Rodrigo and Mario," she said in Spanish.

"I hope we made enough food. They're going to be hungry," replied Guadalupe.

Alba had begun speaking Spanish again since Rodrigo's arrival, something she hadn't done since the beginning of high school. Alba knew it made her mother happy to see her daughter embrace her cultural roots after all these years of trying to blend in with the Anglos in Cotulla and down in Laredo. She knew Guadalupe guessed at her feelings for Rodrigo, and Alba didn't try to hide them. She just wished her father would also accept the budding romance, but Alba had overheard a conversation that made her fear the worst.

"Just leave them alone for the time being," Alba had heard her mother tell Creed. "Your daughter's growing up, and Rodrigo is a fine young man. He's a hard worker, respectful, and you yourself admit you've never seen his equal as a horseman. Let the kids be."

"He's just a wetback," Creed had objected.

"So was your wife, Creed," Guadalupe had reminded her husband.

Creed had grumbled, as was his way, but up till now had said nothing. Alba could tell he was keeping a watchful eye on them, and she was careful not to rock the boat.

The cloud of dust was approaching rapidly, way too fast. Alba caught sight of the pickup tearing along the gravel road with the flatbed trailer bouncing erratically as it flew over the uneven surface of the road. Even at a distance she could see there was only one person in the cab.

"Something's happened," Alba said with concern and ran out to the front porch. Guadalupe hurriedly turned off the gas stove and walked briskly after her daughter, calling out a warning to Creed who was resting his injured leg on the sofa in the living room and dozing under the squeaky ceiling fan.

Creed cursed under his breath and grabbed the crutches. "When it rains, it pours," he said out loud and frowned. He struggled to his feet and made his way clumsily towards the front porch.

By the time he got to the door and limped out on to the creaky, wooden porch, the pickup had stopped in front of the house. Mario was half-carrying, half-dragging a still groggy Rodrigo towards the house. The boy had bled profusely, and his t-shirt was drenched with blood. Creed could see that much from the porch even without his glasses. Guadalupe pressed the corner of her apron over a gash above Rodrigo's eye, trying to stave off the bleeding. Alba held Rodrigo's hand and cried.

"Daddy, can't you do something to stop all this?" she asked sobbing.

Creed didn't answer. He walked purposefully to the telephone and dialed a number he knew by heart.

"Now where the hell is James Brazzle?" he said under his breath.

***

"Let's take a look at these checkpoints you've been telling me about," said Drake Herrin as he and James Brazzle approached the R.A.T.S. roadblock from the north at the Nueces River bridge on the southern outskirts of Cotulla. Drake had flown into San Antonio as planned a few hours before, and James had been there to meet him.

"It's hard to believe Governor Throckmorton would sit on his ass and let the drug traffickers call the shots down here, James. I'm hoping this is a little hyperbole on your part," said Drake, his long white hair pulled back into a pony tail under a Texas Rangers baseball cap. With his aviator sunglasses, he looked more like a drug kingpin than a former intelligence officer.

It was an odd reunion. During their careers, the two retired CIA officers had violated the sovereignty of every foreign country they ever worked in. They unapologetically ran roughshod over the local police and intelligence organizations of allies and foes alike. They sniffed out the weaknesses and vulnerabilities of their targets like human bloodhounds and were relentless in their pursuit of new sources of information. Now the tables were turned, and their own country was on the receiving end of a similarly conceived strategy. Perceived strengths in reality were nothing more than glaring weaknesses and offered opportunities to those who were inclined to take advantage.

The closer they got to Cotulla, the fewer cars were on the highway. No warning signs, no signs of trouble. Just longer stretches of empty highway. Circling vultures added to the ominous desolation and sense of hopelessness the countryside exuded. From a distance the roadblock looked official. Drake saw five or six uniformed guards carrying weapons and standing beside a makeshift booth and a boom barrier. As their pickup drew closer, he realized the booth was a porta-potty, and the boom barrier was a log propped up on stacked concrete blocks. The guards indeed wore uniforms, but with their tattoos, dark glasses, backwards baseball caps, and MP3 players, they looked more like actors from a bad Michael Jackson music video.

"Are we supposed to take this seriously, James?" asked Drake, as his trained eyes took in the roadblock ahead, taking inventory of guards and weapons. "Looks like the ragtag entourage of some third-world warlord," he said.

"That's pretty much what it is, I'd say. But you'll take it seriously if they throw down on you with those M4s," James stated unequivocally. "Wonder where they got them?"

"Buenos dias, caballeros," one of the guards said politely as the pickup slowed to a halt in front of the barrier. *"Sus documentos, por favor."*

"I'm sorry. I don't speak Spanish," said Drake. "I'm not from around here."

The guard look bewildered for a moment and then motioned for one of his colleagues to join him.

"Could I see your documents, please?" the second guard requested in English.

"Who are you? What documents do you want to see?" asked Drake innocently.

"We're border guards for the *República Autónoma de Tejas del Sur*," he replied, pointing to the stenciled initials on his cap. I need to see your identification. Just a formality."

"But I've never heard of anything like this," countered Drake. "I don't know this part of the country very well, but we didn't cross into Mexico yet, did we?"

"No, *señor*," this isn't Mexico...not yet at least. But we have our orders."

Drake handed over his Virginia driver's license for inspection and asked, "Who gives you orders?"

The guard jotted Drake's information down, peering carefully at the driver's license. He looked up from his notebook comparing the photo in the license with Drake's features.

"*El Frente,*" he replied, as if everyone should know the name.

"What's that?" Drake asked again, feigning ignorance.

"Never mind. You talk too much, mister. Okay, we have your name. Next time you come through, bring your passport, or we won't let you by. *¿Me entiende?*" he asked.

"Whatever you say," answered Drake. He looked over at Brazzle who had started to ease the pickup through the checkpoint. "Passport?" he mused out loud.

Brazzle pointed at a pile of feed sacks stacked up beside the porta-potty.

"Those belong to Creed Tucker, I imagine. The bastards stole those sacks of cubes when they beat up Creed's wetback the other day. These might be the ones that did it."

***

"Who do you plan to see in Laredo?" asked Brazzle.

Scarcely a half hour had passed since they crossed through the Nueces River roadblock, and Drake Herrin was deep in thought. He realized that things were worse than anybody in Washington realized and likely to deteriorate further. Austin's inaction was hard to fathom.

"Drake, that was a question," said Brazzle, nudging the older man with his elbow.

"Oh, sorry, James. Just daydreaming. Frank Garza from customs is going to meet me at the bridge. I'll be taking a look at the passports and voter registration documentation they took from the illegals the other day. You heard about that bust, right?"

"Yeah, I don't know what clearer evidence of election fraud you'd want, but we haven't heard a word from Van Slyke. He's not answering phone calls."

"No, I doubt you'll hear from him. By now he's probably wishing he had another job...in a different country."

Herrin looked outside of the pickup window. The scenery was singularly unimpressive. In fact, it was downright inhospitable. Flat, scrub country. Mesquite and prickly pear cactus. Why anybody would want to make a play for this land was beyond him. The drug traffickers must be calling all the shots. If they could control the border and the local governments down here, there'd be no limit to the volume of drugs they could bring in. Drake knew the political rhetoric was just a smokescreen for business considerations.

A couple hundred yards ahead, James saw an older white Toyota Corolla parked at an odd angle on the side of the interstate. The driver side door was open, and both men could see a man's leg sticking out of the car...as if the driver was lying down and looking under the dashboard. Another vehicle, a black Jeep Cherokee with tinted windows, pulled away from the Toyota, accelerating rapidly and entering the far right lane of the interstate. It headed south at high speed.

"You thinking what I'm thinking?" asked Brazzle.

"I'm afraid so. Better check this out," replied Drake.

The men stopped their pickup truck about fifty yards behind the Toyota; just a precaution in case the old sedan was wired to explode. They sat there for a few minutes waiting then cautiously got out of the pickup and walked slowly towards what they knew they would find. The leg still had not moved.

The killers had been economical. The single head shot had been messy but effective. Drake and James looked at the prostrate body of a middle-aged man in the uniform of a U.S. Customs agent. He carried no wallet and no identification. His attackers likely had made off with that. The car's registration also gave no indication who he was. There was only a government name tag that lay on the car floor on the passenger side. Even that was smudged with fresh blood. "Wilson," it read. James Brazzle and Drake Herrin were careful not to touch anything. They returned quickly to their pickup truck and headed towards Laredo.

"Looks like I'll have some interesting news for Garza," said Herrin a few minutes later, the first words spoken since the two discovered the body. "That was his man. Probably ought to call the highway patrol if they still operate in this neck of the woods."

"Forget the highway patrol. You realize what we just saw?" asked Brazzle, a knowing look in his eyes.

"Yeah, I think so. Looks like Mr. Wilson ran afoul of his

paymaster," said Herrin. "Hell of a way to save for retirement."

Brazzle's cell phone rang.

"Bueno," he answered the phone in Spanish. Brazzle listened without saying a word. When he hung up, he looked over at Drake Herrin and just shook his head.

"Just when you think it can't get any worse," he said.

CHAPTER 12

The drive to Laredo took less than an hour even without exceeding the seventy-five mile-an-hour speed limit on Interstate 35. Creed really didn't have much of a choice in the matter. His old pickup shook and shuddered uncontrollably at speeds over sixty, the consequences of a broken axle suffered years ago on Matlock's first solo outing in the aging Chevy at the ripe old age of fourteen. The transition from John Deere tractor to pickup hadn't gone as smoothly as Matlock had anticipated. It would be a few years before Creed allowed him near the truck again.

Driving with the pickup windows down despite the summer heat, wearing his beat-up and sweat-stained straw hat, and a with a cheek full of Red Man chewing tobacco, Creed looked exactly like what he was: an old-school Texas cowboy who resisted modernity with the tenacity of a radical Muslim imam. He had called Rudy Gutierrez the day before and suggested they meet for a cup of coffee and exchange ideas on the security situation in South Texas. Creed suspected that if it hadn't been for the blood they shed together in combat during the Tet Offensive outside of Hue in 1968, Rudy wouldn't have agreed to the meeting at all. In the end, the memory of the drunken blood-brother ritual they invented after the battle held sway over Rudy's radical politics and what Creed recognized as his reluctance to be seen in public with a prominent *gringo*.

Creed set off for Laredo early in the morning and reached the city limits after rush hour traffic had begun to drop off. The outskirts of Laredo were singularly lacking in architectural originality and always struck him as slightly tasteless: strip malls, chain restaurants, and gas stations.

Creed could have been anywhere in the United States except for the overwhelming number of Hispanic residents out on the streets going about their business. He saw a few Anglos, but they seemed to be in a hurry, looking over their shoulders and scurrying for safer digs like field mice eluding the diving shadow of a bird of prey. Young Mexican toughs rode in the back of pickup trucks holding up Mexican flags and blood-red banners with political slogans in Spanish. Horns blared and the thugs shouted friendly obscenities to each other and waved their handguns in salutation.

Rudy had suggested the San Augustin Cathedral for their meeting and Creed didn't object. He made his way slowly through the Laredo traffic and turned left on Grant Street, a couple of blocks from the Rio Grande River and the Mexican border. He drove past San Augustin Plaza on his right, admiring the live oaks that shaded the square. Mothers pushed their infant children in strollers among the trees and he heard the lilting lullabies and their sing-song banter in Spanish from his truck. He turned right on San Augustin Avenue and parked his pickup on the east side of the park.

Creed looked to his left across the street at the bleached sandstone of the old cathedral. The bell tower, Creed knew, was the second tallest building in Laredo. The Gothic Revival architecture was supposed to be historic and somehow spiritually elevating, but for Creed it was trite, a bit of a cliché. It seemed almost pedestrian and far too protestant-looking in its dour modesty. Creed wondered why Rudy had chosen the cathedral for their meeting venue. Probably the privacy, Creed guessed. He hoped Rudy didn't plan to give a sermon from the pulpit on Anglo oppression. He'd heard far too much of that lately.

"You're too late to give your confession," a soft voice said behind him as Creed entered the dark coolness of the cathedral. "Mass is about to begin."

Creed turned at the sound of Rudy's voice and extended

his hand.

"It doesn't matter," answered Creed. "I've no sins to confess."

Rudy took Creed's hand and gave him a Latino *abrazo*, pounding him on the back with his left hand.

"It's been a long time, *viejo*," said Rudy. "You look like shit, by the way."

"With good reason," said Creed. "I've aged ten years in the past month. That's what I want to talk about."

"Kind of guessed that," Rudy said. "Let's sit down and get this over with before people recognize me and start to gossip."

The two men walked down the middle aisle of the cathedral and sat in a pew behind an ornate white column partially concealed from view and continued their conversation in a low whisper. A few elderly women with their hair covered by black *rebozos* sat dispersed throughout the cathedral with their heads bowed deep in prayer, occasionally crossing themselves and fingering their rosaries.

"Rudy, I'm worried about what's happening in South Texas," said Creed bluntly.

"I would be too if I were you," said Rudy. He looked around the almost empty cathedral, suppressing a yawn.

"Rudy, my ranch has been attacked twice and my horse trainer was beaten up by R.A.T.S. thugs at the Nueces River checkpoint south of Cotulla because he didn't have an import permit for cattle feed. I'm sure you've heard about the two Border Patrol agents that were murdered a few weeks ago and all the talk about holding a referendum. I just want to know what the hell is going on. I know you're one of the leaders of the National Front and frankly some of this shit just doesn't sound like it could come from the Rudy Gutierrez that I knew in Vietnam."

"Now you know how it feels, don't you?" replied Rudy.

"Know how what feels?" asked Creed.

"Don't look so innocent, Creed," said Rudy and stared long and hard at his old friend. "You're feeling exactly like most of my Hispanic brothers and sisters have felt ever since they got to this country. Get used to it. This is only the beginning!"

"Since when does Rudy Gutierrez justify outright violence as a means to an end?" asked Creed as he put his hand on Rudy's shoulder for emphasis. "And what the fuck is the end?"

Rudy instinctively raised his forearm and roughly removed Creed's hand with the back of his hand.

"Back off, Creed. There have been some excesses, I'll admit," said Rudy. "You can't make an omelet without breaking eggs."

"But why team up with the damned drug traffickers?" asked Creed.

"That's your only response?" asked Rudy.

"What do you mean?"

"You think you can discredit our whole movement by linking us to the cartels?" asked Rudy. "Surely, you can do better than that."

Creed was flabbergasted.

"Rudy, those bastards tried to bribe me to put an airstrip on my ranch. Don't deny they're involved in all this!"

Rudy stood up and reached in his pocket for his car keys.

"The National Front for the Liberation of Texas is a political movement. We have nothing to do with the drug cartels. You disappoint me, Creed. You used to have your own opinions."

Rudy turned and walked up the aisle without looking back. Creed heard the heavy wooden door of the cathedral open and saw the harsh sunlight streak into the darkened interior before the door closed with an audible thud. He sat for a few minutes wondering how he could have handled that conversation better. Maybe James was right: he utterly lacked diplomatic skills.

CHAPTER 13

"Why hadn't she listened to her father?" she asked herself. She remembered how he took her face in his smooth, manicured hands at the airport, looked her right in the eyes, and made her promise.

"You girls go straight to the hotel and don't use any other taxi except the hotel shuttle.   Understand? Those people down there don't go to the same country club as we do. They don't play by the same rules." The advice was simple enough.

"Sure,   Dad...whatever...now   stop   embarrassing   me; everyone's looking."

Her head banged painfully on the floor of the van, her hands bound behind her back with plastic wrist ties and her mouth stuffed with a filthy red bandana that reeked of human sweat and tasted of salt. She looked across the floor of the van into the terrified eyes of her best friend and sorority sister and saw the mirrored reflections of her own nightmare. Horror, disbelief, and a numbing fear: the anticipation of what might happen next. To her left, a pair of ornately tooled cowboy boots. Another to her right. The conversation was in Spanish and way too fast for her to follow.

***

"¿Qué piensas, buey? You think we got the right one?" Simón Guzmán was nervous. He was tall and skinny for a Mexican. He was known simply as "El Flaco" among his friends, but his English-speaking colleagues called him "Slim". A former federal police officer, Slim couldn't sit still. He was known for his jitters that kept everyone on edge and frightened both his friends and enemies alike. His right cowboy boot was in constant motion, tapping out a bass rhythm that only he could hear. His fingers tapped out a lead guitar riff on the butt of the Beretta 9 mm stuck under his western belt.

"Yeah, she's the right one. Didn't you see her passport?" asked Slim's colleague, who was as short and squat as Slim was tall and lanky. He reached into his rear jean pocket and took out the folded newspaper photograph of the girl and her father from a recent copy of the *Austin-American Statesman*. "Let's take a look at the passport again," he suggested.

Slim unsnapped the breast pocket of his blue and white checkered shirt and grasped the crisp new document between his thumb and forefinger. He slowly pulled the passport out of his pocket as he stared menacingly at the girl, more for the theatrical effect than anything else.

"Lift up her head," Slim ordered. "And take off her gag so we can see her face."

The squat one pulled her dirty blonde hair into a tight pony tail and roughly lifted her head and yanked the handkerchief away from her mouth. Slim held out both photographs and ran his eyes from the passport to the newspaper clipping and to the girl whose eyes were wild with fear.

"*Por favor,*" she mumbled incoherently, gasping for air.

"*Callate,* bitch," said Slim's companion and retied the bandana across her mouth. "What do you think?"

"It's her alright...I hope. You can't tell much from the photos. Her hair was different in the newspaper picture."

"Don't worry. It was the right flight, too. Guillermo saw her get on the plane in Dallas."

"Yeah, it's got to be her," said Slim, trying to sound more confident than he felt.

"Look at them; they're scared to death. One of them pissed herself. Probably afraid we're going to rape them...are we?" he asked hopefully.

"Listen, *cabrón,* don't even think about that. The boss would shoot us if we did. He'll shoot us if we got the wrong girl too." Slim's cowboy boot resumed its uncontrollable tapping.

"Let's at least pull up her t-shirt; take a look at what she's got," suggested the fat one. "I've never seen a pair of *gringa* tits." He reached down and tugged on the girl's Rip Curl t-shirt, laughing with a toothy, obscene grin.

"I told you to cut that shit out," said Slim sharply. "The boss speaks English. If the girls complain to him about being mistreated, we're dead. Get your *campesino* hands off her, *buey!"*

They sat in silence as the van sped across the Mexican countryside. The fat Mexican sulked, and the girls whimpered. Slim tapped his boot. So many things could still go wrong before they reached the boss's ranch outside of Culiacán. They were in Sinaloa, but a few of the local police were honest cops and had refused the cartel's money: a risky thing to do in that part of Mexico. Police officers working against the cartel had very short life spans; especially if they were successful. The driver was careful not to attract unwanted attention, though, and the two cartel soldiers in the front seat armed with AK47s provided added insurance.

The girls had been so gullible, accepting his offer of a ride from the Mazatlan airport to the El Cid Hotel. "The van is much cheaper than a taxi," he had told them. So innocent and trusting. Had he ever been like that? Slim sold his first ounce of marijuana when he was ten years old and ran a small ring of thieves by the time he was twelve, all the while dreaming of becoming a federal police officer. Not to protect the people or enforce the law. Hell no, that's not what the police did in Sinaloa. He wanted to get rich. Work for a major *narcotraficante.* He got his dream job when he turned twenty-one. He was twenty-five now and had every material possession he had ever wanted. But he was still nervous. Afraid of being killed by rival *narcos*, his boss, or even by one of his jealous mistresses. Slim dreamed of saving enough money to buy a small ranch and raising goats. He was tired of looking over his shoulder with fear. Everyone was afraid of something. Fear seemed to rule the world. Look at these poor girls, he thought.

He glanced down at the girl lying on the floor of the van in front of him and saw her looking up at him, eyes beseeching and looking desperately for a hint of sympathy in Slim's expression. He felt his resolve waiver as his eyes briefly met hers and he felt pity and empathy for her plight, but it was only a momentary weakness that quickly disappeared. He raised his hand menacingly, threatening to strike her. He saw her close her eyes instinctively but he dropped his hand.

It seemed like an eternity, but Slim finally felt the van slow down, but then the road became even bumpier. The girls were thrown roughly from side to side. The fat guard just laughed as the three girls moaned loudly through the gags covering their mouths. Then it was over. The van stopped and the rear door opened. They were blinded by the bright, mid-afternoon sunlight of the Mexican Pacific coast. A wave of hot, humid, tropical air hit them with palpable force, abruptly replacing the coolness of the van's air conditioner.

A voice called out, "*Buenas tardes, muchachos.* Did you bring me the product?"

"*¡Claro, que si, Padrino!*" answered Slim obsequiously.

"Take off her gag," said the voice. He stood at the rear of the van dressed in a baggy swimming suit with a brightly colored beach towel wrapped around him. His soft, hairy belly hung over the towel. He examined the passport Slim handed him and compared the photo with the face of the terrified American teenager. He smiled ever so slightly. "*¡Buen trabajo!* Good job!" he said although he never expected anything less from his employees.

He walked back toward the ranch house and the new swimming pool, rubbing his hands together in satisfaction and anticipating the phone call he would make the next day. Francisco Salcido was impressed with his own diabolical ingenuity.

***

Governor Rick Throckmorton wasn't used to be being heckled in public. He was probably the most popular Texas governor in history. He was a successful trial lawyer and a social and fiscal conservative, something which endeared him to his electoral base: white Anglo professionals and the business community. His policies were moderate, though, and his knowledge of Spanish had attracted a surprising percent of the Latino vote in the last elections. Most importantly, though, he looked like a governor. For that matter, many of his supporters thought he looked presidential. Rumor had it he was considering a run for the republican nomination.

But there they were: a group of at least fifty demonstrators stood up suddenly up in the Rudder Auditorium on the campus of Texas A&M University. They completely disrupted the dedication ceremony with their shouting.

"Power to the Republic...Power to the Hispanic Majority", they chanted in unison. Pandemonium reigned as they unfurled large green, red, and white banners that read, "Rights for R.A.T.S." and "Respect the Referendum". One particularly large banner read, "Texas = Occupied Territory".

The campus police responded quickly, but the television camera crews were already there. They recorded the unprecedented demonstration, and the reporters followed the Latino protesters outside for interviews when the police escorted them from the auditorium. The Texas A&M campus authorities weren't used to this kind of disruption. Those things usually happened in Austin, not College Station. It took nearly a half an hour for the city police to arrive with the required number of paddy wagons, more than enough time for the Hispanic protestors to fill the reporters' ears with their side of the story. The evening news broadcasts on local television promised to be spicier than the usual rehashing of convenience store robberies, domestic violence, and apartment fires.

Governor Throckmorton cut his address short, shook hands hurriedly with the university luminaries who had come to rub shoulders with him. His staff hustled the governor out to the official SUV for the short drive to the airport. They had beefed up security, and chase cars created a bubble around Texas' chief executive as the motorcade took a circuitous route to the airport as a precautionary measure. His cell phone rang, an unusual occurrence, since only a handful of people in the entire country were privy to his private phone number.

"Governor Throckmorton?" inquired a male voice on the other end.

"Speaking," replied the governor gruffly. "Who's calling?"

"Please stay on the line for the president," the man replied in a voice that was used to issuing orders.

The governor's pulse began to race. In the best of times the president of the United States rarely called a governor, even one of such an important state as Texas; especially when the governor was a republican and a vocal opponent of the more liberal democratic president. Today, though, the timing was ominous. Everyone from Laredo to Washington was clamoring for action: they wanted a response from Austin to the Hispanic initiatives in South Texas. But the issues were complex. Far more so than anyone imagined.

A series of clicks, a burst of static, and suddenly the familiar voice.

"Governor Throckmorton?"

"Yes, Mr. President."

"Rick, I hope I'm not taking you away from your supporters there in College Station," the president began.

"You're well informed, Mr. President," the governor laughed.

"That's part of my job, you know," the president joked in reply. "Some of my advisors actually know what's going on in your neck of the woods. That's why I'm calling, Rick. I've been getting some worrisome reports about what's happening down there in South Texas. I wanted to get your opinion on the current situation and hear what you're planning to do about it."

"I-I-I've been expecting to hear from you. I'm glad you called," Throckmorton lied. "I won't sugar coat it, Mr. President. It's a complex situation. The municipal governments in South Texas are represented by lawfully elected officials. They have a right to pass ordinances and hold local referendums even if we don't agree with their policies. We're looking into allegations of human rights violations, but there are also constitutional issues at play here. I'm referring to the Texas Constitution of 1876."

"Rick, from what I hear, violations of our country's national sovereignty overshadow any issues of states' rights. I hear the cartels are involved."

Mr. President, we are investigating the situation and I hope to have a report to you within a few days. I need to remind you, though, that the Texas State Constitution provides for the creation of up to four additional states from our current state of Texas. The political demands coming out of South Texas have some basis in law. Our constitution also guarantees the inalienable right for the people of Texas to alter their government in such manner as they might think proper. That's almost a quote."

"If we're going to start quoting statutes, Rick, let me remind you that the federal government is obligated to protect the states against invasion, and it sure as hell sounds like your southern counties are under attack. I can also invoke the Insurrection Act to use our military on U.S. soil to enforce constitutional rights if state authorities fail to act."

"Mr. President, give us a little more time to evaluate our options. I'd like to avoid bloodshed if possible. I remember the last time the federal government took action in Texas. You do remember what happened in Waco, don't you? Texans don't want to see a repeat of that debacle."

"Rick, dammit, you're abusing my good will! I hear they're even talking about holding a referendum on autonomy. I'll give you one week to do something, but it's time for some decisive action. Do I make myself clear?"

"Yes, Mr. President," replied the governor. A click on the other end, and the conversation was over. The governor was breathing deeply and his head was throbbing. He had been candid with the president. The issues indeed were far more complex than most people realized. Especially for him.

CHAPTER 14

Mako Sloane had a love-hate relationship with Mexico City. He loved being surrounded by reminders of its rich history, its Aztec and Spanish heritage. He loved the museums, theaters, and the striking architecture of the capital, ranging from the colonial architecture of the Palacio Nacional in the Zócalo, the main plaza in Mexico City, to the Neo-Gothic designs of the main post office and Palace of Fine Arts. The city's cosmopolitan restaurants were some of the best in the world.

But Mako hated Mexico City for its poverty, crowdedness, and the suffocating pollution that hid the mountains from view most days. The rampant corruption of the Mexican police and governmental institutions was another issue altogether. Although to be lamented, it had been Mako's bread and butter, and it made life in the Mexican capital exciting, unpredictable, and at times, dangerous as hell.

Mako had flown into Mexico City from Managua on a Copa Airlines Boing 737. It never ceased to amaze him how disorganized those flights were. They were a microcosm of the Latin countries themselves: loud, chaotic and confused. He was always relieved when the frenzied and disorderly boarding process ended. It was a pleasant surprise when the airplanes actually took off, flew to their scheduled destinations, and landed safely.

His meeting with the Venezuelan president had gone pretty much as anticipated. Both Hugo Chavez of Venezuela and Daniel Ortega, the Sandinista president of Nicaragua, loved to piss off the U.S. government. They were enjoying the growing crisis in South Texas, and they loved rubbing salt in the *gringos'* wound with their revolutionary rhetoric and self-righteous pronouncements on self-determination. They also were stirring things up in the Organization of American States, trying to rally Latin America against the United States. It remained to be seen, however, whether they had the *cojones* to provoke the "empire" by actually providing military assistance to the National Front for the Liberation of Texas. Mako doubted they did.

A VW bug taxi dropped Mako off on Paseo de la Reforma directly across from the U.S. embassy. La Reforma was built in the 1860s and was modeled after the Champs-Élysées in Paris, a poor man's version of the beautiful French boulevard, but pleasing to the eye nonetheless. He turned onto a narrow, cobblestone street perpendicular to La Reforma and walked down to a small sidewalk café on the left side of the street. He looked up at the sign and smiled. *Mesón del Perro Andaluz,* Tavern of the Andalucian Dog. He took a seat at a table for two facing the street and scrutinized the faces of the passersby. The café was in the Zona Rosa, a touristy area of the capital that had declined in recent years although the quality of food served at its numerous eclectic cafes and restaurants was still first rate.

Mako ordered a bottle of tequila, two shot glasses with a plate of sliced limes and sat back to wait for his lunch appointment. It was mid-summer, the rainy season in Mexico City, and dark, billowy clouds were already gathering in the sky. He welcomed the afternoon showers. The brief downpours brought relief from the choking pollution, at least temporarily. A steady throng of people streamed by the café along the cobblestone street: well-heeled businessmen and their mistresses, diplomats, beggars, and prostitutes; both male and female. Music playing from the adjacent eating establishments competed with loud flamenco music coming from within the Perro Andaluz and added to the cacophony of street sounds. Cars stuck in stop-and-go traffic on the Reforma honked incessantly.

It had been fifteen years since he had seen Félix Aguilar,

in those days a struggling investigator for the Ministry of the Interior, one of the few young lawyers not on the payroll of the narco-lobby in Mexico City. Mako had kept in touch, except for the time spent in prison, and he was looking forward to seeing his old friend, now one of the most powerful men in the Mexican government.

Had it not been for the same jaunty stride he remembered from the old days in Mexico City, he might not have recognized the attorney general as he approached surrounded by bodyguards. Aguilar's coiffured hair was almost completely gray, and his pinstriped, finely tailored European-cut suit shouted "money".

Not bad for a public servant, thought Mako cynically. He wondered if Aguilar would recognize him. It had been a while. He stood up and waved to catch his old friend's attention. Félix broke into a huge grin and dismissed his bodyguards, who retreated to either end of the short cobblestone street.

"Mako, you old sonofabitch!" Aguilar exclaimed in English.

"¡Quiubole, Félix!" Mako smiled in response and the two exchanged a traditional Latino *abrazo,* pounding each other on the back.

"Don't sit down yet, Félix," warned Sloane and handed his friend a shot glass of tequila, the amber liquid reflecting the sun streaming through a crack in the awning over the tables.

"To old times and old friends," proposed Mako. They threw down the tequila, turned their glasses upside down, and bit down on a slice of lime.

A half hour later a glassy eyed Félix Aguilar, attorney general and presidential candidate, turned to Mako and smiled wistfully. Aguilar had switched to Spanish.

"I haven't been in a public restaurant in two years," he said. "My security chief won't allow it. I told him to go to hell today. I told him Mako Sloane's in town."

"I'm sure he was impressed with that," Mako answered and laughed.

Félix looked across the table at Mako. He stared. "What the hell are you doing in Mexico City, my friend? I thought you were retired."

"You need to vet your sources, Félix. I thought I taught you that."

"You taught me a lot of things, Mako. One was not to believe in coincidences. I know you're not just passing through. What can I do for you?" A suddenly serious Aguilar looked at Mako with curiosity. "Let's make it quick, though. I'm keeping the president waiting."

"Well, if you put it that way, Félix...you remember where I'm from, don't you?"

"Of course, I read your file," he laughed. "You're a *Tejano*, and now I think I know what you want to talk about...but what makes you think I know anything about what's going on in South Texas?"

"Because if you didn't, you wouldn't be worth a shit as attorney general. And I know you are," replied Mako. He picked up a tortilla chip and spread fresh guacamole on it. "I know the Sinaloa cartel is involved, and I know you're acquainted with the main players there. Félix, I know how things work down here. You can bullshit the U.S. embassy or a congressional delegation, but you can't bullshit me. I know you and your country, *amigo*."

"What do you want to know, Mako? This is a very delicate subject. Keep that in mind."

Mako looked hard at his old friend. Aguilar had always played both sides of the fence. At one time Mako had paid him a retainer of two thousand dollars a month. He knew what that money meant for a struggling young Mexican official in those days. All Aguilar had to do in return was to meet with Sloane in a hotel room once a month and answer a few questions. Now it was different. Playing both sides these days could cost him far more than his mere political career.

"Is the Mexican government backing the National Front for the Liberation of Texas? Plain and simple," asked Mako and looked Félix straight in the eyes. "That's what I want to know...or is the Sinaloa cartel acting independently?"

Aguilar averted his eyes and sighed. "Of course, I know about the situation," he said. "But most of my information comes from the U.S. embassy. I doubt I have anything new to tell you," he lied.

Mako saw it in his eyes. It was an old habit, but Félix couldn't lie without a slight fluttering of his eyelashes. "Who's running the National Front, Félix?" he asked.

"Mako, that I don't know. That's the truth. But you know there *are* people in our government...powerful people who would love to get a piece of Texas back. They haven't forgotten the humiliation of losing a war to the *gringos* or having their northern territories stolen even though it was 165 years ago. It runs in our collective subconscious. Texas is occupied territory for a lot of us."

"How about for you, Félix?" asked Mako.

A shot rang out and ricocheted off the wrought-iron table where they were sitting. Félix's glass exploded and tiny fragments flew in all directions. Mako reacted instinctively and pushed his friend to the ground, drawing his Browning 9 mm at the same time. A single shooter stood in the center of the cobblestone street and fired several more shots in rapid succession that wounded a matronly middle-aged woman behind them. She cried out and fell to the floor, but Mako saw that she only had been hit in the fleshy part of her upper arm. She was bleeding but it was not a life-threatening wound. Mako snapped off two shots from a kneeling position and saw the shooter crumple to the ground, a scarlet spot on the front of his white shirt beginning to spread. He held his 9 mm in a two-hand grip and quickly scanned the street for other targets. There were none.

Women screamed and people began to stream out of the cafes and restaurants: well-heeled bankers and lawyers dragging their terrified wives and mistresses by the hand, pushing and jostling their way through the crowd away from the Perro Andaluz towards Calle Hamburgo. This was an all too familiar occurrence in Mexico: a public gun battle. Aguilar's bodyguards ran up in a panic and whisked the attorney general away in the middle of a protective shield of bodies.

Mako had time to wave and then Félix was gone. Sirens split the air, and Mako decided to beat a hasty retreat, lest he have to explain the origin of his handgun and his lack of a permit, not to mention the dead body lying on the cobblestone in front of the chic restaurant. He filtered into the frightened crowd and walked briskly in the direction of the embassy.

***

Later that night, a bemused Félix Aguilar sat in his luxurious home in Las Lomas de Chapultepec, an exclusive neighborhood of mostly older, opulent mansions bordering on Chapultepec Park. "The best laid plans of mice and men," he whispered to himself in English. Funny that he would still remember that line from Robert Burns. That's what a Princeton education did for you.

"That Mako is *muy cabrón*. Got to keep him on my side," he said out loud.

One of the maids brought him his nightly cognac with a slice of lemon.

"*Gracias*, Maria," he said as his cell phone rang.

"*Bueno*." He knew who would be calling.

"*¿Qué onda, mi cuate?*"

"*Hola,* Pancho," answered Felix.

"Did you see the news?" asked Francisco Salcido.

"Yes, it's better than we even hoped," stated Félix. "The press is already blaming you for the 'assassination attempt'. They say my strategies are working, and the cartel is feeling the pressure. You were right. This will strengthen my candidacy even more. You're a genius, Pancho."

"Finally, you recognize the obvious," joked Salcido.

"I'm sorry about your man. That was unexpected," apologized the attorney general.

"It was for him too. No worries. That's the cost of doing business." Who the hell was that guy you were with?"

"That's a long story. A retired *gringo* CIA officer. At least I thought he was retired," answered Félix.

"Is he going to be a problem for us?" asked Francisco. "Do we need to do something about him?"

"I'm not sure yet," replied Félix, sipping his cognac. "I'll keep an eye on him and let you know."

CHAPTER 15

Rodrigo winced as he threw his right leg over the back of the paint colt, and he prayed the youngster stood still until he got his foot in the stirrup. His ribs were still sore, and he hoped the green horse wouldn't buck. He had spent more time than usual with the groundwork: longing him in the round pen to take the "fresh" out. When Mario finally saddled him, the colt was soaking wet. White lather foamed up between his back legs, but he looked calm and unconcerned and stood quietly. They might not have to geld this one, Rodrigo thought to himself as he sat quietly in the saddle and stroked the horse's neck.

Despite his half-closed left eye and the bruises on his face, the doctor had given Rodrigo a clean bill of health. He said the ribs weren't broken, and he could ride if it didn't hurt too much. Well, it did hurt. Hurt like hell, in fact, but riding horses was Rodrigo's job, and he had already spent four days recuperating from the beating he received at the hands of the R.A.T.S. border guards. That was enough. Doctors, in this part of the country, it seemed, were no easier on people than the land was.

"*¿Cómo te sientes?*" asked Alba worriedly. She sat in the bleachers above the round pen and watched the training session with concern.

"Better than I thought I would," lied Rodrigo with a smile, trying to conceal a grimace.

Alba hadn't left Rodrigo's bedside for twelve hours after Mario brought him back to the Broken "T", bruised and battered and bleeding. She held his hand the entire time and cried. The doctor set his broken nose, stitched up a few cuts on his face, and pronounced him good to go. Mario appreciated the attention, though, and knew Creed had taken notice. It never hurts to take a beating on behalf of the *patron*.

Rodrigo rode the horse for twenty minutes, trotting and loping circles. At this stage of the colt's training, he just wanted to get the horse used to being ridden, to feeling the weight of the rider on his back. There was plenty of time to put the bells and whistles on later. Patience was the main thing. When he stopped the horse, he pulled back on the reins and subtly shifted his weight to the rear. The horse took one tentative step backwards and Rodrigo released the reins and patted the colt's neck.

He dismounted and turned the reins over to Mario who led the horse away to unsaddle and hose him down. Mario glanced back at Rodrigo who was already climbing up in the bleachers to sit with Alba.

"I'll be right back, Mario," Rodrigo called.

Mario frowned and shook his head. Rodrigo pretended he didn't see Mario's exasperated expression. In a way he felt that his popularity with the *gringos* at the Broken "T" somehow betrayed Mario. He knew that hadn't been the plan when they discussed crossing the river back on the hacienda in Guanajuato, but when he was with Alba, he didn't care about anything else.

Rodrigo and Alba spoke Spanish together.

"I'm worried, Rodrigo," Alba said. "Things were never like this before."

"You mean between you *gringos* and us Mexicans?" joked Rodrigo.

"You stop that," countered Alba. "You know who my mother is. Listen to my Spanish. It's every bit as good as yours, maybe better. I read books in Spanish, you know."

"Like what?" he asked. Rodrigo knew how to read and

write, but he couldn't remember the last time he'd read a book. In fact, the English textbook Alba gave him was the first book he'd ever owned.

"Have you ever heard of Carlos Fuentes?" she asked hopefully.

"I knew a Carlos Fuentes in Guanajuato. He was a chicken fighter. Raised the best *gallos de pelea* in the whole state. But I don't think he's the same one."

"I think not," Alba laughed. "This Carlos Fuentes was a writer. He wrote a novel called *Gringo Viejo*. He's Mexican, but the English translation was a bestseller in the United States. Hollywood even made a movie out it: 'Old Gringo' with Gregory Peck and Jane Fonda."

Rodrigo watched Alba. He couldn't help but smile when he listened to her. She was right. Her Spanish was beautiful. It sounded like poetry.

"It was about two Americans who got caught up in the Mexican revolution. One of them was an old man, a journalist. He came to Mexico to die. He wanted to be killed by Pancho Villa. He said, 'to be a *gringo* in Mexico, ah, that is euthanasia.' I've often wondered what he meant." Alba turned to Rodrigo almost as if asking a question.

Rodrigo didn't say anything.

"So much of our history is intertwined," Alba continued, deep in thought. "What draws *gringos* to Mexico and Mexicans to the United States? How can we love and hate each other so much at the same time?" she asked. "Why would the old *gringo* want to come to Mexico to die in the revolution?"

"Maybe he was tired and bored," speculated Rodrigo.

"Why do you say that?" she asked, leaning against his body. Mario's shirt was damp with sweat.

"Life is easy for most *gringos*...too easy. You get bored of that."

Alba nodded her head in agreement. "But we're free to do and say what we want in this country; don't you think that's important?"

Rodrigo shook his head. "I don't know. The *gringos* talk a lot about freedom. But from what I've seen, the *gringos* don't understand what freedom really is." Rodrigo looked away as if he was embarrassed at what he said.

"What do you mean?" asked Alba.

"Well, here's how I see it. Maybe a long time ago, the *norteamericanos* really fought to be free. They didn't want anyone telling them how to live, what church to go to, or what to say. That was a long time ago. Now, the only freedom they're interested in is the freedom to make money and buy things. The more the better. They're fat and lazy, like cattle. But their souls are in prison, blinded by their own wealth and greed. That's not freedom."

"And in Mexico?" asked Alba.

"In Mexico we're poor. Our government is corrupt, and it steals from the people. We're not free to do what we want. There's always a corrupt bureaucrat we have to pay off, so we can get a piece of paper to take to another bureaucrat and pay another bribe. But spiritually we're free. That's the difference."

Rodrigo looked at Alba, surprised at his own candor. It was dangerous to talk like that to the *gringos*. But Alba was different; she was half Mexican. She had one foot in both worlds. She understood what he meant.

"Alba!" Guadalupe called from the porch of the house. "We have guests. You and Rodrigo come up to the house."

Alba squeezed Rodrigo's arm.

"See, you're already part of the family. Let's go."

***

James Brazzle showed up at the Broken "T" unannounced... again. It was getting to be a bad habit. This time he brought two friends. They were polite enough. The tall, handsome one even spoke Spanish; better than most Mexicans, in fact. That wasn't the problem for Guadalupe. She sensed a hardness surrounding both of them, the worldliness of a world that she didn't want to get to know...ever. But she knew why they were there, and she hoped they had some answers.

Guadalupe heard snatches of their conversation from the kitchen. She gathered that James and the tall one used to rodeo together as teenagers. She suspected they knew each other after that too, probably during James' long absence from Texas. Creed never talked to her about what James really did during all those years. Just said he was working for the government. Guadalupe knew what that meant.

The screen door slammed on the porch. Alba walked into the kitchen and hugged her mother. They whispered to each other in Spanish and giggled like two schoolgirls. Rodrigo stamped his boots on the doormat, kicking off dirt from the round pen. Miniature clouds of dust obscured his boots momentarily and then settled. He followed Alba into the kitchen, his spurs clicking on the red tile floor. Sweat dripped from his temples, and he wiped at it with his sleeve.

"Buenos dias, Señora," he said politely and removed his cowboy hat.

"Good morning, Rodrigo. Go on into the living room and introduce yourself. The men are waiting for you."

***

Rodrigo walked into the next room, nervously holding his

western hat at belt level with both hands. He couldn't imagine what the men wanted with him.

"There you are, Rodrigo," said Creed in Spanish as he caught sight of his horse trainer. "There're a few people here I want you to meet. I think you know Mr. Brazzle...and this is Mr. Sloane and Mr. Herrin."

Rodrigo bowed his head deferentially and waited. The tall one caught his eye. He looked like a cowboy; long and lean and weather-beaten. He looked fit too, and younger than Creed Tucker, at least at first glance...until you looked in his eyes. It wasn't so much the wrinkles. That was to be expected for a man his age. It was more the story the eyes told...or maybe tried to hide. Rodrigo made eye contact with Mako and immediately averted his glance. When Sloane greeted him in Spanish, Rodrigo's teeth almost fell out. He'd never heard a *gringo* speak Spanish like that.

The men quizzed Rodrigo in Spanish about the incident at the R.A.T.S. checkpoint: the number of guards, their weapons, the demands for an import permit. His answers pretty much echoed what Drake Herrin had seen the day before. Mako asked questions about the mood of the Hispanic population in the county: what they thought about the National Front and the proposed referendum. It was Rodrigo's first debriefing by the ex-CIA officers, but it wouldn't be his last.

After Rodrigo left, Mako turned to Drake Herrin.

"I don't know how much of that you got, Drake? he asked questioningly.

"Enough...seems like a fine young man. We can probably use him down the road."

"I'd prefer to leave Rodrigo out of all this, if possible," interjected Creed.

"He's already in it, Creed," countered James Brazzle impatiently. "His own people almost killed him."

Creed looked at James and his face flushed red.

"His own people are not soldiers from the Zetas or the damned Sinaloa cartel," he snapped. "Not all Mexicans are drug-trafficking violent criminals. You know that as well as anybody."

Drake stood up with his hands in the pockets of his baggy tropical-weight khaki trousers.

"You two settle that later. I didn't mean to start anything. Let's continue, shall we?"

Drake looked severely at the two men as if they were misbehaving schoolchildren.

"Sorry," said Creed. "Go ahead, please."

James leaned towards Creed and slapped him between the shoulder blades with rough calloused hands, his version of an apology. Creed sulkily nodded his head in James' direction. Neither could stay angry at the other for long, but words for apologies just weren't part of their lexicon.

"I met with Commissioner Garza in Laredo yesterday. He filled me in on what's been happening on the border, and this morning I talked on the phone for about an hour with Washington...not at liberty to say with whom, but the information comes from the highest level. Here it is in a nutshell..."

Creed shifted his leg awkwardly as he listened. His leg wasn't bothering him that much anymore. His discomfiture came more from the presence in his house of Brazzle's two friends. He hadn't been around men like them since Vietnam. Creed's own experience with death and killing had ended when he got out of the Special Forces. These men had made a career of it, he suspected. They made him uneasy but he sensed they were serious, and that's what the situation required. What did Brazzle say that day on the way to Austin? "Extreme situations call for extreme measures." He suspected these men could ratchet up the ante if necessary.

"Sometimes the federal government can surprise you with its omnipotent intelligence gathering ability and clairvoyance. Unfortunately, this is not one of those times," began Drake Herrin. He walked slowly around the room, his long white hair blowing under the ceiling fan. He kept his hands clasped behind his back like a university professor lecturing.

"The administration forbade the CIA to get involved in this crisis. 'It's a domestic issue,' they said. Well, that left U.S. Customs, the FBI, Border Patrol, DEA: all the federal agencies working the Mexican border. The only problem is they're scared to leave their air conditioned offices...especially after the murder of the two Border Patrol agents and that customs official Hal Wilson the other day. Now they're talking about roadside bombs. They're scared of their own shadows. You don't gather much intelligence sitting behind a desk, gentlemen."

"Jesus," exclaimed Brazzle. "The feds usually beat their chests and tell everyone how badass they are."

"Believe it, James. But it's not just the feds," continued Drake.

"Well, what about the governor?" asked Creed. "We thought he had some balls. Come on; he's a fifth-generation Texan!"

Creed looked at the others for support. Brazzle nodded his head in silent agreement.

"Yesterday the president gave the governor a week to resolve the crisis. Essentially, Throckmorton has about seven to ten days to deploy the National Guard or an armored column from III Corps will drive out of the gates of Fort Hood at the orders of the president of the United States to deal with the FNLT and their ragtag gangs of hoodlums. If the R.A.T.S. rabble resists, people will die. Mako, you've got the floor. Tell us what you know."

Mako Sloane stood up slowly. Creed stared at Brazzle's former colleague. He looked more like an ex-professional surfer than a covert operative on retainer with the CIA. You sure can't tell a book by its cover, Creed thought to himself.

"I've been looking at some of the possible international repercussions of the trouble here in South Texas. Chavez and Ortega are trying to muddy the waters, but they're not going to do much except bluster...unless the rest of the world gets involved in this. That's the problem. The U.S. has left itself open to attacks on the self-determination issue with our support of independence movements inside Russia, the former Yugoslavia, Libya, Nicaragua and elsewhere. Most of the world outside of Western Europe will hop on the anti-Yankee bandwagon and cause us a hell of a lot of trouble if we can't nip this in the bud."

"What about Mexico?" asked Creed. "How deeply are they involved?"

"That's the key question, isn't it? I don't know the answer yet. I do know there are forces in Mexico that support the National Front, but I don't know yet who's running that show. There's a lot of patriotic verbiage out there about recovering the territory the U.S. stole from Mexico in the nineteenth century. How much of that is just political rhetoric, I don't know. My best guess is that the Sinaloa cartel owns a piece of the government in Mexico City and that they're using that historical issue as a red herring to promote their own business interests. It's a lot catchier to say, 'Liberate Texas!' than 'Sell more dope to the *gringos*!' What I don't know is how much direction the National Front is getting from Mexico City."

"So what do we do?" asked Creed.

Drake walked back to the center of the room where he had been studying a trophy mule deer buck mounted above the fire place.

"Don't expect miracles from us quite yet. We've only been

here for twenty-four hours. In general, though, I'd say we need to cut off the snake's head. The problem is, we don't know who the snake is...yet. But I have a hunch he's not in South Texas."

CHAPTER 16

Governor Throckmorton was nothing if not a politician. He knew the importance of covering his ass, and his staff was expert at identifying trends and predicting the ebb and flow of public opinion. As a candidate he had the foresight to vet the myriad of individuals and public organizations donating to his gubernatorial campaign. He was the darling of the Republican Party, and there was no shortage of donors who wanted to see Rick Throckmorton elected governor. But he needed them all to be kosher, with no hidden agenda that would leave him open to accusations of pandering to special interests.

When he learned the Hispanic Conservative Coalition had made a major contribution to his campaign, Rick Throckmorton was pleasantly surprised. The previously unknown Latino organization passed the preliminary due-diligence test of his staff. The contribution was accepted, and the republicans bragged about their appeal to the Hispanic voter.

But only last month a staffer called the attention of the governor-elect to a startling bit of news. The FBI had just arrested the head of the HCC in Laredo and charged him with laundering money for the Mexican drug cartels. Governor Throckmorton immediately disavowed the contribution, instructed his staff to return the money and to avoid media attention.

As he sat in his plush office sipping his morning coffee, the governor skimmed the latest editorial in the *Austin American Statesman* lambasting his administration for inaction on the South Texas referendum crisis. Governor Throckmorton tossed the newspaper on his desk with disgust and rang his secretary.

"Vicky, can you come into my office, please?" he asked politely.

"What's on the agenda today?" he asked his young Mexican-American secretary as she entered his office with her briefing book. Victoria Ramirez was a graduate of the University of Texas with a degree in political science and had received her present job as a reward for her effective work among Hispanic voters during the campaign.

"Okay, let's start with the phone calls. The Hispanic Conservative Coalition called again to express their regret that you won't take their calls. They wanted to apologize for any embarrassment the arrest of their chairman might have caused. They also expressed their concern over the situation in South Texas and hoped that you would respect the Texas Constitution and not listen to the hotheads who want to call in the National Guard."

"Yeah, I've heard that before," said the governor shaking his head in disbelief. "They've got a lot of gall. What else?"

"Well, there's more. They also said you would receive a Fedex package from them today with a more detailed explanation of their position. Then, let's see...no word from your daughter yet in Mazatlan. I've called the hotel, but they claim to have no record of her checking in. I'm calling other hotels on the strip...and your nine o'clock appointment is already waiting in the reception room. He's kind of cute for an older guy...Mako Sloane."

"Oh yeah, the guy from Washington."

"That guy's from Washington? Hmmm...sure doesn't look like the usual politicians that come to see you. I wish I could have met him when he was thirty," she blushed. "And his Spanish is better than mine," she added.

"Show him in, Vicky. Let's get this one out of the way. Let me know what you find out about my daughter. That's number one on your list today," Throckmorton added with concern.

Victoria returned a minute later with the visitor, smiling flirtatiously as she led him into the governor's office.

"If you're here to talk about South Texas, you're wasting your time and mine," Governor Throckmorton said gruffly without looking up as Mako Sloane walked into his office. Mako had driven up from the Broken "T" in Creed Tucker's pickup and was still wearing his dusty Wrangler jeans and cowboy boots. He had taken off his spurs in deference to the office of the governor.

"They told me I needed to meet with you, so I'm meeting with you. Other than that, let's make this short. I've got a lot of things on my plate." The governor finally looked up from shuffling his papers and was taken aback by the intense look in the eyes of his visitor.

"I'm Mako Sloane, governor. That's who the hell I am. I'll leave if you prefer, but then you'll have to explain your lack of manners to the president. I'm here at his request."

Rick Throckmorton froze. He had never heard the name "Mako Sloane", but there was something about the man's physical presence and icy stare that stopped him in his tracks. Did he say the president? How did the president know this dirty cowboy who dared come to the office of the governor of Texas in jeans? The president may have been a Democrat, which didn't hold a lot of water in Texas, but he was still the president. The governor realized he had been out of line. He stood up and extended his hand to Mako.

"I'm sorry, Mr. Sloane," he said apologetically. "Please forgive my rudeness. It's a trying time to be governor. Have a seat."

The governor motioned to several leather chairs around a coffee table in the corner of his office under a portrait of Sam Houston at the Battle of San Jacinto. He stood up and invited Mako to join him.

"But yes, I do want to talk about South Texas," said Mako firmly. "You may not read the *International Herald Tribune*, Governor Throckmorton, but the whole world is watching what you're doing...or rather, what you're not doing."

"Mr. Sloane, what the whole world thinks or says about this situation is of no consequence whatsoever, at least not to me. I only listen to the citizenry of the great state of Texas, and the only arbiter of my actions is the Texas Constitution."

"Well, those are nice words, Rick. May I call you Rick?" said Mako, and without waiting for a reply, continued. "But I'm not registered to vote in Texas anymore, and you're not running for office right now. I'm not interested in empty campaign rhetoric."

The governor looked at Mako with amazement. He was used to visitors kissing his ass. This man, dressed in dirty jeans and carrying a dusty cowboy hat, spoke to him as an equal. Throckmorton wasn't used to that.

Mako paused and looked angrily at the governor.

"Just so you know where I'm coming from, though, let me tell you something. I grew up riding saddle broncs at weekend rodeos in Sweetwater, San Angelo, and a dozen other towns in West Texas. I worked seven days a week, castrating and branding calves, rounding up strays, and breaking colts. I spoke more Spanish than English. So, if you think you're talking to a Washington bureaucrat, get that out of your head right now. I know Texas inside and out. Hell, I sweat Texas. Even if the president hadn't called me last night and asked me to drop in on you, I'd still be worried sick about what's going on. I can probably help you if you want, but I won't listen to any political posturing, even from the governor of Texas. Not when I saw a U.S. Customs official shot dead on the side of I-35 two days ago. You've got a problem, governor. What do you intend to do about it?"

"Mr. Sloane, the situation is far more complex than people

realize. There are constitutional issues at play, but I don't intend to let Mexican drug traffickers take over South Texas. Believe me; all of our options are still on the table including deploying the National Guard if local law enforcement is unable to deal with the problem."

Both men heard a soft knock on the door. Victoria stuck her head in the office.

"Not now, Vicky," warned the governor.

"I think you should see this, Rick," she said and walked straight into the office despite the governor's admonishment. She handed Throckmorton a Fedex envelope, turned on her heels, and walked out.

"What the hell is this?" wondered the governor out loud. He looked up at Mako and shrugged his shoulders. "The Hispanic Conservative Coalition," he read out loud, looking at the return address in Laredo. "What do those bastards want now?" He emptied the contents of the Fedex envelope onto the coffee table: a U.S. passport and a letter.

Throckmorton felt a cold chill originate somewhere around the base of his neck. The chill turned into gooseflesh and ran silently down his back. A lump formed in his throat and he fought a desire to swallow. It occurred to him that the Hispanic Conservative Coalition was no ordinary lobby group.

He opened the passport and saw what he knew he would find: the photograph of his daughter. Lisa Throckmorton, nineteen years old and on her first trip abroad. What had happened?

He glanced at the letter, saw that it was in Spanish, and handed it to Mako.

"I think they've got her," he said, his face ashen and his hand beginning to tremble.

Mako took the letter and read aloud the one-line message.

"*Sugerimos que no envie tropas de la Guardia Nacional a*

la República Autónoma de Tejas del Sur."

"Something about the National Guard?" asked the governor, his fists clenched in helpless fury.

"Seems they don't want you to send in the National Guard, governor," said Mako as he tossed the letter on the coffee table. "Why the hell did you let your daughter go to Mexico?"

CHAPTER 17

Supporters of Félix Aguilar, Mexico's attorney general and leading presidential candidate, arrived in Guadalajara by the tens of thousands. Columns of colorful school buses with religious slogans painted on the sides in gothic letters disgorged crowds of *campesinos* and workers who eagerly collected their handful of pesos for coming to the spectacle. Paying for attendance at political rallies was an age-old tradition in Mexico, and Félix respected the customs of his country.

Campaign workers directed the vibrant throngs towards the entrance of the new Omnilife soccer stadium in Guadalajara where mariachi bands were already playing. Vendors selling soft-shelled tacos, *perros calientes, menudo,* and fried chicken made a month's income in a few hours and counted their devalued pesos with undisguised glee and vowed everlasting allegiance to the candidate. Native dance troupes in colorful costumes and charros on horseback from the *Federación Mexicana de Charrería* congregated near the entrance to the stadium waiting for the signal to perform. Aguilar's political machine wasn't taking any chances. Every appearance of the candidate on the presidential stump needed to be a media event.

In another part of the huge parking lot, plush Land Rover SUVs, Mercedes, and BMW sedans were attended by uniformed chauffeurs and bodyguards. The attorney general's political support defied generalizations. His appeal was broad-based. Félix's audience ran the gamut from dirt-poor peasants employed in the agave plantations of the *Los Altos* region in Jalisco to wealthy bankers from the leading financial institutions of Guadalajara and Mexico City. They all had come to hear the candidate speak.

It was a time of great promise for Mexico. To his backers, Félix Aguilar represented law and order plus economic stability. The spectacular drug seizures he had engineered over the past few years gave reason to hope the government was getting the upper hand in the long, bloody struggle against the *narcotraficantes.* The entire country was repelled by the violence and corruption that had taken so many lives and delivered a crippling blow to the moral fiber of a once dynamic and flourishing people. As one voice, the major newspapers of Mexico lionized the attorney general as a unifying force and practically the greatest Latin American leader since Simón Bolivar and endorsed his candidacy for president without reservation. The recent attempt in Mexico City on Aguilar's life in broad daylight spoke eloquently of the pain Félix's policies were causing the drug cartels. The *narcos* were getting desperate, the newspapers claimed. Félix's backers feared for his life but cheered his candidacy and admired his personal courage. A country that desperately needed heroes had found one.

But today the crowds were hoping to hear something different than the normal political rhetoric of presidential campaigns. Tensions across the border in South Texas were on the rise, and Mexicans watched the unfolding events with an almost obsessive interest. They were proud of their cousins in the United States...more than proud, really. They were in awe of them. The entire country watched with delight as the National Front for the Liberation of Texas stood up for Hispanic rights and thumbed its collective nose at *gringo* threats to bring in the National Guard. The latent sense of inferiority felt by so many Mexicans in regard to anything North American had temporarily receded, replaced by a surge of national pride to be part of *La Raza.* The mood was electric and Aguilar intended to turn the groundswell of support for the National Front into votes for his candidacy.

Félix Aguilar stood on a raised stage at the center of the

soccer stadium. A bullet and blast-proof fiberglass panel surrounded and covered him and his closest advisors. An entire company of heavily armed elite Mexican paratroopers in red berets encircled the stage. Uniformed and plainclothes security guards circulated freely in the stadium looking for possible threats.

As he adjusted the microphone and gathered his notes to speak, Félix saw political activists from the famous Emiliano Zapata Ejido in Jalisco unfurl a huge red and green banner that proclaimed, *"Justicia, Tierra y Libertad!"* "Justice, Land, and Liberty!" He smiled to himself. Right on time, he thought. Political events in Mexico were scripted like Hollywood movies, and directors dispersed among the crowd coaxed Oscar-caliber performances from the actors they supervised. Fifty yards to their left, the labor unions were breaking out their signs and banners. Their slogans would be a little more militant, Felix knew. He had read the script.

"Apoyamos a la República Autónoma de Tejas del Sur!"

"Autodeterminación para Tejas!"

Then the chanting began. It started with the Confederation of Mexican Workers directly in front of Aguilar's lectern and gradually spread throughout the stadium.

"Félix, Félix, Félix," chanted fifty thousand enthusiastic supporters of the attorney general. They punctuated their shouts with sharp upward thrusts, holding tiny Mexican flags on wooden sticks they had received from the outstretched hands of smiling Félix Aguilar campaign workers upon entering the stadium. Television cameras rolled, and journalists interviewed carefully selected political activists for pre-arranged "impromptu" sound bites.

Mako Sloane was one of the few spectators not impressed with the choreographed political demonstration. It reminded him too much of October Revolution and May Day celebrations in Moscow during the 1970s and 80s although, admittedly, it wasn't too different from the Republican or Democratic conventions in the United States.

Felix raised his hands, asking for silence like an evangelical minister appealing to the Lord. The crowds instantly fell silent. He adjusted the microphone and began to speak.

"Mexico today is at a crossroads," he began, pausing theatrically and turning to engage the crowd from all angles.

"Do we continue to live in the shadow of the *Gringo* and fear his every word, or do we follow our destiny and the legacy of Moctezuma and Cuauhtémoc?"

Shouts of "Mexico, Mexico!" were heard over the continued chants of "Félix, Félix, Félix!" Once again Aguilar raised his hands to silence the crowd. The roar of the crowd instantly faded away to an obedient low murmur with the occasional unscripted outburst of enthusiasm from a few *campesinos* who had managed to sneak a ration of intoxicating *pulque* into the stadium.

"The *Gringo* talks about self-determination. He supports this principle of government everywhere except in his own country!" The crowd again erupted in cheers and the irrepressible chant of the attorney general's name. "I say the *Gringo* should practice what he preaches!" As if one person, fifty thousand Mexicans stomped their feet and shouted in a thunderous demonstration of approval.

"Our Hispanic brothers in the United States have opened our eyes! I have only one thing to say today. Mexico supports the just aspirations of the National Front for the Liberation of Texas! Yes to self-determination! Yes to the referendum! No to *Gringo* hegemony!"

The frenzied response of the crowd defied description. Dancing, singing, shouting, and chanting, Aguilar's supporters were ecstatic. He had given them exactly what they wanted to hear. A mariachi band burst into sound and a display of colorful fireworks erupted from the sidelines of the soccer field.

Mako Sloane had seen enough and made his way slowly through the crowd, his cowboy hat drawn low over his forehead to hide his blue eyes. It wouldn't be healthy in Guadalajara today to be recognized by the mob as a *gringo*. Fortunately for Mako, the cheering crowd was distracted by the pageantry of the spectacle down below. A dance troupe in traditional Aztec garb came out on the field to the nonstop shouts and cheers of the crowd and mounted *charros* galloped around the perimeter waving broad sombreros in one hand and holding braided horsehair reins in the other. Even the candidate and his aides danced on stage.

As he drove his rented car towards the airport, Mako mulled over what he had seen. The multitude of craven Aguilar supporters and their fervent support of the autonomy movement in South Texas were worrisome even if the attorney general's campaign *had* bussed in half of them. Public gringo-bashing in Mexico was usually limited to vituperous but impotent abuse in newspaper editorials. The residual anti-American sentiment so evident in the country usually went no further than the print media or an occasional demonstration on Reforma in front of the American embassy. The rhetoric of a few left-leaning politicians and journalists behind closed doors or the occasional rock throwing mob was one thing, but encouraging rebellion in a neighboring country was challenging the generally accepted norms of international relations.

Félix is riding a roller-coaster of public emotion he won't be able to control, thought Mako. Someone is pulling his strings and choreographing his campaign. But who? That's the snake Drake was talking about. That's who I've got to find before it's too late for a lot of people...including Lisa Throckmorton.

CHAPTER 18

Mario couldn't sleep. He peered through half-closed eyes at Rodrigo who rolled over restlessly on the rusty, squeaking springs of an old army cot and reached for his watch on a wooden chair next to his nightstand. Mario saw a brief flash of artificial light as Rodrigo checked the time. His silhouette was barely visible in the faint moonlight that trickled into the bunkhouse through dusty window panes. Mario saw Rodrigo turn in his direction and he closed his eyes, pretending to be asleep. He lay on his back and opened his mouth and snorted softly to complete the subterfuge.

It was almost midnight but it was still hot and muggy. The air was thick. Two ancient floor fans clanked and banged but provided little relief despite their prodigious efforts. Mario lay still, sweating in the sticky stillness of another unbearable South Texas night. He saw Rodrigo gather his t-shirt, jeans, and cowboy boots in his arms, stand up, and carefully tiptoe across the creaking floorboards, pausing after every step to see if he was awake. The high-pitched drone of the cicadas outside the door masked the sound of his slow, shuffling progress towards the door.

Mario opened his eyes but continued to breathe heavily. He didn't want Rodrigo to know he was awake. This wasn't the first time Rodrigo had snuck out of the bunkhouse for a late-night rendezvous with Alba. In fact, it was becoming more the rule than the exception.

When Mario first realized what Rodrigo was up to on these nighttime excursions, it had come as a shock. It had opened his eyes and made him view his own subordinate role on the Broken "T" in much starker terms. Mario felt like Rodrigo and the Tucker family had made a fool out of him. He had become the only "wetback" on the ranch while his erstwhile friend, whom he had led across the Rio Grande like a little brother, was almost part of the Tucker family and Alba's *novio*.

Mario waited for Rodrigo to return. He got up from his cot and paced back and forth across the rough wooden floorboards of the bunkhouse. They were loosely nailed and shifted under his weight. The *click-clack* of the floor fans irritated him. He waited and still Rodrigo did not return. He walked into the tiny kitchen and opened the old, white General Electric refrigerator with the rounded corners. He reached for a bottle of Tecate and used a knife to pry off the cap like the two of them used to do in Mexico. The ice cold beer tasted good going down. By the time Mario heard the sounds of Rodrigo's footsteps approaching, an hour had passed and he had finished off four bottles of the Mexican beer. He was getting angrier by the minute.

Mario sat in the folding metal chair by his bed in the hazy darkness of the bunkhouse, motionless and silent and dressed only in his white underwear which gleamed with a malign phosphorescence. Mario stared as Rodrigo opened the screen door silently and tiptoed into the kitchen with his boots in his hand. Mario still had not said a word and sat expectantly with a bottle of beer in his hand and the empties lined up on the kitchen counter, bearing quiet testimony to his state of mind. Mario saw Rodrigo jump slightly when he caught sight of him.

"Mario, *¿qué pasó?* I didn't wake you up, did I?" asked Rodrigo.

"*¿Dónde estabas?*" asked Mario in an expressionless monotone.

"I took a walk with Alba," lied Rodrigo. "What do you say we get some sleep, *mano*?"

"You take a lot of walks at night, don't you?"

"Sometimes," said Rodrigo.

"Things are really working out for you here, aren't they?"

"I think we're both doing pretty well," Rodrigo replied.

"Not like you," said Mario. "I'm not the *gringos'* favorite Mexican and I'm not sneaking out at night to be with the *patron's* daughter."

"Listen, we've got a whole string of new colts to work tomorrow. We're going to have to get up early and I'm kind of tired."

"I bet you are, *cabrón*," replied Mario sarcastically. "You've been using all your energy banging that *gringa* every night, haven't you? That's why you're so tired in the mornings these days. That's why I have to do all your work."

"*¿Por qué me hablas así?*" countered Rodrigo. "Why are you talking to me this way? I've done nothing to you."

"Because I see what's going on, *buey*," Mario said and stood up threateningly.

"Mario, please, this is the beer talking...*somos amigos*. Don't be like this," pleaded Rodrigo.

"If we were friends, you wouldn't be kissing the old *gringo's* ass and *chingando* that *puta!*"

Rodrigo didn't wait for Mario to throw the first punch. He took two quick strides in Mario's direction and threw a right cross that landed squarely below his left eye. Mario fell to the ground and looked up at Rodrigo in shock. Rodrigo pushed him back to the floor and held him down with his knee pressed into Mario's sternum. He raised his fist again.

"Mario, you talk about Alba that way again, and I'll forget we were ever friends. *Entendido?*"

"*Haz lo que quieras.* It's been a long time since we were friends."

Mario struggled to his feet, cursing under his breath and retrieved his small suitcase from under his cot which he had packed a couple of days ago just in case. He opened the suitcase and changed clothes quickly.

"Mario, wait!" pleaded Rodrigo.

"*¡Traidor!*" Mario hissed through his teeth. He walked out the door carrying the suitcase and let the screen door slam.

***

Mario didn't know what time it was. He hadn't slept much, occasionally dozing during the night while sitting on his suitcase on the side of the highway. The blinding headlights of eighteen wheelers and the howling *whoosh* of their passing on the way to Laredo would startle him back into a groggy consciousness as he sat with his head cradled in his arms. Mario was afraid to lie down. There were too many creatures in Texas that took advantage of the cooler night air to take care of business. Snakes, scorpions, tarantulas, or poisonous spiders; most things in Texas bit or stung or could hurt you in some other way. Mario didn't want to be on the receiving end of that kind of business.

He was too tired to even care about the stray Border Patrol car that might drive by. It didn't really matter. Federal and local law enforcement rarely ventured out on patrol these days anyway. They had received unambiguous instructions to keep a low profile and not to provoke violent incidents. Most of the police officers and federal agents expressed their outrage publically but secretly welcomed the directive. There were too many armed R.A.T.S. detachments patrolling the major intersections and bridges. The once all-powerful federal and state agencies were now outnumbered and overmatched. Handguns and shotguns couldn't stand up to assault rifles and RPGs. They all waited for the inevitable: the arrival of the National Guard.

Mario was headed towards the border for another crossing of the Rio Grande; this time in reverse. He had given it a good try. He had come all the way from Guanajuato, crossed the Rio Grande safely, made it up to La Salle County, and got a job...only to have his best friend betray him. He'd be damned if he was going to take orders from a wetback who wanted to be white. Mario had no doubts about his own identity. He was Mexican, a member of *La Raza,* and he didn't need a half-white girlfriend to make him feel like a man.

There were a few pickups traveling along the highway even at this hour, and as the sun came up, Mario boldly stood on the side of the road flagging down the passing trucks. One, driven by Anglo ranchers slowed down to take a look at Mario but sped up and went on its way when they got a closer look.

A black Dodge Ram 3500 Power Wagon sped by Mario but then screeched to a halt some fifty yards past him and careened towards him in reverse. The truck kicked up gravel as it swerved on and off the shoulder of the highway. A week ago Mario would have run away at the sight of a R.A.T.S. patrol. Now the sight of the approaching truck with four uniformed Mexican youths wearing headbands and backwards baseball caps riding in the bed of the pickup was almost a welcome sight, and he found himself wishing he was one of them.

The truck stopped next to Mario and the four armed thugs jumped out of the back of the truck and pointed their AK-47s at him. An older Mexican, both arms sleeved out with tattoos, climbed importantly out of the passenger side of the truck. He wore a red and green bandana around his head, sunglasses, and had a Browning 9 mm stuck into his belt. This one must be in charge, thought Mario.

"*¿Qué haces aquí, buey?*" he demanded without ceremony. "What are you doing here, asshole?"

Mario was strangely unafraid. He stood up straight with his shoulders back and said, "I'm going back to Mexico. I've had enough of the *gringos* and their country."

"Hey, I know you," interjected one of the gunmen. "You work for old man Tucker, don't you? You and that kid we beat up a couple of weeks ago."

"Not anymore," replied Mario. "They can all kiss my ass. I quit."

"Where's your friend?" the one in charge asked.

"He's back at the ranch sleeping with the *patron's* daughter."

"Put down your weapons," the leader of the patrol said to the others. He turned to Mario and looked him over. "You need a job and a place to live, *camarada*?" He smiled for the first time.

"Maybe I do," said Mario, his spirits rising.

CHAPTER 19

"Vicky, get the National Front on the line!" Governor Throckmorton put down his cup of coffee and leaned back in his overstuffed leather chair paid for by Texas taxpayers. He stared without seeing at the pair of mounted longhorns hanging over the door to his office. Just a few days till the president's deadline arrived. No matter what he did, the proverbial shit was going to hit the fan. He couldn't see a way out of this one. He'd suffered through political crises before but never anything remotely like this. The National Front and the Hispanic Majority Committee refused to even take his phone calls. His fact-finding missions were turned back at the Nueces River checkpoints. And then on top of everything else, they threw the haymaker: a Fedex envelope with his daughter's passport. Lacking subtlety, perhaps, but effective. Lisa Throckmorton, the governor's daughter, abducted in Mexico. But where was she?

"Line one, Rick." said Vicky and discreetly transferred the call.

The governor picked up on line one and heard Mexican *norteña* music in the background.

"This is Governor Throckmorton. Who is this?" The governor tried to keep his voice under control.

"*Buenas tardes,*" answered a soft female voice in Spanish. "*¿Con quién quiere hablar?*"

The governor barely managed to conceal his exasperation. "I want to speak with the head of the National Front."

The receptionist continued in Spanish. "He's out of the office today. Is there somebody else who could help you?"

she asked politely.

"Let me speak to whoever's in charge," the governor responded in English.

"*Un momento, por favor.*" There was a click and the governor realized the secretary had put him on hold. A recording played an old Franco song from the 1980s as he waited...and waited.

Finally, he heard another click and a male voice answered. "*Bueno.*"

"Who is this?" asked the governor yet again.

"This is Rudy Gutierrez, minister of defense of the National Front for the Liberation of Texas. What can I do for you?" the voice said in English.

"Minister of defense? Of what?" the governor almost shouted into the telephone.

"Of the Hispanic majority in South Texas, governor. Or did you stop believing in representative democracy when your lily-white candidates lost in the municipal elections? We're making preparations to repulse the expected *gringo* aggression. How can I help you today?"

"Mr. Gutierrez, I need to speak with the head of the National Front. Unless we find an immediate resolution to this crisis, people are going to die."

"Governor, I'd like to help you, but the chairman is out of town on urgent consultations. I'm in charge in his absence."

"What is the name of the chairman, and how can I reach him?

"The name of the chairman is classified, as is his location. For obvious reasons. You want to deal with the National Front, you deal with me," replied Gutierrez.

"Mr. Gutierrez, I don't know whether you've ever been in the military, but can you imagine what a well-armed and trained

National Guard unit can do to your ragtag army of drug cartel thugs? You need to talk with us about the referendum while there's still time. If we can't reach a negotiated settlement to end the violence and restore order, I intend to cross the Nueces River with troops from the Texas National Guard." The governor saw no reason for diplomatic niceties.

"Well, let's see now, governor. Last thing I heard, you never did put on a uniform for this country, did you? So I'm not sure *you* know what a well-armed National Guard unit can do. Rumor has it you were a little preoccupied with your fraternity parties at the University of Texas while your peers were dying in combat in Vietnam. Ever think of that?"

"I had a student deferment," said the governor, raising his voice.

"Yeah, I bet you did," responded Gutierrez. "Well, I didn't and I spent a year on LURP patrols in Vietnam. Was wounded twice and decorated with the Silver Star. And we have quite a few Iraq and Afghanistan veterans among our 'cartel thugs' as you put it; dozens of Latino veterans who are tired of being spit on by you Anglos. So, unless you want to talk about autonomy for the Hispanics in South Texas, I think this conversation is over. We're ready for you, and the whole world is watching."

Governor Throckmorton opened his mouth to reply but then realized that Gutierrez had hung up. The sonofabitch hung up on the governor of Texas!

***

The governor had been drinking for several hours and was more than a little drunk. It was three o'clock in the afternoon, and he long ago had lost any pretensions to discretion. A bottle of Tres Generaciones tequila stood blatantly on his desk, and he was chasing shots of tequila with cold Modelo Especial beer.

He stared at Major General Monica Mendoza, commander of the Texas National Guard, through glassy eyes. The unsigned deployment order lay in front of him. He looked at the document and saw a death warrant for his daughter, probably a hostage somewhere in the Mexican state of Sinaloa. He had no illusions about Lisa's fate were he to sign the document or even call in the FBI to help get her back.

"As soon as the National Guard crosses the Nueces River, they'll kill her...I know it," he mumbled to himself.

"I'm sorry, governor?" said the general.

Rick Throckmorton waved his hand in apology. He made a conscious effort not to slur his speech. "Just thinking aloud, general...now, what do you know about the disposition of the R.A.T.S. units?"

"The R.A.T.S. deployments have been clever. Someone in charge has military training, that's for sure, but they have no defense against our high-altitude reconnaissance flights and high-resolution photography. We know the location of every unit they have, and the reports are updated three times a day. Starting tomorrow, that'll be every hour."

"How many are there?" asked the governor

"I'd say between 1,000 and 1,250 mainly deployed in small units at bridges and strategic intersections. We've seen several armored vehicles which probably came from the weapons depot they plundered in Zapata. Our guys barely got out alive, and the insurgents got a veritable treasure trove of weaponry."

"What about across the border? Any activity on the Mexican side?"

"As a matter of fact there is," the general replied. "We've spotted a regiment of motorized cavalry moving north towards

Laredo from the interior. We questioned our counterparts in Mexico about it, and they assure us it is nothing more than a security measure to lower tension on their side of the border. We're keeping an eye on it."

"If I give the order to deploy, we have to be very specific on the rules of engagement."

"Yes sir, of course. We've discussed this and we all agree. We won't open fire on R.A.T.S. units except in self-defense. Then our soldiers are free to use deadly force. Our units will seek to occupy key strategic locations, and we'll seek to arrest members of the National Front for inciting insurrection. Hopefully, they'll lay down their arms when they see us coming."

"Were you born in the U.S., Monica?" asked the governor suddenly, eyeing the general carefully.

She paused and glanced at the governor with unconcealed surprise.

"Yes, I was, governor...in San Diego, California. My parents crossed the border illegally before I was born. They're citizens now. Why do you ask?"

"Just wondering, I suppose," speculated the governor. "Do you have any mixed feelings about sending troops into combat against your own people?"

"Governor, your question surprises me. My 'own' people, as you put it, are hardworking, law-abiding citizens of the United States," the general retorted. "I don't have any drug traffickers in my family tree."

"But I mean, your parents weren't always legal citizens, were they? Don't you think there're people like your parents supporting the National Front? Honest Mexicans who crossed the border illegally to look for a better life? People who have been duped by the drug traffickers?"

"Governor, your questions are obviously rhetorical. Of

course, there are honest illegals mixed up with the National Front. Hard-working people just like my parents. Illegal Mexican labor has supported Texas and the whole Southwest for generations. But, governor, times have changed."

"Enough to deny our own cultural heritage?" The governor slurred the word "heritage" and tried unsuccessfully to suppress a belch.

"You're not talking like a conservative republican governor of Texas right now...but yes, times have changed that much."

"You know, my mother lived on a farm near Waelder, Texas as a kid. She always spoke with great affection about the Mexican family that lived and worked on their farm. My grandfather was very close to them as well. He spoke Spanish, or thought he did, at least. He called it 'Messican'."

"Governor Throckmorton, if you don't mind me saying so, you're letting sentimentality crowd out common sense. Look around you. When your mother was growing up, there weren't Mexican gangbangers driving around South Texas who'd just as soon kill you as look at you. The drug business didn't exist. And then there's the issue of corruption. Drug dollars have suborned high levels of the Mexican government and police force, and don't think that all of your own state legislators or political appointees are pristine. The U.S. Customs official they found dead last week was playing both sides of the fence, and there are more where he came from, believe me."

Throckmorton looked at the general with a skepticism he didn't bother to hide. He couldn't imagine being Hispanic and working against Mexicans who were just trying to do the same thing his parents did to get to this country. She was right, though, about the drug trade. That had changed the rules of the game. His thoughts suddenly shifted back to his daughter. He stood up unsteadily from his desk and extended his hand.

"You'll have my decision in twenty-four hours, general," he

said. "Have your troops ready to move."

"Yes sir," responded the general and turned briskly on her heels and walked out of the governor's office.

Governor Throckmorton sat back down in his chair and sighed. He put his head in his hands and ran his fingers through his hair in exasperation. He reached into the top drawer of his desk and pulled out an address book.

"Where the hell is it?" he asked out loud as his finger ran down a list of names and phone numbers. "I know it's here."

Then he saw it. A cell phone number scribbled on a scrap of paper he had discarded in the corner of his drawer, never thinking he would need it. He picked up the paper and stared at his near illegible scrawl. He could barely make out the name...Mako Sloane. He pulled out his cell phone and dialed the number.

CHAPTER 20

"You're pushing your luck with me, Mako," said Félix Aguilar. They sat in the balcony of the Mazurka restaurant in Mexico City on Nueva York Street. A waiter had just brought the ice cold shots of vodka the Polish restaurant was famous for, but neither man was in a drinking mood. A musician sat at the black baby grand piano and played Chopin's "Minute Waltz". Crystal glasses clinked at the tables around them and well-heeled clients sampled the exotic East European cuisine with murmured expressions of approval.

Mako could tell Félix hadn't been pleased to get his call a few days after an assailant broke up their lunch in the Zona Rosa by firing several shots into the crowded patio restaurant where they sat. Mako sensed during their phone conversation that the attorney general's cordiality was strained and knew that his invitation to dinner was an imposition. The attorney general these days dispensed his time sparingly, but Mako knew that curiosity alone would cause him to acquiesce. He wasn't surprised when Félix agreed to meet.

Mako didn't bother with his usual surveillance detection run before the meeting. The only people interested in his whereabouts would already know where he was headed. He exited his hotel lobby in Polanco, and in a rare but intentional absence of tradecraft Mako stepped off the curb into a waiting hotel cab with no attempt to conceal his destination or throw off would-be watchers.

"*A la Mazurka,*" he instructed the taxi driver.

He arrived at the restaurant almost at the same time as the attorney general, who was accompanied by a large retinue of heavily armed security guards. The two old friends chose a secluded table for two in the balcony of the restaurant and sat for a minute without saying anything, listening to the classical music and guessing at the hidden agenda of the other. When Félix finally spoke, Mako was taken aback by the change in tone from their previous cordial meeting.

"Pushing my luck? How so, Félix?" he asked

"I'm not the same young investigator for the *Secretaría de Gobernación* that used to hang out with the junior CIA officer from the American embassy thirty years ago," stated Félix in a particularly inauspicious beginning to the conversation.

Mako nodded his head.

"So, if it's all the same with you, let's dispense with small talk. I don't have much time," continued Félix.

"I know you're not the same man you were thirty years ago," replied Mako. "I heard you speak yesterday in Guadalajara. You've become a cynical politician, Félix. You may be the next president of Mexico, but you're a far cry from the idealistic attorney that used to work for me."

"I told you never to bring that up, Mako. That's ancient history: water under the bridge."

"Listen, we were once good friends, Félix. I'll be straight with you. What you do with your candidacy; who's financing your campaign, or who's pulling your strings is none of my concern.   In fact, I couldn't care less. I don't submit my reports to the chief of station anymore."

"That's reassuring," said Aguilar glancing around the restaurant, pretending to be bored.

Mako ignored the attorney general's sarcasm.

"I don't think you'd be foolish enough to interfere in the internal affairs of the United States, and I'm hoping your blustering yesterday was just political rhetoric. *Gringo*-bashing is always worth votes in Mexico, isn't it? It appeals to the subconscious anti-Americanism of most Mexicans."

"Sloane, get to the point. You insisted on this meeting. Now, spit it out. I don't have much patience for you or your naïve American political analysis." Aguilar leaned back and inhaled deeply from his cigarette, which he held in his right hand. His left hand beat out a disjointed rhythm on the white tablecloth.

"Okay, Félix, let me break it down for you. First, I'll tell you the same thing I told Hugo Chavez and Daniel Ortega last week in Managua. If you actively support the National Front for the Liberation of Texas, retribution will be swift and merciless. Secondly, I'm sure you're aware that the daughter of the governor of Texas disappeared in Mazatlan earlier this week. I suspect the Sinaloa cartel is involved. I want to know who's got her and where she is."

"You're forgetting yourself, Mako Sloane," said the attorney general, pushing his chair back and preparing to leave. "Like I said, times have changed. Unfortunately, you haven't. You *gringos* don't run things in Mexico anymore, and how the hell would I know anything about the governor's daughter?"

"You know why," said Mako.

"Enlighten me," replied Félix. He picked up a shot of vodka with his left hand and pretended to drink.

"You always liked to play both sides, didn't you?" asked Mako, not expecting an answer.

"What's that supposed to mean?"

"Félix, let's make this easy. You tell me what I want to know and I'm gone."

"I wish I could, Mako. Nothing I'd like more than to see you walk out this door. But I'm neither omnipotent nor prescient. There's a limit to what even the attorney general of Mexico has access to. Why should I know everything the cartel does?"

"Because I think you're on their payroll, Félix," said Mako. "I don't think you take a piss without the okay from your cartel puppeteer."

The attorney general looked at Mako and his eyes widened. His jaws clenched and he slammed his shot glass of vodka on the table with a resounding thud. The icy liquid spilled onto the linen tablecloth and left an irregular pattern of spidery wetness which slowly spread in all directions.

"That's it, Sloane. You've got twenty-four hours to get out of Mexico. Then, God help you."

The attorney general got out of his chair and angrily threw his raincoat over his shoulder. As he turned to leave, he bumped into a mortified waiter, who dropped a tray full of pickled herring, black caviar, and other Polish delicacies on the tile floor.

"Get out of my way," said Aguilar dismissively, and the confused waiter paled and beat a quick retreat.

Mako grabbed the attorney general by the shoulder and said in a low voice. "And if I don't have my answer in twenty-four hours, all of Mexico will be talking about Félix Aguilar, the presidential candidate who used to work for the CIA. Look for the story on the front page of *El Universal* and a couple other papers as well. I still know a lot of journalists in this town, and I've got some chits to call in."

"*¡Cabrón!*" snarled the attorney general and stormed out of the restaurant.

Mako Sloane watched him go and briefly glanced at the other tables on the balcony. A matronly woman across from him froze with a spoonful of black caviar poised for insertion into her open mouth. She stared at him and shook her head in mute disapproval. Mako raised his shot glass in a silent toast to the woman and threw down the ice cold vodka. It burned refreshingly in his throat. He placed a hundred dollar bill on the table and walked towards the stairs.

***

Mako had already packed his leather shoulder bag. He sat in his room at the Hotel Nikko on Campos Elíseos in the Chapultepec neighborhood of Polanco. His Browning 9 mm lay in his lap and a Barcardi light rum and coke stood on a glass-top coffee table half empty with the ice slowly melting as he watched *CNN en Español*. Naturally the coverage was about South Texas and the worsening crisis. A comely Spanish-speaking reporter from Argentina was interviewing people on the streets of McAllen, Texas, her tight skirt and low-cut blouse accentuating rather than concealing her vibrant sexuality, so different from her more androgynous counterparts in the United States.

"We'll see in the near future if the United States respects the principle of self-determination on its own soil," the reporter concluded sanctimoniously as she ended her segment. Mako leaned over and switched off the television set.

He knew it wasn't safe for him to stay in Mexico City. He had chosen the Nikko because an attempt on his life would be less likely in a luxury hotel close to the center of town. And, of course, he wanted to give the attorney general a chance to respond to his parting request. Mako had a feeling he would. The threat to reveal Aguilar as a former CIA asset was real and potentially far more devastating than Félix's own threat to merely kill his former case officer.

Just after midnight Mako heard a light tapping on the door to his room. He leapt from his chair and moved silently towards the door, sidestepping into the bathroom on the right, his gun drawn. As he waited, someone slid an envelope under the door, and Mako heard the sound of footsteps retreating down the thickly carpeted hallway. He waited another minute to make sure the messenger had left and then retrieved the envelope.

It was a business-size, plain white envelope with no indication of who the sender might be.   A single sheet of stationery with three typed lines of text was inside.

Francisco Salcido

Rancho "Vista del Mar"

Culiacán, Sinaloa

"*Gracias, Félix,*" Mako said under his breath and reached for his bag. It was time to get out of Mexico City.

CHAPTER 21

Archibald Rutledge woke up almost every morning with one thought in mind: he was a heartbeat away from the presidency. Never mind the fact that he had been the token southerner on the ballot, a mere political afterthought. The presidential candidate himself was from the Midwest and had polled poorly in the South. Archibald's sole mission as the vice-presidential candidate was to balance the ticket. He delivered the votes the president needed from Dixie, and the rest was history. Somehow, an African-American presidential candidacy was more palatable to the white American voter with the quintessential southern gentleman, the junior senator from South Carolina, as his running mate.

Archibald's political career was almost stillborn. When he abandoned South Carolina for Texas and that bastion of liberal education in Austin, his wealthy father had thrown up his hands in disgust and threatened to withdraw Archibald's generous monthly stipend. The old man finally relented and seven years later welcomed the prodigal son back into the fold and rewarded him with a six figure salary in the family law firm. Archibald quickly won election to the Charleston city council, and his political career took off by leaps and bounds.

Archibald had not been a serious student at the University of Texas. Even he wouldn't be rash enough to claim otherwise. On the contrary, he had been a hell raiser and, quite frankly, a study in youthful dissipation. If it hadn't been for his father and the senior Rutledge's generous donations to the new law school library, young Archibald would never have been accepted. He did have the foresight, though, to court Jody Van Slyke, a brilliant and ambitious young woman, whose dual goals at UT were to make sure Archibald graduated from law school and then to marry him. She succeeded on both counts, and her brother Lester Van Slyke and the young rake from Charleston became fraternity brothers, best friends, and then brothers-in law.

Archibald was a born glad-hander, and in between hangovers he cultivated a network of valuable contacts. At the university, his rolodex card file was brimming with the names of future political celebrities, both at the state and national levels. That was one area where Archibald was especially diligent, and his attention to detail, at least that kind of detail, paid off in spades.

***

Lester Van Slyke, on the other hand, lacked the fire of political ambition that consumed his future brother-in-law. He was content to play supporting roles and assist others in attaining their goals of political stardom. One of those was a fraternity brother and good friend by the name of Rick Throckmorton. That investment paid off in the years that followed, and Lester was delighted when the governor of Texas offered him the position of secretary of state. He preferred access to the perks of high office without the onerous responsibility that usually went with them, and the relative anonymity of the position suited him just fine. Given the choice, Lester would choose to stay out of the limelight.

However, the movement for Hispanic rights in South Texas changed all that and upset his plans for milking the system quietly from the lap of obscure luxury. Lester wanted nothing to do with the reporters from the *Houston Chronicle* and *Dallas Morning News* who besieged his office and pestered him with embarrassing questions. He resented accusations that he ignored anomalies in the latest round of municipal elections in South Texas and the vague suggestions of his involvement in election shenanigans. Now, on top of everything else, Lester's brother-in-law had summoned him to Washington for "consultations".

As he approached the Eisenhower Executive Office Building on Pennsylvania Avenue in the car the vice president had sent to the airport for him, Lester pulled out his cell phone and dialed Archibald's personal number.

"I'm here, brother-in-law," Lester greeted the vice president casually.

"Perfect timing!" responded Archibald. "The delegation from the Organization of American States will be here in thirty minutes. I want you to sit in on the meeting. Come on up. I'll let everyone know you're on your way."

Lester sighed. Being brother-in-law to the vice president had its perks, but there were fraternal obligations as well. Lester was aware the president had ordered Archibald to handle all meetings with international delegations seeking to influence the administration or just wanting to express their opinion on the crisis in South Texas. The president's reasoning was crystal clear, Archibald had explained. The commander-in-chief didn't give a shit what other countries thought. They certainly had no right to interfere in the internal affairs of the United States, and the president was loath to waste his time with useless meetings and have to listen to complaints from heads of state and general secretaries of international organizations that were irrelevant outside the third world. That's what vice presidents were for.

As he entered the anteroom of the vice president's ceremonial office, Lester was surprised to recognize several network news anchors surrounded by their cameramen and sound crews. He was even more surprised when they recognized him.

"Mr. Secretary," the familiar face of the CBS evening news anchorman called to him as the receptionist ushered him toward the vice president's office. Lester turned to him out of curiosity.

"Is it true that money from the drug cartels is behind the success of Hispanic political candidates in South Texas?"

Lester felt he was suddenly thrust into the spotlight at a news conference. Before he had a chance to even acknowledge the question, another voice bombarded him without warning.

"Mr. Secretary, has the governor signed the order to deploy the Texas National Guard?"

Lester turned at the sound of the sultry female voice and saw the surgically altered face of the long-time ABC news anchor. What the hell is going on here today? he thought.

"Shouldn't you folks be down in Austin talking with Rick?" said Lester waving. The receptionist opened the door to the vice president's office just wide enough to let him pass.

"What's going on, Archie?" asked Lester, as he squeezed through the door and entered Archibald's office. He motioned with his head towards the television reporters congregating in his reception room.

"The vultures have gathered for a meal."

"What the hell? This is a Texas affair: a matter of states' rights. Texas will handle the crisis the way Texas sees fit," responded Lester self-righteously.

"You're pleading states' rights to the former senator from South Carolina?" laughed Archibald. "Isn't that preaching to the choir? But don't worry; those reporters aren't after you. At least not today. But they'll all be on the ground in South Texas by noon tomorrow. Some god-forsaken place called Cotulla."

Twenty minutes later the delegation from the Organization of American States entered the anteroom of the vice president's office. The throng of reporters deluged them with shouted questions before they disappeared behind closed doors. The media representatives waited like jackals for the expected press conference.

"Miguel, it's good to see you again," said the vice president, embracing the secretary general of the Organization of American States, a career diplomat from Chile who had known Archibald Rutledge at the University of Texas. He greeted the other members of the four-man delegation, all minor functionaries from Central America, and introduced the Texas secretary of state.

"Mr. Vice President, thank you for receiving us on such short notice for an informal consultation." The Chilean diplomat stressed the word "informal". "I regret the president was unable to attend," he added pointedly.

"Miguel, we've known each other long enough to dispense with formality. I'm sure your colleagues will forgive me if I get right to the point. The president was not about to countenance this consultation with his presence. He believes the mere fact that this meeting is taking place at all is a gross interference in the internal affairs of the United States of America. What happens within our borders is our business, and only our business. That is also my view on the matter. The Texas secretary of state might have a different opinion."

Archibald turned to Lester with a knowing wink.

"Mr. Secretary General," responded Lester to his brother-in-law's cue. "The state of Texas will not tolerate interference in its internal affairs from Washington, much less from the Organization of American States."

The general secretary blanched momentarily but recovered quickly.

"But Archibald, it is precisely Article Two of our Charter which empowers us to promote and consolidate representative democracy. The OAS has sent observation missions on more than one hundred occasions in the last forty years to oversee free and fair elections. If the municipal governments in South

Texas hold a referendum on autonomy, our representatives will be there on the ground as observers along with our colleagues from the European Union."

"Miguel, we would tolerate the presence of international observers out of respect and support for the principle of fair and transparent elections. That is a major concession on the part of the president. I must note, however, that the referendum itself is very likely illegal, and that there's no chance in hell it will ever be held. I would add that you're overstepping the bounds of the OAS Charter. That same Article Two calls for respect for the principle of non-intervention, and the United States government expects you to abide by that OAS core value. I thank you for your time, gentlemen." The vice president rose and escorted his shocked OAS colleagues to the door.

Archibald was a master at playing the crowd and that included the group of reporters waiting outside his office. Lester watched in admiration as he walked through the group of prominent telecasters and newspaper journalists, shaking hands, joking, and deflecting any serious questions. He posed for photographs with the secretary general and then waved off requests for an interview, pleading pressing engagements. His one serious statement was succinct and final.

"The administration respects the right of the state of Texas to manage its own affairs. I would direct any specific questions on the situation in South Texas to Governor Rick Throckmorton in Austin. I would also hope that the secretary general here respects the right of member states of the OAS to manage their own affairs without undue interference."

Back in the opulent furnishings of his ceremonial office, the vice president opened the cabinet of a 19th century French provincial sideboard and extracted a bottle of El Conde Azul tequila and poured two shots of the blue agave extract into two crystal shot glasses.

"I apologize for the conspicuous lack of salt and limes,

Lester. You'll have to use your imagination."

The two men touched glasses lightly and threw down the tequila simultaneously. Archibald's eyes teared up, and he turned to his brother-in-law.

"Now Lester, what the fuck are you up to down there in Texas?"

CHAPTER 22

"So, Mario up and left?" asked Creed Tucker. "What brought that on? I figured that boy would be happy just to have a job these days."

"Rodrigo told Alba they had a fight last night. I think Mario was a little jealous of his partner. He thought Rodrigo was getting all the attention," said Guadalupe as she handed her husband a plate of *huevos rancheros*. Creed's morning forays to Cotulla for breakfast with James Brazzle had become less frequent since the National Front set up its checkpoints along the Nueces River.

Creed laughed.

"Well, of course he was. If Mario knew how to ride a horse like Rodrigo, he'd be getting the same amount of attention. I run a cattle ranch and horse training facility here, not a home for special-needs wetbacks."

"Creed, I wish you wouldn't use the word 'wetback'. You know how I feel about that."

"Lupe, don't you think I'm a little old to learn this damned political correctness everyone's trying to cram down our throats? Pretty soon you'll be wanting me to talk about diversity and take cultural sensitivity classes," complained Creed.

"I didn't know you'd ever heard of cultural sensitivity," Guadalupe retorted.

"Well, I wouldn't be surprised if that sonofabitch went over to the other side. He's probably wearing a R.A.T.S. uniform already."

"Maybe, but I hope he's going back to Guanajuato. He was a nice enough kid. Just had a chip on his shoulder. If he stays here, he'll get into trouble and fall in with the wrong crowd. He lacked the backbone Rodrigo has."

"Well, he wasn't afraid to work, and he knew livestock. We're going to miss him around here even if he wasn't perfect. I've got Matlock and Scrap patrolling the fence line half the day, and I'll be a hand short now for vaccinating the cattle. On top of everything else, I'm beginning to worry the National Front might try to hold a referendum after all. It doesn't look like the governor has the *cojones* to send in the National Guard. Time's running out."

"Would the National Front win a referendum?" asked Guadalupe.

"Probably," replied Creed. "From what I hear, though, a lot of the long-time Mexican-American residents don't like the idea of autonomy any more than we do. Plus, quite a few of the Anglos and Mexicans who left will come back to vote if there's a referendum. It may not be enough, but the feeling is the opposition needs to organize and show some fight, especially if the politicians aren't going to help us. A lot of people think we're surrendering our rights and letting the drug traffickers bully us and dictate policy. They'll be coming back in caravans so the R.A.T.S. patrols won't be tempted to stop them. They'll be armed too. The Daltons are coming back tomorrow night, by the way. They'll be staying with us."

"Creed, *¿por qué no me lo dijiste antes?*" asked Guadalupe. "I've got to get things ready and start cooking."

"I didn't tell you about our Mexican guests either, Lupe. The Morales family's coming back too. Their pickup will be right behind the Dalton's. We'll have a full house tomorrow. How's that for cultural diversity?"

***

The three pickup trucks drove north from the Broken "T" Land & Cattle Company ranch. Creed was driving the lead pickup with Matlock in the front seat. They rode in silence. Scrap and Rodrigo crouched down in the bed of the pickup along with Koot. They took the Cotulla exit off Interstate 35 and parked on the south side of the Nueces River Bridge near the Fish Hatchery RV Park about fifty yards from the R.A.T.S. checkpoint.

A line of mesquite trees and thick undergrowth twisted along the banks of the mostly dry riverbed just ahead. An even dozen uniformed R.A.T.S. guards stood idly on either side of the makeshift boom barrier, drinking beer in the hot sun and watching the trucks suspiciously. Mariachi music blared from a cheap portable radio plugged into a jerry-rigged electric line run from a nearby utility pole. The dog sensed the tension in the others and was alert, his prominent ears pointing straight up. He whined and growled when he saw the R.A.T.S. guards in the distance. Scrap took a short piece of frayed rope and tied Koot to the bed frame of the pickup. Scrap doubted the R.A.T.S. soldiers would take kindly to Koot attaching himself to their Achilles tendons.

James Brazzle and another local rancher were in the other two trucks along with their Mexican ranch hands. The group outnumbered the cartel guards at the checkpoint although a few of the ranchers admittedly were a bit long in the tooth. Most had military service under their belts including several of Brazzle's Mexican workers who had seen combat in Iraq. They were all armed but took care to conceal their weapons.

Creed looked at his watch.

"Matlock, dial Jamie Dalton's number, will you? Let's see how far out they are."

Creed meanwhile got out of his pickup and stretched. He could almost count the number of vertebrae he had by the number of times his back cracked. He walked slowly over to James Brazzle's truck.

"Remember, we're here just to make sure the convoy gets through. We're not looking for a fight unless one finds us."

"Dad!" hollered Matlock as he rolled out of the pickup still holding his cell phone. "Jamie says they got five vehicles in Cotulla right now at J.J's Bar & Grill. They've been waiting for our call. They'll be here in two minutes."

"Okay, boys. Mount up and follow my cues," instructed Creed, walking slowly back to his pickup truck. His leg had almost completely recovered from the vicious cow kick and his limp was imperceptible. He could see a caravan of pickup trucks approaching rapidly from the northeast. The R.A.T.S. guards had noticed them too and took up positions on the far side of the boom barrier preparing to check documents and search the vehicles for "contraband". As the three pickups began to creep forward from the southwest, the guards seemed at a loss. They looked back and forth at the trucks coming at them from opposite directions and were clearly confused, pointing at the trucks and calling to each other in Spanish.

"Matlock, tell Jamie to cooperate with the guards and do what they ask," Creed said as his pickup rolled slowly forward, crunching the white gravel on the shoulder of the highway. Matlock still had Jamie Dalton on the line, and he passed on the message. Creed and the others halted their advance about twenty-five yards from the checkpoint and waited. Two of the R.A.T.S. guards faced them with their M4s in the port arms position, casting nervous glances in the opposite direction where their leader had already stopped Jamie Dalton's truck and was examining his identification papers.

Creed and Matlock had taken down the shotgun and SKS assault rifle from the rack in back of their seat for easier access. It was just a precaution, and nobody really expected the weapons to be needed. Of course, nobody thought the

R.A.T.S. patrol would ever try to keep the Dalton convoy from crossing the Nueces River. That would be foolhardy under the circumstances, even for the National Front.

"Dad, Jamie says the guard won't let them through without visas. He's telling them to turn around," said Matlock excitedly, gesticulating with his free hand while holding his cell phone with the other.

"I was hoping those damn Mexicans would be reasonable when they saw they were outnumbered three to one," mumbled Creed. "Tell Jamie to go to Plan B", he said.

"Plan B...Plan B," whispered Matlock into the cell phone.

Creed grimly released the safety on his Mossberg 12 gauge shotgun. He held the pistol grip in his right hand and directed the 18 ½" barrel towards the side window. He put the automatic transmission into 'D'. The pickup moved slowly forward towards the checkpoint followed by the other two trucks. Creed's column of three pickups carried a total of twelve armed men. Fifteen more were in the five vehicles on the north side of the checkpoint. Creed had to hand it to the R.A.T.S. guards. They had some nerve. Their feeling of invincibility had grown over the past few weeks as they ran roughshod over a cowed local population. To make things worse, an afternoon of drinking ice-cold Corona had bolstered their courage. Warning signals should have exploded in their heads at the sight of the mixed Anglo-Hispanic force which now virtually surrounded them. Unfortunately, the Corona had extinguished any smoldering remnants of common sense that might have been present a couple of hours before.

As Creed watched from the south, Jamie Dalton and the other drivers maneuvered their trucks chaotically under the guise of turning around and heading back toward San Antonio. Their vehicles soon stood in a staggered line across the road, providing cover for the men and opening fields of fire. The occupants of the vehicles jumped down from the backs of trucks and clambered out of cabs with their weapons ready.

The leader of the R.A.T.S. guards at the checkpoint watched in disbelief as the large group of Anglos and Hispanics in the trucks morphed into an organized fighting force arrayed against his badly outnumbered band. He looked back, expecting to see his men lined up behind him, only to observe them walking backwards in craven retreat, occasionally tripping over an uneven buckling in the pavement.

Eliseo Morales walked boldly towards the R.A.T.S. leader, who now stood alone some 20 yards in front of his retreating colleagues.

"Drop your weapon!" shouted Morales. A month earlier, Eliseo had watched as R.A.T.S. soldiers slaughtered 120 hogs he had raised from birth on his farm north of Laredo: a less than cordial sendoff for the resilient farmer whose family had lived in South Texas since the beginning of the twentieth century. Eliseo had taken the hint and gone with his family to live with a brother in San Antonio but had eagerly accepted Creed's suggestion to return.

As Eliseo brazenly approached the cartel soldier with his .30-30 Winchester cocked threateningly and pointed at the border guard's chest. Jamie Dalton called out a warning.

"Watch it, Eliseo. He's got something behind his back."

Eliseo turned his head back to look at Jamie. The Mexican guard took advantage of his opponent's momentary lapse and pulled out a handgun tucked in the back of his jeans. He dove to the ground firing and rolled towards a stand of blackbrush at the side of the road. Rising to his knees, he unstrapped the M4 from his shoulder, preparing to take aim at Eliseo who had caught one round in the shoulder and was writhing on the ground in pain. At that moment, three shots rang out in rapid succession from the southeast, and the guard's body spasmodically jerked to his right and fell into the underbrush. He lay motionless. Blood seeped into the parched soil and was quickly absorbed, leaving only a faint dark stain on the ground.

Matlock swung his SKS around looking for other targets.

"¡No se muevan! ¡Suelten sus armas!" shouted Creed.

The R.A.T.S. guards threw down their weapons and instinctively put their hands behind their heads. That was the advantage to dealing with the cartel soldiers. They knew arrest protocol by heart.

Jamie Dalton attended to Eliseo, whose shoulder wound would likely keep him from doctoring cattle for a month or so but would not cause any long-term disability. The Mexican shooter's aim had been off about six inches: an inch for each Corona consumed.

Scrap and Rodrigo found a supply of plasticuffs in a cardboard box by the porta-potty and used them to secure the wrists of the remaining R.A.T.S. guards behind their backs. Creed ordered them to sit in a circle back-to-back on the hot pavement. Other returning refugees in the caravan dismantled the boom barrier and destroyed the guards' porta-potty with an axe.

Creed looked at the pile of feed sacks on the side of the road and pointed.

"Scrap, you and Rodrigo throw those sacks in the back of the pickup. I *thought* we were a little short on feed...those thieving sons o' bitches."

They left the dead cartel soldier where he had fallen in the thick stand of blackbrush. Creed walked up to the group of guards sitting on the ground.

"¡Saludos al Frente Nacional!" he said, resisting an urge to use his shotgun as a club on the head of the nearest guard. "Let's go!" he yelled to the others. "Back to the Broken 'T'."

CHAPTER 23

Rancho Vista del Mar perched precariously on a hilltop just east of Culiacán, Sinaloa and commanded a sweeping view of the surrounding countryside. Francisco Salcido lacked formal military training, but his years as a cartel soldier and a fascination with Carl von Clausewitz's theories on battlefield tactics had given him an enviable understanding of the use of terrain as part of an effective defense. The picturesque ranch immediately had attracted Francisco's attention for its fortress-like potential, and five years ago he instructed his attorney to purchase the property on his behalf. The owner of the ranch at the time was happy to accept the generous offer, especially when he learned who the principal was. It was the proverbial "offer you can't refuse".

Francisco made a number of improvements on the ranch to augment security. He cleared trees and underbrush to improve visibility on the approaches to the property, and he installed an extensive alarm and motion detection system which covered almost a thousand acres down the mountainside. To prevent technical details on the security arrangements from falling into the wrong hands, Francisco first bought the company that sold him the system. Then, six weeks after the system was installed, the lead design engineer was killed in a freak accident. Nobody seemed to find anything suspicious about the explosion that destroyed the new VW Tiguan and immolated the hapless engineer. Certainly nobody had the temerity to connect Francisco Salcido's organization to the tragic accident. The police looked the other way and ruled the death an accident.

Salcido spent over one million dollars annually on security at his ranch. Each of his guards earned a salary that would be the envy of top-echelon banking executives in Mexico City. Francisco knew that money bought loyalty and the lack of it bred treachery. His employees were fiercely devoted to *El Padrino*, and for good reason. A job on the Salcido ranch meant financial security for life. The only problem was that life expectancy in the employment of the Sinaloa cartel was rather short.

Francisco liked to relax in his study late at night and watch the flickering lights of Culiacán in the distance some 600 feet below his ranch. Though he would never think of sampling any of the white powder his organization transshipped to the United States by the ton, Francisco had nothing against an occasional joint rolled with a potent strain of cannabis cultivated hydroponically in the ranch greenhouse. Francisco considered his use of the potent weed strictly medicinal in nature; almost therapeutic. He believed the herb allowed him to examine his *Weltanschauung* from a more critical, detached point of view. He took notes when he was stoned and read them the next morning to judge the depth of his insight.

It was late but Francisco was wide awake. If everything went as planned, the referendum would be held soon, and the *norteamericanos* still had taken no action to prevent it. A few instances of minor vigilante backlash had taken place along the Nueces River as a few Anglos returned from their self-imposed exile, but nothing more.

Francisco had received a phone call that morning from the mysterious head of the National Front. The man spoke fluent Spanish, but Francisco couldn't place the accent. He never identified himself when he called, and Francisco had no way to contact him. When he needed Francisco, he called. Just like the first time they spoke when the anonymous caller revealed his strategy for the "*reconquista*" and asked for the support of Francisco's organization. Taking back the "occupied territories" was the theme in those first conversations. Now it was actually happening, and they were on the verge of establishing the Autonomous Republic of South Texas.

Francisco smiled at the thought. The muffled sound of his favorite *narcocorrido* caught his ear. The ballad was about his famous uncle Cochiloco and was a favorite among the poor of Sinaloa, many of whom had looked up to Cochiloco as a modern day Robin Hood. He wondered where the music was coming from and then felt the vibration of his cell phone in the pocket of his Ralph Lauren khaki trousers. It was his custom ringtone.

"Bueno," he answered, vaguely wondering who could be calling him at this hour.

"Francisco, disculpe la molestia. Sorry to call you so late, *carnal."*

Francisco recognized the voice of the attorney general.

"No hay cuidado, mano. ¿Qué pasó?" He could sense the tension in the attorney general's voice.

"Remember the ex-CIA *gringo* who shot your man in front of the *Perro Andaluz*?"

"Claro que sí."

"It's time to deal with him," said the attorney general emphatically.

"Where is he now?" asked Francisco.

"He checked out of the Nikko thirty minutes ago. My people are following him. I think he's on the way to Sinaloa. He's looking for the governor's daughter. I'll keep you posted."

"He's a dead man, Félix. I'll take care of it."

***

Lisa had begun to look forward to her conversations with

Francisco. It broke up the monotony of her existence locked in a guest room under heavy guard at *Rancho Vista del Mar.* He summoned her every night to his study for long discussions in English on history, politics, and international relations. Sometimes she could smell the pungent aroma of marijuana in the room and knew he had been smoking. He offered her Chilean wines and plates of exotic hors 'd'oeuvres prepared by his kitchen staff. She found her kidnapper surprisingly urbane and gracious; almost apologetic that he had interrupted her vacation and detained her against her will. Lisa could sense he was frustrated that her father had not contacted him to negotiate her release. Her own unease over her father's silence was increasing.

One evening a week into her involuntary sojourn at the Salcido ranch, Lisa's female attendant knocked politely on her door before entering the bedroom. Lisa knew her UT sorority sister was in the adjoining room, but she hadn't seen or heard of her since their arrival at the ranch.

"El Padrino te invita a tomar una copa," she said. "He wants you to come over right away before it rains. There's going to be a bad thunderstorm."

The two cartel soldiers who had abducted her waited outside the room to escort Lisa to the main residence. She hated the way the fat one leered at her and smiled obscenely. When Simón, the tall skinny one, wasn't looking, the fat one would grab his crotch, rotate his hips, and wink at her suggestively. He frightened her, and she dreaded the prospect of being left alone in his presence. Fortunately, that never happened. Simón appeared to be in charge and the two were always together.

The main residence stood about twenty-five yards from the guest house. Simón walked along a cobblestone walkway in front of Lisa while the fat sullen one lurked behind. Lightning flashed ominously in the distance and muffled rolls of thunder drifted up the mountainside. Lisa looked down towards

Culiacán and marveled at the panoramic view of the coastal plains below illuminated by the almost continuous lightning display. She was bemused at her own ability to appreciate the nocturnal view despite her precarious situation at *Rancho Vista del Mar*.

The three of them walked purposefully across the Saltillo tile of the vast living room towards a circular stairway made of beautiful dark mesquite with a hand rail of black wrought iron. Lisa slipped on a thin, hand-woven Oaxaca throw rug and almost fell. The fat one caught Lisa by the elbows and then released her, but not before he had run his pudgy, soft hands over her buttocks and breasts from behind as if by accident. She turned and slapped him hard across the face. As he raised his hand instinctively to reciprocate, Simón turned threateningly and hissed through his teeth. "*¿Qué haces, pendejo?*"

At that moment Francisco Salcido appeared at the top of the stairs dressed like a preppy attorney from the Deep South in a pink Ralph Lauren Polo shirt, khaki trousers, and a baby blue sweater thrown casually over his shoulders, an unnecessary affectation in the humid heat of summertime Sinaloa. Lisa glanced apprehensively over her shoulder, but her two escorts had retreated discreetly back into the living room.

"Lisa, please come on up," Salcido said in excellent, barely accented English.

"You never did tell me where you learned to speak such beautiful English," she asked, taking a seat in a leather chair with steer horn legs.

"Lisa, I've warned you about asking personal questions, you know that...but I'll tell you my secret anyway," said Francisco.

Lisa could tell he had been smoking marijuana. His eyes were red and glassy, and he looked at her with an expression she hadn't seen before. Lisa was surprised to see him reach for a still-smoldering joint in the glass ashtray, which stood on an ornately carved wood coffee table between them. Usually, he was more discreet. He inhaled deeply before continuing.

"My uncle sent me to a private Catholic school in San Antonio for two years. He was a man of great foresight who viewed the United States as all Mexicans should: the enemy. He used to talk about how God had blessed Mexico with a favorable climate and an abundance of natural resources. But he wondered why God had cursed us by placing us geographically next to the North Americans."

"Do you agree with him?" asked Lisa with trepidation.

"Lisa, I'm a businessman. How can I hate my most profitable market?" laughed Salcido.

All traces of humor then disappeared as suddenly as they had appeared, and he peered at Lisa with an animosity that she had never seen.

"To tell you the truth, I see my whole country living in the shadow of a soulless giant. The *gringo* has a rapacious appetite for material goods that impoverishes his own intellect. He mistakes economic success for spirituality. He believes that his values, his desires...represent the absolute 'good' and anyone with a different opinion is by definition 'evil'."

Lisa watched Salcido transform before her very eyes. His usual congeniality had disappeared and had been replaced by a deep bitterness. Francisco paused often and spoke slowly, searching for the right word to precisely express his thoughts.

"The *gringo* government insists that the entire world dance to its fiddle. From Nicaragua and Panama, to Iraq and Libya, you *gringos* believe you have a God-given right to dictate what kind of government other countries should have; how other people should live. Never mind that your advocacy of universal principles such as self-determination and non-interference applies only to other countries and not to your own."

"Francisco, I think you're being harsh," ventured Lisa.

"Am I, Lisa?" he responded. "Look at Texas. The majority of the population of South Texas wants to be autonomous and what do we see? Your father is preparing to send in the National Guard to quash their legitimate aspirations."

"But wait, there's been nothing in the newspapers about the Guard coming in. How do you know that?"

"Lisa, don't be naïve. Do you think I haven't had the foresight to put my own people in the ranks of the Texas National Guard? I receive daily reports on what General Mendoza is doing. Do you see the irony? A Mexican will lead the Texas National Guard against other Mexicans."

Lisa looked at Francisco incredulously. He thought and acted more like a head of state than the leader of a drug cartel.

"Your father blatantly ignored a threat to the health and well-being of his beloved daughter," he continued. "He would rather preserve his political career than preserve the life of his daughter. What kind of a man is that?"

Lisa's hand began to tremble as she raised the glass of Chilean chardonnay to her lips. The conversation had taken an ominous turn.

"Lisa, our relationship will have to change tonight. This is the last time we're going to meet like this. I truly am going to miss our conversations, but business is business."

Francisco rose from his padded leather chair and walked towards the spiral staircase, glancing back at Lisa one last time. The two guards approached Lisa, accompanied by a plump middle-aged woman in a white robe who was pushing a stainless steel tray table on wheels in front of her. She looked like a nurse and in age could have been Lisa's grandmother. Lisa's entire body went rigid, and she involuntarily gripped the sides of her chair until her fingers ached.

Something flashed brightly in the woman's right hand. The two guards grabbed Lisa roughly by her arms and abruptly jerked her to her feet. They carried her kicking and biting over to the tray table the nurse had rolled in to the room.

Lisa called out to Francisco for help, but she heard only the echo of her own voice. A door closed downstairs and she realized Salcido was gone. She turned her head wildly looking for the nurse. A clap of thunder startled her and she gasped as the nurse appeared out of her peripheral vision. Again, something flashed in the nurse's right hand. Lisa stared, scarcely believing her own eyes as the nurse sharpened a six-inch meat cleaver. Lisa clearly saw the word "Henckels" stamped on the blade of the meat cleaver and thought it odd that she would notice a detail like that. Then she screamed.

CHAPTER 24

"Remember, Monica, your troops are authorized to fire only in self-defense. Not all the National Front soldiers are drug cartel gangbangers. There are likely to be a few misguided U.S. citizens among them," Governor Throckmorton said, his voice tense with emotion. "You can imagine the bad press we'll get if we start shooting our own citizens."

"Yes sir," replied Major General Mendoza. "We understand each other perfectly."

"What do your Latino troops think of their mission?" asked the governor.

"There've been a few rumblings, sir. I think that's probably natural. A lot of them, though, live in South Texas and don't like what the National Front is doing. They've been itching to put the drug traffickers in their place."

"Glad to hear it, Monica. You have my authorization to deploy your troops."

"Thank you, governor."

As she walked out of the governor's office, Major General Mendoza dialed the number of her second-in-command on her cell phone.

"Remember the Alamo!" she gave the code phrase that started the Guard's prepositioned Humvees and tanks rolling south towards the Nueces River from Uvalde in the west all the way to Victoria in the east. Remember the Alamo, my ass, she thought to herself and shook her head. Who the hell in Austin came up with that gem?

***

"Sir, I respectfully disagree. If our boys at the checkpoints shoot down a National Guard helicopter with a shoulder-held SA-7 missile, we can expect massive retaliation and heavy casualties. The strategy we all agreed on was to employ guerrilla hit-and-run tactics to keep the Guard off balance and to gain time for the United Nations and other international bodies to demand a U.S. pullback and recognize our right to hold a referendum."

Rudy Gutiérrez couldn't believe his ears. However, the head of the National Front, whom he had never even seen, was adamant.

"Rudy, I changed my mind. This is a direct order. If you don't care to implement the new strategy, we'll find a new minister of defense who will. We're looking for a major headline. We want the attention of the world focused on South Texas, and we need pressure put on the North American governments, both in Austin and Washington. We need it now, Rudy."

"Yes sir."

"The best way to get it is to lose a lot of men in an unequal battle at the very beginning of their intervention. We want to look like the aggrieved party. Anything short of that, the *gringos* will systematically overrun our positions before the world can react. You and all the leaders of the National Front will be arrested and tried for treason or insurrection. Is that a more palatable option for you?"

"Of course not, sir!" Rudy didn't agree with the directive, but he was an old soldier and would follow orders.

"That's better. Pass on the orders. This will be a great day for the new republic and a Pyrrhic victory for the *gringos*."

The office of Minister of Defense Gutierrez in Laredo was a little more than an hour's drive from the R.A.T.S. checkpoint on the Nueces River south of Cotulla. After the shootout at the checkpoint the day before, Rudy decided to send an additional two dozen troops armed with M4s and RPGs to shore up the checkpoint's defenses. That would be sufficient to discourage any repeat of the vigilante violence that had killed the checkpoint commander but would not even begin to slow down a determined assault by a company of Texas National Guard troops. The use of an SA-7 surface-to-air missile would, though. No question about it. That would get the *gringos'* attention. He hated to think what would happen after that, though.

The origin of the missiles the National Front had obtained was supposed to be a tightly held secret, but Rudy saw the wooden crates when they arrived the day before. The missiles were of Russian origin, supplied by Venezuela. No surprise, really. He suspected the Mexican government had been complicit in arranging the transshipment, but he had no proof. Although he was minister of defense, the National Front operated as a clandestine entity, and even he wasn't privy to the sources of the weapons pouring across the Mexican border into the United States to arm his ragtag army.

There had been no time to train his own soldiers in the operation of the new weapon. Instead, Rudy sent several foreign military advisors to key checkpoints along the Nueces River together with his own forces. Each proudly carried a green cylindrical tube over his shoulder complete with a grip stock, thermal battery, and several spare warheads. From the way the advisors spoke Spanish, Rudy guessed they were Nicaraguan and Venezuelan. Except for conducting training sessions in battlefield tactics and marksmanship, they kept mostly to themselves. Rudy dispatched one of them with the reinforcements heading for the checkpoint south of Cotulla. He watched the Nicaraguan get in the back of an R.A.T.S. pickup truck and wondered if the man realized he was on a suicide mission. Word already had reached Rudy that the National Guard columns left multiple kickoff points at the same time and were headed towards the Nueces River. He didn't even know whether the reinforcements would beat the National Guard to Cotulla. He wondered if it mattered.

***

As the reinforcements piled out of the pickup truck an hour later behind the waist-high row of sandbags the cartel soldiers had erected, they could hear the roar of diesel engines approaching from the northeast.

"*Ya vienen,*" said the new commander of the R.A.T.S. detachment. "Here they come. Take your positions."

The column of military vehicles lumbered noisily along the Interstate 35 business access road, and the R.A.T.S. guards were startled to hear the *wap-wap-wap* sound of two AH-64 Apache attack helicopters approaching from the east. One of the helicopters suddenly appeared above the treetops and circled overhead. A loudspeaker repeated a simple message broadcast in Spanish at a deafening volume.

"Surrender and lay down your weapons now!"

The R.A.T.S. guards took what cover they could and turned to their leader for direction. They were ruthless killers when their targets were unarmed civilians or lightly armed gunmen from a rival cartel. Facing an organized and trained military force, though, they were at a loss and were on the brink of throwing down their weapons and hightailing it into the South Texas brush.

The R.A.T.S. commander was paralyzed with indecision and could only stand and watch with morbid fascination as the Nicaraguan military advisor calmly hoisted the green tube to his shoulder and prepared to apply the "half-trigger" to uncage the seeker. The advisor stood behind a large mesquite tree for cover and exposed himself only long enough to fire the missile at the helicopter on the far reach of its elongated circling pattern. The range was too short for the helicopter to take any effective evasive measures or to employ electronic countermeasures.

The unsuspecting pilot, a car salesman from New Braunfels when he wasn't flying helicopters for the Texas Air National Guard, banked the Apache in a steep turn for another approach to the Nueces River checkpoint. He heard the warning signal indicating a homing device had found him and locked on. His last thought was that the signaling device must be malfunctioning. Then the helicopter exploded in a large fireball. Secondary explosions from the fuel tanks spread the wreckage in a wide dispersed pattern over the National Guard column. Steel fragments rained down on the Guard's convoy of vehicles, wounding several soldiers in open Humvees as the weekend warriors and embedded reporters from local news stations watched in stunned horror.

The second pilot reacted more quickly. He had seen the missile rise erratically from the shoulder of a uniformed R.A.T.S. soldier at the checkpoint as it sought its target. He sprayed the area with long bursts of 30 mm shells and Hydra 70 rockets. The damage was horrific. The Nicaraguan advisor, who had been reloading the SA-7 tube, took one of the 30 mm shells in the midsection and his body now lay in two distinct halves. Multiple explosions wreaked havoc on the defensive emplacements and killed more than twenty of the R.A.T.S. defenders, rendering the majority of the corpses unrecognizable. The rest had thrown down their weapons and raised their hands over their heads in abject surrender. The first battle of the Second War for Texas Independence ended as suddenly as it had begun.

***

The governor was in his office anxiously reading the classified emails Major General Mendoza sent him from her mobile command post at a rest area along I-35. The first reports were encouraging. Most of the R.A.T.S. units along the meandering Nueces River had put up only token resistance and had either surrendered or retreated after the first exchange of gunfire when they realized how badly outgunned they were. The governor's relief soon turned to disbelief, however, when he received the three-line synopsis of what had taken place south of Cotulla.

His hands trembled as he read the unexpected news. A flat-screen television mounted on one of the walls in his office was tuned to CNN, which broadcast the same information a scant five minutes after General Mendoza clicked "send" on her encrypted cell phone.

"Nobody said anything about the traffickers having surface-to-air missiles," the governor said out loud as Vicky Ramirez entered the room carrying a small package.

"Rick, here's something without a return address, but it's marked 'Urgent', and it was shipped via overnight service from Mexico City."

"Open it for me, would you Vicky? I'm reading the general's reports right now. It's not good. We've lost an Apache helicopter and its crew at Cotulla. Jesus, I can't believe it," the governor said.

Vicky took a letter opener from the governor's desk and slit open the padded envelope. She pulled out a neatly folded bundle of bubble wrap paper and began to peel back the layers. Without warning she shrieked and dropped the envelope and its contents on the governor's desk. She bent over with her hand to her mouth and gagged. The governor leaped to his feet and rushed to help Vicky. She motioned him away and pointed to the package, unable to utter a single word.

Confused, the governor reached for the bubble wrap with

trepidation and peeled away the first layer, revealing a napkin splotched with dried blood stains. He reached his fingers inside and pulled out the contents. The discolored napkin, still moist with blood, fell to his desk and a severed finger rolled out. Governor Throckmorton stared at the finger in uncomprehending shock and revulsion. He looked closer at the finger and recognized Lisa's University of Texas class ring. He fell to his knees and vomited.

CHAPTER 25

"What the hell was that?" asked Creed Tucker. The windows in the old ranch house shook and rattled in their wooden frames as the *boom* of a distant explosion echoed across the flat plain and slowly receded into the thick, humid air until the monotonous whirring of the ceiling fan in the living room was the only thing he could hear.

Creed looked around at his guests who had returned to La Salle County the day before from their self-imposed exile. Eliseo Morales rested on the sofa with his arm in a sling. The bullet had exited the fleshy part of his upper arm without hitting bone and he refused to see a doctor. James Brazzle sat with a few of the new arrivals, and Drake Herrin stood just out of earshot on the front porch with his cell phone glued to his ear.

"If I had to venture a guess, I'd say the cavalry just arrived at the Nueces River," said Brazzle as he walked over to the window, looking for smoke or other tell-tale signs of a firefight.

"That was a large explosion, James. Somehow I can't see the Texas National Guard opening up with anything that big."

"In self-defense I doubt they'd pull any punches. Maybe they got fired on first."

A few seconds later a wave of indistinct booms reached them, despite the southwest breeze that muffled any sounds coming from the northeast.

"Shit, that sounds like air-to-ground rockets, maybe fired from a helicopter," speculated Creed.

"Sure takes you back, doesn't it?" replied James.

"I haven't heard anything like that since 1969." said Creed grimly. "Hoped I'd never hear it again, and I sure never expected to hear it on Texas soil."

Creed stood up slowly, looked around the room with angry resignation in his eyes. "Alright, get your boys together and man the positions you were assigned yesterday along the east fence line. No telling who might try to cross into the ranch after that tussle. Jamie, I want you to find Scrap and Matlock and tell them what's happening. "

Jamie Dalton picked up his hunting rifle and asked, "What are our rules of engagement, Creed?"

"What do you think they are, Jamie? You see movement out in the brush in front of your position, you shoot to kill. Better them than us, *entendido?*"

"Yup, I understand."

Guadalupe stuck her head around the corner.

"Creed, you men should come into the kitchen. You don't want to miss this."

The men hurried into the kitchen where Guadalupe and Alba were making tamales. They crowded around the old-fashioned Zenith television set that stood on top of a linoleum counter beside the toaster oven. A pair of twenty-year old rabbit ears perched on top of the old contraption like a high-tech accoutrement from the previous century. Creed turned up the volume so they could hear the news over the hum of the floor fan and the mooing of the cattle in the pens outside the house.

They caught the CNN special report just as Wolf Blitzer turned it over to the glamorous, young Hispanic reporter embedded with the 36th Infantry Division of the Texas National Guard. Her face was pale and her eyes wide with fear. Her hands visibly trembled as she tried to steady the microphone by holding it with two hands.

"This is Margarita Lopez with elements of the Texas National Guard just south of Cotulla, Texas at the Nueces River Bridge where heavy fighting has erupted with armed gunmen of the National Front for the Liberation of Texas. I am told that an AH-64 Apache attack helicopter has been shot down by a surface-to-air missile with the loss of all crew members. In a retaliatory strike, a second Apache helicopter has attacked the insurgents' position with cannon and rocket fire. The National Guard infantry now has crossed the river in a mopping-up operation and we can still hear occasional small arms fire. As soon as we can confirm details on casualties, we'll pass on the information. Back to you, Wolf."

The men stood in stunned silence. It was one thing to hear live reports about combat half a world away but quite another to see video of the carnage of battle on Texas soil. Creed, though, wasn't one to indulge his own emotions or anyone else's for that matter. He walked purposefully to the television set and turned it off.

"Nothing new here, boys. Get out to the fence line, and let's make sure the Broken "T" doesn't make tomorrow's headlines."

The men grabbed their weapons and made their way through the screen door and on to the wooden porch. They could see plumes of black smoke rising in the distance and shuddered at the thought that Texans lay dead just over the horizon.

Creed sat down at the kitchen table with a U.S. Army Engineers map of South Texas. He studied the terrain of his own vast land holdings, trying to determine the most vulnerable approaches to ranch headquarters.

"If I didn't hear it from the horse's mouth, I wouldn't believe it," said Drake Herrin as he walked into the kitchen. His cell phone was stuffed in his shirt pocket. He had been on the phone nonstop for the last two hours.

"If you're talking about the governor, 'horse's ass' is more like it, I'd say," responded Creed. He was no fan of the crowd in Austin, and their political capital with him had diminished greatly since the audience with the secretary of state and the governor a few weeks ago. Had it been that short a time? Creed wondered to himself.

"I can't argue with you there," said Drake, walking up to the kitchen table and pulling out a chair. He sat down heavily and groaned. "The governor just informed the president that he is ordering the Texas National Guard to stand down. The troops will advance no further, and he will seek a negotiated solution to the crisis."

"What?" said Creed as he stood up abruptly from the table, knocking over the chair he had been sitting in.

Guadalupe rushed into the room. *"¿Qué pasó, mi amor?"* she asked with real concern.

"Mr. Herrin has received some rather surprising news. It'll be on CNN within the hour, I'm sure. Looks like the cavalry is pulling back. That's what we get for electing a draft-dodging University of Texas teasip for governor."

"There's more to it than that, Creed," said Herrin. "Throckmorton has other problems that nobody knows about, and it looks like they're affecting his ability to govern. The Sinaloa cartel abducted his daughter last week. Today he received her finger in the mail, complete with her University of Texas senior ring. The FBI will be DNA-testing the appendage, but there's no question it's hers."

"Jesus," muttered Creed. "Can't the FBI do anything? Or your CIA?"

"I'd hate to depend on anything out of Washington, Creed. That's why Mako Sloane is down in Mexico right now. The governor finally came to his senses and asked him for help. Mako's on his way to Culiacán, Sinaloa. He left Mexico City half an hour ago."

***

The brass elevator doors opened and Mako Sloane strode confidently into the plush lobby of the Nikko Hotel. He looked around, knowing this was where they would be waiting for him. Mako knew you didn't prance into Mexico City like you owned the place, blackmail the attorney general and leading presidential candidate, and then traipse blithely out of town as if nothing had happened.

No, Félix's men would be there in the lobby. There would probably be around six of them. One or two women as well, more than likely. They would be the ones closest to the elevator. Their job would be to spot Mako and pass him off to the young thugs who would do the actual surveillance, or at least try to. What happened after that was anyone's guess.

But Mako had a few surprises in store for them, and unless Félix showed more imagination today than he had in his CIA surveillance detection course some thirty years before, Mako was confident he could elude whatever the attorney general might throw against him.

As he left the elevator and turned left towards the hotel exit, he caught the eye of an exotically beautiful young woman in the lobby with long, silky black hair down to her waist and large gold hoop earrings. She smiled coquettishly at Mako, who returned the compliment with an appreciative glance at her shapely legs.

There's number one, he thought to himself.

As she turned away, Mako saw her speak into the collar of her ivory colored silk blouse. He saw a slightly built man in his thirties suddenly put a newspaper into a trash can and walk purposefully towards the exit after Mako. "Number two," he whispered under his breath.

Mako exited the Nikko and ignored the bellhop's offer to flag down a taxi. He turned right on Campos Eliseos and walked several blocks without looking back. He knew they'd be there.

When he stopped and turned to flag down a yellow Volkswagen bug taxi that approached slowly in the lane next to the curb, he saw the entire team arrayed in classic surveillance formation including the man he had spotted in the lobby. The third surveillant walked on the opposite side of the street trying to be nonchalant, gazing intently into the lighted display windows of the exclusive boutiques, window shopping at one o'clock in the morning. The stores had been closed for hours.

The VW taxi stopped at curbside, and Mako got in the backseat.

"How many did you see?" he asked the driver, an enormous light-skinned black man dressed in a Dallas Cowboys gray workout t-shirt and a backwards Texas Rangers baseball cap. His arms looked massive in the tight t-shirt, and his huge frame looked incongruent in the tiny taxi.

"You probably spotted the three behind you on foot. There's also a black Jeep Cherokee with three others hanging back about a block. Pretty basic stuff."

"QL, you're always a sight for sore eyes, but couldn't you have found something a little more uplifting than this piece of shit?" Mako motioned with his left hand at the shabby interior of the VW bug.

"Tupelo's arranged a new Land Cruiser for you. It's on a side street just off the Toluca highway. I'm sure that'll be more to your liking, but first we've got to get rid of the Cherokee."

Mako's team of retired CIA operatives had been in Mexico City for a week preparing for this counter-surveillance run. There were three of them, and they had all worked with Mako for almost thirty years in a variety of third-world shitholes.

Quindarius Lee was Mako's closest associate. They had been together since the late seventies when Mako burst onto the CIA scene with his uncanny linguistic skills and quickly made a name for himself in operations against the Soviet target. Quindarius Lee had been the martial arts instructor for the CIA's paramilitary training program and even now in middle age would be a formidable opponent in any physical contest.

QL kept glancing in the rear view mirror. "Hell, they've only got one car on us, Mako. We deserve a little more respect than that, don't you think?" He threw his head back and guffawed.

"Okay, listen to me." QL turned serious and handed Mako a set of car keys and a card with an address in the Tecamachalco section of Mexico City.

"The Land Cruiser is parked in the driveway of our safe house. Full tank of gas. Documents in the glove compartment. We'll keep these clowns busy for a while...buy you some time. When I turn right at this corner, you're out of here. Good luck, Mako. You be careful now; these cartel assholes make the KGB look like a bunch of altar boys. See you back in Texas...now, go!"

QL slowed the VW bug, and Mako saw Tupelo McSweeney walking briskly alongside the car and opening the passenger side door...then he felt Tupelo grab him by the lapels of his leather jacket and QL push him from the other end. He and Tupelo changed places on the move and then the VW was gone in a cloud of black exhaust. Mako stumbled, regained his balance, and ducked into a small bar just as the Jeep Cherokee hurtled around the corner and accelerated in pursuit of the elusive VW bug taxi.

Mako was back on the street thirty seconds later and flagged down a real Volkswagen taxi.

"Tecamachalco," Mako said. *"Tengo prisa.* I'm in a hurry."

CHAPTER 26

Bronc Thornton had been running from the DEA since he was thirty years old. Except for the inconvenient notoriety of being number nine on their "most wanted" list, Bronc could look back at his life and feel satisfied. At sixty-four, he had most things any normal man could possibly desire: unimaginable wealth, a beautiful house, and a devoted wife. Granted, the fact that he flew airplanes for the Sinaloa cartel, lived on a ranch with a clandestine airstrip in the hills east of Culiacán, and was married to a cousin of Francisco "*El Padrino*" Salcido might not meet the criteria for entry into the Kingdom of Heaven laid down by the minister of the First Baptist Church of Del Rio, Texas who baptized Bronc. But hell, you can't have everything.

As a teenager, James Brazzle had known Bronc by reputation on the rodeo circuit back in the 1960s. But who hadn't heard of the young bull rider from Del Rio in those days? His rodeo exploits were the stuff of legend, and his parents' house was full of trophies and the black and white framed photographs of the dozens of bulls Bronc had ridden.

There was a serious side to Bronc, though, that many people never knew, and even his close friends were surprised when he received an appointment to the Air Force Academy in 1963. That was the last thing most people in Del Rio remembered about him.

James himself had barely recognized Bronc in the officer's club when they next met in Saigon in 1970. By that time, Bronc was driving F4 Phantom fighters for the Air Force and already indulging himself in some of that high-quality cannabis Vietnam was famous for. After the war Brazzle tried to convince Bronc to go to Washington with him and join the CIA. Bronc scoffed at the idea of working for a government salary. He was bringing loads of marijuana across the border at Del Rio in horse trailers and had almost the entire U.S. Customs staff there on his payroll. It was the beginning of a long and lucrative career which culminated in his marriage to Francisco Salcido's cousin Consuela. Bronc was more than happy to put his Air Force experience to use flying small cargo planes full of marijuana and cocaine at tree top level into clandestine air strips in Texas, New Mexico, and Arizona. The lack of health insurance and retirement benefits from his employer didn't seem to bother him.

That was over thirty years ago, and Bronc had lived a charmed life as a cartel pilot, eluding both the DEA, U.S. Customs, the FBI, and a myriad of rats and snitches. Some claimed that Bronc was the inspiration for Robert Earl Keen's *Gringo Honeymoon* and actually was the "cowboy running from the DEA" in the song. Things probably would have continued for a couple more years till Bronc retired, had he not become privy to Salcido's plans for the political map of South Texas.

When Francisco was in town, Bronc and Consuela would ride horseback to *Rancho "Vista del Mar"* on Saturday afternoon for dinner. They would usually spend the night and ride back to their own ranch on Sunday morning. Bronc's home was only accessible by horse or airplane. He preferred it that way. Security was an obsession with him and probably the only reason he was still alive.

That was how Bronc learned that Francisco was holding two young women hostage although he didn't know who they were. Hearing Salcido gloat about the National Front's successes in the municipal elections in the southern counties and his plans for the creation of the Autonomous Republic of South Texas rankled Bronc, and he somehow felt violated on a very personal and intimate level. He would have had difficulty rationalizing this feeling of latent patriotism, considering he had turned his back on the United States so long ago. He certainly couldn't have explained why he looked up a "James Brazzle" in La Salle County, Texas on a motel lobby computer during a short layover in San Antonio in the middle of a smuggling mission or why he called the number and spilled his guts to his old friend who listened to Bronc's story in utter disbelief.

Bronc only had twelve hours before he had to fly his cargo plane back to Culiacán, but Brazzle and Drake Herrin had braved the R.A.T.S. checkpoints and hustled up to San Antonio for a long meeting with him. It was a tense negotiation, and Drake Herrin had to use every bit of political leverage he had in Washington to be able to offer Bronc Thornton immunity from prosecution in return for his assistance. Bronc left the meeting feeling as if a tremendous weight had been lifted from his shoulders, and he looked forward to extricating himself from the tentacles of the Sinaloa cartel. Knowing that would entail risking his life didn't bother him. Bronc had been doing that for thirty years. He waited impatiently for the phone call from this "Mako Sloane" character.

The call came much sooner than Bronc expected.

"Bronc, I'm at the Toluca airport. Can you fly your Cessna down here to pick me up?"

He hesitated only for a minute. "No problem, Mako, I'll be there in two hours. Can you wait on me that long?"

"Yeah, I'll be by the ticket counters. They're on my tail, so please hurry."

"Story of my life....I'm walking out the door."

***

"See that hill in the distance, the tallest one over there to the west?" asked Bronc as he maneuvered the twin-engine

Cessna for his final approach to the landing strip. It was just visible ahead through the thick vegetation.

"Yeah, I see it," answered Mako, wishing Bronc would pay more attention to flying. The man had fired up a joint immediately after they were airborne in Toluca and barely spoke to Mako the entire flight, preferring instead to listen to the New Riders of the Purple Sage blaring out of the plane's sophisticated stereo system. You can only listen to *Panama Red* so many times before you start hankering for something more serene, even classical.

Bronc leaned over and switched off the music.

"That's where the girls are," he said significantly.

"That's *Rancho Vista del Mar*?"

"Yep," said Bronc."

"Know anybody on the inside you can trust?" asked Mako, scrutinizing the ranch from the air.

"Well, let's see.   There's ...uh...me.   I'm on the inside, wouldn't you say? Do you trust me?" asked Bronc smiling.

"Don't have much choice on that one, *amigo*. You're the only show in town. Besides that, you come recommended by an old friend of mine."

"The first rule in this business is not to trust anyone, Mako. I wouldn't let any of those cartel bastards mow my lawn."

"Must be kind of a lonely existence," commented Mako.

"To each his own," said Bronc.

The landing strip was clearly visible now, and Mako could see a Caterpillar bulldozer parked to the side. Bronc didn't take any chances apparently. The remote air strip was freshly graded and looked in perfect condition. The man was clearly a professional despite his eccentricities. The Cessna rolled to a stop after a surprisingly smooth landing.

"Bronc, I hate to abuse your hospitality, but do you have a horse I could borrow? One that wouldn't be recognized as yours?"

"Yeah, but if I were you, I'd be less worried about them recognizing the horse as I would them seeing a six-foot gringo riding by cartel headquarters," Bronc answered. "I didn't bring you here to get us both killed, Sloane."

"Got any better ideas?" inquired Mako with a touch of his own sarcasm.

"As a matter of fact I do," said Bronc.

CHAPTER 27

Vice President Archibald Rutledge looked across the desk in the Oval Office at an enraged president of the United States and wondered how the man ever won the nomination, much less the election. The vice president's latent racism bubbled to the surface whenever he dealt with his boss. He despised the president on a personal level but secretly envied his power, erudition, and urbane sophistication. Despite his southern aristocratic credentials, Archibald felt like a backwoods hick in the presence of the president, something nobody who knew him would ever suspect. He masked his inferiority complex with an arrogant and supremely self-confident sham of a façade, but inwardly he chafed at having to answer to a black man.

"We haven't looked this bad in the eyes of the world since we invaded Iraq," said the president, gritting his teeth in anger. "That was bad enough, but this could be even worse. What the hell is the matter with Rick Throckmorton? Did you see this shit?" he asked incredulously.

He handed Archibald the CIA's translation of an article from *Le Monde* in Paris. The vice president glanced down at the report. He knew what it said already.

"La Guerre Civile en Amérique!" proclaimed the headline in bold letters.

"Or take a look at this one." The President handed Archibald another report, this one from *The Guardian* in London.

"Texas Invades Texas!" shouted the British daily. The article claimed that each of the dead R.A.T.S. soldiers carried a U.S. passport. The reporter was a quick study and knew a little bit about American history. He drew a long-winded but mostly fallacious comparison between the situation in South Texas and pre-Civil War conditions in the South. By this time every foreign correspondent in the U.S. considered himself to be an expert on the issue of states' vs. federal rights. There was also the practically mandatory reference to the annexation resolution which became part of the Texas Constitution in 1845 and which retained the right for Texas to divide itself into four additional states.

"Now who the hell leaked that information about the U.S. passports to a foreign correspondent?" asked the president. "Why didn't the sonofabitch also mention that the Mexican drug cartels forged those passports?"

"In all fairness, Mr. President, our people haven't determined that yet," stated the vice president soberly. "All the passports recovered by U.S. Customs in Laredo appear to be genuine. Nobody knows where they came from, but the fact remains: they're real. I suspect the ones recovered on the Nueces River will be too."

The president ignored Archibald's subtle correction.

"And this is what our allies are writing! You can imagine what Latin America, Russia, China, the Middle East, and the rest of those bastards are saying!"

"Yes, Mr. President," replied Archibald. "I've seen the transcripts. I also just got word that we have vetoed a U.N. Security Council resolution condemning our violation of the principle of self-determination in South Texas. Even the Brits abstained. The General Assembly will undoubtedly approve the same resolution. Looks like only Israel will support us. The rest of the world is talking about voluntary economic sanctions against us."

The first African-American president in the history of the United States looked grimly at his vice-president.

"Look at this photo a junior FSO took in Mexico City

earlier today. The crowd almost tore him to bits when they recognized him as an American." He handed Archibald an 8 x 10 photo of a massive demonstration along the Paseo de la Reforma. "The Mexican press estimated the crowd at almost half a million protestors."

Archibald whistled. "Shades of Teheran in 1979," he said softly.

"The jackals and hyenas are gathering, aren't they?" the president said completely without emotion.

"It would appear so, Mr. President."

"You've heard the talk about impeachment, Archibald?"

"It's still just talk, sir."

"They say the Republicans have all the votes they need."

"It's not too late to turn the situation around with some decisive action, Mr. President."

"When are you leaving for Austin?" asked the president.

"Air Force Two leaves in one hour, sir."

"I want you to make them understand that if Texas cannot clean up its own house, the federal government will. Tell Rick Throckmorton this is his last chance. I will send in troops from Fort Hood if the Texas National Guard is not up to the job of restoring order. That's no idle threat."

Actually, Archibald thought that's exactly what it was.

"I understand perfectly, sir," replied the vice president and stood up, trying to wipe a satisfied smile off his face. The specter of impeachment held no fear for Archibald Rutledge. Quite the contrary, actually. He walked down the hallway of the White House, whistling to himself.

***

"What do you make of all this, bro?" asked Bronc. He and Mako Sloane sat on leather chairs in Bronc Thornton's adobe ranch house high on a hilltop east of Culiacán, Sinaloa. They were watching CNN International via satellite and had just learned about the events that took place earlier in the day at the Nueces River Bridge near Cotulla, Texas. Mako heard the news about Lisa Throckmorton a few minutes later when his cell phone rang and he spoke briefly with Drake Herrin. He hurried to get off the phone in case someone was trying to get a fix on his location.

"You want the politically correct version out of Washington, Bronc?" asked Mako dryly.

"Not really. Somehow I can't imagine you uttering anything that would meet the definition of 'politically correct'. Just tell me what's going on in South Texas. How did things get so screwed up?"

"You leave the United States to live in Mexico as an expat and have to ask me how things got so messed up in the U.S.?"

"Yeah, I thought things couldn't get any worse. What's going on?" Bronc asked again.

"Well, offhand, I'd say it's a clear case of political gutlessness. That, along with a healthy dose of Mexican-style corruption thrown in," responded Mako, taking a long pull on an ice cold bottle of Pacifico. "Texas politicians have been corrupt as long as there's been Texas politics. Plus, you've got a governor who thinks everyone plays by the Marquess of Queensberry rules. He's a middle-aged frat boy with lofty political ambitions. He doesn't want to do anything that'll lose votes for his reelection campaign."

"How can he think Salcido plays by any set of rules except his own?" asked Bronc. "What did he think was coming down the pike after he got the first Fedex package with his daughter's passport?"

Mako shrugged his shoulders.

"Hard to say. The man's lived a sheltered life. Before his daughter was abducted, his biggest problem in life was choosing the right country club in Austin. When you live like that, it's hard to see beyond the boundaries of your own fairy tale. Getting his daughter's finger in the mail didn't figure into the equation."

"Poor bastard," mumbled Bronc, trying not to grin.

"Frankly, I envy a man like Rick Throckmorton. I'd love to still be able to view the world through his eyes, but let's talk about that some other day. I'm more interested in your idea; what you started to tell me as we were landing."

"I wondered when you were going to get back to that. I was beginning to think you called me from Toluca just to have a cold beer and shoot the shit," said Bronc.

He snuffed out his joint and suddenly turned serious. He paused, gathering his thoughts.

"Actually, I do have someone on the inside I can trust. I should. Been married to her for almost thirty years."

Bronc paused significantly waiting for a reaction. Mako just reached across the table and put some guacamole on a *totopo* and poured some *salsa picante* on it.

"Consuela works for the cartel?" he asked without showing even a trace of surprise. He didn't want to give Bronc the satisfaction. Bronc was sparring with him. Mako knew it and weighed everything he said as if the conversation were a game of chess.

"Not really. But she keeps the books for one of Francisco's legit businesses. She's over there at least three times a week."

"Why the hell didn't you tell me that before?" asked Mako, frowning at Bronc. "We probably don't have a lot of time."

"You can say that again. Consuela thinks it may be too late already."

"What do you mean?" asked Mako. Getting information from Bronc was like pulling teeth.

"Just what I said," replied Bronc, lighting another joint and popping the cap of a fresh Pacifico. "I hate this Mexican beer when it gets warm," he said in frustration. "It's hard to keep beer cold in this climate."

"Bronc, try to concentrate. We've got a job to do. Your life is going to depend on how we do it. The life of your wife and family too."

The old pilot looked at Mako through bleary eyes and shook his head.

"Look here, Mako. I've flown that converted King Air 200 you saw on the airstrip over a hundred times to Texas since 1982 when I bought it. I was stoned each and every time I took off. Don't worry about me concentrating. That's how I'm still alive. I'm more worried about you."

"Alright, *viejo*. I respect that kind of experience. But listen, you said Consuela thinks it might be too late....why?"

"She thinks they're planning to move the girls. Francisco probably figures his gambit didn't work, so he might as well get rid of them. Personally, I think he'll have them killed, but it'll take place somewhere else."

Mako stood up and started pacing.

"So how does it usually work? How does Salcido transfer his prisoners from death row?"

"Usually in the same van he picked them up with. At night. Two or three guards plus a driver. They take the poor sons o' bitches all tied up to a little compound up the coast highway about fifteen kilometers. They have huge vats of acid there. They put a bullet in the back of their heads, carve up the bodies with chain saws and toss what's left into the acid.

After a few days, there's nothing left but a little hair and a few bone fragments. Can't even do a DNA test to identify the remains. The victims disappear without a trace."

"Can you handle a weapon, Bronc?" asked Mako thoughtfully.

"Sure can," he answered.

"You probably should pack your bags, don't you think? We're going to want to get out of here pretty fast once we've got the girls."

"Let's hear your plan first."

"It's pretty simple. We rescue the damsels in distress, and then you fly us all back to Texas...*de prisa*."

Bronc looked at Mako and stared.

"Sounds like you got all the details worked out," he said.

CHAPTER 28

"Stay tuned for the Bubba Dobbs Show on CNN," said the announcer.

"Creed, get everyone in here," called Guadalupe. "It's Bubba Dobbs in Cotulla!"

"Bubba's come down to gloat," said Creed as he walked into the living room followed by the rest of the temporary population of the Broken "T". "I actually expected him down here a couple of months ago. Wonder what took him so long?"

"Who is this guy anyway? What's he going to gloat about?" asked Jamie Dalton.

"He's a conservative rabble-rouser who's got a hard-on against illegal immigration. It's kind of interesting to listen to him, but the SOB's never lived in South Texas, I'll tell you that. Claims to speak Spanish too, but I doubt it. He was born up in Childress but left when he was still a youngster."

Guadalupe turned up the volume of the television.

"Today the Bubba Dobbs show is on location in Cotulla, Texas, the scene of yesterday's brief but bloody battle between the Texas National Guard and illegal armed units of the non-existent, but perhaps soon-to-be Autonomous Republic of South Texas. The decision by Governor Throckmorton to stand-down the Texas National Guard appears to be just what the National Front for the Liberation of Texas was looking for. According to a communiqué out of Laredo, Texas, the National Front has announced a day of mourning for the 'Martyrs of Cotulla'. Yes, folks, we've got a lot to talk about today. We'll be taking your calls, so stay tuned!"

"I didn't know Bubba was coming to Cotulla. That takes some *cojones*, you got to admit, whether you like the man or not," said Creed. "The National Front would love to have his scalp. I don't agree with him, but I like the shit out of the old bastard."

"I can't stand him," said Guadalupe. "He's hates us Mexicans. He claims we're all parasites and living off the U.S. government, tries to turn the Anglos against us. I'd like to see him on a roofing crew or shoveling asphalt along I-35 when it's 100 degrees in San Antonio."

"Lupe, shhhh! Let's listen to Bubba," pleaded Creed.

"...so while the governor of Texas and the president of the United States hem and haw, illegal immigrants backed by Mexican drug lords have moved in to fill the power vacuum in South Texas. Now they're talking about holding a referendum on autonomy, but Austin and Washington haven't had the stomach to take decisive action against the usurpers. Yesterday's military action by the Texas National Guard ended when Governor Throckmorton ordered the troops to halt their advance after armed cartel thugs shot down a National Guard Apache helicopter. We invited both the governor and Head of the Texas Election Commission Lester Van Slyke to join us today to answer your questions. The governor declined our invitation and Mr. Van Slyke did not deign to return our calls. Would anything like this have taken place if the administration had acted to secure our borders like I've been preaching? Let's hear what you're thinking. Give us a call at the number on your television screen."

"You tell 'em, Bubba," shouted Jamie, laughing.

"This National Guard fiasco is going to work against us," said Creed. "It'll give the National Front the excuse they've been looking for. I bet they announce the referendum any day now. I tell you what I want to know. Where the hell did they get the surface-to-air missile? Those things aren't usually for sale off the rack in the gun stores in Laredo."

"Sounds like Mako may need to make another trip to Managua when he gets back," said Drake Herrin.

"Is Mako making any progress in Mexico?" asked Creed.

"Talked to him an hour ago. He was still okay but had nothing else to report."

"Why the hell hasn't the story about the governor's daughter hit the news?" wondered Creed out loud.

Herrin shrugged his shoulders as if the answer were obvious.

"The governor hasn't gone to the feds with this. He doesn't trust them as far as he can spit. He's counting on Mako, and he's kept it close to his chest. If he hadn't, his daughter would be dead already, I'd say. She might be anyway in a day or two. This is a tough nut to crack, even for Mako."

"Drake, can you imagine what the people of Texas would do if they knew the governor had stopped the National Guard assault because of his daughter?" asked Creed.

"Well, I'm not sure that was the only reason. I don't think anyone thought the R.A.T.S. patrols could shoot down a helicopter. That must have been a shock."

"You think it was a coincidence that the National Guard stood down thirty minutes after the governor received the envelope with his daughter's finger?" asked Creed.

"No, I don't believe in coincidences. That might have been what pushed him over the edge."

"Here's Bubba again," said Creed as the commercial ended and Dobbs' chubby face appeared again on the screen.

"Welcome back to the Bubba Dobbs Show. We've got Lionel Wharton on his cell phone from Uvalde, Texas. Welcome to the show, Lionel."

"Bubba, when are you going to run for president?" said Lionel. "We need someone in Washington to support the middle class and protect our borders."

"Thank you, Lionel. I may have to run if the White House continues to be occupied by effete intellectuals who work against the interests of the middle class. Do you think any of this would have happened if the administration had secured our southern border?"

"Hell no, Bubba. We might as well not have a border. Our prisons are overflowing with Mexican illegals. We got Hispanic gangs on the streets of El Paso and San Antonio; we got illegal immigrants taking jobs away from Americans, and the government's sucking dry the life blood of the middle class to feed and clothe them and pay for their education and health care. And why? Because nobody has the moral courage to call a spade a spade and secure our borders!"

"Sounds like that redneck is reading from a script," said Creed. "I think Bubba's callers are all ringers."

"Thanks for your call and insight, Lionel. Let's look at the results of tonight's poll: 98% of you CNN viewers believe that the crisis in South Texas is a direct result of the administration failing to secure our southern border...surprised? Not me. What *will* surprise me is if the governments in Austin and Washington don't impeach the governor of Texas and the president of the United States over this disaster in Texas. This is Bubba Dobbs on location in Cotulla, Texas. Be sure to join us tomorrow when we discuss the proposed referendum."

"Listen up, everyone," shouted Creed. "I want ya'll to stay on the Broken "T" until we know what the governor's going to do. The National Guard isn't letting anyone near the Nueces River anyway, and the R.A.T.S. patrols are buzzing around like mad hornets. They have it in for the Broken "T", so let's just stay out of their way."

"I don't know why we're going through with this charade. We won't have a chance on winning a referendum if they hold one," said Jamie Dalton.

Eliseo Morales stood up with his arm still in a sling.

"Don't listen to that *pendejo* Bubba Dobbs! Whenever you start thinking it's you Anglos against us Mexicans, then the National Front wins. That's just what they want."

Jamie looked at Eliseo, whom he had known for over 20 years, and asked, "Are you trying to tell me that most of the Mexicans in South Texas aren't following the cue from the National Front?"

"A lot of them ain't just 'Mexicans', like you say. They're American citizens just like you."

Jamie looked uncomfortable. He looked around the room for support. Everyone was quiet.

"Deep down inside, you *gringos* still look at Mexican-Americans as second class citizens. You think we're inferior. That's part of the problem. Mexican-Americans are tired of your racist attitude. That's what it is, pure and simple."

"Now hold on, Eliseo," Jamie retorted. "I never said anything like that."

"You didn't have to," said Eliseo. I can read between the lines. All I'm saying is that if the Anglos would treat the Mexican-Americans like equals, we wouldn't have honest Hispanics wanting to form an autonomous republic. You Anglos are part of the problem!"

Creed stood up.

"That's enough philosophy for one afternoon. You know which section of the fence line you're patrolling. Let's get out there. Make sure you take plenty of ammunition," he said.

Creed put on his cowboy hat and walked to the door. The others followed with their weapons, got into their pickup trucks, and drove towards I-35 in a cloud of dust. Creed finished his cup of hot coffee on the front porch, took a generous pinch of Red Man, and placed it between his cheek and gum.

Shit, turns out you can't even call them 'Mexicans' anymore, thought Creed and laughed to himself. Probably better find a different chewing tobacco while I'm at it too. I got a feeling the name 'Red Man' ain't quite politically correct. I'm surprised Guadalupe hasn't mentioned it yet. He walked down the stairs and off the porch and headed towards his old pickup, a 12-gauge shotgun slung over his shoulder.

CHAPTER 29

The two riders were barely visible in the driving rain. They slumped in their saddles and wore ponchos that slipped over their heads to keep them dry. The cheap garments had long lost their water-shedding qualities and absorbed more water than they repelled. The men sat forlornly in silence and tried to ignore their soaked, dripping clothes. Their faces were hidden by wide brimmed hats that funneled rivulets of water on to the front of their ponchos and down to the ground.

Thunder rumbled in the distance, and lightning occasionally illuminated the night sky, reflecting eerily off the shiny coats of the drenched horses that stood dejectedly with their heads down. It had been a gully washer of a storm, and the rain came down in torrents, driven by a vicious wind off the Gulf of California. The rain had slackened but still came down steadily. It promised to be a wet and miserable night. The dirt road was muddy and slippery, but the horses were used to adverse conditions and to being ridden hard. They would be alright. They nickered to the other two horses tied up under a grove of oak trees some twenty yards from the road, and the riders heard the faint answer, almost inaudible in the steady downpour and gusty breeze.

It was near midnight, and the two horsemen waited under an expansive live oak within sight of the stone entrance to *Rancho Vista del Mar*. They had been there since dusk, waiting patiently just off the narrow road. This was the end of the line for vehicles, and only narrow, barely visible cattle trails crisscrossed the hills to the east. Occasionally, a determined *campesino* might ride down from the highlands with a small pack train of animals to pick up rice and beans and other supplies at a store near Culiacán, but other than that, the country was desolate and remote. Perfect for what the horsemen had in mind.

Finally, the lights of a motorized vehicle flashed haphazardly in the distance as it made its way carefully down the serpentine road from the top of the hill, slowing perceptibly on the hairpin curves. The road had no guard rails, and the slick mud surface and the precipitous, near vertical drops off the side of the mountain made driving a death-defying endeavor. The two riders watched patiently for ten minutes as the vehicle slowly approached the locked wrought-iron gates of the entrance way. Lightning had knocked out power to the ranch, and the electric motor that opened the gate was not operable. It apparently hadn't occurred to the ranch manager to connect the entrance gate to the emergency power supply.

The vehicle, a white, windowless delivery van splashed with mud, stopped in front of the gate, and a short, heavily built man in a yellow rain slicker got out of the passenger side. He walked slowly to the gate, slipping in the mud and cursing loudly in Spanish. He unlatched the gate and opened it manually: first the right side and then the left. The van drove through and stopped on the other side, waiting for the man to close the gate and get back in the van.

As he turned around and took a laborious step through the sucking mud in the direction of the van, the man was surprised to see a horseman appear out of the darkness in front of him. He was even more surprised when a twelve-gauge shotgun appeared from under the rider's poncho. A peal of thunder in the distance muted the blast of the shotgun, but the driver inside the van recognized the sound. He instinctively drew his handgun and threw open the door, intending to deal with his friend's attacker. A second horseman emerged eerily out of the darkness, an implacable and pitiless phantom, and blocked his way. The driver saw the second shotgun leveled at him. This time there was no coincidental roll of thunder to mute the roar of the discharge which threw the driver haphazardly back into the van. The impact of the 2 ¾ inch double ought buckshot load was equal to a nine-round burst from an automatic weapon. Neither man had a chance, and both died quickly and without making a sound.

The riders wheeled their mounts in the mud and dashed to the rear door of the van which flew open to reveal a tall, skinny Mexican with a pearl-handled Colt 45 in either hand and a wild, terrified look in his eyes. The man blanched at the sight of his two adversaries and their formidable weapons which roared simultaneously. The force of the blasts flung his long, lithe body against the rear door of the van, shattering half a dozen ribs. Like his friends, the skinny one was dead before he hit the ground.

One of the riders dismounted quickly, handing the horse's reins to his partner and pointing a flashlight inside the back of the van. Two teenaged girls, gagged and handcuffed, stared out at him with unadulterated fear in their eyes. He saw bulky, bloody bandages wrapped around the right hand of one of the girls. Her face was pale, and she appeared weak and listless even in her fear. Their terror turned to surprise and then to hope as the stranger took out a pair of garden shears, cut their plasticuffs, and untied the gags which their captors had tied around the back of their heads.

He turned back to his partner, who had remained horseback and called out.

"Bronc, get me the two extra ponchos."

He turned back to the girls and said, "How about a little horseback ride, girls? Lisa, your father's waiting for you back in Texas. Let's get you home. I hope you can both ride a horse."

The girls clung to each other desperately, not knowing whether to laugh or weep. Bronc in the meantime brought up the two horses that were tied in the oak grove off the road. He helped the girls into the saddles and took the reins of both horses, waiting for Mako to join him.

Mako walked slowly from body to body. He leaned over each for just a few seconds with the garden shears and removed the ring finger of each man. The bones crunched audibly as he pressed the forged aluminum handles together with all his strength. When he was finished, he tossed the shears into the brush and glanced up the hill towards *Rancho Vista del Mar*.

"*¡Hijo de puta!*," he whispered softly as he sloshed over to his horse, mounted and took the reins from Lisa's horse in his right hand.

"Let's ride," he said without emotion.

CHAPTER 30

One hour after learning of the debacle on the Nueces River, Governor Throckmorton pulled out his Blackberry and punched in the private cell phone of his old fraternity brother and head of the Texas Election Commission Lester Van Slyke.

"Lester, the shit has hit the fan."

"Yeah, I know, Rick. Those Mexicans are crazy. What are you going to do?"

"I've ordered the National Guard to stand down, at least temporarily. We can't afford any more bloodshed. Can't have Americans killing other Americans on Texas soil like what happened in Waco in 1993. I won't preside over a massacre."

"What can I do to help, Rick?" asked Van Slyke.

"Listen, your brother-in-law is flying in this afternoon from Washington for a briefing. I want you to assemble your team and come up with the definitive legal basis for going ahead with the referendum. I need this in three hours. Understood?"

"You'll have it," said Van Slyke obligingly.

The governor hung up and sat in his office staring off into space. He knew the press had gathered out on the street waiting for him to make a statement, but he had no idea what to say. Was his decision to halt the National Guard's advance a humanitarian gesture? That might play well, he thought. But maybe it was just plain old cowardice? Maybe he didn't have the stomach for a fight. Perhaps the gruesome discovery of his daughter's finger prompted his decision to pull the troops back. Her UT class ring on the end of that bloody stub of a finger haunted him. He couldn't get it out of his mind. To make matters worse, Mako Sloane's daily call-in was overdue, and he was frantic with worry.

***

At five o'clock that afternoon Archibald Rutledge, vice president of the United States, sat in the office of the Texas governor and propped his long legs up on Rick Throckmorton's desk, dangling his Weejuns on the tips of his toes. He looked haughtily around the room and suddenly sat up and slammed his right fist down on the desk. The governor, sitting in a chair usually reserved for visitors, jumped and visibly cringed.

"Is this how the Lone Star state conducts its affairs?" the vice president asked scornfully.

Victoria Ramirez, the governor's secretary, chose that moment to enter the office carrying a tray of refreshments. "Is this what you wanted, Mr. Vice President?" she asked smiling, unaware of the growing tension in the room.

Archibald leaned forward and gratefully picked up the frosty bottle of RC Cola with his left hand and scooped up a banana flavored Moon Pie with his right hand.

"Why are you smiling, Vicky?" asked the vice president. "Didn't you know you can take the senator out of South Carolina, but you can't take South Carolina out of the senator?"

Archibald smiled, leaned back in his chair, and tilted the bottle of RC Cola towards the ceiling, taking a long, grateful draught of the ice-cold brown liquid. He opened the blue and yellow plastic package containing the Moon Pie and took a large bite, chocolate crumbles littering the top of the governor's desk.

"Say what you want, but this shit is *haute cuisine*," said Archibald smiling broadly. "It'll make The Peninsula Grill in

Charleston look like Taco Bell." He took another drink of RC Cola and sighed.

"So, Rick, what the hell is going on? The president, to put it mildly, is disappointed over what's happened in Texas. Actually, the black bastard was apoplectic when I saw him in the Oval Office," the former senator from South Carolina said. "Congress is moving to impeach him as we speak. The president would prefer that not happen."

"Mr. Vice President," began Governor Throckmorton as he launched into his rehearsed explanation of the decision to stop the National Guard's advance.

"Cut the shit, will you, Rick?" interrupted Archibald. "We're fraternity brothers, or did you forget? Just tell me in twenty-five words or less what the hell you're doing."

"Okay, Archie. I'm trying. Let me talk, will you?" said Rick.

"First of all," he continued, "I don't want another Waco on my hands. That should be reason enough. But secondly, Lester's team of lawyers thinks the referendum is legal and recommends we let it happen." Rick looked over at the vice president expectantly.

"Sounds like a crock of shit, but by all means continue," said Archibald.

"Now hold on, Archie," said Lester Van Slyke. "Last year's amendment to the Texas Constitution, which approved the referendum and initiative process at the local level, opened a whole new can of worms. Holding a local referendum in the counties that approve and support the measure is legal. There can be no argument about that."

"Not if the result at the regional level affects the rest of the state, Lester," retorted the vice president.

"Our legal specialists disagree," said Lester. "The only 'if' goes back to the issue of dividing the state into four additional entities and whether the entire state has to vote on that issue.

You've got to realize there's no precedent for what's going on now. Again, our legal team decided that a geographically concise region consisting of contiguous counties has that right."

"Whew," whistled Archibald. "I don't know who's crazier: the Mexicans in South Texas or you sons o' bitches. You guys have drunk the Kool-Aid, haven't you?"

"There's no Kool-Aid involved, Archie," said Throckmorton. "We're trying to survive a ticklish situation. I'll admit we drug our feet too long, but the federal government is not without blame here, my friend."

"Oh, you're planning to blame Washington for all your local problems? That's a bit of a cliché, don't you think, Rick?" commented Archibald.

"Well, you tell me then. Who's running immigration and drug policy? Austin or Washington? The defense rests," said the governor defiantly.

"I'll concede that point, Rick, but the president won't. He's hopping mad and wants to send in the army. His job depends on it."

"Yeah, I've heard that before," said the governor.

"This time I think he's serious," insisted Archibald.

"I'll block his way with the 36th Division of the Texas National Guard before I'll let the United States Army dictate policy in Texas," declared the governor.

Archibald looked up quizzically. "I believe the president has the ultimate say on National Guard deployments, Rick."

"I think he'll find Texas to be different from other states on that subject. I may not have a lot of support right now because of the referendum crisis, but there's nothing that'll boost my approval rating like interference from Washington and a threat to deploy federal troops."

"Be careful, Rick. You might have to put up or shut up on that one," shot back Archibald. "You've already shown the world what a 'bloodthirsty' military commander you are. A few casualties and you call a halt to your offensive. But don't push the president too far. He's sensitive about his legacy as the first African-American president in history, and he's not crazy about the idea of presiding over the breakup of the Union. Anything that smacks of secession or states' rights vs. federal authority gets his attention, and you've got it."

"Look, I've got phone calls into the National Front and the Hispanic Majority Committee to negotiate the ground rules for the referendum," said the governor, "but they won't take my calls."

"And why should they talk to you? It's their referendum, not yours, Rick. If there's a referendum, the National Front will probably win. Then what? What the hell do you think the president will do if you lose twelve or fifteen counties to the Autonomous Republic of South Texas? Have you thought about that?"

"I'm trying not to," admitted the governor.

"Well, if the referendum takes place, I'll be flying to Mexico City. I'll be talking to the president down there and to their attorney general. We think they're pretty heavily involved."

"What good will that do?" asked the governor.

"Jack shit, in my opinion," answered Archibald candidly. "But that's what the president wants. In the meantime, try to keep your heads above water. You're embarrassing me and my ties to Texas."

"Archie, if the referendum takes place. What can we expect the president to do?" asked the governor.

The vice president had started to get out of his chair but sat back down with a groan. He looked long and hard at the governor of Texas.

"Well, Rick, this is strictly hypothetical, but if the National Front calls for a referendum and then declares the southern counties autonomous, I think you can expect a visit from III Corps out of Fort Hood and a demonstration of precision bombing that'll make 'Shock and Awe' look like child's play in comparison."

CHAPTER 31

The rain continued throughout the night, turning the roads and mountain trails into a slick, nearly impassable quagmire. The wind subsided, but the clouds hung low over the coastal plains and fog lurked in thick banks among the folds of the hills east of *Rancho Vista del Mar*. Francisco Salcido woke up early to the soothing call of a solitary male mourning dove, which for some reason had not returned north with the rest of the flock that year. He stretched his legs luxuriously and smiled in the semi-conscious satisfaction of his near omnipotence.

The recollection of the unpleasant task he assigned to Simón the night before brought him abruptly out of his reverie. He had hated to do it. Francisco actually had grown quite fond of Lisa. She was intelligent, well-read, and an interesting conversationalist. She challenged him intellectually. That was a hard-to-find commodity among his usual companions in Culiacán, Sinaloa.

Death had a finality about it that repulsed him, but in Lisa's case he had no choice. She was of no further use to him politically, and the risk she represented with her continued presence did not offset the pleasure he derived from their nightly bantering. Of course, those encounters had ended after the crude, but necessary amputation which had taken place in Francisco's study. It seemed too awkward after that to resume those get-togethers. And now, her decomposing body would be resting in a vat of acid.

"¡Padrino, Padrino!" Francisco recognized the almost hysterical shouts of Pablo Gomez, head of ranch security. Pablo was an older, experienced cartel soldier who had shown

exemplary service to Francisco for almost twenty years. That, in and of itself, had qualified Pablo for a more responsible position within the organization. Longevity was an uncommon attribute on the resume of a cartel soldier.

"*¡Aquí estoy, cabrón! ¿Que pasó?*" Francisco called out in annoyance. This was such an outrageous violation of morning protocol at the *Rancho Vista del Mar* that Francisco did not stop to consider the possibility that something extraordinary might have taken place. He removed his eyeshades and instinctively shielded his face from the dim light of the overcast morning, which in comparison with the cocoon of darkness that enveloped him, was the harshest of daylight.

"*¡A la gran puta!*" he cursed out loud. "What the hell is going on?"

Fifteen minutes later he found out. Francisco donned a pair of high rubber boots Pablo had thoughtfully provided and slogged through the mud in disbelief, circling the white van and staring in shock at the bullet riddled bodies of his guards. There was Simón, lying motionless, his long hair matted down across his gaunt face and gaping mouth. Something shiny protruded out of his mouth, and Francisco bent over to take a closer look. A shockwave of recognition jolted him as he caught sight of Simón's finger and his ostentatious ring with the gigantic ruby he was so proud of. The ruby was covered with mucus and looked like an alien embryo emerging from the birth canal of some hideous life form.

The same sight met him as he examined each corpse.

Well, Félix, *pinche chilango,* it appears the ex-CIA man gave your team the slip after all, he thought in a rage he could barely control. He looked again at the four-fingered right hands of his dead employees and understood the message.

"The *gringo* lacks subtlety...so typical of his race. Who is this *puto*, and how did he know we were transferring the prisoners last night?" He spoke softly under his breath, suspecting the worst.

Francisco returned to Simón's corpse and picked up one of his pearl-handled Colts which lay in the mud. He used his rain slicker to wipe off the gun, stuck the long barrel between Pablo's eyes, and pulled the trigger. The sound of the discharge was deafening in the early morning drizzle and echoed endlessly among the hills.

"Your job performance has been unsatisfactory," Francisco snarled as Pablo's body fell to the ground, surprise etched on his already lifeless face.

Francisco tossed the Colt to the ground in disgust, wiped his hands on his slicker, and looked around. He caught the terrified eyes of Pablo's deputy, who stared at the messy remains of his friend and supervisor.

"You've got a new job," said Francisco and motioned with his arm at the corpses. "Come to my office in thirty minutes and tell me how you're going to find who did this and recover the girls."

An hour later, fifteen mounted and heavily armed cartel soldiers rode their struggling horses up the slippery cattle trail into the hills, following the tracks of the four horses from the night before. The fleeing horses had left deep hoof prints in the mud, and the rain had done little during the night to erase their tracks. It was child's play to follow them.

Francisco led the column of desperate horsemen. Nobody wanted to share Pablo's fate. The horses complained and occasionally reared in protest, but the men drove them hard, spurring their mounts viciously with the large rowels typically used in that part of Mexico. Francisco was more used to riding polo ponies, but he was a practiced and trained rider. He thought nothing of driving his horse into the ground if he had to. The main thing was to get there in time.

A few unanswered phone calls, the trail leading directly toward his brother-in-law's ranch, and Francisco knew he had been betrayed. He thirsted for revenge and was desperate to finish the job Simón and his friends had botched. Francisco was thankful for the low cloud cover and prayed the fog wouldn't lift any time soon. The only way out of the mountains was by airplane, and nothing could take off in this fog. They still had a chance to catch up.

***

Mako rode cutting horses almost every day at his ranch in Chantilly, Virginia, but even he wasn't used to riding six hours straight up a narrow, slippery cattle trail at night with his horse digging deep for traction, struggling with each step. The horse balked every thirty seconds in the muddy conditions, refusing to take another step until encouraged by the insistent touch of Mako's spur. Branches clawed at his face as he rode in the darkness. Thorns ripped cruelly at his clothing and left angry red scratches on his hands and arms.

Mako held the reins of Lisa's horse in one hand and led her sorrel gelding up and down the slick hills across the steep ravines and gorges of the treacherous country. He glanced back every couple of minutes at Lisa who sat transfixed on her horse, both hands glued to the wide Guadalajara saddle horn. She hadn't said a word since Mako heaved her into the saddle at the entrance to the ranch. She made little or no effort to get out of the way of the many branches that extended precariously into their trail. Mako called out a warning to her each time they encountered an obstacle, but Lisa barely reacted. Bronc led the horse of Lisa's friend, who was equally silent and unresponsive.

By the time they arrived at the ranch, a creeping band of gray light on the horizon ahead of them to the east heralded the arrival of a cloudy dawn. The interminable ride had brutalized them all. Mako's body ached cruelly and he could only imagine how the girls felt. He helped Lisa out of the saddle, and she collapsed to the ground, unable to stand on her aching knees. He could see that her jeans were drenched in blood where the saddle had rubbed her raw. She had not uttered a sound during the entire ordeal, and her silence continued even now.

Consuela met them and hustled the girls inside. They jerked back instinctively when they saw a Mexican, but Mako calmed them in a soothing voice. The girls seemed to trust him despite their silence. Consuela had laid out clean clothes for the girls, and she helped them wash up and change. Her luggage was already packed, and the family's most prized possessions had been placed in cardboard boxes Bronc had loaded in the King Air, which stood silhouetted against the tree line on the ridge about fifty yards from the house.

Bronc fueled the aircraft before they left on horseback the day before, and everything within his power to control was ready for the flight. Only the weather refused to cooperate. White billowing clouds shrouded the low hills in the distance like an ephemeral shroud of thick cotton candy, and dense fog enveloped the trees on the horizon. Even Bronc Thornton refused to take off in those conditions.

"Wonder what kind of a lead we have on them?" asked Bronc out loud as he stood looking down the trail they had just traversed.

"With any luck they didn't figure things out until daylight. We probably had a four or five hour head start on them. But waiting on the fog to lift is going to eat away at that pretty fast," replied Mako with a concerned glance at the sky. "What kind of a surface you have on that runway?"

"Looks like mud, don't it?" laughed Bronc. "Not to worry, son. That's about an inch of mud or so and then asphalt...2,600 feet of it to be exact. Cost a pretty penny to install, let me tell you. Nothing but the best for the Sinaloa cartel," he said. "It might be a little iffy generating the necessary speed to take off if the runway's too slick, but we have a fighting chance at least. As long as the weather clears," he added.

Bronc looked over at Mako to judge his reaction. Mako took in his inquiring gaze but ignored him.

"Do you have a sniper or deer rifle or something like that?" he asked. "I'm going to walk down the trail to that place where the trees open up. If I see them coming, I'll start firing. Be ready to crank up the engines."

"Mako, relax," he said. "We're not going anywhere till that fog lifts, and we've got a few hours at least until they come up that hill. Nobody heard those shotgun blasts in that storm last night, believe me."

"Well, they'll be traveling faster than we could, that's for sure. Just bring me a damned rifle," insisted Mako.

Bronc disappeared into the ranch house and came back a few minutes later. He handed Mako a brand new M4 with several spare magazines. A lighted marijuana cigarette dangled from his lips. Mako walked down the trail shaking his head. And they think I'm nuts back in Washington, he thought. He was soon pounding his rubber boots against rocks on the side of the trail to knock off the thick mud which caked to the soles and made it hard to walk. Then he was cursing in Spanish and English as he slid out of control on his ass down the muddy path, holding the M4 high in one hand to protect it from banging against the rocks on either side.

As if following the hackneyed script of a low-budget movie, the day played out almost exactly as Mako feared. He sat on a dry boulder for two hours, observing the trail leading up the side of the mountain towards his position. His back hurt, and his neck was so stiff he could barely turn it from side to side.

Mako could see about three quarters of a mile down the winding trail bracketed by stunted oaks, cholla, and ocotillo, and interspersed with rocks and boulders. It was damp but the sun occasionally showed signs of coming through the thick low clouds. Then he would feel the heat of it on his back for a few seconds, and suddenly the temperature would drop as a bank of fog drifted by, obscuring the trail below for long periods of time and lending a distinct chill to the air.

He heard them before he saw them. Their shouts drifted up the hill from far below and startled him. He released the safety on the M4 and peered into the telescopic sights.

Shit, they made better time than we did. Maybe I can slow them down, at least make them take cover and buy us some more time, he thought as he raised the M4 to his shoulder, adjusted the sights, and waited for them to reappear.

Mako waited until the fog bank rolled by and the first horseman suddenly materialized out of the mist far below. The range was extreme, and Mako doubted he could hit a target at this distance. He squeezed off a round and sure enough the shot was off. He couldn't even tell through the sights where the bullet struck. A fraction of a second later the sound of the gun's discharge reached his pursuers and produced an unexpected reaction. Mako thought they would seek cover, but instead they spurred their horses and raced up the hill with renewed energy.

He took aim again, this time with more urgency and squeezed off a second round. Another miss. The lead horse suddenly lost his footing in the mud and slid back down the hill on his haunches, his rider spurring his flanks cruelly in a wild frenzy of excitement. Mako propped the M4 on the large rock in front of him and placed the cross-hairs of the rifle sight on the chest of the rider, hurrying to get a shot off before the horse regained its traction and bounded forward. Just as the gun discharged, the horse reared on his hind legs, and Mako saw a blotch of red appear on his broad chest and heard the horse scream before he collapsed on his side, pinning the rider beneath him.

Damn, the horse got in the way, he thought. Mako watched through the telescopic sight as the two nearest riders dismounted to assist their fallen companion. He heard shouting and several riders pointed up the trail towards the boulder where Mako was hiding. They opened fire in his general direction with semi-automatic weapons, firing ineffectual short bursts. He had seen enough and slung the M4 over his shoulder by its leather strap. He turned and headed back up the trail at a steady jog, trying to stay on solid ground along the edge of the winding trail, jumping from rock to rock to avoid the quagmire of sticky mud.

Halfway up the hillside he heard the unmistakable roar of the King Air's twin engine turboprops as Bronc kicked them into action in response to Mako's shots. As he reached the crest of the hill, he saw Consuela standing by the airplane and waving to him frantically.

That stoned motherfucker better not leave without me, thought Mako as he shed his muddy rubber boots and wet socks and sprinted towards the airplane in his bare feet. He threw his body through the door as Bronc eased the aircraft forward. Low clouds still obscured the horizon, and the mud lay thickly on the homemade tarmac. "I'm way too old for this shit," Mako muttered, lying on his back and sucking in the damp air greedily.

"See you in hell, bro," called out Bronc from the cockpit as the King Air 200 accelerated down the narrow runway. "Can't see a damn thing!"

CHAPTER 32

Lester Van Slyke sensed something peculiar in his brother-in-law's demeanor. He knew the vice president hadn't been drinking, unless Royal Crown Cola International had begun secretly lacing their bottles of RC Cola with some kind of FDA-approved intoxicant; actually not a bad idea, he thought idly. But Archibald didn't seem to be taking the South Texas crisis or yesterday's bloody encounter on the Nueces seriously. In fact, he seemed to be enjoying it.

"Lester, you should have seen the president going through the foreign newspaper headlines. I'm telling you the man's hands were shaking. He's frightened. No, let me rephrase that. He's scared out of his wits. I thought the man had balls, but I was wrong. He and Rick Throckmorton should get together and discuss remedies for their hot flashes."

"How about you, Archie, are you saying you're not worried?" asked Van Slyke.

"Not me. That's the great thing about being a vice president: the buck doesn't stop here," he laughed. "The difference between the president and me is that he looks at this crisis and sees a disaster, a possible end to his administration. I look at the crisis and see an opportunity," declared the vice president. "And so should you," he added.

Lester Van Slyke looked questioningly at his prominent relative across the broad back seat of the limousine but didn't pursue the odd remark. The limo was in route to the County Line on Bee Cave Road, Archibald's favorite eating spot on the west side of Austin. Secret service agents rode in the chase cars, which surrounded the limo on all four sides. Six police cars, lights flashing, led the procession, clearing traffic for this unexpected deviation from the vice president's itinerary. Lester could only imagine the consternation Archibald had caused his staff when he changed the itinerary at the last minute. He knew how much Archibald loved Texas barbecue and how much the view of the hill country from inside the restaurant made him nostalgic for his student days. He laughed to himself when he thought what his brother-in-law would have said back then if someone had told him that one day he was going to be vice president. Probably would have just grinned and tossed back another shot of tequila.

"An opportunity for what? To get impeached or to start a civil war?" Van Slyke finally asked, curious as to what the vice president meant.

"You've got a lot to learn, Lester," replied Archibald. "That's why you're languishing here in the provinces as a mere secretary of state. You say 'impeached'? That very well could happen, but it wouldn't be me, would it? And then where would that leave Vice President Archibald Rutledge?" He looked at Van Slyke significantly. "Your brother-in-law is only a heartbeat away from the presidency! Or an impeachment trial away. How would you like to move to Washington, Lester?"

"What are you talking about?" asked Lester.

"All I'm saying is that impeachment wouldn't be a bad thing for either of us. In fact, it might be in our interest. If we can do something to affect the situation one way or the other, maybe we should give it some thought."

They made their way slowly up the winding driveway to the County Line restaurant and saw police cars blocking the entrance to the parking lot at the top of the hill. Several secret service agents hopped out of the chase cars and stood on the side boards of the limo. Lester could hear what sounded like chanting and shouting even through the limousine's closed bullet-proof glass windows. As the limousine continued up the steep hill, Lester occasionally caught sight of the tops of homemade signs bobbing up and down. At that distance, though, he couldn't make out the print.

As the limo finally hit the top of the rise, a roar went up from two separate groups of demonstrators. On the right side of the packed lot, there were mostly Hispanic protesters. The vice president caught sight of one crudely printed banner that read "ASESINOS".

"Look at that one over there," said Lester pointing to a Hispanic mother with two small children clinging to her long cotton dress. She held up a sign that read, "EXIGIMOS RESPETO".

"Those signs over there are more to the point," Archibald said, pointing to four men who stood in front of the rest of the demonstrators and waved two professionally made banners. The first demanded "AUTODETERMINACION PARA LOS HISPANOS" while the other succinctly stated, "NO A RACISMO".

The vice president laughed. "'Self-determination for Hispanics' and 'No to Racism'. Now that stings a little."

"How did they know we'd be here?" asked Lester and glanced over at Archibald suspiciously.

"What is it they say?" he asked innocently. "Any publicity is good publicity?"

Lester looked at him incredulously.

"But look on the other side of the parking lot. Here're the good ol' boys. They probably drove in from Johnson City... damned rednecks."

A group of Anglo demonstrators dressed in cowboy boots and western hats stood behind a row of Austin city cops and shouted at the two politicians.

"Traitors!" they screamed. A few of them managed to heave a couple of rocks before they were subdued by the police and carted off.

"Mexican lovers!" others shouted. The Anglos weren't as used to organized political demonstrations and hadn't made any banners with catchy slogans like their Hispanic counterparts.

The vice president led his brother-in-law into the restaurant behind a phalange of secret service agents. He appeared to be looking for someone as they strolled through the restaurant towards a large table in the far corner of the dining area. The usual stunning view of the Texas Hill Country disappeared in the blinding reflection of the setting sun to the west.

Archibald greeted a few of the well-wishers inside by name and pressed the flesh, smiling as if he were in the middle of a political campaign instead of one of the most serious crises to affect the United States in decades. A few protesters shouted insults, but the predominately pro-Rutledge faction inside the restaurant hooted them down.

"Archie! Over here!" called out a booming voice from across the room.

"Ah, there's Bubba," said the vice-president. "I hope you don't mind Bubba Dobbs joining us for dinner. He was in Cotulla this morning. Broadcast a hell of a show on the Cotulla Massacre down there this morning...that's what they're calling it already. Didn't pull any punches either."

Archibald waved his arm in greeting and walked purposefully towards the famous CNN television host. The two embraced like old friends and the vice president introduced Lester Van Slyke.

"You've got some guts, Mr. Secretary," said Bubba Dobbs as he took Van Slyke's limp hand in a vice grip. "I mean coming out into the maelstrom like this. You and the governor are at the center of this tumultuous affair after all. The governor hasn't shown his face in a week."

"Just trying to do what's best for Texas, Mr. Dobbs," replied Lester, astounded that his brother-in-law had delivered him into the clutches of the famous anti-immigration television host.

"Well, that's a matter of opinion these days, isn't it?" he asked, slapping Lester on the back like an old college roommate.

"Bubba, what's your take on the situation down there?" asked the vice president. "You were in Cotulla this morning. Great show, by the way. Really enjoyed it."

Lester found it odd that the vice president of the United States was asking a reporter about breaking events in South Texas. Well, maybe that shouldn't have surprised him, he thought. CNN usually scooped the CIA on important issues, especially in recent years.

"It looks pretty clear to me, Archie. Whoever's running the National Front is a lot smarter than the governor of Texas."

Bubba ordered a Shiner Bock draft from the pixie-like waitress who approached the table. The others seconded his choice, and in ninety seconds they were clanking their mugs and drinking the ice-cold beer.

"I wish I could have met ol' Kosmos Spoetzl," suddenly announced Archibald.

"Who the hell's that?" asked Lester.

"He was the brewer that started Shiner. I think he was German, maybe from Bavaria. Should be on the Texas state flag," he joked.

"Yeah, it's good beer, but I actually prefer a few of the Mexican brews," claimed Bubba. "But you guys keep that a secret, will you?" he pleaded.

"So anyway, if you want to know my opinion," he continued. "If a referendum takes place, the majority of the citizens of the southern counties will vote in favor of autonomy. Within twenty-four hours the National Front will announce the formation of the Autonomous Republic of South Texas and schedule elections."

"Would it be a landslide?" asked Archibald.

"You mean if the administration continues sitting on its ass and lets it happen?"

"Strictly hypothetically, Bubba. Would the National Front win a referendum by a landslide?" Archibald repeated his question.

"You'd think so, but my sources tell me otherwise," replied Bubba. "There's been a late groundswell in favor of a middle ground in the last couple of weeks. You guys ever hear of Creed Tucker?" he asked as he studied both Archibald and Lester.

They shook their heads.

"He's a rancher down there, a big landowner south of Cotulla. Married to a Mexican woman. Apparently, he's getting a reputation as the voice of moderation in South Texas. His people were the ones involved in that little dust-up a few days ago when R.A.T.S. guards at the Nueces River crossing tried to stop a mixed Anglo-Hispanic caravan from coming into the 'republic'. They say his son was the one who shot and killed the R.A.T.S. guard. It was allegedly self-defense."

"He's a political activist? Haven't heard mention of him," commented Archibald.

"No, he's no activist. In fact, he's probably not even aware of his own popularity," explained Bubba. "But he's stood up to the cartel a couple of times and repelled a few attacks on his ranch. He's like the archetypal frontiersman in the middle of Indian country holding his ground. He's a tough old bastard from what I hear. Played tight end at A&M and was in Vietnam. The ironic thing is that at one time he was close to Rudy Gutierrez, one of the founders of the National Front. I hear they fought in Vietnam together."

"Here come the local reporters, Bubba. It'd be better if we

weren't interviewed together. I'll catch up with you in Cotulla tomorrow, what do you say?" proposed Archibald.

"Good idea. I'm out of here. Good to see you, Lester. Let's stay in touch."

Bubba Dobbs hurried out of the restaurant just ahead of a crowd of reporters and television cameras the secret service agents held at bay.

"Lester, you were born in McAllen, weren't you?" asked Archibald.

"Yeah, you know that. Why?"

"Well, that might make you a citizen of the Autonomous Republic of South Texas if the referendum is held," said Archibald cryptically and stared at his brother-in-law.

Lester laughed.

"And...?" he asked.

"And if it all comes down the way Bubba thinks it will, I want you to run for president of *La República Autónoma de Tejas del Sur*," explained Archibald and fixed his stare on Lester Van Slyke.

"Have you lost your mind?" asked Lester, his eyes wide in disbelief.

"No I haven't, but I'm not so sure about you. By the way, brother-in-law," Archibald began coyly. He paused and let Van Slyke squirm. "How's your bank account in the British Virgin Islands doing?"

Van Slyke looked at Archibald in dismay.

"What are you talking about?" he asked.

"Don't play games with me, Lester. I know you don't make much as secretary of state. I don't blame you for trying to line your pockets. But let's not dwell on that for the moment. I need you to run. Don't worry, I don't want or expect you to win, but it's all part of the grand strategy. I'll remember you when I'm president."

CHAPTER 33

He almost died that night. As he drifted in and out of consciousness, Francisco thought of the irony of his plight, and for the first time in his life he felt sorry for himself. The sudden reversal of fortunes didn't fit into the certainty of the familiar algorithms that governed his life. The bewildering turn of events had caught Francisco unawares, and he chafed at the knowledge that he had lacked foresight; that his enemies had outmaneuvered him. Francisco missed a move in a deadly game of chess, and he felt like a fool.

In his rage at being beaten at his own ruthless game, Francisco had led the helter-skelter charge up the mountain, thus violating one of the most important principles he usually applied to his own actions. "Reason and calm judgment are the qualities belonging to a leader," he used to preach, quoting a first century B.C. Roman senator. He had forgotten that principle, and had paid the price.

The bullet had penetrated the horse's chest cavity, ricocheted off a rib and lodged in the animal's heart. The beast threw Francisco rudely to the ground. Adding insult to injury, the dying stallion then fell on Francisco, pinning him on top of a large rock in the trail. His right leg snapped audibly several times, and as Francisco's luck would have it that day, he did not lose consciousness. He would never forget the pain.

Ironically, it was a 20-year old cartel assassin who saved his life. The boy turned killer had been a medic in the Mexican army and recognized that Salcido was slipping into shock. He applied the basic textbook measures he had learned in the *Escuela Médico Militar* in Mexico City, and they were enough to keep the drug lord alive until morning when a Bell 212 Twin Huey arrived after the fog lifted. The absurdity of the fact that the attorney general's office had dispatched the emergency aircraft from its anti-drug base in Los Mochis to save the life of the head of the Sinaloa cartel was not lost on Salcido. He smiled when he saw the insignia of the *Procuraduría General* on the helicopter door. It helped to have friends in high places.

Surgery was scheduled at the *Rancho Vista del Mar* a few hours after the helicopter landed. With gunshot wounds a constant occupational hazard, Salcido installed a sophisticated ER unit years ago, never thinking it would come in handy for his own personal emergency. A discreet phone call to the office of a well-known physician in Mexico City, a hurried flight to Culiacán in the attorney general's private jet, and the prominent orthopedic surgeon was piecing Francisco's splintered leg back together before nightfall. The prognosis was good although the surgeon suspected Salcido would always walk with a limp, a permanent reminder-to-be of his tactical defeat at the hands of the mysterious ex-CIA officer.

As Salcido began to regain consciousness following surgery, his eyelids fluttered and opened for a few seconds only to close again as he fell back into a deep, paralyzing sleep. A vaguely familiar face drifted in and out of focus every time his eyes opened, and its constant presence gave him comfort and somehow made him feel safe and protected. Francisco knew he was hurt, but in his morphine-induced delirium he couldn't put all the pieces together from yesterday's events. Trying to focus his thoughts nauseated him, and he soon gave up trying to solve the riddle of where he was and what disaster had befallen him. He kept his eyes closed tightly and sought refuge in the heavy curtain of darkness that lay over him like a thick and opaque fog.

Gradually, as the anesthesia wore off, the events of the last twenty-four hours began to fall into place, and he was able to make sense of what had happened to him with more clarity than he would have preferred.

"Francisco, *¿cómo te sientes?*" asked a familiar voice.

The voice startled him, and he looked around wildly, trying to identify the source. The terrifying thought that he might be someone's prisoner briefly entered his mind but dissolved quickly as he recognized the concerned features of Félix Aguilar in a chair beside his bed.

"You had us all worried, *carnal,*" said Félix, motioning to the nurse to leave the men alone. Francisco was fully conscious, but the painkillers disoriented him, and his attention span was limited.

Francisco listened to the profusely apologetic attorney general. Aguilar explained to him how the incompetent surveillance team had lost Mako Sloane shortly after he left the Nikko Hotel and how the taxi they had been following turned out to be carrying an American, but not Sloane. And then the untimely storm in Sinaloa, knocking out cell phone service right when Aguilar needed to inform Salcido that Mako had eluded his surveillance and was probably headed to Culiacán. It's always preferable to blame someone else for near disasters, but Francisco was still too groggy to follow Félix's rambling explanation, much less be angry with him.

"Félix," Salcido called out, his voice stronger.

"*Si, compa, estoy aquí contigo*"

"When you become president, we have to make some changes," said Salcido.

"Anything you want, *compa,*" replied Aguilar.

"I'm one of the richest and most powerful men in Mexico, but a *gringo*, a mere *funcionario* from the North American government, can still come into Mexico like a *filibustero* from the nineteenth century, commit crimes against our people and fly out whenever he wants. That must never happen again."

"Have patience," said Félix. "The *gringos* will pay for their arrogance...and soon."

***

"Mako, I'm looking down at the Rio Bravo, or as you *gabachos* call it, the Rio Grande."

"Welcome back to Texas, Bronc," replied Mako Sloane, waking up from a nap and yawning. "You're one hell of a pilot; you know that? You ever flown sober?"

"I try not to if I can help it. But we've got another problem."

"No such thing as problems, Bronc...just challenges. Isn't that what they say?"

"Well, you tell me what this is. I'm looking out at an F-16 on either wing. I'm hoping the DEA has not acquired fighter jets in my absence from the U.S.A., and that these are friendlies."

"It's a good bet they're from the Texas Air National Guard. Lisa's father knows we're flying in. He probably sent them up to meet us. Just follow them on into Lackland. We'll have a welcoming committee unless I'm mistaken."

When the King Air finally taxied to a stop on runway #1 at Lackland Air Force Base, even Mako was surprised at their reception. He leaned over Bronc in the pilot's seat to get a better look out the side window and recognized Governor Throckmorton and his wife standing just beyond the crowd control barriers the ground crew had hastily thrown up around the airplane. The governor was surrounded by uniformed soldiers, and Mako guessed they were from the Texas National Guard. Why they were there, he couldn't imagine.

"Lisa, your father's here waiting for you," Mako called back to Lisa and her friend. Lisa still hadn't said a dozen words to him since he hauled her out of the van at the entrance to the *Rancho Vista del Mar*. She looked out of one of the King Air's passenger windows and Mako saw tears streaming down her face.

"Mako, what the hell is that?" Bronc said. He pointed to several cars waiting beyond the governor's contingent and a group of six men obviously armed and wearing DEA vests.

"I thought we had a deal," said Bronc. He still hadn't killed the King Air turboprops. "Tell me now if we don't, you sonofabitch, and I'm out of here."

"We do, Bronc. I don't know what's up here, but I'll take care of it."

"That's reassuring, Mako," said Bronc, lighting a leftover roach. "I always thought you looked like a narc."

"I'd wish you'd give that a rest," said Mako with a frown, pointing to the joint. "This isn't exactly the time." He loaded a magazine in his M4, shouldered the weapon, and made for the exit door, ducking his head.

"You're lucky I'm stoned, Sloane. I might be pissed off otherwise," Bronc said.

Mako opened the door to the King Air and looked out at the unexpected welcoming committee.

"Throckmorton!" he yelled. "We had a deal. What's the DEA doing here?"

One of the DEA agents walked forward holding up his badge. "We're here to arrest Bronc Thornton," he yelled over the roar of the King Air turboprops. "We've got no interest in you, Sloane. Put your weapon down!"

"Like hell, you are!" called out the governor of Texas. "You're on Texas soil, and you are subject to our laws!" the governor said emphatically. "Put away your badge. You're not arresting anyone here today."

"This is a United States airbase, and we have jurisdiction," countered the DEA agent. "You can be charged with obstruction of justice, governor!"

"Major, disarm these men and taken them into custody," commanded the governor as the National Guardsmen shouldered their assault rifles and moved menacingly towards the federal agents.

"You haven't heard the last of this, governor!" shouted the DEA agent threateningly.

"I hope you have permits for those weapons," countered the governor. "Bronc Thornton has been pardoned by the president of the United States, and you are exceeding your authority."

"We'll see about that!" mumbled the agent as the National Guardsmen disarmed and handcuffed him along with his colleagues. Mako saw the federal agents herded into a Humvee on the tarmac not far from Bronc's King Air.

"Where's my daughter?" shouted Rick Throckmorton.

Bronc Thornton killed the King Air engines and reached for an ice cold Modelo Especial in the ice chest behind the pilot's seat.

"Consuela," he called out to his wife in the rear of the aircraft. "*¡Bienvenida a Tejas!* We're home!"

CHAPTER 34

At first Rodrigo thought he heard gunfire coming from the direction of the Nueces River. He and Alba lay together on a blanket on top of the square bales in the hay barn, shreds of dried grass sticking through the blanket and scratching their bare skin. It was hot, and their naked bodies glistened with perspiration and itched from the hay.

"Don't tell me they're fighting again!" exclaimed Alba in Spanish, sitting up with alarm and cocking her head and listening. "I feel like this is the beginning of a war, just like in the movies."

"No, those aren't guns, Alba. Those are firecrackers. Sounds like they're celebrating," he decided. "I can tell the difference."

"Well, I better get back to the house. The fireworks probably woke up my parents too," Alba said worriedly. "We can't let my father find us out here." She kissed Rodrigo and started to slip her clothes back on.

Rodrigo watched her admiringly in the dim light as she slipped a t-shirt over her naked torso. He could just barely make out the outline of her breasts as they disappeared under her clothing. Rodrigo had been in love with Alba since the first time he laid eyes on her. He almost knocked her down when he and Mario ran around the corner of the barn, desperately dragging a hose from the well to put out the fire the R.A.T.S. patrol started. It seemed like half a lifetime ago, instead of a few months.

***

Alba tip-toed up the steps to the house just as the lights in the living room came on. When Creed and Guadalupe came out on the front porch into the stifling air, they found Alba already there, looking off to the northeast where brilliantly colored fireballs shot high into the dark sky and burst into descending petals of colored light like a psychedelic rain shower. They heard an occasional boom and the *rat-tat-tat* of firecrackers exploding.

"What are you doing out here at this hour, Alba?" asked Creed.

"I heard the fireworks and thought they were shooting again," she replied. "I was scared."

"That's strange. I was drinking coffee in the kitchen… couldn't get to sleep. I didn't even hear you get up," he said. Creed brought his ceramic coffee cup to his lips and peered at his daughter, the question on his lips unspoken but obvious.

Alba felt a lump in her throat. The hair on the back of her neck stood up and she felt a tightening in her scalp as she sensed her father's intense scrutiny. Or was it just her imagination? She looked over to her mother for help, but Guadalupe stood watching the fireworks and pretended she wasn't listening to the conversation.

"I thought you were asleep and I didn't want to wake you. I tiptoed through the house," Alba lied. "I guess I didn't notice the light in the kitchen."

She could feel the blood rising to her face and she felt suddenly hot and flushed and she knew it wasn't from the heat of the warm humid night air. Her lie was altogether too transparent and she knew her father wasn't buying it. Alba saw Creed staring at her, and she knew her strained voice betrayed her and she couldn't bring herself to look at him. She glanced at a few shreds of dried hay clinging to the damp cotton of her t-shirt and knew her father had seen them too.

She might as well just blurt it out, "I've been having sex with Rodrigo in the barn!"

"And the straw on the back of your shirt, young lady?" Creed asked. "What have you been up to? And where the hell's Rodrigo?" he added and squinted and looked towards the barn and bunkhouse which remained shrouded in darkness. The blackness outside swallowed whole the narrow beam of light from the porch lamp, and its hazy radiance made little impression on the night.

"Creed, *basta!*" said Guadalupe as she stepped between father and daughter and took Creed's hands in her own. "Alba is old enough to make her own decisions. She's a grown woman now if you haven't noticed!"

"Yeah, that's what I'm worried about. Now where is that damn wetback? He and I are about to have a conversation." Creed's voice was strained and Alba saw that he was struggling to keep his temper in check, usually a losing proposition.

Creed freed his hands from Guadalupe's insistent grip and stormed off the porch, almost running down the creaking wooden steps. He headed at a brisk walk across the courtyard towards the bunkhouse, its outline looming in the faint moonlight that unexpectedly filtered through a broken cloud cover and illuminated the outbuildings for a brief moment.

"Rodrigo!" he shouted.

"Momma, stop him!" pleaded Alba.

"Creed, don't you lose your temper!" Guadalupe warned but she could do little more than hug Alba who by this time was crying inconsolably, her body convulsed with sobs and collapsing in her mother's arms. "You were young once too, don't forget!" Guadalupe called out to her husband.

Alba tried to break away from Guadalupe's embrace, but her mother held her tightly from behind and refused to let her run to join Rodrigo. Alba knew that her presence would infuriate her father even more but she wanted to protect Rodrigo. Guadalupe took her daughter by both elbows and forced her back into the house.

"*Está bien, Alba. No te preocupes,*" she said. Alba knew she didn't mean it.

***

Creed reached the bunkhouse. No lights were on and there was no sign of life from within. He stopped to catch his breath. Creed knew he should turn around and return to the house. There would be time enough to speak with Rodrigo tomorrow after he calmed down. But what Creed knew he should do was a theoretical, almost abstract concept with only the vaguest link to reality. He could have no more postponed this conversation than he could have commanded the tides to submit to his will. He pounded on the door with this fist.

"Rodrigo!" he shouted. "Where the hell are you?" Creed cupped his hands around his eyes and peered into the two dusty rectangular windows of the front door to the bunkhouse.

"*Aquí estoy, señor.*" Creed heard a soft voice almost at his side and turned to see Rodrigo standing before him, fully dressed with his western hat held in front of him at belt level.

"You ungrateful, backstabbing wetback!" shouted Creed and grabbed Rodrigo by the front of his shirt.

Rodrigo offered no resistance as Creed shook the smaller man like a leaf and backhanded him once hard across the mouth with his left hand. Rodrigo stumbled but regained his footing and approached Creed quietly. He stood directly in front of Creed, looking at him almost serenely and wiping a thin stream of blood from the corner of his mouth with his sleeve.

"*La amo, señor,*" he said.

"Love?" almost shouted Creed. "You bastard!"

This time Creed hit Rodrigo with his fist and Rodrigo fell to the ground and stayed down for a few moments before forcing himself to rise again and stand once more in front of Creed, unsteady and swaying slightly. He made no effort to defend himself and didn't say a word.

"I take you into this house and give you a job and you sneak behind my back and take up with my daughter," said Creed as he grabbed Rodrigo by the shirt yet again.

"*Voy a casarme con ella,*" said Rodrigo. He refused to bow his head or apologize.

"You'll marry her over my dead body," said Creed through his teeth and pushed Rodrigo roughly away. He turned abruptly on his heels and walked back towards the house, his hands trembling.

As Creed got closer to the house, he saw the Dalton and Morales families walking up from the guest house. The fireworks had woken them up too.

"You might as well come on in," called out Creed. "Let's turn on the television and see how bad the news is."

His rapid breathing gradually subsided as he climbed the stairs to the porch and held the door open for his visitors. Creed's legendary temper was usually a short-lived phenomenon, and he had already begun to feel a little sheepish about his outburst. Rodrigo was a damn good ranch hand, and he knew his daughter could do far worse. He'd have to eat some crow tomorrow and have a talk with both of them. That wasn't going to be easy, but Guadalupe was right as usual.

Creed entered the house and looked for Guadalupe, intending to get the first apology out of the way. He was feeling worse with each passing minute, but Guadalupe and Alba were in the back of the house in Alba's bedroom, and they wouldn't even answer Creed's knock on their door. He hated the silent treatment, but the apologies would have to wait until tomorrow, he guessed.

CNN was in crisis mode, broadcasting live from Cotulla and interviewing anyone who had the slightest connection to South Texas. Both the governor of Texas and the president of the United States, though, were conspicuously absent.

"Shhhhh! Here he is!" said Jamie Dalton as the familiar round face of Bubba Dobbs appeared on the screen.

"Folks, we're back reporting live from Cotulla, an unlikely venue for what I can only describe as the most momentous day in United States history since the bombardment of Fort Sumter, South Carolina by Confederate forces in 1861. And, speaking of South Carolina, in a few minutes I will be speaking with Vice President Archibald Rutledge, who has ignored the warnings of his own security advisors to be with us today."

"That sonofabitch has a knack for getting people riled up, doesn't he?" observed Creed.

"So the governor backed down. What now?" wondered Jamie Dalton out loud.

"Your guess is as good as mine," said Creed. "I wish James Brazzle was here. I always like to hear his opinion."

"Where is James, anyway?" asked Dalton.

"He and Drake Herrin are up in San Antonio picking up that Mako Sloane fellow. From what I hear, Mako brought the governor's daughter back from Mexico...minus one finger."

"Holy Shit!" said Jamie Dalton.

"The news is back on," said Creed. "Let's listen."

"We expect the National Front for the Liberation of Texas to call for a referendum on autonomy for the southern counties along the Mexican border. The Organization of American States has already recognized the National Front as the de facto government in South Texas, and I believe that most of the countries of the world which are inimical to democracy and liberty and the American way of life will follow suit by morning. In my opinion, today represents a dark day in our history. A criminally incompetent administration in Washington has failed to secure our borders, and as a result we are witnessing the Mexicanization of the United States. In other words, the contagium of a failed state has now legally crossed our national border."

"Jesus, I didn't realize it was that bad!" Creed said. "Old Bubba sometimes takes it too far, doesn't he?"

"In my view we can expect to see the same kind of movements in New Mexico, Arizona, and California. This is nothing more or less than the implementation of the Plan of Aztlan, the reconquest of the southwest United States by Mexico."

"Whew, the man has been smoking some powerful shit," exclaimed Jamie Dalton.

"He's just as bad as the National Front people," said Guadalupe who had come into the living room and joined the guests crowding around the television.

"One bright spot in this crisis is a voice of reason in South Texas who has acquired a reputation for common sense and moderation, a unifying force between Hispanics and Anglos. I'm talking about Creed Tucker, a La Salle County rancher who has stood up to the cartel but seeks integration rather than separation. We expect to hear more from Mr. Tucker in the future."

Nobody in the living room said a word. Creed looked around the room in disbelief. The others stared at him as if they were seeing him for the first time.

"Did I just hear that right?" asked Jamie.

"*¡Creed, están hablando de ti!*" said Guadalupe. "Too bad

he couldn't have seen you a few minutes ago. Unifying force, ha!"

"I'll talk to them both tomorrow, Lupe," Creed replied. "I was wrong."

The rest of the visitors look at both Creed and Guadalupe with curiosity but had the good sense to stay out of what they knew was a family issue.

"I didn't realize we were sitting in the same room with a genuine celebrity," said Jamie Dalton.

"How the hell does Bubba Dobbs know anything about me?" Creed asked. "But forget about me for a minute. Here comes the vice president," added Creed.

"Ladies and gentlemen, we're back with Vice President Archibald Rutledge, a former senator from the state of South Carolina, who just happens to have received his education at the University of Texas in Austin. Welcome to the program, Mr. Vice President."

"Thanks, Bubba," said the vice president. "I'm proud to be a guest on your show."

"And what is the administration's view on the crisis, Mr. Vice President? The silence from Washington has been deafening."

"Well, Lou, as a tenth generation South Carolinian and a former senator from that great state, I am particularly sensitive to the issue of states' rights as you can imagine. The president and I sometimes diverge on issues involving the extent of federal authority, I must tell you. But we're really not talking about South Texas seceding from the Union. This is not a repetition of 1861. This is a crisis involving complex internal legal issues of the state of Texas. Legal minds far more competent than yours or mine have decided that holding a referendum on autonomy for South Texas would comply fully with the tenants of the Texas Constitution. As Americans, we have to trust in democratic values and the wisdom of the electorate to decide such global issues as the right to self-determination. These are issues that cannot be decided by intimidation or force."

Bubba Dobbs face began to turn red and he looked almost apoplectic.

"Mr. Vice President," began Bubba as he stuttered and searched for words to adequately express his outrage at what he just heard.

"D-D-Democratic values?" he asked in shock. "Am I speaking with the vice-president of the United States? I think the American people would want to know what 'democratic values' have in common with a referendum on autonomy that the Mexican drug cartels are shoving down the throats of the citizens of South Texas at gun point!"

"I've seen enough." Creed looked around the room in disbelief and walked over to the television and turned it off. "Who's side is Rutledge on? The sonofabitch sounds like he's running for office. So does Bubba Dobbs for that matter. I think I need a drink."

CHAPTER 35

"Well, get a load of this, will you?" said Creed as his pickup crossed the Nueces River Bridge into Cotulla for breakfast at Angelina's. "Surprise, surprise."

Several trucks and a dozen cartel soldiers were manning the checkpoint at the bridge, but they waved Creed by without a challenge. James Brazzle sat beside Creed in the front, and Drake Herrin and Mako Sloane rode in the back seat of his extended cab pickup. *Norteña* music blared from a loudspeaker at the crossing, and one of the guards hurled a string of lit Black Cat firecrackers in the general direction of the white pickup truck with the Broken "T" Land & Cattle Company brand stenciled on each front door. Creed winced as the firecrackers exploded in an erratic volley.

"I wonder how long the bastards intend to celebrate," speculated James. "Most businesses in town have been closed for three days already."

"It's not every day that you make the governor of Texas and the National Guard back down," said Creed.

Creed braked and slowed down as they crossed the city limits. A red pickup full of young tattooed Mexicans, all wearing backwards R.A.T.S. baseball caps, raced by with its horn blaring. The passengers leaned out the truck waving their arms in jubilation, their fingers forming the traditional "V" for victory. The driver emptied an entire magazine as he fired his 9 mm into the air. A few pedestrians could be seen walking along the sidewalks in Cotulla. Several waved to the early morning revelers and shouted encouragement in Spanish, but most tried to ignore the R.A.T.S. soldiers and looked away as their pickup truck roared by.

Creed parked his truck in front of Angelina's and the four men started to climb out of the truck. The red pickup in the meantime had circled the block and approached Creed's truck at high speed before the driver slammed on his brakes and screeched to a stop about five yards away.

"Hey old man," the driver said to Creed in Spanish. "We know who you are."

The driver stepped menacingly out of his pickup, and four others jumped down from the back of the truck. Creed saw handguns protruding from the back of the cartel soldiers' baggy jeans under their t-shirts. They had been drinking, and one of them threw a beer bottle carelessly towards the four men.

"*Buenos dias, caballeros,* how can I help you this morning?" Creed said affably, staying within easy reach of his 12-gauge Mossberg, which he had wedged up against the driver's seat next to the door in the pickup. Out of the corner of his eye he saw that his three companions had appraised the situation correctly and also had their weapons close by.

"You can start by getting the fuck out of Cotulla," said the leader of the R.A.T.S. soldiers. "This is our town now." He was a tall, stocky man with a belly that refused to be covered by a mere t-shirt. His long goatee was sparse and scraggly, and he wore an expensive pair of ill-fitting sunglasses, which he had to adjust every few seconds as they fell down on his bulbous nose.

"Well now, let's look at that logically," said Creed, still smiling and staying close to his shotgun. He answered the R.A.T.S. soldier in Spanish. "Strictly speaking, we haven't had a referendum yet. But anyway, Cotulla is north of the Nueces River and would still be part of Texas no matter what the referendum decides. I can show you a map if you don't know Texas geography."

"Fuck your map, old man. You old bastards belong in a

home for senior citizens in San Antonio. Maybe you can play shuffleboard all day instead of shooting Mexicans. You need to get back in your truck and leave...now! We respect the memory of the Martyrs of Cotulla. No *gringos* on the streets of this town!"

Creed shouted, "Now!", and all four "senior citizens" threw down on the cartel soldiers with their 12-gauge Mossberg "Cruiser" model shotguns with short 18 ½ inch barrels for use in close quarters.

"On the ground, *cabrones!*" Creed shouted in Spanish. "*¡De rodilla!*"

"*Manos atrás de la cabeza,*" added James Brazzle menacingly.

The R.A.T.S. soldiers dropped immediately to the ground and put their hands behind their heads.

Drake Herrin went from solider to soldier, disarming each man and frisking him. Creed walked slowly over to their red pickup, cocked his shotgun, and calmly began to blow out each tire. Each deafening blast was followed by a loud hiss of escaping air as the pickup slumped further towards the ground with each shot.

"*¡Idiota! Lo vas a arrepentir!*" shouted the leader of the Mexican thugs.

Mako walked over to him nonchalantly and slammed the butt of his Mossberg into the man's jaw. The cartel soldier collapsed to the ground without a further word, blood oozing from the corner of his mouth. His companions stared at Mako in shock.

Sloane turned to the rest of them and said in perfect Spanish, "Give my regards to *El Padrino*. Tell him you ran into Mako Sloane. Now take off your shoes and socks!"

In disbelief the R.A.T.S. soldiers hurriedly took off their Chinese-made Nike and Adidas knockoffs, fumbling at their shoe laces and glancing fearfully up at Mako.

"Now get out of here, *hijos de la chingada,*" Mako said.

The Mexicans picked up their still groggy leader and double-timed it down the street, half-dragging and half-carrying the overweight thug, occasionally hopping on one foot and cursing in pain from the burning asphalt.

Creed looked at Mako as if seeing him for the first time.

"Jesus, Mako, I like your style. Now I know how you brought Lisa Throckmorton out of Mexico alive."

"Let's eat breakfast," replied Mako. "You say Angelina has good *chilaquiles?*"

***

That afternoon the four men sat in the shade under a large mesquite tree between the Broken "T" Land & Cattle Company ranch house and the round pen where Rodrigo trained horses each morning before it got too hot to work the young colts. A blue and white ice chest stood under a round iron table painted green. Creed had welded old John Deere tractor seats on to metal posts buried in the ground, creating rustic, though uncomfortable chairs which he arranged in a circle around the table. A persistent breeze from the southwest blew hot and dry on the men's faces, but they preferred to sit under the tree in the open air rather than breathe the cool air-conditioning in the house.

Creed reached in the cooler which contained several different kinds of Mexican beer in addition to a few native Texas brews. He pulled out a can of Lone Star.

"I used to be mighty partial to Mexican beer. I still prefer it, to tell the truth, but now I think it's almost treasonous to drink anything other than Lone Star or Shiner," said Creed.

"Not me," said James Brazzle and reached in the cooler for a Modelo Especial and leveraged off the bottle cap with the flat blade of his Swiss Army knife.

"Mako," why'd you knock out that gangbanger today in Cotulla?" Creed turned serious and looked at Mako with curiosity.

"It's purely psychological, really," replied Mako. "Those cartel gunmen are ruthless, but they're not particularly brave unless they're in a group. That's why they joined the R.A.T.S. army. It's just another gang to them. But if they think you're crazier or more violent than they are, you'll have the advantage. They respect extremism even if it comes from the other side."

Creed nodded his head in agreement.

"It seems that extremism's all we've seen recently," he said.

"You haven't seen anything yet, I'm afraid," said Drake Herrin. He looked tired and drained as if the drama of the past few weeks had drained him. He was pale and his face looked gaunt in the harsh shadows of the mesquite tree.

"You know something we don't?" asked Creed.

"I might," said Drake and looked at the others as if he was trying to decide if they could be trusted with what he knew.

"Well, spit it out," said Creed. "We're on the front line of any future military action. I think we deserve to know."

"Politicians are craven sons o' bitches," Drake said as a preface.

The men sipped their beer slowly and watched him without saying anything. Nobody disagreed with Drake's preamble. They waited as he collected his thoughts.

"The president has run out of patience with Throckmorton. He's sending in III Corps from Fort Hood with air support from a squadron of A-10 Warthogs and Apache helicopters he's pre-positioned at Lackland Air Force Base. Gentlemen, the proverbial shit is about to hit the fan."

"I'd heard the rumors," said Creed. "Frankly, though, I didn't believe it. I don't think that's the right decision. There's nothing that will get Texans riled up more than interference by Washington in their affairs. It'll piss Throckmorton off too. This could get out of hand and be worse than the damned referendum!"

"Throckmorton's beating his chest and saying he's going to block their way with the National Guard," said Drake.

"Yeah, I like that," laughed Creed. "A few third-world thugs make the governor pull his troops back and now he wants to face III Corps? He's off his rocker!"

Creed stood up suddenly and looked east towards the horizon. The others followed his concerned gaze. Through the waves of heat rising from the brush and cactus along the long gravel road that led to I-35, they could see a faint but large cloud of dust that was rapidly moving towards them.

"Lupe, call Scrap and Matlock in from the barn, please. Tell them to bring their weapons. Find Rodrigo and tell him the same thing. Let's move. It looks like we may have company, a lot of company," said Creed.

The four men reached down beside their chairs for their weapons. They instinctively took up positions behind cover with clear fields of fire. Scrap and Matlock came running up with assault rifles and Rodrigo carried a deer rifle.

"You three get behind those round bales by the barn. Stay out of sight unless there's shooting. I want you to be a surprise for whoever's coming," instructed Creed.

Guadalupe went back into the house. James Brazzle threw down the rest of his Modelo Especial and turned to Mako Sloane.

"This wasn't exactly what you signed up for, was it Mako?"

"The job description *was* a little vague," replied Mako. He took up his position behind an old Ford pickup and waited.

As the cloud of dust grew closer, the men could see a caravan of pickup trucks weaving its way towards ranch headquarters. Creed counted at least fifteen trucks, and he could see men crowded in the back of each truck. He estimated they would be facing at least fifty to sixty cartel soldiers. Guadalupe ran back out of the house, carrying extra boxes of ammunition. She carried a Remington 30.06 and crouched down beside her husband behind their old white pickup.

"Lupe, get back in the house right now," Creed hissed in Spanish.

"Too late, *mi amor*," she answered. "Looks like I'll have to stay here with you."

"Where's Alba?" he asked.

"Over with Rodrigo, I imagine," she said.

"Keep your head down, Lupe," said Creed quietly. "These are not good people."

The lead pickup truck stopped about twenty yards from Creed's position. Scrap, Matlock, and Rodrigo were now behind the enemy and separated from the rest of the men by the entire caravan of trucks. The driver's door opened, and an older Mexican, wearing a cowboy hat pulled down over his eyes and dusty boots with spurs, stepped out. He stretched, took off his hat, and wiped his brow.

"Creed, *no seas pendejo*. Come out from behind there. I see you crouching there thinking you're Davy Crockett or someone like that."

Creed stood up as he recognized the old *vaquero*. "Is that you, Lolo? What the hell are you doing here and who are all those people with you?"

"These are my friends, Creed. We're all Mexican-Americans. There are people here from Laredo, Zapata, Brownsville, Alice, Kingsville. We're all from South Texas, but in a week or so we might be saying the 'Autonomous Republic of South Texas' unless we do something about it."

"Yeah, so I heard," Creed said, still wondering what Lolo Gonzalez was doing on the Broken "T".

"Creed, most of us Hispanics here in South Texas are hard-working, honest citizens of the United States. The National Front is driving a wedge between us and the Anglos. We can't let that continue."

"Lolo, I agree."

"That's why we're here, my friend. We want you to lead us. Help us stop this referendum. But if there is a referendum and the National Front wins, we want you to run for president."

"What?" asked Creed. "You can't be serious!"

James Brazzle walked out from behind his pickup truck.

"President Creed Tucker! Now I've heard everything. Might as well make Koot secretary of defense while you're at it."

CHAPTER 36

"Whose brilliant idea was this anyway?" asked PFC Alfredo Jimenez as he strolled through the front line dispositions of Company B with his squad leader. A stray yellow dog wandered down the line after them, hobbling on three legs. Her ribs showed clearly through a mangy coat of matted hair. She tucked her tail between her hind legs and glanced furtively at the young men, ready to either dodge a rock or accept a crumb offered in pity. The sudden appearance of the 36th Infantry Division in her neck of the woods was an unexpected opportunity for some caloric largess. It might even keep her alive until the weather cooled off.

"Since when is a half-ass roadblock across Interstate 35 in Dilley, Texas, with a couple of rusting Humvees from the Texas National Guard, going to stop III Corps when it comes storming out of Fort Hood?" Jimenez spat on the ground in disgust and looked at his squad leader for affirmation.

"Why're you asking me?" answered Sergeant First Class Juan Quintero. "I'm on your side. I hear the regular army's going to throw the damned Seventh Cavalry Regiment against us. Shouldn't take long to break through these lines, should it? Hell, I'd rather be back in Afghanistan."

PFC Jimenez was glad to have a sympathetic ear. He was scared. As a matter of fact, most of the guardsmen were scared. They all had jobs and families back home. That's where they were supposed to be. Since when was it the mission of the Texas National Guard to fight the U.S. Army, and what chance in hell did they have when you came right down to it?

"The Seventh Cavalry Regiment? That's Custer's old unit.

They're probably going to treat us like the Sioux and Cheyenne after Little Big Horn; maybe even put us on a reservation just for Mexicans. Maybe we'll get to open a casino, eh? I think I'd like to deal blackjack."

"Maybe," said Sergeant First Class Quintero. "I wouldn't put it past them, would you? We're nothing to the Anglos, even when we're bleeding for them in their own wars. My father said it was like that in Vietnam too. *¡Carajo!*" The sergeant kicked a rock with his hot-weather combat boots.

The enlisted men in the company heard the sound of diesel engines and looked up to see trucks approaching from the north along I-35, bringing in more National Guard infantrymen. The young soldiers, mostly Latinos, jumped out of the trucks one by one and lined up in formation waiting for orders. Their Anglo company commander gathered the platoon leaders together and briefed them on their mission.

"What kind of war is this supposed to be anyway?" PFC Jimenez continued to grumble. "Texans versus other Americans! A lot of those boys in the Seventh Cav are from Texas too. You know they are! I can't believe they'd fight us."

PFC Jimenez opened the wrapping to a beef burrito from the Gonzales Taco Stand. The tacos were taking the place of ready-to-eat meals during the first days of the Guard's latest deployment in South Texas. The Dilley fast food restaurant owners were some of the few local inhabitants who appreciated the presence of the Texas National Guard in their vicinity. The prospect of a miniature Civil War was doing wonders for business even though three days of Mexican fast food had given most of the soldiers the shits.

"That *pinche* Governor Throckmorton must be out of his mind. First, he says we're going to kick ass all the way to the Rio Grande, and so we rush down to the Nueces River. Then, a helicopter gets shot down, and we blow away some *narcotraficantes.* So, what does he do? He retreats! And now he wants us to stop the U.S. Army from interfering in Texas' internal affairs?" PFC Jimenez threw up his arms theatrically. "I got nothing else to say."

A single shot rang out in the distance, and everyone crouched down instinctively, looking around wildly for the source of the shooting. The yellow dog opportunistically grabbed a soft-shelled beef taco in her mouth and scooted out of harm's way, lying down at the base of a prickly pear cactus to enjoy the spoils of war.

"Now what?" said Sergeant Quintero, as something caught his eye to the south along I-35 at the roadblock his men had thrown up hastily just north of the Gulley Ford Tractor dealership. He heard excited shouting in both English and Spanish coming from a crowd of people and several vehicles in front of the checkpoint. He hurried towards the commotion, loading and locking a full magazine in his M4 just in case.

As he approached the confused scene, he saw a group of civilians armed with assault rifles and shotguns confronting his own men. Neither group seemed inclined to back down and the shouting grew louder and more insistent.

"Drop your weapons!" shouted a Latino corporal. Four guardsmen stood beside him with their weapons pointed at the group of civilians. Some of the civilians, a mixed group of Latinos and Anglos, had gotten out of their trucks while others remained inside. There were four trucks and at least three or four men in each truck.

"Where's your commanding officer? And don't point those guns at us. I doubt you even know how to use them!" The voice belonged to a tall Anglo in a cowboy hat who held an SKS assault rifle casually in his right hand pointed at the ground.

"What's going on here?" asked Sergeant Quintero as he walked over to the armed men. "Everybody calm down," he said.

"We want to speak with your commanding officer," repeated

the cowboy.

"Yeah, I heard you the first time. Talk to me first. I'm Sergeant First Class Juan Quintero. This is my squad. Men, put those weapons down," he ordered and turned back to the group of civilians. "State your business," he said crisply.

"My name's Matlock Tucker, and these men are all from the People's Army of South Texas, or at least that's what we're calling ourselves. We're all vets, and we don't like the idea of federal troops telling Texas what to do. We've come to help."

The young Tucker examined the small National Guard force and their shoddy defensive positions and snorted. "By the looks of it, you can use all the help you can get."

"By whose authority are you here?" asked the Sergeant First Class.

"By whose authority? Are you nuts? Did Buck Travis ask the Gonzalez reinforcements who authorized them to come to the aid of the Alamo? I've got one hundred more men at the Broken "T" Land & Cattle Company ranch waiting on a phone call from me for the okay to come to your assistance, sergeant. So get your head out of your ass and get your commanding officer over here."

***

"Rick, it's the president again," said Victoria as she stuck her head into the governor's office. Her face was pale as she delivered the message. "You've got to take his call. Nobody hangs up on the president like you did!"

"Alright, put him through, Vicky," replied Governor Throckmorton.

He sat back and stared at the blinking light on his phone. He knew his own political career was over. His indecisiveness in a crisis situation had surprised everyone, himself included. His own daughter had paid the price of his helplessness and had become one of the first victims of the conflict. She would have died if it hadn't been for Mako Sloane. And now he was about to oversee the breakup of Texas, and the president of the United States was personally calling to threaten him. How could it get any worse?

"I'm listening," said the governor, picking up the phone. He had closed the blinds to all the windows in his office and turned out the lights. An unopened bottle of Jose Cuervo Tequila Gold stood on his desk, beckoning. It was tempting. Alcohol had a way of masking the stench of his own problems. Like a sicky sweet aerosol. It usually worked: at least for an hour or so until his head started to ache.

"Rick," said the familiar voice. "I'm having trouble believing you're in complete possession of your faculties. How are impeachment proceedings against you moving along, by the way?"

"With all due respect, Mr. President, I could ask you the same question. You're threatening to send federal troops into South Texas against the wishes of the governor of Texas? You don't know much about us, do you, sir? And to answer your question: since I told you to go to hell on the national news, the impeachment motion has been withdrawn."

"All I know is that you've allowed a situation to get out of control and made this country a laughing-stock in the eyes of the world."

"Mr. President, we've had this conversation before; several times, in fact. If the federal government's drug and immigration policies hadn't allowed the Texas border to become a haven for the Mexican drug cartels, none of this would have happened! You're more concerned about giving driver's licenses to illegal aliens than making immigrants comply with the law and securing the border."

The governor reached for the tequila with his right hand, put the bottle between his legs and somehow managed to unscrew the bottle cap. He didn't bother with a glass. He drank straight from the bottle.

"That's obfuscation, pure and simple, Rick...hold on for just a minute, I've got Lieutenant General Buchanan on another line."

The governor heard a click and realized he was on hold.

Buchanan? he thought with a start, and he felt the little hairs on the back of his neck stand up straight. He reached for the tequila bottle and wet his lips again. Tommy Buchanan, the Commanding General of III Corps at Fort Hood! He heard another click and knew the president was back on the line.

"Rick?" he asked. "Sorry, I'll talk to the general after we get through. Now where were we?"

"I think you were accusing me of obfuscation, Mr. President," the governor reminded him.

"That's putting it mildly, governor. Do you know that your secretary of state is a person of interest in an FBI corruption investigation involving electoral fraud?"

"Lester?" asked the governor, his mouth agape. "Electoral fraud?" Governor Throckmorton was momentarily taken aback.

"Can that really surprise you, Rick? Didn't you ever wonder about the municipal elections back in March? Did you ever ask yourself how it was possible that the number of registered Hispanic voters increased by 50% over just a couple of months? Do I have to spell it out for you?"

The governor caught his breath and almost choked. His throat felt dry. He raised the bottle of tequila to take another swallow and poured most of it down the front of his denim shirt. He wiped his chin with the back of his bare hand and stared out into space. He felt the cool of the tequila as it soaked through his jeans onto his crotch. Since Lisa's return, he had started wearing jeans and cowboy boots to the governor's office. Somehow it made him feel more masculine and in control. He realized it was an illusion.

"Rick, are you there? This is not an issue of states' rights vs. federal rights. This is an issue of Texas refusing to clean up its own mess."

"I respectfully disagree, Mr. President. This is an issue of Texas having to clean up a mess created by the incompetence of the federal government. And you cannot intimidate us by the mention of Tommy Buchanan or any other U.S. Army commander."

"Don't be a fool, governor. There's still time to reconsider."

"Reconsider what? Let me give you a heads-up, Mr. President. I don't think you want to preside over the unfortunate precedent of federal troops firing on soldiers from the Texas National Guard."

"It'll be on your conscience, Rick. Think about it. You're about to give away South Texas to some nebulous political grouping, whose leader has never made a single public appearance. We don't even know who they are."

"My conscience? How dare you, Mr. President? Let me tell you something: civilians will come out in droves along with our own troops to meet Tommy Buchanan's III Corps. If you want to take South Texas, you'll be killing Texans to do it. How do you think that'll play on CNN and Fox News? You *were* hoping to get reelected, weren't you?"

CHAPTER 37

"After the referendum, the National Front will need to select a presidential candidate," stated Félix Aguilar emphatically. "He must be Hispanic, and he must be under our control."

"*Por supuesto,*" agreed Francisco Salcido. He had insisted on getting out of bed and sitting at his desk on the second floor of the ranch house despite the persistent pain in his leg. Fortunately, the Otis elevator he originally installed for his now deceased mother allowed him the mobility to use both floors of his elegant home. His stamina was still limited, and the post-operative pain he experienced sapped his strength. Francisco refused to accept any more morphine after the first twenty-four hours and wanted to be as alert as possible for both the conversation with the attorney general and the phone call he expected at any time. He raised the heavy cast on his leg with both hands, readjusting it to find the most comfortable position. He gasped with the unexpectedly sharp pain that shot all the way up to his hip.

"He must also have an impeccable record on corruption and can't be linked back to Mexico, especially to your organization, *carnal.*"

"Well, everyone knows the mayors of Brownsville and Laredo. That's why I suggested them as candidates," said Francisco. "They've taken orders from us for years. They're discreet, and we can trust them. If you don't like them, we've got a dozen more in our pocket. What more do you want?"

"That's the problem," laughed the attorney general. "They've been on our payroll too long. If the U.S. government ever forced the British Virgin Islands to reveal the names of North-Americans with offshore accounts in their banks, those two mayors would have a lot of explaining to do. So would a lot of other prominent people."

"You can't eliminate everyone who takes money from the cartel, Félix. Not many people work for us altruistically, do they?" he managed a smile despite his pain.

"Fortunately not. That kind tends to be a little too independent and self-righteous."

"Well, at any rate, we can only make suggestions. We don't have the final say. The head of the National Front will pick the candidate. It's his show after all, and he's supposed to call me this morning."

Francisco smiled to himself. He enjoyed mentioning the head of the National Front in the attorney general's presence. He knew Aguilar couldn't stomach the idea of sharing power with anyone, and he liked to yank his chain occasionally. But Francisco was impressed at the enormous political power in South Texas the anonymous leader of the National Front seemed to wield. He could orchestrate carefully choreographed political events, planned down to the minutest of details. He was like a Hollywood director with South Texas as his provincial stage. Most of the work was outsourced, though, and his labor pool was the Sinaloa cartel.

"So, who do you think he is?" asked the attorney general.

"I think he's a fucking genius, that's who. I don't need to know any more than that. I don't even know where he's from, Félix. He's not Mexican. I can tell you that, but not much more. He asks for money; I give it to him. He asks for people and weapons; I send them over in my trucks. In return, he's giving us the Autonomous Republic of South Texas, and soon the North Americans won't be talking about a 'porous' border anymore. It'll be leaking like a sieve. I'm just happy he chose me as his partner and not one of the other cartels."

Francisco heard the first faint bars of the Cochiloco *corrido* and then felt his cell phone vibrate. The call startled him and he banged his broken leg painfully under the desk.

"¡Cabrón!" he hissed, wincing as he answered his phone. "¡Bueno...si!"

The attorney general looked over at his friend who held the cell phone to his ear and listened attentively without saying a word. At one point in the conversation Francisco took out a pencil and paper and jotted down some figures in his notebook.

"I'll take care of that this afternoon," he said and then looked quizzically at the cell phone. "The *chingón* hung up without even saying goodbye. He does that every time," he stated as if his feelings were hurt. "Who does he think he's dealing with?"

The attorney general shook his head.

"I don't like it, Francisco. How can we take orders from someone we don't even know? I need to sit across the table from people I work with. I want to look them in the eye. Look right into their soul and see what they're made of."

"As long as Mr. "X" keeps his promises, I'm on his side."

"What did he want?" asked the attorney general.

"Five million dollars wired to this account." Francisco held up his notebook and showed the attorney general the bank coordinates for an account in Banco Azteca in Panama.

"Five million dollars? What the hell for?"

"For the electoral campaign of Rudy Gutierrez, the National Front's future candidate for president of the Autonomous Republic of South Texas...after we win the referendum. Looks like the issue was decided without consulting us."

"You mean that chicano who's minister of defense for the Front?"

"That's the one. He was born in the States and was a war hero in Vietnam. He also hates Anglos with a passion."

"I don't like it," the attorney general blurted out.

"*¿Por qué?*" asked Francisco. "He's got all the qualities you mentioned and then some."

"A war hero could get sanctimonious with us. He might have too much backbone," speculated the attorney general.

"Not like you and me," responded Francisco. "Is that what you're trying to say?"

"This broken leg has improved your sense of humor, I see."

Francisco eased himself out of his chair into the wheelchair that stood next to the desk. The attorney general hurried over to help.

"Any news on who might run against Gutierrez if we do win the referendum?" asked Aguilar.

"Yeah, there's talk a couple of Anglos might run. One of them is Lester Van Slyke, the secretary of state of Texas who helped us in the municipal elections in return for a small monthly retainer. You remember him, don't you? That'll probably split the white vote and make it more likely for Gutierrez to win," Francisco said looking at the attorney general. "Our friend thinks of everything: a real politician, didn't I tell you?"

"For five million dollars we *better* win the election," groused the attorney general.

"*Callate, buey,*" he said. "It's not your money."

***

"Scrap, you and Rodrigo are in charge of the ranch while I'm down in Brownsville. I'm going to do an interview with Bubba Dobbs on the referendum," announced Creed at breakfast. He hated to leave the fate of his beloved tiger stripe cattle in someone else's hands even though Scrap had worked cattle since he was in elementary school and knew the business as well as his father. He hated even worse to leave Guadalupe and Alba at the ranch while he was off politicking. The Nueces Strip had become about as lawless as the Mexican state of Sinaloa, and there were people out there who'd love to do his family harm.

"What about Matlock?" he asked. "Where's he going to be?"

"Matlock's one of the commanders of this motley crew they're calling the People's Army of South Texas. A bunch of trigger-happy veterans if you want to know my opinion. I think Matlock misses Afghanistan. Either that or he has a death wish," replied Creed, taking a bite of a large flour tortilla filled with *huevos rancheros* and hot sauce.

"Where are your partners in crime, by the way?" asked Scrap.

"You mean Mako and James?" he asked.

Scrap nodded his head and took a swig of Guadalupe's fresh orange juice.

"They should be here any minute. James is coming with me to Brownsville and so is Mako if he gets back on time. That old spook is on his cell phone all day, and then he slips across the border into Mexico at night and doesn't come back till after dawn. Bronc Thornton should be back any day too. What a group that'll be!"

"Lupe, thanks for the breakfast. It was delicious as always," said Scrap as he got up to leave, kissing his stepmother on the cheek. "Where's my sister?" he asked.

"Where do you *think* she is, *mi amor*?" she answered cryptically, glancing over at her husband. "Find Rodrigo, and you just might find your sister too."

"What are you trying to say, Lupe?" asked Creed and he

winked at his wife. "I hope you're keeping an eye on those two."

Creed's talk with Alba and Rodrigo had been tense but in the end he reluctantly given his blessing to their relationship... with a few caveats, of course.

"What's the matter, Creed?" said Guadalupe. "Don't want another Mexican in the family?" she asked.

"Is there something going on I should know about?" asked Scrap suspiciously.

"Don't worry about it, son. You just make damn sure our people patrol the fence line on the east side of the ranch while I'm gone. I'm depending on you to take care of security on top of everything else. With me out campaigning against the referendum and gone half the time, this family's more of a target than ever."

"We'll do the best we can, but we need more men to cover all that ground," said Scrap.

"You'll have to get by with what you've got. Good men are in short supply these days."

Scrap stood at the door looking at his father.

"We need to stop this referendum, Dad. South Texas needs a little common sense. We're sure not getting any from the National Front or Governor Throckmorton."

"South Texas needs something; that's for sure. I just don't know what the hell it is."

CHAPTER 38

"This is Bubba Dobbs for CNN with La Salle County rancher Creed Tucker in Brownsville, Texas. Creed, thanks for taking time out of your busy schedule to speak with us about the referendum today."

"Bubba, I'm a long-time fan of yours. It's good to be here."

"Well, if you're a long-time fan, you know I don't beat around the bush with my questions, so let me start with the obvious one. The vast majority of the citizens of South Texas are Hispanic, and an awful lot of them appear to support the National Front. What makes you think you have a chance in hell of convincing them that a referendum on autonomy is a bad idea?"

"You do get right to the point, don't you?" replied Creed.

"It's just that when I look at you, I see a lily-white cattle rancher who probably exploited undocumented immigrants most of his life. Aren't you just about the last person that either the United States federal government or the National Front with their Hispanic supporters here in South Texas wants to represent their interests?"

"Well, Bubba, don't you think you're being a little hard on an old man?" replied Creed, biting his tongue and trying to look congenial. "To begin with, down here it doesn't matter what the federal government thinks. We manage our own affairs. Always have even before all this talk about a referendum. But I did earn a Silver Star and two Purple Hearts for the U.S. government a few years back. I doubt they'd be so ungrateful as to share in your unkind characterization of me."

"Now Creed, I didn't mean anything personal. I'm a

journalist, just trying to get to the bottom of a complicated story."

"Secondly, Bubba, this referendum isn't about Hispanics vs. Anglos. It's about what's best for all of us. And so what if I've employed undocumented immigrants on my ranch? There weren't any Anglos lining up to fill out job applications at the time. I don't apologize for that."

"There've been plenty of political candidates and appointees who've had to resign just because of that," said Bubba.

"Not me, Bubba. It'll be a cold day in hell before you find me marching in step with this political correctness crap. Mexican manual labor has carried the Southwest on its shoulders for generations. It's been a symbiotic relationship, and maybe it's time to end the hypocrisy. I understand that's an unpopular point of view today in your circles, but that's my opinion."

Creed leaned back and spit a stream of foul-smelling brown liquid into a Dixie cup. He preferred the taste of Red Man to coffee and didn't seem to notice the amusement of the camera crews when he placed a pinch of the leaf tobacco in his mouth before the interview began.

"By the way, Bubba, were you ever in the service? Did you ever put on a uniform for your country?" asked Creed.

"I'll have you know I had a student deferment and wasn't called to serve. But I've used my education…"

"Yeah, your education. That's all I need to know, Bubba," Creed interrupted. "Thanks for your candor. I know who I'm talking to now: another rabble-rousing conservative arm chair warrior. I've had my fill of your type in the media and in Washington."

"Now hold on, Creed!" Bubba didn't get a chance to finish his sentence.

Creed glanced towards the studio window in time to see a disembodied arm appear out of the murky semi-darkness of the small guest auditorium, pointing what appeared to be a handgun in Creed's general direction. The discharge came a fraction of a second later, and it was earsplitting in the confined quarters of the studio and continued to reverberate long after the shot rang out.

The shooter fired a 9 mm round from his Baretta 92S-1 at a muzzle velocity of over 1,000 feet per second. The bullet shattered the soundproof glass window separating the KRGV television studios from the tour group which had arrived to view the airing of the Bubba Dobbs Show on CNN. Creed was momentarily stunned by the noise and splintering glass but then dove instinctively for the cover of the leather chairs the men had been sitting in.

Out of the corner of one eye, Creed saw Bubba Dobbs fall to the floor, a bright red splotch of blood appearing on his starched white shirt between his neck and shoulder. At the same time Creed heard multiple cracks of small arms fire and saw Mako Sloane and James Brazzle both firing their handguns at Bubba's attacker, a well-dressed young Hispanic man dressed in a conservative navy blue suit and tie. Four rounds fired at almost point blank range threw the body of the attacker into what remained of the glass barrier. His body crashed through the weakened glass window and he came to rest lying face up, suspended over the wooden frame of the glass window like an upside-down letter "U".

The glass diverted the trajectory of the 9 mm round enough to save the life of Bubba Dobbs, who lay on the floor of the studio, bleeding profusely from the superficial, but painful wound in his left trapezius muscle. A few inches lower, and CNN would have had to find a replacement for the cantankerous old television host. Creed rushed to Bubba's side, ripping his shirt open to see how serious the injury was. There was a lot of blood, but he was relieved to see that the round passed through the muscle without hitting any major arteries or veins.

"I didn't mean to piss you off that much, Creed," said Bubba smiling weakly.

"Wait till you see what happens when I really get riled up," replied Creed, crumpling his sports jacket and placing it under Bubba's head for a pillow.

Creed insisted on accompanying Bubba to the Brownsville Medical Center. James and Mako rode with them in the ambulance, their weapons concealed in Serpa drop-leg holsters.

"You lost a lot of blood, Bubba, but you're way too ornery to die on us," said Creed. "Besides, you owe me a new shirt from the men's department of Walmart," he said, looking at his own blood-splotched shirt.

Bubba managed to raise his head slightly.

"As much as my ego would like to think I was the target of that assassination attempt, I think that boy shot the wrong man. They were trying to kill you, Creed."

***

Alba thought she felt familiar hands touch her hair and shoulders. She smiled to herself, half asleep, and stretched luxuriously like a cat being stroked. Then she opened her eyes with a start. Why was Rodrigo taking the risk of coming into her bedroom? Their rendezvous always took place in the hay barn after her parents were asleep. It was better that way; safer, especially now.

She saw the sinister silhouettes of several figures standing around her bed in the opaque darkness, but before she could cry out, one of them rudely stuffed a balled-up handkerchief in her mouth and another bound her arms painfully behind her back. Two men lifted her out of bed, one holding up her neck and shoulders, and the other lifting her legs. The third walked ahead with a shotgun. She kicked her legs, struck out at her abductors, and received a hard slap across her face and a hissed warning for her efforts.

A fourth intruder was waiting on the front porch holding the kitchen screen door open as the other three carried Alba outside. Alba caught a glimpse of Koot lying on the front porch, twitching slightly and foaming at the mouth. The screen door closed silently and the wood planks of the porch barely creaked as the men carried their prize down the stairs and then rapidly strode across the front yard. The dark moonless sky did nothing to illuminate their path, and they tripped constantly over the uneven gravel road that led towards the interstate, cursing in shouted whispers.

A Ram pickup was waiting a hundred yards down the road, and the men carefully deposited Alba on the back seat between two other men who were waiting for her. Through terrified eyes, she saw that all the men were armed and wore backwards R.A.T.S. baseball caps. They smiled luridly at her, and she smelled alcohol on their rancid breath and their clothes stank of cigarette smoke. Someone started the pickup and drove slowly down the road without turning on the lights. The abduction had taken scarcely three minutes. Once the pickup reached the last cattle guard before the interstate, the driver sped up and turned right onto the access road heading south towards Laredo. It was still three hours till sunrise.

CHAPTER 39

"Mexican Standoff in South Texas," shouted the headlines of the *Houston Chronicle*.

The *Dallas Morning News* boasted, "Throckmorton Stands Up For Texas....Finally!"

The *San Antonio Express News*, though, spoke for most Texans when it asked succinctly, "What the F...?"

Elements of III Corp's Seventh Cavalry Regiment made the short hop from Ft. Hood over to I-35 and began to roll south down the interstate at first light. The national and state media had talked about nothing else for several days and the deployment was expected. Tens of thousands of Texans, Hispanic and Anglo alike, lined both sides of the highway in San Antonio to wave the Texas and Mexico flags, jeer, and throw rocks at the federal troops. A group of fifty to sixty women from the New Daughters of the Texas Revolution and the Hispanic *La Mujer* Women's Network blocked all south-bound lanes of the interstate at the I-10 exit towards Houston. Most of them had small children with them, and they sat in a long row with their children in their laps, blocking the freeway and singing "Solo le Pido a Dios" by Leon Gieco in Spanish and "We Shall Overcome" in English. They displayed a banner that spanned all four lanes of the highway that read, "DON'T MESS WITH TEXAS!"

The frustrated troops also encountered indignant protesters from the same militant women's organizations at the I-35 exit to Interstate 410, the beltway around San Antonio. On the south side of the I-410 interchange, a group of Latina women, dressed in desert camouflage fatigues, combat boots, and brown berets charged the Second Battalion Humvees and managed to throw several Molotov cocktails before they were arrested by military police and carted off.

Soldiers from the lead battalion had to physically remove the women from the interstate at each blockade. They carried the women and their children kicking and screaming out of the convoy's path while television cameras from both local and national news stations whirred and journalists recorded every controversial moment. Texas state and city law enforcement units were conspicuously absent as the federal troops moved through the city, and calls from Lieutenant Colonel Stanley Overstreet, commander of the Second Battalion, to the San Antonio police chief for assistance went unanswered. It was a field day for the press, and the Second Battalion's public affairs officer lost track of a number of his embedded journalists when they abandoned the convoy to interview the protesting women.

Many of the soldiers riding to confront the Texas National Guard were veterans of Iraq and Afghanistan, but the bewildering presence of so many "hostiles" along the highway, who also happened to be fellow citizens, was disconcerting to say the least.

Specialist Johnny Rodriguez, a six-year veteran from Mission, Texas was a 19D, a Cavalry Scout. He drove the lead Humvee of the Second Battalion as the column of military transport trucks moved slowly in the direction of the Texas National Guard position north of Dilley, Texas. His longtime friend, "Chapo" Zavala, manned the M60 machine gun installed on the weapon mount of their M1043 configuration Humvee. Since the appearance of the surly welcoming committee in San Antonio, neither had said a word. It was one thing to be hissed and booed by a resentful and occupied foreign populace, but these were fellow Americans.

"Chapo, ¿qué coño está pasando aquí?" asked Johnny, shouting above the roar of the diesel engine. "Why are these people pissed? I thought they wanted our help! Isn't that what ol' General 'Tom' said?"

"Man, I guess 'Old Tom' knows Texas about as well as he knew Iraq. Remember how they were all supposed to welcome us there too? Shit, Johnny, there were mothers with babies in their arms yelling at us and throwing rocks back there in San Antonio! Did you see the Latinas in the brown berets? And this is Texas, bro!"

"I know, homes, something stinks here." As they approached the northern outskirts of Dilley, a sleepy interstate town of 3,500 souls, Specialist Rodriguez noticed movement ahead on the highway. He downshifted and slowed his Humvee, keying his helmet transmitter. "I see something up ahead blocking the interstate. Can't quite make it out, but I think I've got the National Guard force in sight," reported Rodriguez. "What are your orders?"

"Advance to within 1,000 yards of the enemy line, stop your vehicle, and await further orders," came the answer from the Second Battalion communications officer. "Do not open fire."

"Roger that...do not open fire."

Rodriguez clicked off his microphone and obediently slowed and then stopped his Humvee, waiting for further instructions. He and Chapo sat in a choking cloud of diesel fumes, looking across an expanse of burning highway at an indistinguishable mob of Texas National Guard soldiers and civilians. The temperature hovered around 101°, and there wasn't a hint of a breeze in the air to provide relief.

Johnny raised the binoculars to his eyes for a better look. Shimmering heat waves rising from the asphalt in the distance created a ghostlike spectacle that sent chills down his back. The entire Texas front line drifted in and out of focus, distorted by the rising hot air. Johnny caught his breath. He turned to Chapo and simply said, "You're not going to believe this shit." His voice trembled slightly. The day had begun badly and was getting worse.

As far as he could make out to the south and for a quarter mile on either side of the highway, Specialist Rodriguez saw massed throngs of defenders, some in uniform, entrenched behind sandbagged bunkers, but mostly armed civilians in cowboy hats and baseball caps standing behind pickup trucks and SUVs and waving their weapons defiantly: thousands of them. They appeared, disappeared, and transformed eerily on the blurred horizon like a phantom horde out of someone's nightmare.

As he stared in disbelief, two huge flags were unfurled slowly to a bellicose roar that slowly increased in volume until the two banners were waving in a belligerent challenge. The voices of thousands of reluctant warriors thundered across the barren brush country. Johnny recognized the Texas and Mexico flags, which came as no surprise. From their enormous size, Johnny surmised the rebels had borrowed the flags from local car dealers.

A horseman in a coonskin cap galloped erratically back and forth in front of the warlike host, waving what appeared to be a sword of some kind. A chant began faintly and gained in decibels until it clearly could be heard over the roar of the dozens of diesel engines behind Specialist Rodriguez' Humvee. The sound lagged behind the upward thrusts of the horseman's sword, but Johnny realized he was egging the mob on: a martial cheerleader rousing the rabble for the upcoming melee.

"Tex-as, Tex-as, Tex-as," came the chant, rumbling across the open plain.

Johnny couldn't see who started it, but he heard the single crack of a shot fired from a deer rifle, followed almost instantaneously by the firing of hundreds of rifles, both military and civilian. Johnny knew that the effective range of the National Guard M4s was only 500 or 600 yards, but some of those ranchers' deer rifles could reach them if the shooter got lucky. Stray bullets kicked up little bits of asphalt in the highway in front of them and plunked harmlessly in the dust on either side of the road.

"Those motherfuckers are crazy," said Johnny as he did a tight three-point turn with his Humvee and retreated out of range. The vehicles behind him were slower to react, and the resulting traffic jam sowed panic among the young soldiers as the occasional accurate, long-range shot pinged off the aluminum panels of the Humvees. Those closest to the Texan front line abandoned their vehicles and fled on foot to the chagrin of their commanding officers and noncoms who shouted futile orders for them to hold their positions. It was an embarrassing moment for the famed Seventh Cavalry Regiment, and thousands of Texas irregulars cheered with pugnacious delight as they saw the confused federal soldiers retreating on foot. The chanting continued non-stop.

***

"Tex-as, Tex-as, Tex-as!" Despite the distance that separated the two forces, the constant din was intimidating, and the soldiers of the Second Battalion exchanged nervous glances. After conferring with his company commanders, Lt. Colonel Stanley Overstreet hoisted a white flag in his command Humvee and drove slowly forward with his driver and two-man retinue of aides-de-camp.

The appearance of the Second Battalion's command Humvee under a flag of truce provoked a new round of cheering and chanting from the Texans. Many of the civilian irregulars had been drinking and refused to submit to anyone's command. In fact, the Texas front line far more resembled a confused mob than an organized fighting force.

"Tucker!" called the Texas National Guard commander, Colonel Ignacio Cruz, as he saw the approaching Humvee and white flag.

Matlock Tucker strolled casually over to the Colonel and saluted, almost in jest. "What's up, Iggy?" he asked.

"Nothing funny about this, Tucker," replied the Colonel, who five days before had been filling cavities and performing root canals at his dental clinic in Ft. Stockton, Texas. He didn't appreciate Matlock addressing him by a nickname that nobody had used with him since the two knew each other in Afghanistan.

"You seem to have some authority among these ranchers and South Texas trailer trash. Think you can get them to hold their fire? You might hint subtly that their lives depend on it," he suggested. Matlock commanded a contingent of over one hundred and twenty-five well-disciplined veterans, and he passed on the order to his men.

"Spread the word! Hold your fire!" Matlock's men double-timed it down the line in both directions with the order. The chanting continued as the Second Battalion command Humvee approached. It was deafening and Matlock had to raise his voice to make himself heard.

Colonel Cruz, accompanied by two National Guard company commanders and Matlock Tucker, walked towards the slow-moving Humvee which stopped five yards in front of them, belching black smoke. Lt. Colonel Overstreet got out slowly and approached them warily with his two aides-de-camp.

"Colonel," he said, addressing the commander of the Texas National Guard unit. "What is the meaning of this reception?" he asked, looking towards the Texas line. The chanting had subsided, but a low murmured roar continued like the pounding of the surf and the irregulars continued to wave their weapons menacingly. He stared in disbelief at the horseman in the coonskin hat who raced back and forth in front of the Texas line.

"Lieutenant Colonel," replied Colonel Cruz, emphasizing the word "lieutenant". "I must request that you turn your troops around and return to Ft. Hood. You are interfering in the internal affairs of the State of Texas. I have orders to resist if you try to continue your way south."

"Who issued your orders?" asked Lt. Colonel Overstreet, still staring in disbelief at the colorful sight in front of him.

The flag bearers had begun to march back and forth in front of the mob, waving the two flags frenetically to the incessant cheers of the ragtag multitude.

"I am acting at the direct order of the governor of Texas."

"My sympathies," said Lt. Colonel Overstreet.

"And who are you taking your orders from?" asked Colonel Cruz.

"From the president of the United States," replied Overstreet self-righteously.

"Well, I guess we're even then."

Lt. Colonel Overstreet looked towards the mob of defenders in front of him with contempt. "Do you know how much firepower I can call to bear if I give the order?" he asked.

"I know exactly how much, but let me ask you something. Do you want to go down in history as the commander who ordered his troops to open fire on the civilian defenders at Dilley, Texas?"

Cruz looked out at the endless line of Humvees and military transport trucks from Ft. Hood and tried to exude more confidence than he felt.

"Who are those civilians?" the Second Battalion commander asked pointing at the Texan line.

"Tell him, Matlock," said Colonel Cruz.

"Well, we've got my boys from the People's Army of South Texas..."

"The *what* Army?" Lt. Colonel Overstreet exclaimed.

"You heard me," Matlock retorted. The 'people' have had to take things into their own hands down here in South Texas because their governments have done nothing but talk. Besides us, there's also about four or five thousand regular folks who'd rather take care of their own affairs than have Washington tell them what to do. Every one of these men can shoot, and most have been in the military. The women too," Matlock added. "I believe we can make you sorry you came to visit us plain folk down here in South Texas."

"We'll see about that. In the meantime, control your men. If they fire upon our position again, we'll open up with everything we have. I'll be in touch."

The Lt. Colonel spun around on his heels and walked back to the Humvee. Colonel Cruz turned to Matlock and asked, "Now what do we do?"

"Wait for the cavalry to rescue us, I guess."

"We *are* the cavalry, Matlock!"

"Then pray," Matlock suggested.

CHAPTER 40

Matlock sat in his pickup truck on the left flank of the Texas line with his men from the People's Army of South Texas. The sun was approaching its zenith in the mid-day sky, and his troops were hot, irritable, and hungry. Most had been up since before dawn and had gone without breakfast to get to Dilley on time, coming from as far away as Rio Grande City, Brownsville, and South Padre Island. They didn't come to defend the referendum or to support the idea of an Autonomous Republic of South Texas. Most of them didn't want any part of that, but they sure didn't want Washington to decide the issue for them either.

There were practically no trees along the Texas front line, and the men strung up plastic tarps between trucks for shade. The sun was merciless, and the hot, uncomfortable morning turned into a torrid, unbearable afternoon. Matlock's men reluctantly took turns pulling guard duty, switching off with the National Guard soldiers. Most of the "independent" irregulars were still in a rowdy, hell-raising mood and couldn't be bothered with the more mundane tasks of soldiering. They seemed more concerned about keeping ice in their beer coolers and listening to the Houston Astros baseball game on their truck radios. As much as a confrontation with federal troops, the stand-off was a tailgating opportunity for the farmers and ranchers that made up the "irregular" contingent of the Texas line of defense.

George Strait's "Amarillo by Morning" blared from Matlock's car stereo. A group of middle-aged Hispanic ranchers three trucks down listened to Vicente Fernandez croon, *"¿De que manera te olvido?"* Matlock got out of the truck, opened the white Igloo ice chest in the bed of his Dodge Ram and removed an icy bottle of Dr. Pepper. He opened the bottle with a pocket knife and drank half of the bottle before coming up for air. It was getting hot.

Some of the men had gone into Dilley and brought back enough tacos and burritos to sicken an entire company of Texas irregulars. The fast food restaurants in Dilley were operating twenty-four hours a day and were starting to run out of ingredients. Food wholesalers in San Antonio were having a hard time keeping up with the demand, and the Gonzales Taco Stand and Dairy Queen in Dilley were running their own vans back and forth to the Alamo City in a veritable frenzy to keep the opposing armies supplied with junk food. The Second Battalion allowed the supply trucks to pass in return for first dibs on the hamburgers and tacos. The "standoff" was proving to be an economic bonanza for the local economy.

Colonel Cruz sauntered over to Matlock's sector of the line and motioned to him. The Colonel was wolfing down a hamburger and had a chocolate milkshake in one hand.

"Iggy, I'd stay away from those milkshakes if I were you," said Matlock. "I can just see that crap clogging up your arteries. Makes me sick to imagine what your insides look like."

"Give me a break, Matlock. I eat Mexican food three times a day at home, so when I'm away, I like to try white man's food."

"So what do you make of the situation?" inquired Matlock. Out of the corner of his eye, he caught sight of Governor Throckmorton heading their way, wearing jeans, cowboy boots, and a western hat. "Oh shit, here comes John Wayne," he said with a groan.

"Afternoon, Governor," nodded Colonel Cruz politely in the governor's direction.

"Howdy, boys," replied the governor. "How's the morale of

the troops?" he asked.

"Troops?" answered the Colonel. "Is that what they are? You're being generous, don't you think?"

Governor Throckmorton looked at Colonel Cruz with surprise. "These men have answered the call to defend Texas against the federal incursion. I think we can at least refer to them as 'troops'," he said.

A group of partying Texas volunteers chose that moment to organize a "mass mooning" of the federal line. Fifty mildly intoxicated irregulars in baseball caps took a few steps forward in front of the Texas line, turned their backs to the Second Battalion, bent over, and dropped their Wranglers down to their knees, exposing buttocks of varying sizes, shapes, and colors to the disbelieving opposing troops. The cat-calls and whooping from the Texans drowned out the smattering of applause that drifted 1,000 yards from the Second Battalion in the stifling heat.

"Do you hear that spontaneous cheering?" asked the governor proudly. "That's what I mean when I say 'morale'. Our boys know what they're here for, and they're fired up."

"Yes sir," replied Colonel Cruz, trying not to roll his eyes.

The governor gave a perfunctory salute. "Carry on, men. Texas is proud of you."

Matlock and Colonel Cruz watched the governor continue his inspection of the "troops". They glanced at each other in silence.

"We may have to put that sonofabitch in a straitjacket before it's all over," ventured Matlock.

"Come on, Matlock. That man is the commander-in-chief of the Texas National Guard."

"Not for long, I suspect," replied Matlock. "He's lost it; thinks he's William Barrett Travis at the Alamo."

"Maybe that's what Texas needs," ventured the Colonel.

Matlock's cell phone rang.

"Excuse me, Iggy," he said. "Don't go away." Matlock took a few steps away to talk in private.

***

The cicadas suddenly shrieked in unison as if a toggle switch had activated their shrill whine. They added to the bedlam of noise, vying for the lead with country and mariachi music and the sound of gasoline and diesel engines. Colonel Cruz finished his hamburger and slurped the last of the chocolate milkshake. He gave a deep sigh, wondering whatever possessed him to join the National Guard in the first place. He thought it would look good on his resume, he guessed. Show the Anglos he was one of them. It wasn't going to take much time, they told him, and the extra money wouldn't hurt either. But first it was Iraq, then Afghanistan. And then when you think you've paid your dues, you're called back to active duty: this time for combat duty in Texas, of all places. The world was going crazy, he thought as he saw Matlock approaching, his face ashen.

"What's happened, Matlock?" Colonel Cruz asked with concern.

Matlock stared without saying a word. He turned to Ignacio Cruz and grabbed him by his shoulders.

"They've got Alba!"

***

The mood was grim and somber at the Broken "T"

Land & Cattle Company ranch headquarters when Matlock and twenty men from the People's Army arrived later that same afternoon. The ranch was on high alert, and a group of armed men intercepted Matlock's pickup shortly after it exited Interstate 35 before it even arrived at the entrance to the Broken "T".

"Is that you, Matlock?" called Jamie Dalton, stepping forward out of the thick cover of blackbrush and mesquite. His long-sleeve shirt was dripping wet from perspiration and stuck to his body like a second skin. He took off his western hat and wiped his brow, flinging a stream of sweat to the cracked ground. He carried a 12-gauge shotgun and wore a gun holster around his waist.

"Yeah, Jamie...it's me. What's going on?"

"They're all waiting for you at the house. No news yet. They're expecting a phone call with the demands."

"Who else is there?" asked Matlock.

"James Brazzle, Mako Sloan, and that old bull rider Bronc Thornton, who flew the governor's daughter back from Mexico, plus a few locals you know."

"How's my father?"

"Like a raging bull looking for the red cape."

"And Guadalupe?" he asked, not wanting to hear the answer.

"Not so good, Matlock." Jamie replied, looking at the ground.

"Okay, Jamie. Thanks." Matlock gritted his teeth. He drove on towards the ranch house slowly, watching the trailing pickup trucks in the rear view mirror. Clouds of dust occasionally obscured one or two of the last vehicles in the caravan for a few seconds at a time. Here and there a nondescript gray lizard ran across the road, braving the blazing sun and the Michelin radials to get to the other side. Buzzards circled overhead and Matlock caught the stench of something dead lying out in the pasture. From the smell, the poor creature had been there for a while. He subconsciously hoped it wasn't one of their calves. It was a hard country, and it took a toll on the animals that tried to eke out a living on it.

Matlock drove through the entryway of the ranch, crossed the last cattle guard with a rumble, and doubled his speed, gravel crunching under the tires of his dually. He tapped his fingers nervously on the steering wheel, no particular tune in mind but just needing to stay in motion, even just a part of him. He knew that finding his sister was going to be the hard part, maybe impossible. They could have taken her anywhere, even Mexico.

"Where's Lupe?" he asked without bothering to greet anyone as he walked into the kitchen, banging the screen door behind him. James Brazzle was standing in front of the portable television set, watching the local news report from Dilley. Rodrigo stood quietly off to one side, his western hat held shyly in front of him. He nodded at Matlock.

"She's with the veterinarian and Koot in the bedroom," James replied.

"What the hell's the matter with Koot?" he asked almost in a snarl. If it wasn't one thing, it was another, he thought angrily.

"Well, how you think those cartel bastards got into the house? They poisoned the dog. He's in pretty bad shape."

"Damned cowards!" Spittle flew from Matlock's mouth as he tried to control himself. "Where's Dad?"

"He's in the living room with the big boys, waiting on a phone call that'll never come, in my opinion," James answered, exhausted from the stress of the campaign and the assassination attempt on Creed in Brownsville the day before.

"Why won't it come?" Matlock stopped in his tracks and looked over at James Brazzle with concern.

"Because they know your father can't be intimidated by words. They won't bother with blackmail. I'm afraid they mean to show him this is only the beginning if he refuses to leave South Texas and stop campaigning against the referendum. That's why we have to move quickly."

"Ah, there you are, Matlock," called out Creed as he came into the kitchen followed by Mako Sloane and Bronc Thornton. Creed embraced his older son in silence. Matlock approached the other men and shook their hands, nodding his head in a wordless greeting.

"How are things in Dilley?" Creed asked almost absentmindedly.

"Mexican standoff, Dad. Apart from the governor acting like a damned fool, it looks like the Seventh is just waiting on orders from General Buchanan at Fort Hood. They could cut through us like butter if they're willing to take the political heat for it."

"How many men did you bring?" asked Creed.

"Twenty or so...all vets."

"Good," replied Creed. "We may need them."

"How'd they get through our patrols?" asked Matlock.

"Hell, we just don't have enough men. We can't cover the whole ranch all the time. They poked through a hole; that's all."

Matlock glanced over at Mako.

"Mr. Sloane, you're the big shot from Washington, right? Got any idea about this one? Can you bring Alba back like you brought back Lisa Throckmorton?"

"It's too early to say, Matlock. We don't know what we're facing yet, but I'll do my best."

"Your best? Is that all you can offer, Mr. Sloane?"

"Matlock, watch your mouth, son!" interrupted Creed. "Mr. Sloane's on our side. He and James Brazzle probably saved my life yesterday. If Alba can be rescued, they'll get her back."

The men heard shouting outside in front of the house and walked to the porch to see what the disturbance was. They saw Jamie Dalton and two others standing beside the open door of a pickup, reaching into the back seat and dragging a body out, legs first.

"We got one!" called Jamie excitedly.

The man was conscious, but his head lolled from side to side, and he made no effort to walk. Jamie's men hauled him across the bare ground between the round pen and the house, his legs dragging behind him. Creed stood on the porch watching and could see from the man's bloody face that he had been roughed up a bit. He looked Mexican.

"Jamie, what do you got there?" asked Creed.

"A damned cartel soldier, by the looks of him," replied Jamie. "Caught him climbing through the wire in the east pasture."

"Did you have to beat him up?" Creed asked angrily. "Three against one?"

"What do you mean, Creed? He's a Mexican, and he was trying to get close to the house," said Jamie. "Since when do we have to start playing fair with these bastards?"

Jamie let the Mexican drop in the dirt in front of the porch. He lay groggily on the ground and tried to raise himself to his knees. He lifted his head and mumbled something in Spanish. Rodrigo had joined Creed and Matlock on the porch and peered intently at the intruder.

"Mario? *¿Eres tu*?" he asked and rushed down the steps.

"Rodrigo!" exclaimed the ragged figure. *"¡Yo sé dónde está la muchacha!"* he whispered hoarsely.

Rodrigo turned to Creed who stood motionless on the porch, watching.

"It's Mario," he said in English. "He knows where Alba is!"

CHAPTER 41

Félix Aguilar slammed his fist down painfully on the top of the mahogany desk in his office at the *Procuraduría General de la República* in Mexico City. A tray with an elegant set of Talavera cups and saucers rattled threateningly, and hot coffee splashed out of his cup onto the carefully lacquered finish of the antique desk. He resisted a desire to smash his cell phone or even his head against the wall.

"¡A la gran puta!" he exclaimed in fury. "What the hell is going on? The last thing I heard, we were in favor of the candidacy of two Anglo candidates, right? They were going to split the non-Hispanic vote and ensure the election of our candidate when the referendum was approved. Wasn't that the ingenious strategy? Now all of a sudden you're trying to kill one of the candidates without even consulting me, and you shoot the wrong man? Can't I depend on you anymore, *carnal*?"

The attorney general's relationship with Francisco Salcido was changing. He would never have allowed himself to speak with the cartel leader in such familiar terms even a few weeks ago. Chinks were appearing in Salcido's armor, though, and after his accident in the mountains and the escape of the hostages, his aura of invincibility had faded. Now, with the blunder in Brownsville, Francisco had screwed up yet again. That wasn't like him, and the attorney general was concerned. Félix was used to a seemingly unending string of successes, and two tactical setbacks in a row at the hands of his North American friend-turned-nemesis had been frustrating to say the least. Francisco's erratic behavior did not bode well for his own election, he thought.

"It was your friend, again, Félix. The description matches. I wish you had taken care of him in Mexico City instead of losing him like a small-town cop."

"Small-town cop? *No digas tonterías, amigo.* Don't underestimate Mako Sloane. He was a CIA legend in his day; the best they could put in the field, and it appears age hasn't diminished his skills. You found that out yourself, didn't you? Twice now if my count is right." The attorney general wasn't about to let Francisco's barb go unanswered.

"Mako Sloane is a footnote. A mere annoyance: like a buzzing gnat. I *will* take care of him. The important thing, Félix, is not to lose sight of our main goal. Rudy Gutierrez must win the election in South Texas for us. But this Anglo rancher is proving to be more of a political threat than the National Front anticipated. He has widespread support among the moderates, and he's campaigning fiercely to stop the referendum. His popularity is growing. He's got to be stopped, no matter what it takes."

"You've spoken with our friend, I take it?" asked the attorney general.

"Yes, he wanted to try a more subtle approach now and suggested a change of plans."

"Oh?"

"I've already implemented the change. We 'borrowed' the rancher's daughter yesterday. Stole her right out from under the old fart's nose. This time we'll send more than a finger in the mail," Francisco laughed. "We'll see how important his new political career is to him."

The attorney general brightened up.

"That's subtle?" he asked. "Now that's more like the Francisco Salcido I know."

"Life is full of ups and downs, *mi cuate.* It's like baseball, my friend. Everyone gets in a slump, but you keep swinging, and eventually you start hitting the ball again."

"I never knew you played ball, Francisco!"

"I didn't, but I've read about it," he laughed.

"Turn on Univision.   I'm giving a live interview in five minutes."

"*Suerte, carnal.*" The attorney general heard a click, and his friend was gone. He combed his hair hurriedly and buzzed his secretary. "I'm ready," he said.

It only took the Univision crew a few minutes to set up their television cameras and lights in the attorney general's office. Georgina Ramos, the Spanish language network's news anchor, was resplendent with her long raven hair, tight-fitting Dolce & Gabbana dress and mostly exposed breast implants. Félix Aguilar ogled her appreciatively, relaxing behind his desk and sipping hot coffee from an elegantly hand-painted Talavera cup. She glanced at the attorney general and nodded, ready to start the interview.

"Félix," she began, "The United States government has accused Mexico of encouraging the movement for self-determination in South Texas and aiding the National Front for the Liberation of Texas. How would you respond to these accusations?"

"Georgina, the United States accuses Mexico of many things. It's an old story. Every time we see a rise in violence along the border, the U.S. embassy pays me an official visit to complain. The North Americans sometimes remind me of small children who refuse to take responsibility for their own actions."

"But, Félix, what about specific allegations that Mexico has provided financial and logistical support to the National Front through the Sinaloa cartel?"

"First of all, the government of Mexico has nothing to do with the drug cartels. We wage a relentless war against them and kill and imprison their members on a daily basis. But to answer your question regarding Mexican policy towards the National Front, I would emphasize that our government has been scrupulous in its support of the principles of self-determination and non-intervention all over the world. I see no reason to drop that support just because we're talking about the United States."

"Is this the beginning of a regional movement in the United States; a Hispanic demographic explosion that results in the birth of similar movements throughout the southwestern United States?"

"I don't want to sound chauvinistic or take populist, anti-*gringo* positions just to get elected, Georgina. Let me make that clear. However, Mexicans do have a long, collective memory, and nobody has forgotten how the United States acquired the territories that comprise its southwestern states. But besides observing the situation with concern, Mexico has no interest in promoting instability along its northern border. Furthermore, the *'reconquista'*, as it is known, and the 'Plan of Aztlan', are terms coined by Hispanic citizens of the United States. Mexico has nothing to do with that. This is a homegrown movement of U.S. citizens."

"One last question, Félix," said Georgina, adjusting her long, black hair with a sideways flick of her head. "Right now outside of the town of Dilley, Texas two armed forces are facing each other in an unprecedented confrontation between North American state and federal troops. What is the official position of the Mexican government regarding the situation, and what do you think is going to happen?"

"Georgina," began the attorney general, enjoying his role of rubbing salt in the self-inflicted wounds of the North Americans. "We regard the current crisis in South Texas as strictly an internal affair of the United States. Our only interest and fervent wish is that the government of the United States respects the principle of self-determination on its own soil.

When the *gringos* insist on adherence to this vital principle of government in so many corners of the globe, yet trample this universal right in one of their own states, we begin to doubt their sincerity on other issues as well."

"Mr. Attorney General, we appreciate your time today. Ladies and gentlemen, this is Georgina Ramos for Univision with an exclusive interview with the attorney general and possibly the next president of Mexico with a plea to the United States government: 'Respect the principle of self-determination in South Texas'."

CHAPTER 42

When it happened on Christmas Eve in 1914 during World War I, they called it "fraternization". German and British troops in the Ypres Salient put aside the mandatory requirement to kill each other and instead sang Christmas carols, embraced, and in one unforgettable incident, even played a game of soccer together. The troops' commanders, however, were horrified at this drastic departure from standard military procedures and threatened courts-martial for the offending troops should the fraternization ever occur again. The truce ended, and the soldiers reluctantly returned to the more politically acceptable practice of butchering one another.

In Dilley, Texas the fraternization began a little differently: with the exchange of a bottle of Cholula chipotle-flavored hot sauce. Specialist Johnny Rodriguez of the Second Battalion of the Seventh Cavalry Regiment unwrapped his order of fish tacos from the Gonzales Taco Stand and made a horrifying discovery.

"¡A la verga!" he shouted. "This is the second time those culeros at the taco stand forgot the chipotle sauce. Man, you can't eat a real fish taco without chipotle. You might as well order a fish taco from Cracker Barrel."

Johnny and his Humvee gunner, Chapo Zavala, had managed to smuggle a case of Tecate in bottles from Super S Foods in Dilley, and they were each on their fourth beer. Chapo took out his Ipod and hooked it up to the radio speakers inside the Humvee.

"How about a little Calle 13, Johnny?"

"Horale, Chapo. Turn the motherfucker up, homes."

Chapo selected "Artists", then "Calle 13" and clicked on "Shuffle".

Johnny recognized *"Atrévete, te, te""* right away, and both he and Chapo raised their best reggaeton voices in accompaniment.

Cambia esa cara de seria

Esa cara de intelectual, de enciclopedia

Que te voy a inyectar con la bacteria

Pa' que des vuelta como machina de feria

The other Latinos nearby recognized the popular lyrics and eagerly joined in for the chorus. They all were bored to tears and welcomed any diversion.

Atrévete, te, te, te

Salte del closet, te

Escápate, quítate el esmalte

Deja de taparte que nadie va a retratarte

Levántate, ponte hyper

"Mierda!" cursed Johnny after the song ended. "I refuse to eat a fish taco without chipotle sauce. "Where's that white flag?" he asked.

"The old man left it in our Humvee," answered Chapo.

"Bring it to me, my friend, and I'll get us some chipotle," Johnny declared, opening up a fifth Tecate and tilting his head back for a long draught of the ice cold beer. Chapo hustled off to the Humvee and came back waving a small white flag on a tent pole.

"Gracias, carnal! Let me show you how it's done," said Johnny and marched towards the Texas lines, holding the

white flag as high as he could. Shouts erupted from the National Guard sentries as they spotted Johnny walking slowly across no-man's land.

"Hold your fire, men!" shouted Colonel Cruz of the Texas National Guard as he watched a solitary figure approach from the federal lines under a flag of truce. At times the figure blended into the heat mirage on the horizon and became an indistinct blur and then seemed to appear suddenly out of the haze. It was a long walk, but the figure finally stopped about twenty-five yards from the Texas positions and seemed to look for something up and down the line.

"*¿Qué onda, camaradas?*" he shouted. "Anybody here from Mission, Texas?"

"*Aquí estamos, compañero,*" came the answering shout. "Over here! We're from Mission. What's your name?"

"I'm Johnny Rodriguez. Maybe you've heard of my mother. Everyone calls her 'Yolanda'. She has a *taquería* on South Mayberry."

"You got a cousin named 'Danny' in the Zetas?"

"*Simón, vato*...but nobody's supposed to know that!" he laughed, tossing his empty bottle of Tecate on the ground.

"I went to school with your cousin, man. He's a bad motherfucker!"

"*¡Horale!* Listen, anybody here got any chipotle salsa? The *culero* at the taco stand forgot to put the Cholula in my bag."

"Hey Speedy Gonzales, how about some Grey Poupon?" shouted one of the Anglo ranchers.

"I'll try that too," cried Johnny, sharing in the joke. "*Pinche gringo,*" he added in a voice nobody could hear but himself.

One of the Mission Latinos left the Texas defensive positions and walked out in the open towards Johnny, carrying a bottle of chipotle-flavored hot sauce.

"Soldier, get back to your position!" ordered Cruz.

"Chupame la verga, cabrón," retorted the volunteer from Mission.

"Shit," mumbled Colonel Cruz under his breath. "What am I supposed to do? Shoot the sonofabitch?"

Governor Throckmorton was standing near the Colonel and witnessed his dilemma. "Colonel, let this play out. It could be to our advantage," suggested the governor.

Chapo Zavala in the meantime saw his friend Johnny chatting amicably with a group of Texans and decided to join him. He threw the rest of the beer in the Humvee and drove slowly towards the Texas line, music blaring. Three other Latino soldiers from the Second Battalion jumped into the Humvee with him for the short ride to join Johnny. One by one, men began filtering out of both lines and walking towards the impromptu gathering in between the two opposing forces, bringing food and beer. By the time Colonel Cruz noticed the first National Guard soldiers leaving their positions and heading for the spontaneous revelry, it was too late to recall them. He had lost control of his men. Soon, Anglos from the opposing armies were also discovering old friends and mutual acquaintances in the ranks of the "enemy", breaking out guitars, and popping cans of Shiner Bock and Lone Star. Frisbees were flying overhead, and a discordant mix of songs by Texas country artists vied with *Calle 13*, *Maná*, and *Los Tigres del Norte*. It was bedlam.

***

Lt. Colonel Stanley Overstreet stood up in his command Humvee and watched the scene in front of him in utter dismay and disbelief. His company commanders reported to him grim-faced and sheepishly shrugged their shoulders when he asked for an explanation of how several hundred men from the Second Battalion happened to be fraternizing with the enemy.

"This is an absolute goat-fuck!" he shouted. "Get the MPs up here...fast!"

It had been an odd day for the military police attached to the Seventh Cavalry Regiment, and it would get even stranger. Hauling off screaming women and children who were attempting to block a military convoy on its way to battle in South Texas was bad enough. Having Molotov cocktails hurled at you by Hispanic women dressed in fatigues and brown berets took the experience to yet another level, but attempting to break up a festive gathering of fraternizing troops from opposing armies was asking too much even of professional military police. Discipline broke down utterly and irreversibly once Johnny handed a Tecate to one of the MPs when the latter attempted to arrest him.

"Ah, what the hell! *Me da igual!*" said the Mexican-American MP and emptied the ice cold bottle of Tecate in one long appreciative gulp. "Got any chips and salsa, man?" he asked.

Grills were hauled out of the backs of pickup trucks, and soon the smell of cooking meat and sausages mingled with the stench of diesel fumes, sweat, and Coppertone Sport Lotion. The thump of heavy bass from the sophisticated car stereo systems of the Texas volunteers added to the overall impression of unreserved pandemonium. Residents in Dilley heard the muffled sounds of the bacchanal and assumed that hostilities had commenced. The fast food restaurants closed their doors temporarily, and the entire population drove out of town in the direction of the ominous rumbling in their Silverados, Rams, and Toyota Corollas to witness the historic battle. It would have been reminiscent of the picnickers at the First Battle of Bull Run in the Civil War were it not for the conspicuous absence of any battle to observe.

Lt. Colonel Overstreet watched the unprecedented

developments and saw his military career going down the proverbial drain. West Point, the First Gulf War, Iraq, Afghanistan; it had all been in vain. His career would end here and now on the mesquite plains of South Texas with his famed Second Battalion unabashedly fraternizing with the enemy and ignoring orders to cease and desist. It was mutiny. He stood helplessly with his arms at his sides and didn't notice the battalion's public affairs officer addressing him in a panic-stricken voice.

"Colonel," he practically shouted. "My embedded reporters are up there filming and interviewing the troops! The mutiny is being broadcast 'live'!"

"Get General Buchanan on the line, now!" ordered Lt. Colonel Overstreet.

In fact, any thoughts about damage control at this point were too late. A shell-shocked General "Tommy" Buchanan had just hung up the telephone after a catastrophic reckoning at the hands of the president of the United States who just happened to be watching CNN with his national security advisor in the White House when the regularly scheduled programming was interrupted by a live feed from Dilley, Texas. The president watched the television screen with disbelieving eyes as soldiers from the Texas National Guard swayed arm in arm with the elite troops of the famed Seventh Cavalry Regiment to the sounds of a Puerto Rican reggaeton band.

"No way, man," said Specialist Johnny Rodriguez into the CNN microphone held by embedded reporter Margarita Lopez. "No way us Latinos are going to fight other Latinos. Americans against other Americans? What for, man? So some asshole in Washington can say he's tough on immigration? Fuck that! I'm in the U.S. Army, but I'm from Texas. Let Texas decide! If our leaders can't get it right, the people will!"

"There you have it from Dilley, Texas. Soldiers from the Seventh Cavalry Regiment, the Texas National Guard, and the People's Army of South Texas plus thousands of Texas irregulars send a resounding message to their military and civilian leaders. Americans will not fight other Americans! And to think, it all started with a bottle of Cholula chipotle-flavored hot sauce. This is Margarita Lopez for CNN. Back to our studios in Washington."

CHAPTER 43

"Bring that boy in here, and get him cleaned up," said Creed. "Now!" he added, his voice tense with emotion. "I need to talk with that Mexican sonofabitch!"

Guadalupe heard the shouting and ran out to the front porch. She gasped when she saw Mario's swollen features and gasped again when she heard him say, "*Yo sé donde está la muchacha!*" She had the men whisk Mario into the house, gave him some cold water to drink, and cleaned his cuts. She took several Blue Ice packs out of the freezer and applied them to Mario's left eye and nose which appeared broken. She shooed Jamie Dalton out of the kitchen after a few carefully chosen words in Spanish.

"Jamie, *¿qué hiciste? ¡Eres un animal!*"

"Lupe, I'm sorry! We didn't know who he was," said Jamie. He looked down at his own skinned-up, painful knuckles.

Creed walked briskly into the kitchen. "Lupe, we don't have that much time. Can he talk with us now?"

"*¿Estás bien, mi hijo?*" she asked, holding the ice pack to Mario's cheek. Tears streamed down her face.

"*Si, señora…estoy bien. Muchas gracias.*"

***

Mario stood up on his own, a little shakily at first, but then followed Creed into the living room where the men were waiting. He groaned quietly as he eased himself into a chair next to the fireplace. Rodrigo and Matlock stood in the doorway, listening. Jamie looked over their shoulders, trying to hear what Mario might say.

"Jamie, I think it might be better if you stayed out of sight. I doubt he's too favorably disposed towards you right about now," suggested Creed. "Better get back to patrolling, and try to be a little more careful about who you beat the shit out of."

"Sorry, Creed," he said. "I was just trying to do my job." He turned on his heels and walked downtrodden out of the room. The screen door slammed, and Creed heard Jamie's truck start up and pull out of the driveway.

"I'm going to speak Spanish with Mario now," said Mako. "Stop me if you're having trouble following us."

Despite the circumstances, both Creed and James laughed out loud. "Mako, you're in South Texas. We fart in Spanish down here," said James.

"So much the better," Mako answered. "I won't have to waste my time translating for you old *pedos de buey*." He pulled up an old wooden stool and sat down directly in front of Mario. He leaned forward and looked intensely at the young Mexican.

"Mario, is Alba alright?" asked Mako in Spanish.

"She was when I left her this morning," answered Mario. "She's tied up, but they haven't hurt her."

"Is she in any immediate danger?"

"*Si, señor, la van a matar esta noche!*" declared Mario. "*Por eso vine.*"

Creed stood up from his chair. "Where is she, you sonofabitch!" he shouted, reaching for Mario with his outstretched arms.

"Creed, sit down! Mario's here to help!" James Brazzle leaped to his feet with the reactions of a retired athlete and intercepted Creed before he got to Mario.

"Sorry, boys," Creed muttered. "You heard him, didn't you? He says they're going to kill my daughter tonight!"

James grabbed Creed by the shoulders and sat him down roughly. "Just let Mako work, will you? He's knows what he's doing."

"Where is she, Mario?" asked Mako patiently.

"At *Rancho Las Aguilas*."

"Creed, you know what that is?" asked Mako.

"Hell, yes. It's a 5,000 acre ranch owned by Grupo Zima, a big Mexican tomato grower. It's about four or five miles out Ranch Road 133 west of Artesia Wells. Only about 20 miles from here. That's a stroke of luck, I'd say. I was afraid they had taken her into Mexico."

"Maybe, maybe not. Drake, get some satellite photography going. We may be busy tonight, boys. Creed, what time is sunset this evening?" asked Mako.

"Not sure; somewhere about seven-fifty, I think. We still got an hour and a half."

Drake retrieved his laptop computer and quickly brought up his secure link to a CIA mainframe in Langley, Virginia. He downloaded overhead photography of South Texas from the latest pass of the KH-12 reconnaissance satellite, and within five minutes he had "Las Aguilas" on the screen.

"This doesn't look much better than Google Earth," James noted. "The CIA can't do any better than that? No wonder we keep fucking things up wherever we go."

"Drake, zoom in on those buildings, will you?" requested Mako, ignoring James' comment. Drake moved his courser to the ranch headquarters and guest houses. He clicked twice.

"Whoa, that's more like it," said James, catching his breath. "Shit, I see four pickup trucks parked in front of the house...

and I can almost see the label on that guy's bottle of beer!"

"Technology has advanced a bit since you last had a job, James," said Drake.

"Alright, four pickup trucks...at least ten men, I'd say, maybe a few more," said Mako. "That's pretty much what Mario said. He says they're waiting for some big shot to get there from Mexico before they kill Alba. There's supposed to be some high-level meeting tonight. See that airstrip to the west of the house? Something tells me they'll be using that tonight."

"Matlock, make sure your men have enough ammunition. Take some of ours if you need it," Creed ordered. "Have the men ready to move in thirty minutes. Give Rodrigo a Mossberg and meet us at the trucks. Rodrigo's riding with me. James, I'd prefer it if you'd stay here at the ranch and keep an eye on Guadalupe."

"Whatever you want, Creed," answered James Brazzle.

"Drake, can you print out a copy of this photo?" asked Mako as he studied the overhead photography of the house. "We'll take a copy with us to study on the way."

"How do you want to approach this, Mako?" asked Creed, looking over his shoulder at the computer screen.

"Well, offhand I'd say we'll have to park the cars by this gas compressor station...right here. Looks to be about a mile from the house. Think you can make it that far on foot, old man?"

Creed barely reacted to Mako's attempt at humor. "You're almost as old as me. If you can make it, so can I."

"We'll approach through the brush on foot and surround the house. We'll take out the guards one by one and break in as quietly as we can and kill whoever's inside. Mario knows what room she's in. Should be a textbook extraction. The only problem is, there's no such thing as a textbook extraction.

Something always goes wrong," Mako said.

"But how many of those yahoos have experience in this kind of operation?" Creed asked worriedly, motioning with his head in the direction of Matlock's men.

"About zero, I'd say. That's what I'm here for, Creed," said Mako and dialed a number on his cell phone. "We're going to deploy them as backup to cover our withdrawal." Creed heard the faint ring on Mako's phone and then a muffled voice on the other end.

"QL, bring Tupelo and meet me at the intersection of Interstate 35 and Ranch Road 133 at seven-thirty. It's the exit to Artesia Wells. Bring your weapons and the RPG just in case."

"Who's that?" asked Creed.

"Some old friends of mine from a previous life. They helped me down in Mexico a few days ago. I'll introduce them as soon as they get here."

"Why haven't you brought them to the ranch?"

"They're shy, Creed. They prefer to keep a low profile."

"I've seen your brand of shyness, Mako. You're a regular wallflower."

***

The sun set quickly, and the vague suggestions of pink and purple in the clouds on the horizon vanished suddenly and emphatically. Darkness crept over the barren landscape, turning the monotonous panorama of the flat plain into nothingness. Six pickup trucks pulled off the Interstate 35 access road to the narrow shoulder, parked, and then waited.

About the same time, Quindarius Lee and Tupelo McSweeney

conducted a drive-by reconnaissance of the white Austin-stone entranceway to the ranch to make sure the approaches to *Las Aguilas* weren't covered by video or motion detectors. Satisfied they would not encounter any electronic surveillance as they entered the ranch, QL called Mako on his secure cell phone.

"It's a go," he said softly into his phone.

"Roger that, QL," replied Mako and pulled out slowly from the shoulder of the access road at the Artesia Wells exchange and turned due west on Ranch Road 133. The hot air rising from the black asphalt even after dusk was heavy with humidity, and the faint stench of skunk along with the persistent drone of the cicadas kept the men's nerves on edge. Each secretly welcomed the distraction of the clanking diesel engines that erupted when Mako gave the signal to move out.

One by one the pickups doused their lights and crossed through the stone entrance, rumbling noisily across the cattle guard on the other side. QL and Tupelo were waiting in their truck about seventy five yards into the ranch around the first curve in the gravel road. Creed stopped his pickup, and Mako got out and walked slowly over to his team.

"You ready, boys?" he asked.

QL nodded his head. Mako looked over at Tupelo who was smiling broadly. His teeth reflected blue in the dashboard lights.

"What are you smiling at?" asked Mako.

"Just happy to be alive."

"Make sure you stay that way."

"Whatever you say."

"It's time," Mako said and walked back to his truck.

QL drove slowly forward in low gear, leading the way. At

the compressor pump station the trucks made a tight U-turn and parked in single file pointing back towards Ranch Road 133. As Mako had instructed, each driver left enough room between his vehicle and the truck in front to allow him to pull out freely in case they were missing any drivers on the way back.

"Matlock, you and your men are staying here," Mako said. "I want you to set up an ambush fifty yards up the road towards the house. Have your men spread out twenty-five yards on either side of the road. If you see people coming, though, you damn well better challenge before you open fire. Keep your phone handy, and I'll try to call and give you a heads-up when we're on our way back. Understand?"

"Got it," replied Matlock.

Creed took Mako by the elbow and pulled him aside. He smelled stale beer and garlic on Mako's breath and felt the sandpaper roughness of his unshaven jaw as he leaned forward and whispered in his ear.

"Mako, that's my daughter in there. We take it slow and easy, understand? None of your CIA cowboy shit this time," Creed said.

Mako pulled back and looked at Creed in amazement.

"I know your reputation," Creed added.

"Don't worry. We'll be careful," Mako said and turned to Mario. "V*en conmigo.*"

Mario followed obediently, his hands trembling. His knees were weak and almost buckled at every step.

Mako and his team moved slowly. It took them forty-five minutes to cover the scant mile to the ranch house. It was a moonless night, and the men felt their way through the maze of cactus and mesquite, tripping frequently and cursing quietly. They tried to stay on an old cattle trail Mako had seen in the overhead photography, but the path had been easier to identify from several hundred miles above the surface of the earth than it was walking in the pitch black on the uneven ground.

The *Las Aguilas* ranch house was lit up like a *Cinco de Mayo* fireworks display. The aura from the bright lights pierced the blackness of the surrounding night and emanated in hazy rays through the prickly pear cactus, cholla, and scrub vegetation around them. As they drew closer to the house, Mako slowed their pace even further, and they began to seek the cover of the clumps of mesquite and cactus instead of avoiding them. About seventy-five yards out from the house off to their right side, Mako suddenly caught the smell of cigarette smoke wafting towards them on the barely perceptible breeze. QL and Tupelo smelled the smoke at about the same time and instantly dropped into a low crouch. Mako nodded his head at QL who silently moved out in the direction of the smoker. A few minutes passed and they heard the sounds of a slight scuffle and then the approaching footsteps of QL. For a big man his movements were almost catlike, and he was almost upon them before they realized he was back.

"There was just one," QL whispered and handed Mako a R.A.T.S. baseball cap. "Might come in handy," he explained. Mako nodded his head and put the cap on backwards.

Ten minutes later the men reached the pipe fencing that encircled the compound at a distance of about 50 yards from the rambling one-story house. They lay on the ground, silently observing two guards who stood smoking between the parked pickup trucks and the front door to the house.

"Show me which room Alba's in," whispered Mako as he low-crawled over to Mario, propelling himself with his elbows and knees.

"There's a guest bedroom off the living room on the left side of the house. That's where they're keeping her. There'll be a guard outside the window," Mario replied.

"*Vale*, Mario. Here's what we're going to do. You're going to pretend to be my prisoner. They're going to think I'm that guard back there on the ground...but not for long. I'm too tall. But that's all we need, just a few seconds."

Mako motioned to QL and Tupelo, and they moved out quickly to the right, hugging the ground. They crossed through the pipe fence and moved in closer, keeping the pickup trucks between them and the guards. Mako pulled the R.A.T.S. cap down on his head and stood up, pushing Mario in front of him. Creed stayed back and kept the guards in the sights of his SKS.

"Hey, look who I've got here," Mako called out in Spanish to the guards.

"Who is it?" they asked in response, drawing their pistols and walking towards the approaching figures of Mako and Mario.

"I've got Mario, the *pinche* deserter." Mako tried to stoop over to conceal his height. He saw QL and Tupelo circling the guards, already within pistol-shot range. He had to give them time to get closer. They had no silencers and couldn't afford to make any noise.

"Mario, *lo siento*," whispered Mako and struck Mario hard from behind, knocking him to the ground. "*¡No te muevas, pinche traidor!*" he said just loud enough for the guards to hear.

"*Horale,*" where'd you find him? replied one of the guards. "We'll kill him along with the girl. *El Padrino* will enjoy the entertainment. Maybe he'll give us a bonus."

The guard laughed and turned to his companion to share the joke. For an instant he stood mesmerized by the sight of a huge figure standing over the prostrate form of his friend whose head lay at an odd angle on the ground. Then he felt a pair of rough hands grabbing his chin from behind, jolting him out of his own shocked paralysis. He threw his right elbow back, hard into Tupelo's abdomen, but it was too late. A jarring, twisting motion of Tupelo's two hands, a searing pain in his neck, and it was over.

Tupelo and QL moved out in opposite directions around the house, weapons drawn. Mako motioned Creed and Rodrigo in from the fence line while he and Mario knelt in the shadows of the front porch. Mako slipped the strap of his Heckler & Koch MP5 off his shoulder and adjusted the 100-round Beta C-Mag.

Creed looked at him with surprise.

"What the hell's that?" he asked in a whisper.

"So I don't have to change magazines in the middle of a conversation," Mako explained. His cell phone vibrated and he listened for a few seconds and hung up.

"You ready?" he asked Creed.

"Let's get Alba."

CHAPTER 44

Carl Von Clausewitz wrote that surprise on the field of battle confuses the enemy and deprives him of courage. It's a simplistic truth, but the nine Sinaloa cartel soldiers who died in the hail of automatic weapons fire directed at them by their attackers who burst through the front and back doors of the ranch house at *Las Aguilas* never had time to put that tactical principle to the test. They died before they could even draw their hand guns, and surprise never registered in their brains.

The angry roar of more than one hundred rounds fired in the small enclosed area was disorienting, and the echoes continued long after the last cartel soldier fell. Mario pointed to the bedroom door a few yards down a short hallway that led away from the living room where nine dead men now lay motionless in unflattering poses: mouths agape, limbs akimbo and twisted at unlikely angles.

"Follow me," Mario said. He walked rapidly down the hallway up to the bedroom door holding his Mossberg at his side, pointing at the floor. Mako and QL followed closely behind, but Mario had a head start and reached his hand out for the door knob, calling to Alba.

"Mario, wait!" warned Mako, but the young Mexican was intent on finding the girl.

"Alba, it's Mario, we've come to get you," he cried out, pushing the door open and taking one step into the room, an expression of vindication already spreading across his features. Without warning, Mario's body flew back across the hallway at the same instant as the unmistakable roar of a shotgun discharged at close range exploded in the enclosed hallway. He hit the wall on the other side of the corridor in the air, and his body fell, sliding down into a crumpled heap on the floor, his abdomen ripped open by the double ought pellets fired at point blank range. Before the shooter had time to eject the spent shell and chamber the next round, Mako and QL both burst into the small room. They hesitated momentarily to locate Alba and then opened fire on the hapless shooter who suddenly found himself outnumbered in the small bedroom. The first rounds hit him in the chest as he belatedly cocked the shotgun and started to bring the weapon to bear. His errant shot hit the ceiling and produced little more than a heavy shower of dry wall particles which fluttered down harmlessly on his two assailants. His body still twitched on the floor as Rodrigo and Creed ran past him to free Alba who sat gagged and tied to a small chair in the corner of the room. Mako and QL turned and ran past Mario's twisted body to the aid of Tupelo who had started to clear the house room by room.

"Mako, we need prisoners to find out who's behind all this," called out Creed as Mako sprinted out of the room. "Take it easy now!"

"Got to protect my men!" shouted Mako as he took an M67 grenade from the ammo bag hanging from his belt and motioned with his head towards the first room. QL kicked open the door, and Mako pulled the pin and tossed in the grenade. Following the deafening explosion, Tupelo burst into the smoke-filled room and opened fire with his Heckler & Koch MP5, just in case. The men's ears rang with the sounds of the explosion and automatic weapons fire, and they did not hear the panicked voices coming from the oak-paneled study at the rear of the house. They moved on to clear the next room.

***

Francisco Salcido, aka *El Padrino,* had been enjoying a glass of Woodford Reserve bourbon, a gift from his guest of honor, when the shooting started. His initial alarm turned to panic, and he looked at his guest with a jolt of déjà vu, convinced that he had been betrayed by the man sitting across from him.

"Is this a setup, *cabrón*? Who the fuck *are* you anyway?"

Francisco heard the first explosion and recognized the thunder-clap of a fragmentation grenade. He knew the intruders must be going room-to-room and that it was only a matter of a few minutes before they reached the study. He opened the middle drawer of the desk where he sat and removed a fully-loaded 9 mm Browning which he pointed at the chest of his guest.

"Are you DEA? Answer me!" shouted Francisco and threw his glass of Woodford Reserve at the fireplace. Somehow the glass struck the blunt corner of the wooden mantel above the fireplace and bounced harmlessly on the colorful Oaxaca rug on the floor without breaking. The wool quickly absorbed the expensive liquid which spread silently in a spidery array, causing the red dye to run messily into the white border of the faux Navajo pattern. This infuriated *El Padrino* even more, and the detonation of the second grenade in the adjacent room threw him into an uncontrollable rage. Without hesitating, he pulled back the slide mechanism on the 9 mm and at a range of three feet aimed one round into the face of his guest who fell back, blood gushing from a symmetrical hole almost exactly in the center of his forehead.

"Nobody double-crosses Francisco Salcido," he said and emptied the rest of the 13-round magazine into his erstwhile business partner's chest.

***

Mako and his team heard the unmistakable sounds of the 9mm in the adjacent room. They looked at each other in silent agreement.

"After you," mouthed Mako. QL kicked in the door and Tupelo charged into the room looking for targets. He saw a well-dressed Mexican standing behind a desk in the elegant, wood-paneled study, desperately trying to load another magazine in his Browning. A short burst caught the Mexican in the left side of the chest, and he fell backwards over his chair to the floor, knocking down a pair of crutches which were leaning against the wall. Mako ran over to him and looked down at the mortally wounded man. Francisco's eyes were open, and he looked up with a sudden gasp of recognition at Mako's face looming above him.

"*Puta madre!*" he said, blood oozing from the corner of his mouth. "The photograph...it's you!"

"*Buenas noches, Padrino,*" Mako said. "What brings you to Texas?"

Francisco tried to speak but coughed up a stream of crimson foam. Mako leaned over to pick up what he was saying.

"Don't you mean the Autonomous Republic of South Texas?" Francisco whispered. He tried to laugh and coughed convulsively, a pink spray of phlegm and blood discoloring his shirt. Mako looked down at the prostrate figure and saw the cast on his right leg and the crutches on the floor.

"I think we've met before, Francisco," he said, feigning politeness.

"*Chinga tu madre,*" hissed Francisco...and died. His head fell to one side, and his eyes stared lifelessly and without purpose at a point in space nobody else but he could see. Mako stood silently over Francisco's corpse, staring at his expressionless eyes.

"Looks like we've cut off the snake's head," said Mako. "By

accident."

"Mako, you need to come over here," called QL, standing on the other side of the desk and looking at the body of Francisco Salcido's guest. "You're not going to believe this."

Mako walked around the desk and saw QL kneeling beside the prostrate body of a middle-aged man dressed in a pink polo shirt, Duck Head khaki trousers, and fashionably weathered Topsiders.

"What do we have here?" Mako asked. "The U.S. banking connection for the Sinaloa drug cartel?"

"Look again, Mako," said QL quietly.

Mako peered over QL's shoulder at the familiar features and stood in stunned silence as Tupelo joined them after a quick check around the room to make sure all the potential shooters were down. Tupelo looked down at the dead man.

"Jesus Christ, isn't that Vice President Archibald Rutledge?"

"It was," said Mako, looking down at the shattered body of the vice-president.

"What the hell do we do now?" asked Tupelo.

"Punt, I reckon," replied Mako.

CHAPTER 45

Creed rushed into the study and stopped abruptly. He saw Mako, Tupelo, and QL standing strangely silent over a motionless figure on the floor, whose outstretched arms were flung clumsily to either side of his body. His torso was crisscrossed with bullet wounds and a small hole in the middle of his forehead still oozed blood.

Another lifeless form lay next to the fireplace on a blood-soaked rug, ignored by the men. Creed's eyes shifted back and forth across the room between the two corpses, trying to process the images. Tupelo took a step backwards and Creed caught a glimpse of the first victim's face.

"Jesus! Is that who I think it is?" he asked, pointing at the body of Archibald Rutledge and looking reluctantly to Mako for confirmation.

"Yeah, I'm afraid so. Looks like there's an immediate vacancy in the West Wing of the White House," said Mako. "Interested?"

"How in hell...?" Creed started to ask.

"Rain check with the questions, Creed," interrupted Mako. "I've got no answers. Right now get Alba and Rodrigo out of here. Call Matlock and have him pick you up. Tell him to bring our truck up too. We'll all rendezvous at the Broken "T"."

"What are you going to do with the vice president's body?" he asked.

"I'm still thinking, Creed," answered Mako. "Didn't I tell you there's no such thing as a textbook extraction? Now get moving. It's not safe here."

Creed took Alba by the hand and walked briskly out of the house. Rodrigo stood over Mario's body in the hallway in disbelief.

"Rodrigo, *vamonos*!" shouted Creed.

Rodrigo knelt down and closed his friend's eyes.

He picked up the inert body, carrying it in front of him like a new bride.

"Leave him," called out Creed.

"No, *señor*, he comes with us!" Rodrigo insisted.

***

"Mako?" QL looked up from the body of the vice president with a question on his lips.

"I haven't the slightest idea," replied Mako. "No matter what you were going to ask, I don't have the answer."

"That's reassuring. You've always been an inspiring leader."

"Thanks for the vote of confidence, but save your barbs for later. It's just the first time I've seen a dead vice president of the United States.

"You and me both."

"In the meantime, you might want to take some photos, QL. They may come in handy and keep us out of prison."

"Hope they work better than last time," replied QL.

Mako pulled out his secure cell phone and ten seconds later had Drake Herrin on the line.

"Drake, here it is in a nutshell. Creed's on his way back to the Broken "T" with Alba. Mario's dead. About a dozen bad guys are down. A couple of other unexpected casualties as well. "

"Let's hear it," said Drake.

"That's the interesting part. The meeting Mario alluded to? It was Francisco Salcido, aka *El Padrino,* and a guest. The guest was Vice President Archibald Rutledge. They're both dead."

"Archibald Rutledge is dead?" asked Drake Herrin.

"Yeah, we heard shots as we were going room to room. It looks like Salcido shot the vice-president. Probably thought he had been set up."

"Any theories?"

"We might be talking about a two-headed snake. I'm thinking Rutledge might have been the head of the National Front."

"Good God, man! You can't be serious. But why?"

"Let's talk later. We're getting out of here and bringing in a few bodies."

"I'll get Bronc Thornton over here for a positive identification."

"Make sure you have something on ice for us, Drake. We're going to need a few drinks after this."

Two hours later Bronc Thornton climbed up into the bed of QL's pickup with a can of Tecate in one hand and looked down at the body of Francisco Salcido, which had been covered by a black tarp. A Ferragamo designer shoe stuck out incongruously from under the tarp, a reminder of the drug lord's expensive tastes.

Mako pulled back the tarp, revealing the frozen features of the Culiacán native.

"Yeah, that's Pancho alright. Never looked better in my opinion. Not very sporting, though, to shoot a man with a broken leg, is it?" asked Bronc.

"He didn't leave us much choice," answered Mako. "We found him to be distinctly lacking in good manners."

"Looks like his friend here would share your opinion," said Bronc as he glanced at the body of the vice-president. "I recognize Pancho's handiwork," he commented, pointing at the entry wound in the forehead. "Who is he? Looks like a preppy lawyer from Austin."

"Good call. Yeah, he was a preppy lawyer, alright," replied Mako.

"Anyone I'd know?" asked Bronc.

"Not unless you read the newspapers, watch television, or listen to the radio." said Mako.

"Bronc, do you know why Francisco would be meeting with the vice president of the United States?" asked Drake.

"Is that who that dead motherfucker is?" Bronc asked. "Christ, Francisco knew his business, didn't he?"

"What do you mean?" asked Drake.

"Well, all you hear about in the U.S. is Mexican government corruption and collusion with the traffickers, and you're telling me the whole time the vice president of the United States was working with the Sinaloa cartel? That's funny as hell," Bronc suggested.

"Yeah, a real hoot," said Mako. "Only I'm not sure we're talking about a penetration. Rutledge had his own agenda, you can bet on that. My guess is that they were both using each other."

Mako pulled the tarp back over Salcido's corpse and the three men jumped down from the back of the pickup. Bronc was the only one who seemed to find humor in the situation.

"Have you checked their cell phones?" asked Bronc.

"Rutledge's phone was shot to pieces. We're looking at Salcido's," replied Drake.

"Well, I can tell you whose numbers are in that phone," claimed Bronc. "Start off with the next president of Mexico and then use your imagination. Better have a thick notebook when you start to jot the numbers down."

"You're talking about Félix Aguilar, I presume?" asked Mako.

"Yep, the man owes his political career to Francisco. He'll be sorely disappointed to hear of *El Padrino's* demise. Mexico's lost a real patriot," he said cynically.

"Were they friends?" asked Mako.

"A man like Francisco doesn't really have friends, Mako. How could he? He had to watch his back twenty-four hours a day. He trusted Félix, though, at least as much as he trusted anyone," explained Bronc.

He drained the can of Tecate and tossed the empty in the back of the pickup truck. The can bounced off Salcido's corpse and rattled until it came to rest along a corrugated steel ridge in the bed of the pickup.

"How about Salcido? Was he behind the National Front?" asked Drake.

"Yeah, he was behind it. At least in some capacity. But he had a partner in the U.S. who would call him and ask for money, men, and sometimes even weapons. I overheard some of those conversations. But here's the kicker: Salcido didn't know who it was," said Bronc, scratching the four-day stubble on his chin.

"Until tonight," speculated Mako.

Drake looked sharply at Mako. He took off his navy blue Texas Rangers baseball hat, pulled his long white hair back into a pony tail and tied it with a rubber band.

"Pancho loved to be the moving force behind political candidates and movements," continued Bronc. "He did the same thing in Mexico with the attorney general. Money can move mountains; change villains into heroes. He wanted to expand his empire, and he hated us *gringos*," added Bronc.

"It's still pretty farfetched to think that Rutledge might have been behind the National Front," said Drake.

"You have another explanation of why the vice president of the United States was having a tête-à-tête in South Texas with the head of a Mexican drug cartel?" asked Mako. "Come on, Drake. You're usually way ahead of me on these things."

Drake grasped the bill of his cap and looked up at the sky.

"It's just such an elaborate scheme. I mean, the National Front isn't just one man. It's an entire organization. It's like a shadow government with huge popular support. How could one man have organized it?"

"How could a debauched, spoiled frat boy become vice president?" asked Mako. "The man was ambitious, and he had organizational talent. A few hours ago I would have agreed it couldn't be true. Now I'm not so sure."

"Doesn't a vice president have a secret service retinue?" asked Bronc. "Where were they?"

"Rutledge had a reputation for sneaking out on his own," explained Drake. "They caught him once in a strip club in Moscow all by himself chatting up a Russian hooker. He wasn't exactly a role model for America's youth, you know. They're probably looking for him right now in the clubs near his hotel in Austin."

"So what the hell do we do?" asked Mako. "Get rid of the evidence?"

"That's going to be up to the president," said Drake. I'm more interested in something else." Drake paused, deep in thought.

"I'm waiting," said Mako.

"Bronc, did the attorney general ever talk personally with

the head of the National Front?" asked Drake.

"I doubt it, but that'd just be speculation on my part. Francisco wouldn't have shared his contacts with anyone. The attorney general encouraged him, of course. He even referred to the movement as the beginning of the *reconquista*. You know, when Mexico takes back the land we stole from them after the Mexican-American war."

"Mako, I think this might be an opportunity to employ an old-fashioned 'false-flag' approach," said Drake.

"What are you talking about?"

"Well, I think the president would like to know how involved the Mexican government is in all this," said Drake. "I know I would. If we can get to Aguilar, I'd say we have a chance to find out."

"So what are you thinking?"

"The National Front has lost its anonymous leader, right? If we named his successor, Aguilar would never know it's not the same man, would he?"

"I guess not," said Mako. "But I've burned my bridges with him, Drake. He'll have me killed if I show up in Mexico again. Find someone else," he suggested.

"I have," replied Drake. They heard the screen door slam, and both looked over to the ranch house where James Brazzle was coming down the stairs and walking in their direction.

CHAPTER 46

"So it's true?" asked Félix Aguilar.

"*Si, desgraciadamente es la verdad. El Padrino está muerto!*" reluctantly confirmed Salcido's younger brother Antonio.

"But how can you be sure?" asked Félix into his cell phone.

"We've got a witness. There was a raid on *El Padrino's* Texas ranch to rescue the girl. You know...the *gringo's* daughter. There was a housekeeper in the guest quarters. She called the emergency phone number."

"She saw *El Padrino's* body?" asked Félix.

"No, the *gringos* took him away, but he's dead. We're sure of that."

"*¡Ay caray!*" lamented the attorney general. "What now?"

"What do you mean? Nothing changes. Nothing ever changes. I'm the new *Padrino* and we keep working together".

"But what about the National Front?" asked the attorney general.

"Ah, now that I don't know. Francisco never shared his political plans with me."

Félix threw his cell phone on the thickly carpeted floor of his office and cursed. He leaned back in his chair and stared blankly at the wall.

He had been delivering a stump speech the night before in Zacatecas when the rumor hit with the force of a Julio Cesar Chavez body punch. *El Padrino* had supposedly been gunned down in a shootout in South Texas. The Mexican news media and the Spanish language networks in the United States spoke of nothing else. News of the death of the vice president of the United States in the same gun battle gave rise to a plethora of conspiracy theories. Frankly, though, the attorney general could have cared less about the vice president of the United States. He had hitched his horse to the Francisco Salcido bandwagon, and the possibility that the source of unlimited funding for his political career might have suddenly disappeared was not a pleasant thought.

As much as he regretted Francisco's death, Félix realized that now he had the opportunity to manipulate the events in South Texas as he saw fit and to plan strategy for the next stage of the *reconquista* movement. Aguilar's own ambition for the movement extended far beyond the borders of South Texas. He intended to provide the spark to ignite smoldering resentment towards Anglo supremacy elsewhere as well. He would turn the localized movement for autonomy in South Texas into a general conflagration that consumed the entire Southwest, but to accomplish that he desperately needed to establish contact with Francisco Salcido's political ally, the head of the National Front.

Félix cancelled his scheduled appearance at the quarterly meeting of the Princeton Alumni Club at the Maria Isabel Sheraton Hotel and returned to his residence in *Las Lomas de Chapultepec.* The almost daily thunderstorms that accosted Mexico City during the summer rainy season had drifted off to the east, leaving the capital's normally noxious air almost breathable, admittedly a relative concept for the smog-choked city.

Félix sat alone on his terrace, his domestic staff scurrying to make the attorney general comfortable and bringing trays of traditional Mexican hors d'oeuvres and a selection of his favorite alcoholic beverages, including several brands of French cognac, Bacardi rum, and ice-cold bottles of Modelo Especial. The attorney general accepted the lavish attention as his due and indicated with a slight inclination of his head and a subtle movement of the index finger of his right hand that he would prefer a Bacardi rum and coke. Félix then dismissed his obsequious staff with an imperious wave of his hand and sat back, savoring the Cuba Libre, mixed to perfection with just the right amount of fresh lime juice.

He looked down into the courtyard of his neighbor's house. On weekends his neighbor's young trophy wife had the habit of sunbathing topless in plain view of the terrace and didn't seem to mind the attorney general's undisguised interest in her anatomy. The thirty-year old bleached blond bombshell recently returned from Los Angeles with an exaggerated bust line and paraded endlessly back and forth between her reclining chair and the swimming pool, proudly displaying the latest advances in North American plastic surgery. At the moment, though, there was nothing in his neighbor's backyard to hold Félix's attention beyond a tasteless collection of imitation Aztec and Mayan statues depicting grotesque genetic crosses between reptiles and human beings.

The attorney general was deep in thought and didn't notice that night had descended upon *Las Lomas.* He sat in the darkness, the occasional bolt of distant lightning briefly illuminating the terrace and the trays of food he hadn't touched.

Félix nodded off briefly. His chin bounced off the top of his chest and he woke up with a start, cursing under his breath. Falling asleep in his chair made him feel like an old man. It had been a stressful day, he thought, or maybe he really was aging. As he stood up from the lounge chair, trying to get his bearings in the pitch black, his cell phone suddenly rang. Félix did not recognize the number but saw that the country code of the caller was "1", the United States. He pushed the green button.

"*Si,*" he said.

The voice he heard spoke fluent Spanish, but with a slight accent the attorney general couldn't place.

"Is this Félix?" the caller asked.

"In the flesh," the attorney general quipped. "Who's this?"

"Francisco Salcido gave me your phone number and suggested I call you if anything ever happened to him. It appears the man was clairvoyant."

Félix caught his breath. This was a turn of events he hadn't expected. He sat back down in his chair and tried to control his breathing.

"Do you represent the National Front?"

"I *am* the National Front," the voice continued.

"Then we need to talk," suggested the attorney general.

"When can you come to Laredo?"

"I can be there in a few days. Can I call you at this number?"

***

The initial outrage over Vice President Rutledge's murder in South Texas and the bellicose rhetoric about punitive air strikes against cartel targets in Mexico soon gave way to shock and indignation when the details of his death began to trickle in. Speculation inside the beltway over the vice president's relationship with the head of the Sinaloa cartel kept the administration preoccupied and in extreme damage-control mode in the days after the shootout at Rancho Las Aguilas. Even the republican opposition in Congress was more interested in exposing corruption in the democratic administration and harvesting political capital from the crisis than exacting retribution for a murder nobody really understood. To the amazement of everyone south of the Nueces River, the crisis in South Texas was put on the back burner as insiders in Washington pointed fingers and blamed each other for the colossal goat fuck.

In La Salle and Webb counties, on the other hand, things were heating up. The National Front began an aggressive propaganda campaign to promote the referendum, and its spokesmen had been holding town meetings and gatherings in local high school gymnasiums virtually non-stop since the shootout. The Front continued to function as a well-greased machine, a tribute to the organizational and conspiratorial skills of its late founder. Even Rudy Gutierrez, though, had no idea his organization had lost its leader. He was curious when the daily phone calls from his superior ceased, but the Front's operating account was flush, and Rudy was too busy campaigning for the referendum to worry.

Creed Tucker led the movement in opposition to the referendum on autonomy, and he used every opportunity to counter the anti-Anglo rhetoric of his former Vietnam "blood brother". To everyone's surprise, Creed's message took root and his support grew in leaps and bounds as the hard-working Mexican-American middle class in South Texas grew tired of the radicalism of the National Front.

A week after the shootout that took the lives of the vice president and the head of the Sinaloa cartel, Creed Tucker and James Brazzle sat under the tall mesquite tree in front of the Broken "T" ranch headquarters. The extended drought had decimated the mosquito population in South Texas, one of the few positive results of the dry spell. The pesky insects had practically become an endangered species and sitting outside at dusk would have been almost pleasant for a change if it hadn't been for the John Deere tractor seats which passed as lawn chairs. It hurt to sit in them. The two men squirmed uncomfortably, trying in vain to find a position that didn't exacerbate their old rodeo injuries. Clouds had gathered on the eastern horizon as Tropical Storm Janis pushed valiantly against a high pressure system, trying to make her way inland through Port Isabel. The ranchers agreed they would gladly accept some wind damage in return for five inches of rain.

"I still think you ought to reconsider and talk to Bronc

Thornton before the debate," suggested James. "You know drug trafficking is going to be a major topic, and you don't know shit about it." James reached into the cooler and rummaged around for the last Modelo Especial. "If you're going to argue against a referendum, you'll need to know what you're talking about."

"Listen, I know all I need to know about drug trafficking. The bastards subverted the democratic process and finagled this cockamamie idea of holding a referendum on autonomy, killed Texas National Guardsmen, kidnapped my daughter, and murdered the vice president of the United States. You need more?"

"Well, don't forget that the vice president might have been as corrupt as anyone. He could be at the root of the whole problem."

"That remains to be seen, I'd say," said Creed. "But if it's so damned important to you, I'll talk to Bronc."

That was all James had been waiting for, and he raised his aching body slowly from the John Deere seat and stretched.

"Creed, you give Texas hospitality a bad name with these tractor seats. I don't think you could have made more uncomfortable chairs if you had tried. Alright, I'm going to get Bronc. Last time I saw him he was sober."

Creed watched James walk stiffly down to the round pen where Rodrigo was giving a few tips on horsemanship to Mako and Bronc.

"Bronc!" called James as he peered over the cedar posts of the round pen. "Come give us your sage advice. We've got problems of state to resolve."

"This I got to hear," said Mako, following Bronc as he opened the creaking gate of the round pen and followed his new friend towards the house, the slick soles of his cowboy boots slipping on the sparse dead grass, his spurs jangling like wind chimes. Rodrigo dismounted and led the stud out of the round pen towards the barn. Alba climbed out of the bleachers and took Rodrigo's hand, kissing him lightly on the cheek.

Creed watched the three men approach, as unlikely a group of heroes as you'd ever want to see, he thought. Why does South Texas have to depend on two over-the-hill ex-CIA types and one ex-pilot for the Sinaloa drug cartel?

"Sit down, Bronc," he said gruffly.

Bronc made himself as comfortable as possible in the John Deere tractor seat directly across from him. Creed didn't like talking to Bronc, and he hurried to get the conversation over with.

"Bronc, let me tell you something. If you hadn't flown Phantoms in the war, and if old James Brazzle here hadn't convinced me to talk with you about drug trafficking, we wouldn't be having this conversation." Creed looked long and hard at Bronc with critical eyes.

The two men were silent for a moment as Bronc pulled out a joint from his shirt pocket and lit it.

"Well, Creed," drawled Bronc, inhaling deeply. "If your wife didn't have such delectable tits, I doubt if I'd still be hanging out on the Broken "T" talking with you, so I guess we're even. I'm partial to brown women, you know."

James was out of his seat and grabbed Creed by the shoulders before the old rancher had time to raise his fist. "Sit down you old fart. You started that one," said James, his temper rising. "You are one crotchety old son of a gun, aren't you? Always looking for a fight."

Creed sat back breathing heavily, trying to compose himself. Bronc pissed him off just being Bronc, much less bringing in Lupe's name, even if he *was* just trying to get a rise out of him. Creed felt the men's eyes on him, and somewhere deep inside he knew his grouchiness had gotten the best of him and made him look foolish...again.

"Okay, touché, Bronc, let's talk business. James here thinks you can educate me on the drug problem in the country," said Creed grudgingly.

"Depends...what do you want to know?" said Bronc, helping himself to one of Creed's Lone Stars.

"Do we have a problem?" asked Creed.

"I don't, do you?" countered Bronc.

"Bronc, cut the shit, will you?" demanded James. "Tell him what you were telling me yesterday."

"Alright, alright," Bronc said, putting down his joint and picking up a bottle of Lone Star. "Now where were we?" he asked.

"The War on Drugs?" Creed reminded him.

"Oh, yeah. All I was telling James was that nobody really wants to win the War on Drugs. Let's be honest for a minute, can we? Nobody, not the DEA, the FBI, U.S. Customs, not even the president. The War on Drugs is a cash cow! It's the feeding trough for thousands and thousands of government workers: from street cops to DEA agents to prison hacks all across the country. You know what the worst nightmare is for both the drug cartels and the U.S. government? Legalization, that's what! It would put them all out of business. But think of the savings in government spending. Think of the tax revenues! It's a no-brainer, but government agencies don't want their rice bowls broken."

Creed looked at Bronc and rolled his eyes.

"It's actually not as crazy as it sounds," said James. "More and more Latin American countries are looking seriously at legalization as the only solution to the violence associated with drug trafficking."

"May I remind you the vice president was killed last week in a shootout with Mexican drug traffickers? I don't think the country is ready to consider that kind of radical policy," Creed said. "I know I'm not. Besides, this is Texas, not the People's Republic of Massachusetts or somewhere like that."

"Maybe," said James. "But 80% of the population in South Texas is Hispanic. They think differently than the Bible Belt voters in the rest of Texas. Keep it in mind when you debate Rudy."

CHAPTER 47

Rudy Gutierrez loved political campaigns. He was in his element whether sampling Mexican food at a gathering of his militant political base in Brownsville with mariachi music playing in the background or giving a speech in a packed high school football stadium in Laredo. He had a message for the Hispanics of South Texas and his audience was receptive.

When the head of the National Front called the week before and told him he would be the Front's candidate for president of the Autonomous Republic of South Texas once the referendum was approved, Rudy was thrilled. Then, when the campaign contributions began flowing like an oil gusher into the Front's account in the Falcon International Bank, Rudy's optimism over the future of his cause turned into sheer exhilaration. With that kind of financial support, Rudy knew the referendum would be held and that he couldn't possibly lose the election.

The crowds that gathered to hear his fire-breathing, anti-Anglo rhetoric were effusive in their support of the National Front. He flaunted his Vietnam wartime credentials and used them to lambast what he referred to as "Anglo racism". He recounted his experience during the Tet Offensive in 1968 when a North Vietnamese machine gun position had his mostly Hispanic squad pinned down in the rubble of Hue. His Anglo company commander had refused to come to his aid, he said, and his squad was all but wiped out. Gutierrez limped to this day, a memento, he said, of Anglo moral hypocrisy.

Rudy urged Hispanics to stand up for themselves and take back what the "soulless" North Americans had stolen from their ancestors. To do otherwise, he challenged, would be the moral equivalent of betrayal and surrender. He called upon his Latino brethren to rise up in New Mexico, Arizona, and California and throw off the shackles of Anglo racism.

Rudy's personal security apparatus consisted of the reconstituted Laredo chapter of the Brown Berets, mostly Vietnam, Iraq, and Afghanistan veterans with one thing in common: a commitment to the *reconquista*...first South Texas then the rest of the Southwest. Before the referendum, most had been under FBI surveillance as subversives and suspected terrorists. Now they wore the distinction as a badge of honor.

Rudy was a born leader, but he didn't mind taking instructions from the head of the National Front, a man he actually had never seen. His respect for the man's political acumen had grown dramatically following the Battle of Cotulla when he overrode Rudy's military advice and supplied the R.A.T.S. defensive forces with Russian surface-to-air missiles. As predicted by the anonymous head of the National Front, the Texas National Guard victory indeed proved Pyrrhic in nature, and the sacrifice of the Martyrs of Cotulla had turned world opinion in their favor. The death of the vice president had further muddied the waters, but the resulting paralysis and finger-pointing in Washington played into the National Front's hand and bought them the time they needed to campaign in favor of the autonomy referendum. In fact, the vice president's death was proving so fortuitous for the cause of South Texas autonomy that Rudy wondered whether the mysterious head of the National Front had planned that as well.

When the almost daily phone calls from Rudy's mentor suddenly ceased, he wasn't concerned. With several million dollars in the National Front's operating account, there was more than enough money to finance an elaborate campaign and orchestrate a media blitz before the referendum which Rudy viewed as a foregone conclusion. When Rudy's personal assistant delivered the newspapers early one morning and pointed excitedly to the headlines in disbelief, Rudy was as flabbergasted as anyone, but he failed to connect the dots or draw a connection between the sensational news and the coincidental disappearance of the head of the National Front. Instead, his political instincts told him to prepare a rebuttal against possible accusations of National Front involvement in the atrocity.

In South Texas the death of Francisco Salcido brought out mixed emotions. The more radical elements of the *reconquista* movement, including most of the R.A.T.S. soldiers and recent illegal immigrants, were alarmed. They knew where most of their political support came from, and many were concerned about the future flow of money and weapons to their cause. On the other side of the political spectrum were the more conservative Latinos: those who had bitten the bullet and bowed their heads for years in resignation. They had worked hard and fought tooth and nail for their citizenship and middle-class status. They were elated over the news. They had no desire to see South Texas degenerate into a lawless region where unwritten arbitrary rules were upheld at the point of a gun: a North American Sinaloa.

Rudy Gutierrez entered the studios of Telefutura 21 in Laredo, Texas accompanied by his entourage of Brown Beret bodyguards, stout mustachioed men carrying a variety of semi-automatic weaponry and with handguns bulging out from under their shirts. They wore distinctive brown berets, some of them worn and tattered, probably relics from their days as political activists in the 1960s. Most sported tattoos, and the younger ones were sleeved out. Rudy on the other hand had undergone a complete makeover, exchanging his Vietnam-era combat fatigues and Che Guevara t-shirt for a conservative business suit. He had even shaved his Daniel Ortega look-alike mustache. Rudy appreciated the contrast between his new conservative exterior and radical political persona and was sure the "new look" would be good for a few thousand more votes in support of the referendum and autonomy.

Rudy looked around the studio expectantly and caught sight of Creed Tucker and two middle-aged Anglos about his own age talking with CNN moderator Bubba Dobbs, who had left a Brownsville hospital that morning. Dobbs wore his left arm in a sling and still looked pale from his ordeal.

"Bubba!" Rudy called out as he approached the group. He motioned to his Brown Berets to stay behind and greeted the three men as if he were getting together with fellow members of the Laredo Kiwanis Club.

"Who are you trying to fool with that business suit, Rudy?" asked Bubba. "This is the first time I've ever seen you with a tie. Where's that wrinkled Che Guevara t-shirt you usually wear?"

"That just shows how little you know me, Bubba," said Rudy. "Even Che wore a suit every now and then."

"Hello, Rudy," Creed said. "I'd like you to meet my advisors."

Rudy shook Creed's hand and looked at his two friends. They returned his appraising stare without flinching and greeted him in fluent Spanish. He recognized the type although it had been awhile.

"Where's Van Slyke?" asked Rudy. "Aren't there supposed to be three of us here to discuss the referendum?"

"Rudy, my contacts in Texas have informed me that the FBI picked up Mr. Van Slyke this morning for questioning," replied Bubba Dobbs. "He won't be gracing us with his presence tonight."

"For questioning? About what?" asked Rudy.

"I think you know the answer to that one, Rudy," said Bubba with an edge to his voice.

"You overestimate me, Bubba," said Rudy. "But I assume I'm going to hear the old litany of accusations of electoral fraud tonight? I was hoping you *gringos* would come up with something new to accuse us Latinos of, but I guess I was wrong."

"I'm just the moderator," Rudy, objected Bubba. "Although I do have a better idea than I used to about how ruthless the drug lords are." He pointed to his bandaged shoulder as evidence. "I can't speak for Creed although I understand he's had a few encounters with the drug traffickers himself."

"You *are* arrogant bastards, aren't you? Let me make one thing clear right now, and I'll repeat it as many times during the debate as I need to. Our movement has nothing to do with the Mexican drug cartels. It has everything to do with Hispanic civil rights and reclaiming our dignity which was stolen from us by you *gringos* along with about half our country."

"This should be an interesting exchange of views," said Bubba. "Okay, we're on in thirty seconds. James, you and Mako can join the audience. Rudy and Creed, let's take our seats in the studio."

The men hurriedly took their seats, and Bubba watched the producer for his cue.

"Good evening. This is Bubba Dobbs from Laredo, Texas, the future capital of the Autonomous Republic of South Texas if Rudy Gutierrez and the National Front have their way. The last few weeks have witnessed some momentous events in the history of the United States, not the least of which was the murder last week of Vice President Archibald Rutledge, whose bullet-riddled body was found on a ranch south of Cotulla, Texas. I stand before you tonight with my arm in a sling, another victim of Mexican drug cartel violence in this lawless region."

Bubba stood up, took off his suit jacket and melodramatically displayed his "badge of courage," turning around for the cameras to make sure the television audience saw his bandaged shoulder and arm in a sling.

"Bubba, let me say one thing to start with," interrupted

Rudy. "The National Front condemns violence as much as any other political grouping in South Texas, and we have nothing to do with the Mexican drug cartels. We believe in the democratic process, and that's why I'm here tonight."

"Okay, Rudy, let's go ahead and start with you," said Bubba. "What exactly does 'autonomous' mean to you?

"That's an excellent question," replied Rudy. "We're all Americans. We're not looking to become a separate country. But because the overwhelming majority of the population of South Texas is Hispanic, we're just saying that our interests have not been protected or represented by the predominately Anglo governments in Austin and Washington. We think we can do a better job. We will secure our own borders, police our own territory but still remain loyal Americans: Hispanic Americans with our own autonomous identity. We believe we should have the right to determine our own future. The referendum would give us that voice."

"Creed, would you care to comment on anything Rudy mentioned?"

"Yes, indeed," replied Creed. "First of all let me say that I don't question Mr. Gutierrez' claim that he and his supporters are loyal Americans. I'm familiar with Rudy's military record, and it's impeccable. I would only suggest that Rudy perhaps is not aware of the influence the drug cartels have had in pushing for the referendum...at gunpoint. Quite frankly, I think that's the crux of the matter here."

The rest of the debate went as expected. Rudy appealed to emotions of the Hispanic majority in the border region of Texas and Creed spoke to the economic realities of autonomy and the very real threat of massive military intervention by either the Texas National Guard or the U.S Armed Forces, something he predicted would occur within the week, once Washington had recovered from the dual shock of the "Mexican Standoff" and the murder of the vice-president. Creed wanted to prevent a bloodbath, and he attempted to paint a stark contrast between the chaos and poverty in Mexico and the prosperity and security of the United States. He ended his closing monologue with a telling statement, or at least he thought so.

"Some of you were born here, but many of you crossed the Rio Grande looking for a better life. Have you forgotten why you came or what you wanted to leave behind? A vote for the referendum and autonomy is a vote for the past and what you left behind," Creed declared passionately.

When Creed sat down and Rudy Gutierrez stood up for his closing remarks, a commotion erupted in audience that slowly grew in volume until half the audience was standing up and cheering wildly. Creed at first mistook the excitement for an unexpected show of support for his position, but as the shouts grew more insistent, Bubba's producer burst into the studio.

"They're pulling back!" he shouted.

"What?" asked Bubba, stunned at the brazen interruption.

"The U.S. Army is retreating!" he repeated.

***

Johnny Rodriguez of the Second Battalion had become an overnight media sensation. A You Tube clip of Johnny venturing into no-man's land between the Seventh Cavalry Regiment and the Texas lines asking to borrow a bottle of Cholula chipotle-flavored hot sauce went viral with over ten million views in twenty-four hours. Even before General "Tommy" Buchanan ordered the Seventh Cavalry back to its barracks in Fort Hood, a Cholula advertising executive posing as a reporter from "Univision" infiltrated the Second Battalion's forward positions looking for Johnny and waving an advertising contract in the air.

"You want me to do what?" asked Johnny in amazement.

"We want you to be Cholula's spokesman. Sign this contract, and you'll be on every Spanish-language television station in the United States within thirty days. We'll guarantee you a six figure minimum during the next twelve months."

Johnny had drunk a lot of beer in the last twenty-four hours, and he was rolling a marijuana cigarette with Chapo Zavala. "Hey Baby Qué Pasó" by the Texas Tornadoes blared at full volume from a battery-powered MP3 speaker, and he wasn't sure he heard right.

"Say what?" asked Johnny. He sat cross-legged in the shelter of a two-man canvas tent with a pair of earphones glued to his ears.

"You're a star, Johnny!" declared the Cholula executive. "We want you to be our spokesman for Cholula's 'Give Peace a Chance' campaign."

"Give Peace a Chance?" he repeated. "Shit, why not?" he sighed. "Can you get me out of my 4-year enlistment?" he asked hopefully.

"Something tells me, they'll be glad to get rid of you, Johnny!" laughed the Cholula representative. "It might be the only way to avoid putting you before a firing squad. And they don't need any more bad publicity."

***

One thousand yards to the south, the mood of the National Guard troops and the Texas irregulars was ebullient. A rumor that the Second Battalion had been ordered back to Fort Hood spread like wildfire through the Texas lines. By noon federal soldiers were dismantling their temporary shelters and loading equipment into their trucks. An hour later dozens of diesel engines were belching smoke as the federal column prepared to leave the scene of the bizarre standoff and return to its barracks.

When the first Humvees turned around and headed north on I-35 towards San Antonio, rousing rebel yells and Mexican *gritos* resounded in waves along the Texas front line. A thundering crash of gunfire echoed across the flat plain as thousands of celebrating and relieved farmers and ranchers fired their weapons into the air. The realization that this motley crew of Texas patriots had forced the mighty III Corps to back down was intoxicating. Local residents lined either side of the interstate to jeer the federal troops on their humiliating return to Fort Hood. Symbolically, the civilians held up the now-famous bottles of Cholula Hot Sauce and chanted the new Cholula slogan, "Give...Peace...A...Chance!"

Governor Rick Throckmorton stood by Colonel Ignacio Cruz of the Texas National Guard and beamed. He pounded the Colonel's back and did his best imitation of a Mexican *grito*. Half a dozen ranchers approached the governor and hoisted him to their shoulders, marching back and forth along the rapidly disintegrating Texas line and shouting, "Rick...Rick... Rick!" The horns of several hundred pickup trucks honked incessantly.

A little over one thousand six hundred miles away, the president of the United States sat with his national security advisor in the Oval Office and watched the live television feed from Dilley, Texas.

"From goat to hero in forty-eight hours," the president mumbled. "There was a method to his madness after all."

"When does *our* metamorphosis begin?" asked the national security advisor.

"Never, unless we can somehow wade out of this shit smelling like a rose," said the president gloomily.

At that moment CNN's Margarita Lopez approached Governor Throckmorton amid the noisy jubilation of the rejoicing troops in Dilley and thrust a microphone into his face.

"Governor, tell us what you're feeling in your moment of triumph," she demanded.

"First of all Rita, let me just say that this is a victory not only for Texas, but for the country as a whole. Cooler heads have prevailed, and I want to express my gratitude to General "Tommy" Buchanan and the president of the United States for their decision to 'Give Peace a Chance'!"

The local residents, who had crowded around the governor to hear his interview, howled with glee and raised their bottles of Cholula Hot Sauce as if on cue.

"Give...Peace...A...Chance!" they shouted in unison. The Chapala Advertising Agency from Guadalajara, Mexico had rushed in a camera crew the night before to shoot some raw footage just in case the Cholula-sponsored peace campaign continued to catch fire. They couldn't believe their good fortune as Dilley residents and the Texas irregulars waved their bottles of hot sauce and chanted.

"Governor Throckmorton, what message would you like to give to the president of the United States?" asked the CNN reporter.

"It's very simple. I would like to work with the president to begin the healing process. Violence only begets more violence. Texas has always been different from the rest of the country. We must look for an alternative path to confront the dual problems of illegal immigration and drug trafficking. With the president's help, Texas will point the way for the rest of the nation."

"There you have it, ladies and gentlemen. Governor Rick Throckmorton extends an olive branch...or should I say a bottle of Cholula Hot Sauce for peace to the president. This is Margarita Lopez reporting for CNN from Dilley, Texas."

The president clicked off the television with his remote control and sat back with a sigh. "Texas politicians are all full of shit, aren't they? The country hasn't seen this kind of political theater since LBJ," said the president. He paused and looked over at his national security advisor. "Are you thinking what I'm thinking?" he asked.

"Well, there *is* an immediate vacancy in your administration, sir. It would be seen as a gesture of reconciliation, that's for sure. I'd say it's something to think about."

"And then we just let the situation in South Texas run its course? We let Mexico's failed state drift northwards. Where does it stop? At the Red River?" The president wadded up a sheet of paper in frustration and tossed it into a trash can next to his desk.

"No, actually there's some hope in South Texas," replied the national security advisor. "An Anglo rancher named Creed Tucker is campaigning against the referendum and is showing unexpected strength in recent polling even among Hispanics. He's got a fighting chance to win."

"Is he pro-Texas?"

"Very much so."

"Well, I wish him success, but if the National Front decides to hold the referendum under some pretext, we're going back in with surgical air strikes with or without the approval of Throckmorton," said the president.

"We've got to get Congress focused again. This witch hunt for offshore bank accounts and cartel moles is costing us a lot of political capital."

"I'd say that'll take a few more days. In the meantime..." The president leaned over and pushed the button on the office intercom system.

"Yes, Mr. President," his receptionist answered.

"Could you dial Rick Throckmorton's private cell phone,

please?" the president requested.

CHAPTER 48

Rain fell at the Broken "T" Land & Cattle Company Ranch for the first time in almost a year as the remnants of Tropical Storm Janis bullied their way into South Texas. The arid, parched ground greedily soaked up every drop of moisture and begged for more. Within an hour, water began to pool and run off into shallow arroyos and gulches that hadn't held water for what seemed a lifetime. Even the horses welcomed the storm and stood in their overgrazed pastures with their hindquarters pointing to the wind, tails between their legs. Sheets of wind-driven rain cascaded down their backs, and their manes ruffled in the stiff breeze.

Scrap Tucker pulled up in his pickup, windshield wipers waving frantically, and parked in front of the house. The truck's rugged all-terrain tires left deep ruts in the mud across the ranch, but the relentless downpour promised to obliterate any trace of the truck's passing. Scrap and Rodrigo got out of the truck and ran for the shelter of the screen porch. Creed was waiting for them inside and held the door open as the two men stomped up the wooden stairs in their Wellington rain boots. It had been nine months since Guadalupe ordered the sixteen inch rubber boots from L.L. Bean, and this was the first time the men had even tried them on.

"Where's the over-the-hill gang?" asked Scrap.

"Inside having breakfast," Creed answered. "Rodrigo, take your boots off and go find Alba for your English lesson. She's waiting for you."

Rodrigo nodded his head and headed for the living room where Alba was waiting with her CD player and notebooks.

"I'd say you're going to have a new brother-in-law before too long, Scrap," said Creed, appraising Rodrigo as he left the porch. "What do you think of that?"

"It's probably more important what you think of it, Dad," replied Scrap.

"She could do worse," Creed said, never one to waste words.

Scrap took off his muddy boots and tossed them into a cardboard box in the corner of the porch. "Tanks are starting to fill up," he said. "I thought we were going to have to start hauling water soon for the cattle. This rain is a godsend."

They heard voices in the kitchen and turned to see Mako Sloane, Drake Herrin, and James Brazzle ambling around looking for the coffee maker. Creed took off his windbreaker and hung it up on the deer antler clothes rack in the corner of the porch. He opened the screen door and joined the others.

"You boys make me nervous when you get together like this. I know chaos and mayhem aren't far behind," said Creed in his typical grumbling manner.

"Chaos and mayhem?" laughed James. "Hell, Creed, you are hard to please. What can you possibly find to criticize with civil war, kidnappings, and assassinations to keep you entertained?"

"Yep," Creed replied. "What do my political advisors have planned today?"

"How does a meeting with Rudy Gutierrez grab you?" asked James.

"I doubt he'd agree to that," Creed replied. He looked around the kitchen and realized the others knew something he didn't.

"He already has, Creed," said Drake Herrin.

Creed frowned. He didn't know whether he liked being

out of the loop like this. He was starting to feel like a real politician with his staff making all the important decisions with him just smiling and shaking hands...a figurehead.

"What'd you do? Threaten to kill his family? How'd you get him to agree to see me? He pretty much hates our guts. Made that pretty clear during the debate, didn't he?"

"He did, Creed," James said. "But he also made pretty clear his opposition to the drug traffickers."

"And you believed him?" asked Creed, rolling his eyes.

"I did. That's why you need to see him. To convince him he's playing into their hands."

"I'd hate to burst the man's bubble," said Creed seriously. "Besides I don't recall we have any real proof. It seems obvious to me, but it'd just be my word against his."

"Creed, we've got something you can show Rudy. It might get him thinking at least," said Drake Herrin as he handed several sheets of paper to Creed.

"Just tell me what it is, you bunch of conspirators," said Creed and thrust the paper back at Drake.

"Damn it, Creed, if you're going to be a politician, you've got to get used to reading a written report every once in a while," said James.

"Who says I want to be a politician, but anyway, that's what I have you high-powered advisors for."

Creed reluctantly took the documents from Drake and sat down on a stool at the breakfast bar in the kitchen, glancing at the report and trying to make sense out of the numbers, dates, and dollar amounts.

"Well, I see some bank account numbers, wire transfers, and dates. What's it all about?"

Drake took the documents and pointed to an account number at Banamex in Mexico City.

"Headquarters tells us this was the day-to-day operating account of Francisco Salcido. It's in the name of one of his legitimate businesses he used to launder money."

Drake pointed to a recent international wire transfer made from that account.

"You see here that a couple of weeks ago, five million dollars, give or take a few thousand, were transferred to a Banco Azteca account in Panama from Salcido's account in Mexico City. Now, here's where it gets interesting. Just twenty-four hours after those funds arrived in Panama, the National Front's account at Falcon International Bank in Laredo received an incoming wire transfer in the sum of two million dollars from that same Banco Azteca account. We don't think it's a coincidence."

"Sonofabitch!" exclaimed Creed. "That's pretty close to a smoking gun, isn't it?"

"It is in our eyes, but it wouldn't stand up in a court of law," said Drake.

"That's why we want you to meet with him. Make him realize he's being used by the drug traffickers; that his 'brown power' platform is just a vehicle for the cartel to move its operations north," said Mako.

"Why don't we just tell him about Archibald Rutledge and Salcido?" asked Creed.

"We don't think he even knew who the head of the National Front was," said Mako. "It'd just be our word against his, and he's not likely to believe us."

"Alright, I'll see what I can do," agreed Creed. "When do you propose this meeting take place?"

"He'll be here in thirty minutes," said James.

Creed looked sharply at his old friend.

"That's the last time you schedule my time without

coordinating with me first, you understand? I'm running the show down here, not you or Langley or anybody else."

***

Scrap stood lookout on the porch wearing his rain slicker and cowboy hat covered with a plastic rain cover. Wind battered the screen enclosure and a heavy spray penetrated the fine mesh that normally served to keep out irksome insects. Water dripped from the brim of his hat as he kept his eyes peeled for the expected arrival of Rudy Gutierrez and his entourage.

"Here they come," Scrap called out to the men inside the dry kitchen.

A heavy squall partially obscured three sport utility vehicles slowly making their way along the long gravel road from the interstate. They drifted in and out of view as opaque sheets of rain poured down from the leaden sky and then dissipated, only to be replaced by others marching purposefully towards them from the Gulf of Mexico.

"Show them in when they get here," said Creed. "But don't walk out that door with a weapon. It might be the last thing you do."

"Great, I can already see the headline: 'Scrap Tucker Gunned Down by Brown Berets While Offering Doughnuts and Coffee.' Are you sure about this, Dad?"

"I am," Creed said. "Bring them all in. His bodyguards can have coffee with the CIA."

Things started off well enough. Rudy's bodyguards agreed to leave their weapons in the kitchen by the door to the porch and sat down to have a cup of coffee with Scrap and the over-the-hill gang. Creed led Rudy into the living room for a private exchange. Neither man was hopeful about prospects for a meeting of the minds, but when you lower expectations, you're less likely to be disappointed.

The conversation, though, could have gone better. In fact, it would be hard to imagine it going any worse unless fisticuffs had been involved. Rudy Gutierrez carried a chip on his shoulder the size of the Enchanted Rock in Llano County, Texas and didn't mind letting everyone know. The men in the kitchen heard raised voices almost immediately, but other than a few knowing looks passed back and forth, they said nothing. They just sipped their hot coffee and ate corn tortillas drenched with Guadalupe's homemade *jalapeño* and *tomatillo* hot sauce.

"So how many wetbacks do you exploit on your ranch, Creed?" asked Rudy to begin the conversation, continuing the confrontational tone he had taken during their meeting at the cathedral and then during the televised debate in Laredo.

Creed knew he had to keep his temper in check although the fingers on his right hand involuntary twitched and slowly formed a fist at his side.

"Oh, let me count. I guess it'd just be my wife, daughter, and her fiancée," he replied. "Oh, wait, there *was* one more," Creed added sarcastically. "But Mexican drug traffickers killed him two days ago. The bastards kidnapped my daughter, and he was with us when we rescued her."

"Your daughter was at the same ranch as Francisco Salcido and Archibald Rutledge?" asked Rudy. "What the hell was she doing there?"

"Kidnap victims usually don't have a lot of say about where they're taken. Are you telling me you didn't know about the abduction?"

"Creed, I don't appreciate your insinuation. Like I said at the debate, we have nothing to do with drug traffickers."

"Well, Rudy, I don't doubt your word, but I think you've

been paraded around like a show bull with a ring in his nose. They're using you, son. You've been misled."

"The only misleading thing that's going on in this campaign is Creed Tucker trying to convince Hispanics in South Texas that he's on their side. If it wasn't so pathetic, it'd be funny."

"Rudy, don't you see that you're letting your hatred of Anglos cloud your reason? Plenty of bad things happened in Vietnam. They didn't all have to do with race or ethnic background."

"It wasn't just Vietnam, Tucker. The life of every Hispanic in North America is full of daily examples of discrimination and oppression by you Anglos!"

"Then take a look at this and tell me what's going on!" said Creed and thrust the bank documents at Rudy.

"What the fuck is this?" asked Rudy, abandoning any pretense to civility.

"This is the smoking gun, I'd say."

"What are you talking about?" asked Rudy.

"You know that two million dollars you received in the National Front's bank account in Laredo? This shows where it came from: the Sinaloa drug cartel and its late great leader Francisco 'El Padrino' Salcido."

"What are you bastards doing? Spying on us? Let me see that," Rudy replied and grabbed for the documents. He peered at the text for several minutes and looked up at Creed, momentarily at a loss for words.

"This doesn't prove anything, Tucker. Where does it say that Salcido or the cartel is involved?"

"The CIA has identified that Banamex account as belonging to Salcido. It's a front company used to launder money. That's where your campaign money comes from. You're being used, Rudy. You're nothing but a pawn." said Creed."

"You expect me to believe the CIA? *Vete a la chingada, pinche gabacho!*" hissed Rudy as he stood up to leave, hurriedly stuffing the documents in his shirt pocket.

"You're forgetting yourself, Rudy Gutierrez. Just be thankful you're a guest at the Broken "T" today."

"You're right, Tucker. I apologize for my lack of manners. See you on referendum day."

Rudy was already out the door followed by his retinue of bodyguards splashing through the mud puddles in front of the house before anybody said a word.

"Creed, you missed your calling," declared James Brazzle. "You should have been a professor in conflict resolution or maybe an ambassador."

"Relax, boys," Creed said, the color slowly returning to his face. "Mission accomplished. Rudy took the documents. Believe me, he'll check out that information. Now what else did you have in mind for the day?"

CHAPTER 49

"This is a good place to meet," said Félix Aguilar in Spanish as he looked around the dark interior of the Cosmos Bar & Grill.

"Well, I didn't think I could impress a *chilango* with the quality of food here in Laredo, Texas," said James Brazzle. "Mexico City restaurants are the best in the world, in my opinion, so I went more for discretion and anonymity."

"I appreciate the thought you put into it," Félix added, nodding his head in acknowledgement. "I apologize for being late, but the storm delayed all Aeromexico flights into Nuevo Laredo from Mexico City. I'm lucky I made it at all."

"Don't worry about being late. That's a minor consideration compared to the importance of the business we need to discuss."

James sat back and idly looked at the bartender, a rotund Hispanic man in his fifties with white shaggy hair combed straight back from an unusually low hairline. Contrasting black, bushy eyebrows protruded from his lower forehead like two interconnected awnings. A roll of neck fat sagged over his white, starched collar, and his short stubby fingers struggled to encircle the oversized bottle of wine he poured. A short skinny waiter brought their drinks on a tray and served them attentively.

"*A sus ordenes,*" said the waiter and backed away deferentially.

"*Salud,*" proposed Félix, raising his glass of Malbec and clinking glasses lightly with James' gin and tonic.

Brazzle looked over at Félix in his fashionable Italian silk suit and realized how right Mako had been when he insisted James haul out the Brooks Brothers relic from his wardrobe. He hoped he didn't look as awkward in it as he felt. It had been a few years since he had worn a business suit.

"I didn't realize Francisco had friends in such high places," James said. He was following the script he had carefully rehearsed with Drake Herrin and Mako Sloane before the meeting.

"Congratulations. I see you recognize me," said Félix. "I'm impressed."

"It would be hard not to. I read several Mexico City newspapers every day," replied James. "I would be embarrassed not to recognize the next president of Mexico."

Félix beamed at the compliment.

"So, you're a North American. That surprises me," declared Félix. "Your Spanish is excellent. I would never have guessed you were a *gringo* from speaking with you on the phone."

"My mother was from Buenos Aires," James said, adhering to the legend Mako had suggested to explain James' proficiency in Spanish. "We spoke both Spanish and English at home. My father was an American cattle rancher. We lived on a large *estancia* in the province of San Luis in Argentina. Over the years my accent has become a little confused, I guess." he said.

"You know my name, friend, but I'm afraid I still don't know yours," said the attorney general and looked questioningly at Brazzle.

"Let's keep it that way if you don't mind," suggested James. "My activities wouldn't be understood by the authorities here, to say the least, and I'd prefer to remain anonymous. Francisco and I were able to work very well together on that basis. I took care of organizational and political matters, and he provided financial and logistical support. Our interests seemed to overlap. I didn't threaten his business activities, and he promoted my political goals."

James saw the attorney general bristle momentarily at his refusal to identify himself. However, in the end Aguilar said nothing and seemed to accept the unequal arrangement.

"You'll find that I'm more interested in the political ramifications of our project than Francisco," the attorney general stated. "I'd like to have some input in your '*reconquista*' strategy. Other than that, our goals are the same. I do find it curious, though, that a *gringo* would be interested in addressing past wrongs committed by the North Americans against my people."

Félix looked around the lounge at the mostly Hispanic clientele. He sipped the Malbec and looked at James, waiting for his answer.

"It's not that really. I sympathize with Mexico's plight, of course, but history is rather Darwinian, don't you think? The loss of Mexico's northern territories was inevitable, in my opinion. My motivation is of an entirely different nature. Suffice it to say that there are political forces in this country that don't agree with the present administration. They would stop at almost nothing to discredit the president and replace him with a candidate of their choosing," said James carefully.

James had to force himself to be patient. The conversation was going much better than he had anticipated, and he hoped the miniature transmitter taped under their table was functioning as well as it had been earlier in the day.

He glanced up from his gin and tonic and added, "Your direct participation in my project would fit in well with my plans. I'd welcome another point of view and your advice as long as I can still count on the financial support Francisco gave me."

"Nothing will change in that regard," Félix assured him.

"My relationship was with Francisco's organization as much as with him. They will want a quid pro quo, of course."

"Naturally. Francisco and I often spoke of the mutually beneficial nature of our relationship. What exactly are they looking for?"

Félix looked around the almost empty room and lowered his voice conspiratorially.

"Francisco was an entrepreneur, as you know."

"Yes, of course," James interjected.

"In return for specific quotas on seizures and arrests, Francisco's organization will need guarantees to move agreed-upon quantities of product into the future Autonomous Republic of South Texas...unhindered. It's as simple as that."

James nodded his head and made a dismissive gesture with his left hand as if discounting the significance of what Aguilar had proposed.

"I have no problem with quotas as such," James replied. "I had expected as much, but the future president of the Autonomous Republic and his administration will deal with those types of day-to-day issues. I'll be more than happy to recommend to Rudy that he agree to the quotas, but you will need to meet with him personally."

"You're sure Gutierrez can win an election?" asked Félix.

"Well, let's not get ahead of ourselves. We've got to hold the referendum first," James said. "But, yes, I think he can."

James stared at Félix, pausing a moment to reconstruct the dialog he had rehearsed with Mako and Drake. It was time to probe the government's involvement in the autonomy movement, he thought.

"Can I expect any overt assistance from the Mexican government during a Félix Aguilar administration?" asked James.

"Only rhetorical help. When the movement spreads into New Mexico and the rest of the Southwest, we will provide moral support and vote against the United States wherever we can in international forums, but anything substantive will be provided clandestinely."

"From the government or from the cartel?" asked James, trying to pin down the attorney general.

"Do you really think there's a difference?" the attorney general replied.

James raised his glass in appreciation at the attorney general's observation.

"Does the outgoing president know anything about your plans?"

"Of course not," Félix laughed. "The man's a dinosaur. He still believes in stopping corruption, defeating the cartels, and that *La Virgen de Guadalupe* is looking out for him. He's an anachronism. Francisco wanted to kill him, but I persuaded our friend that winning the election would be the more efficient way to rid ourselves of the self-righteous prick."

James forced himself to laugh.

"Sometimes the most effective form of retribution requires patience and subtlety. I like your style."

"*Así es,*" agreed the attorney general.

"May I offer you a ride to your hotel?" James asked considerately.

"No, thank you. I'll be taking a taxi," he replied. "Maybe I should meet with Rudy Gutierrez before I fly back to Mexico City."

"An excellent idea," said James. He took out his billfold from the inside pocket of his suit coat and rummaged around, making a show of looking for something. "Here's Rudy's business card with his coordinates. I'll let him know to expect a call from you."

"Perfect. I look forward to our next meeting," said Félix, rising from his chair and extending his hand.

"Give Peace a Chance," he suddenly said, laughing. "That was brilliant, by the way: sheer genius. I'd say Cholula owes you a fortune in consulting fees for that gem. Call when you need me."

James nodded in reply but didn't think it necessary to disabuse the attorney general of his assumption that the National Front was behind the Cholula campaign. If it made him look good, James would accept the compliment. He watched the attorney general stroll confidently, almost arrogantly out of the restaurant. He saw the momentary flash of neon lights out on the street as Félix opened the door to the outside, and then it was pitch dark again, the lounge owner's idea of chic ambience. He reached his hands under the table and unfastened the battery-operated transmitter.

"Call Rudy," he said quietly into the tiny microphone.

***

Rudy Gutierrez was pretty sure that Creed Tucker's "advisors" were either current or former CIA officers. They had that look. He wouldn't put it past the agency to get involved in some kind of covert action in South Texas to derail the campaign for autonomy. That would be just like them, he thought, even though he seemed to remember some kind of prohibition against their involvement in domestic affairs. Linking the National Front to the Sinaloa cartel and its deceased leader Francisco Salcido would be an effective way to discredit Rudy and his campaign.

He studied the documents which purported to trace the origin of the large wire transfer the National Front received earlier in the week. That was certainly the National Front's bank account number, and they *had* received that amount in a wire transfer from Panama. That much Rudy couldn't deny. The big question mark in Rudy's mind was Creed's allegation that the Banamex account belonged to the Sinaloa drug cartel.

The problem was the CIA's credibility, he thought. It had none. There was nothing the CIA did better than lie. He had seen that in Vietnam, and he had no way of knowing if the "smoking gun" Creed showed him was just another lie or not. The lingering doubt gnawed at Rudy, and he telephoned his accountant even though it was getting late and most of the campaign workers had already gone home.

"Oscar," he said, "I've got something for you to take a look at. Can you come over to my office, *por favor?*"

"¡Claro que si!" came the reply. Rudy had chosen his accountant well. Oscar was a CPA from El Paso, who as a younger man, had served eighty percent of a sixty-month sentence in federal prison on a money laundering conviction. Rudy figured correctly that Oscar knew the ins and outs of international banking and would be able to keep the National Front's campaign financing on the right side of the law. So far he had.

"Oscar, take a look at these documents, will you?" Rudy asked when Oscar came into his office. "Does anything look fishy to you?"

Oscar put on his thick glasses and studied the money trail shown in the documents Rudy gave him.

"Where'd you get this, Rudy? Are we under some kind of surveillance or something?"

"Just tell me what you think. Do you think our money originated from this Banamex account?"

Oscar buried his face in the documents once more. He was

incurably nearsighted, and his glasses only partially corrected the problem.

"Maybe," he said, "but it's circumstantial. It could be just a coincidence."

"Do you think this could be drug money?" asked Rudy.

"Rudy, there's no way to tell. Look here, this account belongs to some company called Grupo Zima. It looks legitimate, but I suppose it could be a front company used to launder money."

"Do you know anybody at Banamex in Mexico City to ask?" inquired Rudy hopefully.

"Rudy, those aren't questions that you want to be asking publically or privately if you want to stay healthy. Where were you told the money came from?" asked Oscar.

"I wasn't," Rudy admitted.

"Your guess is as good as mine, then."

"*Señor Gutierrez?*" Rudy's secretary stuck her head inside the door. "Three men are here to see you. One of them is Creed Tucker. I recognized him from the television debate."

"Alright, Oscar. That'll be all," said Rudy as he escorted his accountant to the door. He looked out and caught sight of the three familiar figures of Creed Tucker, Mako Sloane, and James Brazzle.

"Jesus!" he exclaimed in exasperation. "Here comes the CIA. You guys never give up, do you?"

"You mean these two old farts? Hell, they're harmless. Look at them. They couldn't even pass a piss test right now. High as a kite on Geritol," joked Creed but then turned serious. "Rudy, I've got something else for you. Got a minute?"

"Do I have a choice?" he asked. Rudy turned his back on his guests and walked back into his office.

Creed took a small MP3 player out of its case, laid it on Rudy's desk, and handed him a pair of earphones.

"I think you're going to want to listen to this," he said.

"What do we have here, Creed, another CIA fabrication?"

"I almost wish it were," replied Creed.

"Let me spell it out for you," interrupted Mako. "We don't have a lot of time. You're going to get a phone call shortly, we believe, from the attorney general of Mexico. He's going to ask to see you this evening. About an hour ago, he met with James Brazzle here, who posed as the head of the National Front. The real head of the Front is dead, Rudy."

"Surely, you can do better than that!" Rudy retorted, visibly paling.

"Yeah, it sounds crazy, but that's all we can tell you right now," said Mako. "Put on these earphones and listen to the conversation. Then believe what you want."

CHAPTER 50

An hour later Rudy sat alone in the National Front headquarters with his alligator-tail cowboy boots propped up on the desk in front of him. Besides an old skinny janitor from Chihuahua, who was slowly making the rounds from office to office emptying trash cans, Rudy was the only one still on the job. He felt like a journeyman boxer who's just taken a vicious beating for ten rounds with nothing to show for his efforts but a swollen, disfigured face and sore, bruised ribs.

He sat quietly for a few minutes and let his mind wander, recalling for some reason a bullfight he had seen as a child in the famous *Plaza de Toros* bullring in Mexico City. He couldn't have been more than ten or eleven years old at the time, but he remembered wondering why the bull kept charging the cape over and over and falling repeatedly for the *torero's* sleight of hand instead of going for the man himself. He had wanted to call out and explain the ruse to the bull, but he hadn't, and in the end he had shouted "*¡Olé!*" with the rest of the spectators who cheered the *matador* and lusted for the beast's blood.

Rudy stared at the proposed flag of the future Autonomous Republic of South Texas hanging on the opposite wall. The Mexican-American designer from Santa Fe he hired had done a clever job, he thought, creatively blending elements from both the Texan and Mexican flags. In his mind the concept of the Autonomous Republic was just that: an amalgam of two worlds, a merger of two rich cultures. Only now the parentage and legitimacy of the new republic-to-be had been revealed to be a farce, something worthy of a cheap political thriller, the kind you buy at the airport newsstand on the way to your departure gate and then leave unread in the pocket of the seat in front of you as you disembark.

A teetotaler most of the time, Rudy was not in a teatotaling mood. How could he be after realizing what a fool he had been. Or was just plain "ass" a better word? What hurt most of all was having that ill-tempered Anglo rancher with his CIA advisors have to point out the obvious: Rudy had been duped. He had taken the bait hook, line, and sinker. He had fallen for the sleight of hand trick like the bull of his childhood, and just like then, there had been nobody to call out a warning until now, and now it was too late.

He walked down to the Del Norte liquor store and bought a bottle of El Conde tequila. Why mess around? he thought and gladly shelled out the $62.95 for the 750 ml bottle. Returning to his cramped office, Rudy leaned back in his discount Staples office chair and chased his shots of tequila with Mountain Dew from an icy green can he bought in the vending machine down the hall.

Rudy's cell phone had rung a scant fifteen minutes after Creed Tucker and his friends left the headquarters of the National Front. His custom ring tone from a popular *Los Tigres del Norte* ballad made the hair stand up on the back of his neck when it pierced the silence of his office. The predictions of the apocalypse were coming true one by one.

Rudy knew Mexican politics and couldn't help but recognize the distinctive voice of the attorney general on the other end of the line. Normally, he would have been flattered by a call from Félix Aguilar. Rudy had become enthralled with the attorney general's candidacy after hearing his rousing address at the Guadalajara soccer stadium when he voiced support for South Texas autonomy. It seemed the attorney general dared to say out loud things most Mexican politicians had only whispered in the past. Tonight, though, was different. Rudy crossed himself before he answered the phone, hoping it was anybody but Aguilar. Even a call from his hated ex-wife would have been a welcome distraction.

Rudy looked at his watch. It was time to move if he was going to be on time to the meeting. He swung his legs off the desk and stood up, taking a deep breath and finishing off the can of Mountain Dew. He unlocked the bottom right hand drawer of his desk and removed his loaded Glock 17 nine-millimeter pistol and stuck it down the back of his jeans.

***

Félix Aguilar sat in the same dimly lit room of the Cosmos Bar and Grill where he met the "head" of the National Front just a few hours before. He preferred that the rabble not recognize him in public and decided he couldn't improve on the anonymity offered by the unabashedly old-fashioned drinking venue. There were a few more committed alcoholics in the establishment than there had been earlier in the evening, and a Mexican pop singer crooned on stage for a private party in an adjoining room. The same overweight bartender refilled drinks for his regular late-night customers who leaned over the bar, resting their Sunday-go-to-meeting cowboy boots on top of the brass foot railing. Business was brisker now, and beads of perspiration perched precariously on his fleshy forehead as he feverishly mixed cocktails and washed glasses. Overhead track lighting illuminated the bar with soft diffused light while overworked scented candles on the tables attempted to penetrate the murky, smoke-filled darkness of the lounge.

On the other side of the room a heavily made-up, older Hispanic woman cupped her breasts in the palms of her hands and lifted them into a tight counterclockwise orbit as she argued with her escort. Felix had noticed them drinking tequila when he first walked in, and the waiter had already refilled their shot glasses and beer chasers several times.

"What do you mean they don't look real?" she cried out

in Spanish, raising her voice in protest. "I had them done in Buenos Aires. Can you imagine how much that cost?" she asked her escort.

"Son hermosos, mi amor," said her companion, trying to mollify her. He leaned over drunkenly and attempted to kiss the exposed portion of a breast as it reached its apogee, with just the hint of nipple jutting out of the woman's lace brassiere. A deceptively quick right cross landed squarely on his left cheek bone, spinning the ill-fated lover out of his chair and on to the floor.

"Cochino!" shouted the woman in outrage. *"No soy una cualquiera,"* she said emphatically as she burst into tears, carefully returning her mostly exposed breast to its hiding place.

Two bouncers appeared quickly and showed the star-crossed lovers to the door, the woman still weeping inconsolably. The attorney general smiled to himself, appreciative of the melodramatic distraction. Like any male, he loved female histrionics, as long as they were directed towards someone else. This display was worthy of a Mexican soap opera.

Félix had arrived at the Cosmos a few minutes early and waited patiently for Rudy Gutierrez to arrive. He knew Rudy's platform by heart and had even listened to a couple of his campaign speeches. The attorney general recognized a rare combination of political acumen and street smarts in Rudy that made him a dynamic and effective candidate. He approved of the emphasis Rudy put on a separate Hispanic identity, and naturally, Rudy's consistent theme of Anglo perfidy towards Mexicans struck a chord with Félix. He considered Rudy a political diamond in the rough and wasn't surprised at his strong showing in the polls.

***

Rudy had more than a slight tequila buzz as he threw open the door to the Cosmos a few minutes later and strode boldly into the bar, limping only slightly from the lingering effects of old war wounds. He stopped, waiting for his eyes to adjust to the darkness inside and surveyed the customers. He immediately recognized Félix with his perfectly coiffured hair and wearing one of his trademark Italian silk suits. He saw Félix stand up and motion to him. Rudy approached the table warily and the two men shook hands. Rudy gave him a perfunctory Latino *abrazo*, clapping the attorney general familiarly on the back.

"What a pleasure to finally meet you, Rudy. Your courage in the struggle for autonomy has been an inspiration to all Mexicans," began Félix. "Could I offer you a drink?"

"Un tequila," Rudy replied curtly.

"It's been a long day. I think I'll join you," said Félix and called the waiter. "Two tequilas," he said. "And bring the bottle."

The conversation died briefly as Rudy stared at the attorney general in silence. He struggled to keep his emotions in check and knew the tequila wasn't helping. It never did, which was why he had quit drinking years ago. He studied the man, staring at his custom-tailored suit. Even his selection of a vaguely purple shirt to go with his matching Charvet striped silk tie spoke of a level of sophistication and urbanity he found hard to reconcile with what he now suspected about the leading candidate for the Mexican presidency. He stared at Félix's carefully manicured nails and soft hands and saw in him the very antithesis of a predatory drug lord. Maybe the CIA was wrong about him after all, he thought.

"In a few weeks you could be the president of Mexico," said Rudy, interrupting the silence.

"In a few weeks we *both* could be presidents," Félix replied.

"Salud," he proposed as they touched glasses and threw down the shots of tequila.

"If I win the election...," Félix began.

"You mean 'when', don't you?" interrupted Rudy.

"Yes, but I'd rather not jinx myself," Félix laughed.

"You're not superstitious, are you?" asked Rudy.

"We make our own luck, I like to think, but I'd rather not tempt fate at this point."

"I agree," said Rudy. "Fate can be fickle...but you were saying?"

"I was starting to say that if I win the election, the Mexican government under my administration will likely offer foreign aid to the future Autonomous Republic of South Texas. That should ruffle some feathers in Washington, don't you think?"

"Hold on, now," said Rudy. "I know how these games are played. Why would Mexico risk pissing off the Colossus of the North? What would you want in return? We don't have a whole lot to give, you realize."

"That's where you're wrong," Félix countered. "You've got a 1,254 mile long border with Mexico. That's worth more than you can imagine."

"A border's a border, unless you're a drug trafficker," said Rudy, never one for excessive subtlety. "Then it's a business opportunity."

"Precisely," Félix said. "The supporters of our cause and those who offer us financial assistance come from diverse backgrounds. But that shouldn't be news to you."

"I'm not quite sure what you mean by that." Rudy answered and threw down another shot of tequila without waiting to clink glasses with the attorney general.

Félix put his shot glass down and stared at Rudy.

"Rudy, are we going to be children and pretend we don't know where all the money for the National Front comes from? Or the manpower and weapons for the R.A.T.S. military wing?"

"I assume the money comes from Hispanic organizations and like-minded brothers and sisters who support our cause," stated Rudy stubbornly although inwardly he shuddered at the direction the conversation had taken.

"I don't doubt that the National Front has its ideological supporters and well-wishers. But do you honestly think that charitable bingo games and raffles raised the two million dollars you received last week for your campaign? How about the SA-7 missile that shot down the National Guard helicopter? Did that come from groups of concerned citizens? I don't think so, Rudy, and I don't think you believe that either."

"Félix, how well did you know Francisco Salcido?" asked Rudy bluntly.

The attorney general shifted uncomfortably in his chair and looked around the room nervously.

"That's not a name you should mention in public, Rudy," Félix admonished.

"I take it Francisco was a Mexican patriot and a benefactor of the cause?" Rudy asked disingenuously.

"You might say that," responded Félix. "I'm not sure what you're driving at, Rudy. There's no reason to play cat and mouse here. I'm here to tell you that Mexico and her friends will support your administration and do everything possible to make the autonomous republic a viable entity."

"And in return?" asked Rudy. "Can I get a straight answer from you?"

"Alright, here it is in black and white. In return, my friends would expect your cooperation in meeting their annual export goals. Of course, they would concede a certain volume of product in seizures and sacrifice personnel in pre-arranged arrests."

"Of course," said Rudy, his heart drumming loud enough to be heard over the Julio Iglesias "wannabe" in the next room. So old Creed Tucker and his CIA cronies had it right, he thought. The attorney general of Mexico just spelled it out to him with unexpected candor, confirming everything Rudy had feared. The tequila he had been drinking for the last several hours buzzed annoyingly in his head, and his thoughts were hopelessly muddled. He stared at Félix with expressionless eyes and wished there could be a different denouement to this tragicomic script.

"In return our friends are prepared to be very generous. Look what we've been able to achieve together so far, Rudy. What do the North Americans say? 'If it ain't broke, don't fix it.' I don't see any point in changing a strategy that has worked so well, do you?"

Rudy didn't answer. He turned away and stared at the flickering candle on the next table.

"Rudy, listen," the attorney general began. "There's no room here for idealism. Sometimes the end *does* justify the means. We couldn't have achieved our political goals without the financial and logistical backing of our friends. That's the long and short of it."

"And now what?" asked Rudy.

"Now we solidify your gains in South Texas and move the '*reconquista*' westward: all the way to the Pacific Ocean."

"You're ambitious," replied Rudy.

"History is cyclical," explained Félix. "Our time has come. Demographics are on our side. We're just providing the catalyst," he laughed and belatedly tossed back his shot of tequila. He reached for the bottle and poured two more glasses.

"Félix, *estás muy equivocado,*" Rudy said, raising his tequila in a silent toast. "You're very wrong, my friend. Our entire movement *is* based on idealism, and nothing can justify the means you're talking about."

"You misunderstand me," the attorney general began.

Rudy cut him off with a preemptive wave of his hand.

"No, I understand you perfectly, and that's the problem. You know, ever since I was a kid, I wondered why the Anglos looked down on us. It hurts to be called a 'greaser' or a 'wetback' when you're ten years old. We were poor, but my father worked hard in the citrus groves, and my mother cleaned house for a rich Anglo family in McAllen. They eventually got their citizenship, but they were still 'dirty Mexicans' to the Anglos. I joined the Army and went to Vietnam in 1967. I thought that fighting for my country would buy the equality I wanted, but I was wrong. My blood was the same color as theirs, but they still looked down on me. I got back, finished college on the GI Bill and went to law school. You know what they said? They said I wouldn't have got into law school if it hadn't been for affirmative action! *¿Qué mierda, no?* You can't win for losing in this country."

The attorney general tried to interrupt, but Rudy held up his hand.

"You've opened my eyes today, Félix. People laugh at Mexico, don't they? '*Mexico, lindo y jodido,*' they say. And you know why Mexico is screwed? Because of people like you, Félix. The crime, corruption, chaos, and violence. You use it to feed your own greed and further your personal ambition. You've tried to use our movement the same way. You've perverted everything I believe in, but I'm not going to let you get away with it."

"Don't be naïve, Rudy. If you won't cooperate, the head of the National Front will just replace you. That's the best case scenario. More likely, they'll just kill you. You can't change anything. *¡No seas pendejo!"*

"I only see one *pendejo* at this table: a *pendejo* with a Princeton education."

"Rudy, this is your last warning. You're forgetting yourself," said Félix sternly.

"Am I, Félix? Is that what this is all about? You're here to put me in my place? Think again, *puto*. Does the name Archibald Rutledge mean anything to you? It should; he was the real head of the National Front! But he's dead, along with Francisco Salcido."

"Listen to yourself, Rudy. You're delirious."

"Is that right?" responded Rudy. "Here's what makes perfect sense: the man you spoke with today is a retired CIA officer, a friend of Mako Sloane. Does that ring a bell?"

"Mako Sloane?" repeated Félix and sat up straight in his chair. "Don't tell me you've been listening to that sonofabitch?" Félix stood up and tossed a hundred dollar bill on the table. "I see it's too late for you, Rudy. You're a fool."

Rudy made a quick motion with his right hand behind his back and pulled out the Glock from under his jacket. He pointed the pistol at the attorney general's chest.

"Sit down, Félix. I'm not through with you yet."

"Rudy, you're about to throw away everything you've worked so hard to achieve over the last twenty years."

"¡Callate, buey!"

Félix sat down obediently with both elbows on the table.

"Don't you understand?" asked Rudy. "Mako Sloane lured you to Laredo. He set you up like a street-corner dope dealer in a pathetic sting operation. What's this, Félix? Your hands are shaking. Don't tell me you scared now?"

The attorney general sat and stared at the Glock. His eyes

made the visual loop from the pistol to Rudy's face and back again.

"Now listen to this, and tell me who's the bigger fool," said Rudy.

Rudy took out the MP3 player and pushed the "play" button.

Félix paled as he listened to the incriminating dialog recorded three hours ago with James Brazzle. He put his head in his hands and sat motionless as his own words recited the indictment.

"This kind of information is radioactive," said Rudy. "Can you imagine what the press could do with this? Or a U.S. federal prosecutor?"

"What is this?" interrupted Félix. "Some kind of amateurish attempt at blackmail?" he asked.

"It may be amateurish, but blackmail? No, that's not my style, Félix. Can't you see where this is going?" Rudy paused for effect, the latent actor coming out in him as if he were playing the lead role in an action-packed thriller. "I'm going to kill you," he said. "It's a more permanent solution."

"No!" whispered the attorney general. "Don't do it Rudy. It's not too late; you can become wealthy beyond your wildest dreams! Think what you're doing, *carnal!*"

"You're not my brother!" Rudy shouted.

He leveled the 9 mm at the attorney general's abdomen and squeezed the trigger. The Glock boomed. Again and again. Customers dove under the tables and a woman screamed. Félix's hand flew up instinctively, trying to block the unrelenting salvo of bullets. His body jerked back convulsively with the impact of each round, his face reflecting pain and confused disbelief. Words gurgled out of his crooked mouth in a trickle of dark red blood. He was still alive as he slid off the chair and lay on the floor in fetal position on his right side, rapidly bleeding to death. He raised his left arm as if pleading for his life and tried to speak again. Rudy fired once more, and the attorney general's arm fell to the floor and lay outstretched over his head.

The sound of the shots still rang in Rudy's ears as he sat looking at Felix's body and his lifeless eyes that stared at the ceiling. Sixty seconds passed like an eternity as Rudy contemplated a dozen permutations of possible exit strategies. Each scenario offered but a single resolution. He heard the distant sirens of the Laredo police approaching the lounge at high speed. Out of the corner of his eye he saw customers rushing towards the exit in terrified relief that this madman did not seek more victims. He sat alone in the bar with Felix's corpse, the Glock still in his hand, wondering how he had let himself be so pathetically used. He heard loud voices in the adjoining room as the police arrived and prepared to confront him.

"Sir, put your gun down!" he heard a Laredo cop command.

Rudy turned and looked scornfully at the overweight policeman. He quickly stuffed the Glock in his mouth and jerked the trigger.

EPILOGUE

Two days later at dawn, the roar of a pair of A-10 Warthogs woke Creed from an exhausted sleep as the indestructible "flying guns" dove towards the R.A.T.S. checkpoint on the Nueces River south of Cotulla, Texas and opened fire with 30 mm GAU-8A Avenger cannon at a fixed rate of fire of 2,100 rounds per minute. Drake Herrin's phone call to Washington about Félix Aguilar's death and the late Mexican attorney general's role in the conspiracy finally tipped the scales and woke the sleeping tiger.

Although the White House later denied that the Warthogs had dropped cluster bombs on the National Front defenders, Creed Tucker and James Brazzle could find no other explanation for the carnage they discovered when they reached the checkpoint site. They found the black, charred hulks of a dozen pickup trucks and unidentifiable body parts dispersed over an impact zone more than 150 meters in diameter. Indeed, it would take several days before state and federal authorities, finally working together, were able to make even approximate casualty estimates. Mako Sloane's warning to the late Mexican attorney general about "swift and merciless" retribution finally had come true.

Similar reports soon began to filter in from the remaining R.A.T.S. checkpoints along the southern bank of the Nueces River. The air strikes had been simultaneous and the devastation was monotonously similar at each location. The few survivors from the Warthogs' bombing runs rushed madly towards the border in pickup trucks in a desperate race against death itself and attempted to cross into Mexico. Heavily armed intercept teams from the 36th Infantry Division of the Texas National Guard deployed by helicopters along the border stopped and arrested most of the retreating survivors, whose bravado and cocksureness had instantly evaporated in face of the concentrated firepower of the air-to-ground attack aircraft. At about the same time, National Guardsmen specially trained in urban warfare tactics burst into the headquarters of the National Front in Laredo and took everyone in the building into custody including a confused, elderly janitor from Chihuahua who figured *La Migra* had finally tracked him down. Those who resisted died instantly in a remorseless hail of semi-automatic gunfire.

When local newspapers on both sides of the border broke the bombshell story of the Mexican attorney general's murder in Laredo complete with a transcript of his conversation with the "head of the National Front", all murmurings of outrage over *gringo* aggression faded away, and the local populace joined in the effort to drive the drug trafficking gangs out of South Texas. Vigilante action by incensed citizens was swift and brutal, and the United Nations General Assembly threatened to investigate the numerous cases of summary executions and lynchings that allegedly took place in the days following the overwhelming show of force by the U.S. military and the Texas National Guard. The president's and the governor's approval ratings, however, shot through the roof when they each answered the United Nations' protest with an undiplomatic and unprintable expletive.

International observers, who had arrived with plans to witness the inevitable referendum on autonomy, sheepishly returned in a long caravan of SUVs to Houston's George Bush Intercontinental Airport where they boarded the first available flights to their respective capitals. Most of them were able to leave the country before the 24-hour deadline for their departures imposed by the Department of State expired. Several irate members of the delegation from the Organization of American States, however, were detained for overstaying their welcome, and the Venezuelan delegate was arrested for striking a TSA inspector at the airport. Local authorities conveniently ignored his protestations about diplomatic immunity at the explicit order of the president whose patience with the rest of the world had run out.

As Washington awoke from its impotent stupor, sabers rattled in Congress and armchair hawks struck dramatic poses on television news programs and called for military reprisals against Mexico, whose government quickly disavowed the disgraced attorney general and denied any knowledge of the conspiracy.

Creed Taylor and James Brazzle became overnight celebrities when news of their role in breaking the back of the National Front became public. A steady stream of journalists and television news correspondents laid siege to the Broken "T" seeking interviews with the two ranchers in their now familiar sweat-stained western hats and cowboy boots and spurs.

When an overly inquisitive reporter from *People Magazine* happened to see Alba and Rodrigo exchange a furtive kiss as Rodrigo headed to the round pen to saddle his first two-year old of the day, their photograph was plastered in every tabloid newspaper in both the United States and Mexico and on every entertainment and gossip website on the internet. Within twenty-four hours a producer from Univision showed up at the Broken "T" and offered to buy the rights to the story of their romance for a new Mexican *telenovela* to be called *"Los Enamorados de la Reconquista"*.

Mako Sloane and Drake Herrin, on the other hand, were more circumspect in their reaction to the unexpected limelight, and they managed to sneak out of South Texas unnoticed and unheralded before the media onslaught began. They knew what awaited them in Washington and neither was looking forward to what was sure to be a lengthy debriefing process. Mako's detractors on Capitol Hill demanded details on the shootout at *Rancho Las Aguilas.* A few even had the temerity to suggest that Mako's precipitous attack on Francisco

Salcido's South Texas hideout might have caused the death of Vice President Rutledge. It was back to the dirty business of politics in Washington.

Antonio Salcido, Francisco's younger brother and the new head of the Sinaloa cartel, wasted no time and put out a contract on Mako's life and offered five million dollars to whoever brought him Sloane's ring finger as proof of his demise. The irony of Mako's not-so-subtle message left at the entrance to *Rancho Vista del Mar* was not lost on the new cartel leader, and he swore on his brother's memory that he would kill Mako Sloane within a year and mount his appendage as a trophy on the wall of his study. Mako shrugged his shoulders at the news which he took philosophically. Death threats and assassination attempts had been part and parcel of his career since the mid-1970s. Nevertheless, for once in his life Mako decided to err on the side of caution and planned to take a lengthy leave of absence in a "safe and secure" location following the debriefings. He was either getting old or had wised up, perhaps even both.

To nobody's surprise, the president of the United States chose Rick Throckmorton for the vacant vice presidency. Both politicians had deftly managed the goat-to-hero metamorphosis and were enjoying unprecedented bipartisan popularity. Much of Western Europe and the Third World whined, complained, and tried to ridicule the Americans' penchant for self-righteous drama, violence, and political theater, but as the late Vice President Rutledge once put it: "The president doesn't give a shit what the rest of the world thinks."

With the gubernatorial election looming in Texas, speculation naturally turned to the possible candidacy of Creed Tucker. Both political parties sent delegations of partisan luminaries to the Broken "T" to explore the possibility with Creed, who began to feel like a Texas blue-chip high school football prospect, but the only official announcement he made was to say that he would make his decision after Alba's wedding later in the year.

Within a month following the crushing defeat of the leaderless National Front for the Liberation of Texas, isolated protests broke out in Laredo and McAllen over alleged cases of racial profiling by the now emboldened Border Patrol, DEA, and U.S. Customs agents. Once again local news and radio stations debated the immigration issue, and the state of Texas and the federal government pointed fingers at each other regarding the origin of the mess. Loads of marijuana and cocaine again began pouring across the border and drug-related vendettas and turf battles between rival gangs and cartels raged with renewed intensity, often spilling over onto the streets of Texas cities. The governments of the United States and Mexico looked on in frustration, and the leaders of the two countries shrugged their shoulders in feigned impotence.

The Sinaloa cartel licked its wounds and continued to pay off U.S. federal agents from Brownsville to El Paso and to reap immense profits with their across-the-border trade. Antonio Salcido, however, was not satisfied with mere financial success and dreamed of political stardom on the international stage, something which had eluded his brother.

The rains stopped, the grass withered and dried, and the parched ground cracked open in protest over the catastrophic shortage of life-giving moisture. Ranchers met for their morning coffee at local restaurants and spoke of the draught in hushed apocalyptic whispers. Things had finally returned to normal in South Texas, but nobody, least of all Creed Tucker, believed that the status quo would last.

ABOUT THE AUTHOR

Clabe Taylor is a fifth-generation Texan and former intelligence officer who spent most of his career abroad in Europe and Latin America. He speaks Russian and Spanish in addition to his native English. You can read more about Clabe and his novels at www.clabetaylor.com and you can follow him both on Facebook and Twitter.

NOW AVAILABLE

Mako Sloane is a CIA legend, but his dizzying rise to stardom in Moscow is matched by his precipitous fall from grace after he discovers a secret that vested interests in both Russia and the U.S. want to keep quiet. Ten years after Mako's mysterious disappearance, investigative reporter Max Crandall is writing Sloane's unauthorized biography. Max's research inadvertently dredges up ghosts from the past, and he finds himself the target of a manhunt as unidentified operatives try to derail his project. Max lures Mako out of self-imposed exile, and the two discover the truth behind a bizarre conspiracy that threatens to send the world spiraling into a superpower confrontation of unprecedented proportions.

www.ingramcontent.com/pod-product-compliance
Lightning Source LLC
Chambersburg PA
CBHW050537260626
47157CB00002B/337